TIME OUT

NASHVILLE STEEL BOOK TWO

STACEY LYNN

Time Out

Nashville Steel Series

Book Two

Stacey Lynn

Copyright © 2023 Stacey Lynn

Content Editing: My Brother's Editor

Proofreading: Virginia Tesi Carey, TK Rapp

Cover Design: Shanoff Designs

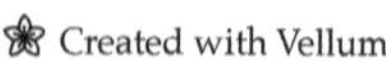 Created with Vellum

CHAPTER 1
DAVIS

"We're headed out. Are you coming?"

I tossed my bag over my shoulder and ran my hand through my hair. "I'm not sure, man. I think I'm out."

Mason Yeets's jet-black eyes doubled in size. "You're bowing out of heading to Broadway? But it's bachelorette season."

Yeah. I surprised myself with that one. "Nah. I'm good. Think I'm going to head home."

"But we won."

So some of us guys had created the habit of partying on Broadway after a win at home. As football players for the Nashville Steel, our stadium was a short ride away from the infamous country bar and rock music-lined streets of Nashville where millions visited every year. Frankly, I thought the street smelled like armpits after a three-hour workout in ninety-degree weather, but that didn't mean the street wasn't a blast. And being football players, we were often offered premiere VIP seats and bottle service purely for the purpose of bringing more fans—mostly women in their early to mid-twenties into the bars.

I'd had more than a few hangovers after a night out, but tonight? I wasn't feeling it.

Made no sense, but there it was. I'd just helped bring my team a win in my very first Monday Night Football matchup, prime time television, in my rookie season. The press couldn't stop talking about my speed and ability to read the field and block a half-dozen tackles on my way to the end zone.

Typically, that'd have me being the one to offer to buy first round, get the party started. I'd had no problems taking advantage of the perks of finally making it to the pros. And still, even Mason and Cortland pleading with me, along with our backup quarterback, Sam Denmark, making a pouty face in the background, didn't have me changing my mind.

Odd.

I shook it off and slapped Mason's shoulder. "Pretty sure you and Denmark can handle it for me. Wouldn't want to take the attention off you."

"*Shit.* You wish. You're the one who gets my leftovers."

Probably true. I was too pretty boy to be considered sexy. Too innocent. Too *Nebraskan*, as my last college girlfriend had told me, whatever the hell that meant.

I spent a few minutes talking with the rest of the players, including our quarterback Cole Buchanan before he headed to the family room to grab his girlfriend, Eden, and his son Jasper. I went to the private player parking lot and slid into my brand-new Tacoma truck. As far as vehicles went, it wasn't flashy, but my family had rarely been able to afford anything new and if it was, it wasn't a vehicle of any kind. More likely tractor equipment or clothes or shoes.

God, I needed to shake off this lingering morose sensation. It wasn't normal. I was the fun guy. The life of the party. I was smart as hell and could use my engineering degree if football didn't work out, and there I was, crawling through the dark streets of Nashville on my way to my penthouse and somehow—all of the success I'd earned, all the money I made, and the fancy screen on my truck didn't mean a damn thing.

I was *lonely.* Ironic, considering I'd just bowed out of a night with guys who were quickly becoming my brothers.

But there was a difference between being alone and lonely… and screw it.

I jerked my truck into the underground parking at my high-rise condo building, climbed out, and hustled across the street to Lou's.

From Louisiana, Lou claimed to be straight from the Bayou, but where he was from didn't interest me. His po'boy sandwiches with shrimp and roast beef did.

He was not only the owner, but the main nighttime bartender during the week. Relief swept through me as I entered the bar, televisions playing on two different walls—twelve different screens. Since the game had ended well over an hour ago, most of the crowd that would have been there to watch the game was gone, leaving Lou alone at the bar, wiping off the top of the gleaming granite countertop with very little customers.

I took a seat near the far corner, my back to the televisions. I'd been there. Didn't need to see the plays or read the criticisms.

"Hey there, kiddo."

Kiddo. I heard it enough in the locker room. "What's the good word, Lou?"

His bar had all the best post-game gossip and news.

"Whole damn bar was on their feet with that touchdown you scored."

"Which one?" I had been pretty awesome.

My second touchdown of the night was a hell of a score, a forty-yard breakaway run when our team went for it on fourth and two. Should have been a quick few yards to set us up for a field goal before I saw the hole in the blockers. Still, I liked needling the guy. He reminded me of my grandpa sometimes, always quick with a laugh, sarcastic comment, and a sprinkling of wisdom.

He whipped his towel at me, laughing as he barely missed. "Kids your age. No smarts, all smart-asses. The one where you hurdled the safety."

Huh. Not the second one. "Ah. That last one. Wasn't so bad, eh?"

"Not bad at all. Your ankle okay?"

"Right as rain." Twisted it coming off that touchdown, wobbling after I hurdled Levi Harrison, Seattle's safety. It pulsed with a dull pain but was manageable. I'd had worse.

I ordered a beer, Miller Lite, because I wasn't into fancy drinks or hard alcohol. Might have been the Nebraskan in me, but simple and easy still tasted better than pretentious and expensive.

Lou and I talked about the game some more. He'd never made a fuss about knowing who I was, but the night I stopped in after our first home pre-season game, he'd told me I played good. Figured Lou didn't give a lot of compliments, and *good* was a euphemism for *fucking incredible,* which was how I was feeling that night. I'd been coming in for three months, almost once a week, for a po'boy and beer or two, sometimes with Dawson, my team's tight end, or Mason, and Lou had never said a word. Figured, since it was Nashville, most locals were used to the parade of celebrities and country musicians and stars of all forms, but I appreciated it. I'd been well-known in Clemson and a small-town celebrity back in Nebraska. For once, it felt good to not be all that known or noticed while I was at the local Target grabbing a pack of new underwear.

Like usual, we chatted about football for a few minutes, and then he steered the conversation to his grandkids in high school and college after he brought me my sandwich. I munched on fries and got a fresh beer, but even then, that anxious knot in my chest still wouldn't go away.

What in the hell was it?

I was living my dream. Should have been flying off that win and how well I was playing.

I wasn't caving to expectations or any stress from media who wrote I was still too soft, too young, too *not perfect enough* to sustain the energy I'd shown this early in the season.

Doubters were everywhere, but they always had been. I was used to it.

My phone rang, and some of that concern vanished as my sister's face, smooshed up to kiss her youngest, soon-to-be middle child on the cheek, appeared on the screen.

Thank goodness it was quiet enough that I didn't have to step outside to take her call.

I'd never miss this.

I brought the phone to my ear. "Hey Annie."

"God. You suck so much. Slowest person out there." She deadpanned the insult, her highest form of praise, and I took a sip of my beer.

"I know. It's a shame. I should be sent back to Clemson to start all over."

She snorted. "No shit. Your ankle okay?"

Because nothing came faster after her insults than a big sister's worry. God, I loved her.

Missed her. Maybe this was my problem... I was used to not seeing my family much, but they'd always been at my games. Then Annie and Avery had to go and get married and start populating the next generation's offensive lines, and everyone's visits to my games became less.

"It's good. Sore, but nothing major."

"Shouldn't have pretended you're a track star instead of a semi-mediocre football player."

"I think semi and mediocre is redundant."

"Are you moonlighting as an English teacher now, too?"

"Someone has to impress Mom and Dad."

"Please. I'm their favorite because I keep giving Mom more grandbabies. She might like you too if you have a kid."

"As if."

No way. No, thank you. No how. Not anytime soon.

Kids were several years down the line for me. While most of my old classmates in Nebraska got married after college, if they even finished or went, and started popping out kids, I had other things I wanted to accomplish first.

Like make a Pro Bowl. Go to—and hopefully win—a Super Bowl. Join the two-thousand-yard club by rushing that many yards in a single season. Break a few records.

Girlfriends and wives and kids and responsibilities could stay on my back burner.

"Mom loves me," I huffed.

"Yeah, I know," she grumbled. My sister. My biggest supporter and largest pain in my ass. "You're all she talks about at church and the grocery store. *'Our Davis. He's so special. So important. Makes millions, and he's barely old enough to shave.'*"

"Too far." I laughed, managing not to spit out my beer. "I shave."

Occasionally. There was a reason my teammates called me kiddo and baby face.

"You're touching your chin, aren't you?"

I dropped my hand from my chin, didn't even realize I'd done it. "No."

"Liar." She munched on something crunchy, probably an apple because as of last week, that was her current baby craving.

"How's the kumquat treating you?"

She groaned. "Please stop calling my baby a kumquat. It's gross."

"So is how you got that thing inside of you."

"You're a pest. Always have been, and I need to go. David is currently running through the house naked, refusing to put clothes on. I just wanted to tell you good game."

"Ah… so my namesake does take after me."

"Your name is Davis, not David, dumbass."

"Potato, potahto, and you can tell me good game whenever you're ready."

"I already did. Told you, you suck, same thing."

"Love you, snotface."

Lou slid me a fresh beer and shook his head at me.

"You too, boogerhead."

"Sister," I told Lou after I set my phone down.

"Annie or Avery?"

"Annie."

The door opened, and we both turned our heads in the direction, and swear to God, my cock acted like a sex-seeking missile device and immediately shot a warning to my brain that something beautiful was nearby.

In walked a gorgeous woman, my age at first guess, in cutoff denim shorts so short her ass cheeks would probably show when she took a seat, tits popping out of the V-neck, ripped gray shirt cropped and tied at her left hip. *Nashville* was plastered and stretched to the max over her chest. The tiniest strip of skin appeared between that shirt and her rolled-over denim shorts, and

I was pretty sure I swallowed my tongue as she ran a hand through her long, thick chocolate-brown hair that shone beneath the bar's overhead lights.

She huffed toward the bar, glancing at me, before taking a seat several down and propping her elbows on the shining wood top.

"Hello there, young lady." Lou approached with his standard greeting. Eighty or twenty, he called them all young. "How's your night?"

That same huff, exasperated mixed with maybe amused, came from her full, red lips.

Cherries. They'd taste like cherries if I were to bite into them. Full, red, and undoubtedly soft and sweet.

"Well, I'm soon to be homeless and as of five minutes ago, unemployed, so I'd say it's not so great. How's yours?"

Lou's bushy gray brows rose. Like the experienced bartender he was, and definitely male—there was no way he was touching that one. "Whiskey or beer?"

She reached for her back pocket. The move twisted her toward me, pushing those full breasts in my direction. It took effort, massive effort, to yank my eyes up right as ours met.

"I've got her tab, Lou."

"No, you don't." Those full cherry lips pressed into a thin line.

"Save the money. Sounds like you'll need it."

"And what do *you* want for being so nice to me?"

It was delivered with a sneer, telling me most likely she'd already dealt with enough shit from men tonight.

I shrugged. "Not a damn thing."

Wasn't like her few drinks and maybe a meal would break my bank.

"He's good for it," Lou said. "And if not, it'd be on the house anyway since it sounds like you've had a hell of a night, and before you ask me what I want, just that you get home safely. You do have a safe place to go tonight, right?"

This time she laughed, shook her head, and another flip of her hand with her hand. "Amazing. Yes, I have a place to go."

"Pick your poison then." He gestured to the bar.

She slid her gaze in my direction, arched a brow in question, but

I wasn't going to stop her. "No strings, except I'd like your name, but that's up to you."

Her red lips pushed to one side, and she glanced back at the wall lined with liquor. "Two shots of Patron, no lime or salt, and a beer. Whatever he's having." She nodded in my direction without looking at me. "Maggie."

Lou grabbed her drinks as *Maggie* rolled around in my head. Was it a nickname for something? Margaret?

Once Lou was done, he headed my way, and I leaned over the bar. Maggie was shooting her first shot of tequila, thumb scrolling on her phone screen.

"Any chance you can change the screens off sports?"

If she hadn't seen my face yet, I didn't want her to. Sure, it was the easiest way to get a girl's attention, but I didn't need my post-game interview showing up on the ninety-two-inch screen behind me either.

"You got it."

He grabbed the remote, and as he turned on the guide, Maggie's attention drifted to that same massive screen. "Your choice, Maggie," he said. "Got a preference?"

"You guys really know how to make a girl feel at home." It was said with the same amount of distrust as earlier, but whatever. I had no clue what her night or week had been like.

Lou kept scrolling, and I took a drink from my beer.

"No preference. Not like anything can help after tonight."

She scowled and then drowned in her drinks, and for a very brief moment, I swore there was fear in her eyes before she blinked it away.

"What do you mean?"

She had no obligation to tell me anything, but if my sister said something like that to me, I'd be ready to *ride at dawn* in a heartbeat.

"Nothing."

Lou, however, did not let that go. "Somebody hurt you?"

He was a big guy, round in all the old guy places, but he also had five daughters. A protective bear was Lou.

"Nothing that doesn't typically happen at bars around here. It's whatever." She flipped a hand through the air and grabbed her second shot. "It's fine."

"That's not fine. And it's not whatever. You telling me somebody touched you, and you got fired for it?"

She cringed. "It might have been me breaking a bottle on the bar and shoving it in his face that was the part that got me fired."

Well fuck that.

And now I wasn't just seeing a curvy, exceptional looking woman with a mouth I wanted to taste and breasts I wanted to get my hands on. I was looking at a woman, barely over five feet, who'd been harassed and suffered the consequences for it.

As she spoke, steel hardened her tone.

"Good," I said, and she probably didn't care, but I continued with, "I'm proud of you."

CHAPTER 2
MAGGIE

had no intention of taking anything from anyone, but when you had the night I'd had, hell, the last three years I'd had, where every time I thought I was getting ahead, the universe laughed and knocked me right back to my backside, I'd take the alcohol the incredibly cute and sexy guy at the bar offered.

There was grit in his voice as he said *good*, and I had to force myself to stay on track.

Save money for a deposit so once Belle and Lance moved in together, I'd have a place to go. Sure, she'd said I didn't have to leave, there was space for all of us, but the apartment we were living in wasn't nearly as big as Belle's heart.

She and Lance were getting married in less than a year.

They needed their own home.

It wasn't her fault my temper got the best of me, and I tended to lose my jobs quicker than my mama could drop to her knees and pray for my wayward soul, if she even bothered anymore.

No, once again, I was the sole bearer of responsibility for my own impulsive decisions.

The guy was cute. The kind of boy I could have taken home to Mama before they kicked me out of my small Christian college and refused to allow me to return home. I'd become nothing if not resourceful, so I used the five grand in my checking account, hopped into my car—the only possession they allowed me to keep

—and headed to Nashville so I could chase my dreams instead of following someone else's plans.

Fat lot of good it'd done me in the three years since I'd been here. I was too busy chasing my tail to get around to chasing those big dreams I had.

"Where were you working?" the bartender asked.

He reminded me of a guy who'd ride motorcycles and forget to shave for years at a time. He was big, burly, with a belly that said he liked to eat and probably cooked well, too.

"Franco's."

"Ugh. That place is a shithole." That came from the man near the end of the bar. "Rough crowd."

"Well, we can't all work a pretty nine to five at some bank or something." That's what he had to do. Probably an accountant or something. So clean cut.

So—cute. No, that didn't do him justice at all, but with the dress pants and the buttoned popped on the collar on his gray dress shirt, he gave off young finance slash banker vibes for sure.

He choked on a laugh and covered his mouth with his fist. "I look like a banker?"

"Best thing I've heard all night," the bartender muttered. "After hearing you call your sister a snotface."

"Charming." But I was grinning.

Mostly because he was blushing.

"She started it," he said, and I laughed a little harder. "She also said I suck at… my job."

He cleared his throat and turned back to me. "It's the shirt, isn't it?"

"And the hair." Which was glossy. Swept to the side and neatly cut around the ears. Cute ears, too, which was *not* something I usually noticed in men, but everything about this man was like someone said, *"Draw me perfection who looks like they open car doors, says please and thanks and prays before their dinner meal"* and dropped him straight into it.

"I'm not a banker." His hand went to his hair, sweeping it to the side, and when he caught me watching him, dropped his hand back to the bar.

"So what do you do?" Impulsivity was scratching at my temples, teasing me to move toward him, maybe run my fingers through his hair to see if it was as soft as it looked from here.

He glanced at the bartender. Then me.

Ah. A guy who didn't want to be honest. Not my first rodeo.

"I work for Nashville Steel."

"Football team? Wasn't there a game tonight?"

"Yeah. There was a game." Another slight curl of his lips like he was hiding a secret and in no hurry to get to the punch line.

Usually it'd irritate me, but his lips were full and his teeth bright white and there were muscles in his arms that told me he probably could have easily taken out the asshole at Franco's who grabbed my tits while saying, "*I'll give you a tip. And if you're good, you'll get more than just the tip.*"

"So what are you? Their social media manager? Or do you work in their finance department?"

He was not. Couldn't be. But I hadn't felt the urge to flirt with anyone in months. Broadway brought out the worst in men. I'd seen it time and time again since moving there.

But this guy wasn't on Broadway—he was at some off-street sports bar talking to the bartender like they'd been friends for years. Hell, maybe he was the guy's son or something.

Not that I cared enough to ask. Truly.

A loud, booming laugh came from the other side of the bar.

The banker shot him a sheepish grin while scratching the back of his neck.

"Shut it, Lou."

Ah, so the Santa Claus biker lookalike was Lou. Made sense. The place was his, which explained the belly on him.

"My daughters are going to love this. Hell, get your sister back on the phone. This will make her year."

"You're a pain in the butt, Lou." Not-banker dude fidgeted in his seat, still grinning that sheepish smile when he swiveled on the stool in my direction. "I am, in a way, involved in their social media."

He was lying. It came in the twitch of his left eye and that look that said he still had a punchline to deliver.

I was getting tired of being at the mercy of other people's jokes, even if this was the most intrigued I'd felt toward anyone.

I shifted my attention to the bartender. "Lou, is it?"

"Yes, young lady?" He had a wide smile, slightly yellowed teeth, and lips that disappeared into his full beard.

"You want to tell me what I'm missing?"

"Better if I showed you."

"Lou." The guy groaned and dropped his face into his hand, elbow now propped on the bar.

Lou ignored him and grabbed the remote. In seconds, I was staring at the guy who had offered to buy me drinks, no expectations. Sweat beads pooled on his forehead with football pads on.

Oh my goodness. Bury me in the back parking lot. Lance would *kill* me for not knowing who this guy was.

That his name appeared beneath his smile, and a microphone was shoved into his face and the words *Rookie Davis Hall scores three touchdowns in Monday Night Football Madness.*

I turned to him, heat creeping up on my cheeks, and tried to salvage my dignity.

It was hopeless. Lance said his name almost as often as he told Belle he loved her, and he loved her a *ton.*

"I can see the resemblance," I teased, bringing my beer to my lips.

He followed the action with a completely different look than was now behind him on the big screen. No wonder he had asked Lou to change the channel earlier.

"Is that your brother?"

Lou's laugh was boisterous, almost shaking the walls of his own bar.

Davis's smile, on the other hand? Charming. Completely disarming with a hint of roughness to it, and that gleam in his eye was no longer embarrassed.

It was heated.

Made my toes curl in my platform heels.

It was undeniably sexy.

"I have two sisters. No brothers." As if I hadn't just completely offended him.

"Huh."

He turned to Lou, requested two more beers, one for each of us, although the shots had warmed my stomach, and the beer was going straight to my head, leading to only bad decisions.

This guy played professional football. He made millions.

I was in no place to be breathing his same air, much less flirting with him… or doing anything else that impulsive itch suggested every time he smiled, and my insides fluttered.

"That's it? That's all you have to say? I mean, you're in the presence of *greatness*, and I get a completely unimpressed 'huh'?"

Oh, I was impressed. With his muscles and his smile and his hair and those teeth and lips and that straight nose… I hadn't looked down, but given the top half of him and now knowing his profession, I had a feeling he'd be ripped and muscled everywhere. Didn't quite care about football, but the rest of him was on a level of greatness I'd never touched before.

"I should go live on the TikTok or the Facebook with this. This is liquid gold."

Davis flipped his coaster at Lou like it was a frisbee without peeling his eyes off me. "What would it take, then?"

"What would what take?"

He leaned closer. There were four seats in between us, but we might as well have been pressed up against each other for all the heat he was giving off.

I shivered from the heat in his gaze.

"What would it take to impress you?"

———

Impulsivity won.

We stumbled through the door to Davis's condo, thirty floors in the air, a tangle of limbs entwined, and our mouths fused together.

He kicked off his shoes, I stumbled out of my heels and he laughed against my mouth as I dropped three inches lower.

"Damn, you're short," he muttered right before his hands that had been at my waist slid to my backside and with a quick move, I was lifted, legs wrapping around him.

"Prefer fun-sized."

He chuckled against my lips before pressing them to the hinge of my jaw. "Well, let's see how much fun we can have."

"Yes," I rasped, right as he bit down at that tender flesh of my shoulder, making the already heated storm within me burn brighter. Dear goodness, I did not have to go home with a football player on my *Bingo* card for the year, but I was not regretting my choices.

Yet. I'd see what tomorrow would bring.

In moments, I was clinging to him, inhaling the musky scent of his cologne or shampoo as he bent down and laid me out on his couch.

"Can't make it to the bedroom," Davis murmured. He leaned over me, one foot braced to the floor, one knee between my thigh and the couch, and began undoing the buttons of his dress shirt.

Like hell, I cared where I was to get to enjoy a view like this.

"Next time."

I was still staring at his chest, but my gaze rose as he said it. "There's more?"

I lifted a hand as his chest was exposed, pushed it beneath his opened shirt as he released the final button and took in the delicious view. His oh-so glorious six-pack and a thin trail of light brown hair that dipped beneath his waistband against a beautiful, tight and toned tan skin.

"If you're up for it."

"Let's see how good round one is first." My fingers went to his belt. I opened the clasp, but instead of going to the button of his pants, I slipped my fingers between his waistband and yanked him toward me.

He fell forward to me with a surprised gasp and a smile that lit up his carved cheekbones. One hand settled next to my shoulder, the other on the cushion. "It's going to be great, Snickers."

"Snickers?"

"Mm-hmm." His lips brushed over mine, back against my jawline. "My favorite fun-sized treat."

He silenced my laugh with a kiss, and his hands went to my shirt. "Need this off. Been wanting to touch you ever since you walked into Lou's tonight. First thing I thought of was if you'd taste like cherries."

More likely I tasted like sweat and bad decisions but thankfully he didn't seem to mind.

I lifted my arms as he pushed up my shirt, and for a moment, our eyes locked right before his dropped to my breasts that were testing the lacy confines of my bra.

A low, pleased groan slipped from his full lips before he glanced back at me. "You still sure you're okay about this?"

I was more sure given that he was kind enough to ask. "Yes."

"Good." His hand splayed flat to my soft stomach. "Then stay right here. I'll be right back."

"Thought you couldn't wait?"

He stood from the couch and shot me a wicked look that made my toes curl into the cushions beneath.

"Safety first."

CHAPTER 3
DAVIS

Never been so damn thrilled to not head to Broadway. Whatever was messing with my head dissipated after the call with my sister and then evaporated altogether as Maggie and I sat at Lou's until he kicked us out so he could close up. It was only then I suggested we head back to my place, if she'd be okay with that.

She'd fired off a quick text to a friend and slid off the stool.

As soon as we hit the elevators, I stopped holding back, and now I couldn't wait to get back to her, explore every inch of her short and curvy body. I grabbed the box of condoms I had in my nightstand and shucked out of my pants and socks before I hurried back to the living room.

Maggie was a vision, spread out with one leg bent on my couch, her hair a pillow of dark, stormy waves beneath her. Goddamn, she was gorgeous.

She caught my movement and turned her head in my direction, and it was then I noticed where her hand was. Where her fingers were… slipped beneath the band of her shorts and *moving*.

Oh dear God. Yes… this woman was everything.

"Show me," I grunted, nodding at her fingers doing the work I couldn't wait to help her out with.

Her laugh was low and husky, and when she went to pull her hand out from her shorts, I shook my head. "Stop."

"Which one do you want?"

I wanted her bent over this couch. Riding my face. Riding *me*. I wanted us so damn exhausted she'd stay tomorrow and so damn sore I couldn't walk right when I had to report back to practice on Wednesday.

I tossed the condoms onto the coffee table and retook my perch on the couch. In quick movements, I had her shorts undone, flung to the floor, and was staring at the wetness soaking through her white silk thong.

"Can I?" I curled my fingers around the edges of that frail fabric.

She lifted her hips, and I pulled them down slowly, anxious to be inside of her, still wanting to torture her.

It'd be fair play.

She'd been torturing me since the moment she walked through that door tonight.

She was shaved bare beneath her thong, and as I slowly tugged it down her thick, gorgeous fucking thighs, a shiver rolled through her. Her fingernails were white-tipped and I groaned as she pressed them to her clit, through her slit, and then made two circles as I finally slid her thong off her and it joined her shorts on the floor.

"What do you like? Hard and fast? Slow?"

"This. You right here, watching me."

Ahhh… an exhibitionist. I'd keep that in my pocket for later.

Except no. That wouldn't happen. Before I'd brought her here, I'd made it clear.

Tonight was for tonight. One night only. I had too much going on to be capable of more.

I'd been honest and gentle. Reminded her that I had no expectations. The drinks I bought and the plate of nachos we ended up sharing did not mean she owed me anything.

Except she'd agreed, finishing her last beer and licking her lips. *"That's good. I agree. I have too much to figure out myself."*

Later wouldn't come. That was okay. Perfect, even.

Except now that her cute little moans were filling my ears and her hips were rolling, making her breasts tremble, there wouldn't be nearly enough time for me to explore this body in all the ways I'd already dreamed of.

"That's enough," I said and my hand covered her fingers. "Let me see."

"Davis…"

"Shhh." I brought her fingers to my mouth, enthralled with the pink blooming on her cheeks and the gasps from her parted lips made as I wrapped my own lips around her fingers, and *holy sweet divine.*

"Not cherries," I whispered and bent down to kiss her to see if she'd be willing to taste herself. "Perfection."

My tongue slid into her mouth, wrapped with hers and her thighs pushed apart, allowing room for me between them. Her body melded to mine, hips rolled to meet me.

As I began to lose myself in her, relieving her of her bra and bringing my mouth to her pert, firm, and full breasts, I regretted my hasty decision.

One night wouldn't be enough.

She was too damn delicious.

———

The sun was rising over the horizon, and I hadn't spent a single minute with my hands not on some part of Maggie's body in hours.

And the things I'd learned about her. The shy hesitation she showed when I went down on her the first time. The way she screamed as she came and then asked me to do it again. We'd rested only for water and it was during our last break, Maggie sitting naked on my kitchen counter, me standing between her legs and swirling my tongue around her nipples in between sips of water when she'd tilted her head toward my private pool on the rooftop patio.

"Can we go for a swim?"

We didn't make it to the pool. I'd carried her out to the hot tub and sat her down on my hardening dick.

The thing should have been broken by now, useless, except

every touch from Maggie had turned me into a machine needing minimal recovery time in between rounds.

Water splashed around us, the bubbles from the hot tub only allowing the tips of her nipples to appear above the water before sinking back down, and her breasts were as perfect as I'd first thought. Round, firm, and full, I could use them for pillows and never sleep better.

"That's it. Nice and slow, Maggie."

She had her hands at my shoulder, riding my dick—*finally*—and with the sun rising behind me, the glow made every inch of her skin glisten, her eyes, cornflower blue, closed, and she dropped her head down as if she wanted to see me filling her.

"You feel so good. It's like… it'd just… so damn good…"

It was fucking perfection. Never had a woman made me feel this insane. I tightened my fingers against her ass, loving the soft flesh, and yanked her down.

She let out a cry, unhindered by being outside with every noise she made.

Screw any neighbor who could hear us.

Her thighs began shaking, that telltale sign she was close, and then she was biting down on my shoulder. A sharp pain ripped through me as she came, clamping her teeth against me and I moved her harder, slower, so deep inside of her I could feel the end of her until I groaned out my own release. That bite was going to leave a mark and screw anyone who gave me shit about it.

I'd worked my ass for it.

Slowly her orgasm receded, and I held her against me. I let her go with one hand and reached for the hot tub's remote control to turn the jets off. My body was liquid, burning, and not entirely from the early morning sun or the water.

"We should get out of here and dry off."

Her arms wrapped around my shoulders, and she hugged me tight. "Can't walk. Carry me?"

I doubted my own legs could handle it right now.

I'd had girlfriends in high school. A few in college that lasted longer than six months, and I'd had more than my share of one-night stands, but I'd never had this connection. This sense of something so damn right at the absolute worst fucking timing in my life.

I couldn't keep her.

She'd agreed to one night and was as set on it as I'd originally been.

But we'd just spent hours together, and I wasn't ready to let her go.

So I stood, groaned as I climbed to my feet, and managed to get us out of the hot tub. I always kept a shelf of towels outside, so I grabbed one for her and wrapped it around her back, tucked it between us before I wiped off my feet and stepped inside.

"I need to go get dried off and dressed." Probably needed another shower.

A six-hour recharge nap.

"I'll be right back, okay?"

She clung to the towel and tipped her head up. She was shorter than I originally thought, and all five feet two of her that was more than a foot shorter than me looked up at me.

"Okay."

I kissed her forehead and hurried back to my bedroom. My sheets were a disaster. We'd spent rounds two through four on the bed. Memories that would stay with me when I was on the road and only had my hand for pleasure. It didn't take me long to grab a quick shower, dry off, and tug on a fresh pair of shorts.

I'd talk to her. Maybe I couldn't promise much but I could see her again? Spend the day with her? One more night…?

I'd ask.

But then I returned to my living room, and she wasn't where I left her standing.

Her shorts that had spent all night and early morning puddled on my floor were gone. Along with the rest of her clothes. The towel I'd given her was draped over the back of the couch.

"Maggie?"

Nothing. Not even a muffled response from the hall bath behind me, but I already knew it was empty since the door was open.

Not a sound except for the gentle hum of the air conditioner.

She was gone.

"Well, shit."

That sucked.

CHAPTER 4
MAGGIE

My stomach tied itself into a thousand knots, and I couldn't peel my gaze off the growing pile of plastic sticks on the coffee table in front of me.

It was rare I wished I could go back to the simple life I'd known growing up the first eighteen years of my life, but today was definitely one of them. As if I'd ever be welcomed. If there was a slight chance of it before, it evaporated into mist now.

"What am I going to do?"

Belle, my sweet friend who'd welcomed me into her apartment after she found me sleeping in my car almost a year ago, smiled in a way that said everything would be okay.

Because she'd make it so.

If only I had her confidence.

"We'll tell him. He seems like a good enough guy, and you know where he lives."

She knew *all* about him. Between Lance's obsession with the running back and my admission I'd slept with him after that night in October, Belle knew more about the man than anyone outside his own mother, probably. And I'd spent the last seven Sundays out of the apartment at game times so I didn't have to see his face on the screen or hear Lance talk about him. Not that that mattered—I'd certainly done my fair share of stalking.

Belle was right, like usual. He definitely seemed like a decent guy. He'd at least given me a night of fantasies I wasn't sure I'd ever recover from. Who in the world could compete with his stamina? It'd taken me four days to walk without a limp again.

I fiddled with the threads of my worn T-shirt. "Maybe I don't have to. He doesn't have to know. I could—"

"Could you?"

No. I was already shaking my head. I couldn't.

"It's okay."

Belle always smelled like lemons and sunshine, and she did now as she climbed off her perch on the couch, joined me on the floor where I was still staring at the scattering of pregnancy tests she'd run to the drugstore to purchase for me. She wrapped her arm across my shoulders and pulled me to her until my head hit her shoulder.

"It'll be okay. We'll give you some time to figure things out. It's okay to take a few days or whatever if you need it. And then you guys can figure out the rest."

I was twenty-two years old, pregnant, knocked up by a stranger, and had spent the last year living in my friend's guest room after being evicted from my last house due to my horrifically crappy roommates. Belle and I had met when I worked at a karaoke bar. She'd actually heard me sing when no one in the crowd wanted to go up, and then afterward, I was fired for dropping an entire case of glasses all over the floor. I'd been living out of my car, when she chased after me to talk about my singing. She insisted on helping me, and after I turned her down with singing help, she'd refused to leave me alone until I stayed the night at her house. That one night, when I was exhausted and couldn't fight her turned into months of staying with her and the best friendship I'd ever had. Since the night I couldn't stop thinking about, I finally found an apartment of my own, as dingy and unsafe as it was. I was trying to find a better apartment, and I'd resigned myself to trying to find a roommate. Now that I was pregnant? What stranger wanted to take *that* on?

I picked up one of the pregnancy sticks and tilted it back and forth, but it was the same digital readout of the word I'd dreaded seeing for the last two weeks since I realized my period was late. It wasn't until I almost puked out of nowhere this morning that reality became clearer.

I was twenty-two without a full-time career or a college education and moved to Nashville to make it big as a country singer and so far, I'd bounced around living arrangements, had at least a dozen jobs, and not once had I been able to do anything more than step on stage at karaoke bars.

"I can't believe this is happening. I mean… how?"

Belle snorted and gave me a shove. "When a man…"

"Shut up. I know *how*." And boy, did I vividly remember. "We were careful."

"Every time?"

"All five of them."

"I still think you're fibbing about that."

"The couch." I held up a finger and Belle laughed.

"Shut up, you brat. I've *heard*. Trust me, but a man that good shouldn't be real. Puts the rest of them to shame."

Exactly. How would I ever move on from that night? More than once, before I thought I was pregnant, I'd considered stopping by his place for a repeat. Or heading to Lou's to leave my number for him. They'd seemed close.

I'd felt desperate.

That was probably a weekly occurrence for him. I would have been forgotten the next day, which was why I'd snuck out before that awkward goodbye could happen or before I could suggest I give him my number and have him either take it and never call or politely turn me down.

Next to me, Belle stood and started cleaning up my pregnancy sticks and boxes. "Do you need anything?"

"A better family?" The joke fell flat as Belle's smile.

"You have me and Lance and my family. We'll make sure you're taken care of."

"He's moving in with you and you're starting your own life together. I need to figure this out on my own."

Just like I'd been doing since I'd gotten pulled out of my conservative Christian college after my resident adviser found a boy in my room.

We'd only been kissing, but it was after curfew. The fact that Jacob had brought beer, which was a huge no-no, was the second mark on my record. The school had called my parents, and they'd yanked me out of school. When I refused to return home to our small town in the middle of Nowheresville, Missouri to repent from my sins, they told me I was on my own.

"Should have named you Jezebel, you harlot. You may return to the fold when you're ready to repent of your sins."

Yeah… no thanks, Mom.

My father had only been slightly less hurtful. *"That's what happens without the protection and leadership of a man over your life."*

I could hear him scratching his next sermon, probably a warning to all the women in the congregation. They'd use me as a warning, and many of the young girls would probably never be allowed to leave home if they were still single.

The only people I missed were my younger siblings, mostly my sisters. Their life would only get harder because of my screw-ups.

"Knew we never should have sent you to school. Knew the world would sink its evil claws into you."

"Hey." Belle shook my shoulder and stood, grunting as she stood. "Come on. Lance and I will never turn our backs on you. We may not be blood, but you're stuck with us forever."

"Thanks."

She took my hand and pulled me to my feet. "Let's get some food in you. We'll have this all sorted in no time."

Right. It'd be so easy to go talk to a professional football player, show up at his door and say, "Hey, remember me? Well, you're stuck with me forever now."

I might have grown up in an ultra-conservative Christian family where I hadn't been allowed to wear jeans until I was exiled, but I'd lived enough in the last three years.

That night I'd spent with Davis Hall, had been the best night of my life, and that was before the sex that lasted all night. He was funny. He'd offered me a reprieve from the anxiety running through my mind like a hamster on a wheel. We'd laughed and teased, even in the midst of passionate, limb-wrecking sex. I'd never felt so free. Heck, I'd allowed him to go down on me when I'd only let one other guy do that. Enjoyed the hell out of it too.

My core pulsed at the memory. That first swipe of his tongue against my already swollen and ready clit, and I shivered. Damn, he was *good*.

"Right. It'll all be sorted. Everything will be fine. My future is mine for the making."

"That's the spirit." Belle laughed. "Keep saying it and you might believe it."

I had to. The belief I could make something of myself, on my own, was the only thing I had left.

Well, other than a mostly stranger's DNA growing inside of me.

———

"I can't believe we're doing this. And on Christmas."

Belle wove her car through the streets of Nashville.

"It's Christmas Eve, and they had a game today. He'll have to be home."

"Yeah, with a house filled with friends or something. Or worse… family."

Pregnant after a one-night stand. I wasn't exactly nailing the *take home to mom* material.

"Stop worrying. Everything will be fine."

She had said that for the last three days, ever since that first positive sign showed up and every minute after. Sure, easy as that. Stop worrying. Easy peasy. Done.

If only…. She turned down his street. Lou's lights were on across the way and a frog jumped into my throat as the high-rise condominium complex loomed overhead.

This was stupid. It was seven o'clock at night on Christmas Eve.

My life couldn't get any more strange.

"At least they won the game." I hadn't avoided today's game. Anxiously pacing for three hours knowing what we were doing tonight was my afternoon exercise. My feet were sore, and I was pretty sure, swollen. "It'll put him in a good mood, right?"

Belle squeezed my hand as the automatic doors slid open to us and *wowzers.*

This was luxurious. From the artwork to the crystal hanging chandeliers, this building screamed modern and *expensive.* The tan leather couch with a gold chrome frame probably cost more than my father made as a pastor in six months. It was more gorgeous than I remembered it, but last time I'd only had eyes for a blue-eyed devil with apparently very virile sperm.

"It'll be fine. You said you guys had a great night. He does a ton of volunteer work with kids and his background couldn't be anymore paper-perfect. This is not the kind of guy who's going to throw you to the streets."

Raised in Nebraska. Played football at Clemson. His dad was a factory worker, his mom a dental hygienist, and he was the youngest of three with two older sisters. Thanks, Wikipedia, for giving me my baby daddy's background so easily. Now we didn't need to have the *"tell me about your family"* conversation.

Just jump right into *"so you're going to be a dad, how's that feel?"* conversation.

Should be easy enough.

"Yeah, but he has the money to fight me for custody or something."

"Let's just talk to him first, okay? Before you spiral into another panic attack?"

"It wasn't a panic attack." I freaked, sure, but who wouldn't. I blamed the hormones coursing through my body at higher than average levels.

"You say potato…"

"May I help you young ladies?"

A gentleman, old enough to be my grandfather with the same shining white hair and dressed in a deep red suit coat with black lapels stood behind a marble security desk. The hair was the only thing he had in common with my grandfather—I'd never seen mine give a smile this guy was doing. Friendly and open and lacking extreme judgment.

"Yes." Belle pulled me toward him while I followed. "Can you please tell us if Davis Hall is here? We need to speak with him."

CHAPTER 5
DAVIS

"Make sure you take care of yourself and rest." My dad's face was a blurry mess on my phone's screen. Behind him, my mom kept moving in and out of the frame.

"I'm good. Only mildly sore."

Tonight's game had been brutal and I'd taken a few hard hits. One midair while I was trying to hurdle a defender who must have crouched down to prepare for what was becoming my signature move because Boston's safety stood right as I was over him and knocked me flat on my back. So hard it'd taken me a few seconds to move.

Still held on to the ball and scored the touchdown though.

"I miss you!" My sister, Annie, jumped into view and gave me her profile, running her hands down the side of her massive belly. "I'm so sorry I stole Mom and Dad from you on Christmas."

"You're too big to travel, and I had a game to play. It's okay. Next year."

"Next year." A grin broke out on her face, and Mom and Dad were shoved out of view completely as my nephews, Annie's oldest two boys, jumped up and down. Their ginger hair bounced on their heads.

"Hey boys. Ready for Santa to come?"

"Mommy said bad boys get coal, not toys." Luka shoved out his lips into a pout.

"That's true." I nodded seriously. Being an uncle was sometimes serious business. "But you've been a good boy all year, right?"

Behind him, Annie snorted.

His six-year-old face scrunched up. "Mostly?"

"Then I don't think you have to worry about coal, Luka." I wiggled my finger in the screen for him to come closer. "And if you *do* get coal from Santa, don't forget that Uncle Davis sent you something, too, okay? I promise you'll have presents."

His blue eyes went wide and bright. "A *Jeep*?"

He'd been talking about that ride-on toy since his birthday in April, and Annie forced me to hold off on getting it for him until Christmas. They lived a simple life on Duke's farm and refused to allow me to spoil their kids throughout the year unless it was something necessary, like books, but on Christmas, I was allowed to go wild.

So yeah… Luka was getting a Jeep and an Escalade because what good were ride-on toys on the farm if you couldn't race against friends or your younger brother?

"Can't say. But make sure you're extra good for your mom tonight. Maybe read a book to your baby sister you'll meet soon, and we'll see what happens in the morning, okay?"

He didn't hear a word I said, lost in Jeep excitement. "Love you, Uncle Davis! You da' best."

"All right. Put Grandma back on the phone, would you, kiddo?"

My mom's phone swung through the air giving me a blurry look inside Annie and Duke's one-hundred-plus-year-old farmhouse before my mom's gentle smile came into focus.

"Love you. You going to see anyone tomorrow?"

I'd been invited to my buddy Cole's place with his girlfriend, Eden, and Cole's son, Jasper. Cole was our quarterback, and he'd taken me under his wing, even letting me stay with him for a couple weeks when I first moved to town. He lived in his hometown, a small town north of Nashville, and I usually loved going there. Our tight end, Dawson, had mentioned us getting together and hanging out, and having some drinks, and Yeets, one of our wide receivers, invited me over to his family's cookout. He had his entire family visiting from Alabama and one more mouth to feed out of the thirty who'd been in the stands earlier would be nothing. The idea of Yeets's cookout made my mouth water at the mere thought. His Southern mama could *cook*.

"I've got places I can go."

Outside the food, I wasn't feeling any of them though. All that love and mushiness and familial drama. Something had been missing lately, and it'd all started that night in October....

Probably had to do with this being my first year not making it home for Christmas or being around family at all.

Or could be…

No. Maggie was a great time. I'd enjoyed her. Had I thought about her and the sounds she made when I slid deep inside her since? When I wrapped my hand around her hair when she was on her knees at the edge of my bed? What man wouldn't? She'd been short and curvy with massive tits I could have played with for hours. I hated she'd walked out when I'd wanted her to stay. The sting of that hadn't quite left me.

It was one night of fun. *Great* fun. I needed to remember that— and soon, go find someone else.

It'd be easier if I could stop thinking of her.

"Okay. We'll call you tomorrow once we unbury ourselves from the mountains of presents sitting in Annie's garage."

"Love you, Mom."

My dad's voice came through, muffled from a distance. I didn't need to hear him to know what he said. "And tell Dad I'll go soak in the hot tub."

"Love you, too. Davis. Sleep well, and Merry Christmas."

I shoved off the couch and was careful as I made my way to the kitchen to grab an ice pack from the freezer, because I might have been a fully grown adult, but my dad's advice was always sound. My shoulder and ankle, and lower back were sore as hell. College football never did me dirty like this.

My phone rang as I went over to the freezer, digging through frozen vegetables, looking for ice packs, and I didn't bother glancing at the screen first.

It was Christmas Eve. My phone had been ringing off the hook with invites to head to other player's houses or Coach's.

"Yeah?"

"Mr. Hall, sir, it's Roger at the front desk. I have a young woman here to see you."

I mean… could make for a great Christmas gift from one of my friends on the team, but not really my style.

I gave up on finding the ice pack and grabbed a bag of peas, closing the freezer door. "Not expecting anyone, Roger."

"That's what I told her, sir, but she's insistent you'd want to see her."

"I've told you a thousand times to call me Davis."

"Can't do that, Mr. Hall."

Mr. Hall was my father, a great man. I could only hope to someday live up to half of his awesomeness. I was only twenty-three years old. I wasn't Mr. Anything except maybe Mister-Great at running forty yards in four point two four seconds.

Thank God I chose a secure building, especially if she wasn't a gift from a player but a fan. "What's her name?"

"Maggie, sir."

Maggie. It couldn't be. And after I'd just been thinking about her? After she vanished? No way.

More memories flashed. Her plump ass in my hands while she sat on my face. Her breasts bouncing, visible in the mirror above my dresser while I took her from behind. Her mouth on my —

"You sure?"

"That's what she says, sir."

"She look like someone who has an ass you want bent over your kitchen table?"

We hadn't done that, but I'd wanted it.

A cough sputtered through the line. Might have given dear old Roger a heart attack. Oops. My bad.

"Sir—"

"Davis."

"Um. Davis. I'm not sure…"

"Just tell me, Roger. Yes or no." Because if it was her, we had a lot to talk about.

"Uh. Well, yes, sir. If I was thirty years young and hadn't had that hip surgery…"

Perfect. "I knew you were a dirty old man. Send her on up."

Well, hot damn.

Merry Christmas to me, after all.

————

Bag of peas forgotten, I hurried to the bathroom. I'd had to dress in a suit before heading to the field this morning from the hotel the team stayed in before game nights. Lucky for me, the hotel we used for the season was only two blocks away, so it wasn't really an inconvenience. I'd walked over to the hotel in athletic wear yesterday, my suit in a hanging bag draped over my shoulder. After I got home from the game today, I'd tossed my suit and overnight bag in my laundry room and changed into a pair of gray sweatpants and black Steel T-shirt. Our logo, a red outline of a football with flames wrapped around it, was stamped across my chest, and a quick look at my hair showed I wasn't looking too shabby at all.

A normal guy who had a house of his own.

Sure, if normal guy meant I was the first-round draft pick, and I lived in a penthouse with my own private rooftop deck with a pool and hot tub on the thirty-eighth floor of a downtown Nashville apartment building overlooking Broadway and our stadium. But what really was normal, anyway?

When a quiet knock came from my front door, I was pacing back and forth in front of the entryway, waiting, worrying.

I'd wanted her to stay, thought about going to Franco's, the bar she said she'd been fired from to see if they'd give me her last name and look her up on Instagram or something but hadn't.

She'd left. We'd only agreed to one night. So why was she here…

My hand shook as I opened the door. A number one high school recruit and a first-round draft pick, and I got nervous around beautiful girls. If only the media could see that side of me—on second thought…

Nope.

I opened the door and stood in the doorway, and there she was.

Maggie.

Thick head of shining chocolate-brown hair. Completely natural with a curvy body and those tits….

Damn, those suckers were otherworldly. So full. Round. Plump.

"Snickers," I choked out. And made sure I hadn't actually been saying hello to the *girls* but to the girl…

Well… the girls. "You are?"

The blonde standing off to Maggie's side shrugged. "Moral support."

"Hello, moral support." The new blonde rolled her eyes.

I dismissed her for the girl who'd appeared in more than one dream in the last two months.

As our eyes met again, Maggie shuffled on her feet. Not exactly the excited look of what I would have preferred. "How are you?"

"Can we talk?" she asked, and I was pretty sure those light-blue eyes of hers had a sheen of wetness in them.

No good conversation ever started with tears and a need to talk. "Sure."

I stepped back, and they entered, the new blonde more confident and at ease, while Maggie's eyes roamed the open floor of my condo. Straight ahead from my front door was the city's skyline with an entire wall of floor-to-ceiling windows that overlooked my two-story deck. Although she'd already seen it. Was she thinking about what we'd done out there? Or on the couch in her line of sight or at the kitchen counter?

Hell, we'd defiled ninety percent of the interior.

Her eyes rounded larger with everything she took in, and her face paled.

What the hell?

I mean… she'd come *here*. Moral support headed to the kitchen counter, dropped her purse and hopped up onto one of the black leather stools. "Merry Christmas, by the way, and good game today."

Confusion and excitement whirled together, slicing through my stomach as something else took root.

Worry. Who *were* these women, and what in the hell were they doing here, and worse… why had I let them in?

CHAPTER 6
MAGGIE

was so vastly out of my league.

In all my worry over the last several days, I'd forgotten the most important thing.

He was filthy rich and living a high-profile life.

I was the exact opposite and hadn't taken a single step to accomplish what I wanted most in life.

What in the hell did we have in common besides a mixture of our DNA forming into something that would soon resemble an alien swimming in my uterus?

"Um. I know this is a surprise and all, but I swear neither of us are crazy."

"Speak for yourself," Belle snorted. "Lance tells me all the time I'm a certified nut job."

Davis's thick, blond brows tugged together, and his gaze slid from me to her.

"Not helping, Belle."

"Ah. So moral support has a name."

"Hello." She waved from her perch where she'd made herself at home in the kitchen. "Got anything to drink?"

"No offense, but I think I should know why you're here, so maybe we can start with that?"

"It's her story." Belle slid off the stool. I swear... she got away with everything. "I'm thirsty." She had a hand at the fridge's door handle and waited for Davis's go-ahead.

He was still giving me that constipated, worried, and maybe… slightly happy look. I'd wipe that last one away soon enough. "She always like this?"

"Belle doesn't know the meaning of the words stranger or boundaries."

"Truth."

Without tearing his eyes off me, he nodded. "Go ahead. Water only and no phones."

"No phones?"

"Not until I know you two didn't come here to snoop through my things or sell pictures of my home to the highest local gossip rag or whatever, so yeah. No phones."

"Like I need the cash. I've made more money sitting in this kitchen in thirty seconds than you have in three months, and yes—I know your salary. Which is public information before you really do think I'm short a few marbles."

Awesome. She was spiraling out of control. "Belle! Can you please shut up?"

"Well, he should know." She twisted off the top of her water bottle and placed a second one on the counter. "That's for you, Mags. You should fill your stomach." She turned to Davis. "My great-grandfather's family started, and my family still runs WWMP. I'm *old, homegrown Nashville money*. Trust me, any peanuts I'd make off selling pics of you to gossip rags—which neither of us would *ever* do—would be tossed in the donation plate at next Sunday's Mass. If I still went to church, anyway."

Davis blinked rapidly and then scrubbed his hands down his face. "What in the hell is going on right now?"

"Sorry." Although I didn't really think he was talking to me. "She's a lot, but I needed to see you, and she wouldn't let me come alone."

"Right." His hands fell to his hips with a heavy sigh, and he blew out a breath so hard his hair blew up at his forehead. "Let's get back to that, and maybe the rest of this might start to make sense."

It was go-time. I'd practiced this a million times once those sticks started coming up positive. Now I was there—chin tilted up to look him in the face, and he still had to look down at me. He was everything I remembered. A slight wave to the thick but neatly trimmed and cut hair, longer on top. An innocent-looking face and a body that spoke of sin, he'd definitely proven he was no innocent.

"She's pregnant," Belle blurted.

Davis's head whipped in her direction, and mine followed.

"What?" She shrugged and swallowed a gulp of water. "You were taking too long."

Dear God, please forgive me for all my sins and take me now.

"What'd you—" He turned to me. "What'd she say?"

"Merry Christmas, you're going to be a dad?"

Which was *not* the way I'd decided on how to let him know—it just came out.

Davis sputtered. Swiped his hand over his hair and down his face again. It was too early to be those pregnancy hormones raging I'd already read about, thanks to Belle, but it did something to me. Maybe it was being here again. Seeing him. He was utter perfection carved straight from marble with the cheekbones and those lips and muscles…

Two months ago, I walked away because I feared how much I'd felt for him after that night. And it wasn't the sex. Not entirely. It was the laughter and the respect and the fun and the freedom I'd had to be myself, to try new things. To do things I'd only ever been curious about before and have him love every damn minute of it.

"We were safe. Every damn time."

"Studies show condoms don't always hold up in the heat of hot tubs."

Davis's head whipped toward Belle, who I was pretty certain needed a knife to her throat, and then back to me. "What?"

"It's a theory she has," I said quietly. This was not at all how I wanted this to go. Probably should have left Belle at home.

I'd been right, though. He was definitely not looking happy in any way, shape, or form, and as he stood there, gaping at me, his tanned skin paled with every heated, silent moment that passed between us.

"You're not lying," he finally said, and the words came out of his mouth thick with grit.

Pretty sure regret was in there as well.

"No." I shook my head, unable to say anything further. What else could I say? We'd agreed to one night—not a lifetime of being connected to each other.

"I need a minute."

Davis stalked off, palm of his hand pressed to his forehead, eyes glazed over. I spun on my feet as he threw open the sliding door to his deck and then slumped into one of the lounge chairs right outside the door.

His feet hit the ground, elbows to his knees, and his head fell forward, staring at his hands, the cement floor. More likely, he wasn't seeing anything except the end of his life as he envisioned it.

"You should have stayed quiet," I told Belle and grabbed the water bottle she'd slid across the island to me. "You *promised* you'd stay quiet."

"I'm sorry. Forgive me?"

"Never." Of course I would.

She'd been there for me when no one else was, and without Belle in my life, I had no idea where I'd be, but it wouldn't still be in Nashville that was for certain. Although, then I wouldn't be in this mess in the first place.

"I can leave. I really am sorry."

"Don't leave yet." She was my ride, after all, if he came back in and told me to get the heck out.

She nodded and glanced outside. "Think we should go see if he's alive?"

A very unladylike snort escaped me. Belle was bonkers. I turned to see Davis hadn't moved an inch since he collapsed into that chair, but as I ran my fingers through my hair, his head lifted, and our eyes met. His steely dark eyes slammed into mine and stole my breath with the intensity. The worry. The fear. The *anger*.

He pushed off the chair, and this time he was gentle when he opened the sliding door. It closed behind him, and he shifted that look of his to Belle.

"I'd like to talk to Maggie alone."

I immediately changed my mind about needing a ride. I'd call an Uber if I had to, but this was something I should have done on my own in the first place.

"I'm good," I told Belle. "You can go."

"I can wait in the lobby?"

I was already shaking my head. "It's okay."

"You drove?" Davis asked, and the question was for Belle, but he was still staring at me.

"She did."

"I'll get her home. I swear she'll be safe with me. Besides…" His lips quirked, that first hint of his playfulness returning as he smirked at Belle. "I'm guessing you not only know where I live but what I do and where I work and probably my bosses' names and my entire family's history?"

She smiled with no shame. "Not your *entire* family history. Things get hazy before your grandparents on your mother's side."

"Of course." At least he was being a good sport about Belle's insanity. He chuckled and settled his hands on his hips. "You okay with staying here with me so we can talk?"

Not in a long shot. Hard conversations were never my strong suit, and this was sure to be a doozy. "I'll be all right."

"I'll leave then." Belle grabbed her purse and walked toward Davis. "But hurt her, and I can bury your body. I have connections. Besides, she's been through enough."

His jaw fell open, and she walked away, winking at me before squeezing my shoulder. "You'll be good."

The click of his door closing after she left brought with it a heavy silence.

We spoke at the same time.

"I'm keeping it."

"Are you sure it's mine?"

And then again.

"Okay."

"Yes."

A nervous laugh fell from both of us, and Davis swiped his hand over his mouth before that glazed look in his eyes returned.

"I'm not sure what we even need to talk about, to be honest. Do you need anything? Something to eat? Drink?"

"I'm good."

"Should we sit?"

I moved toward the couch with trepidation. I'd been spread out all over that thing, thigh draped over the back while his fingers drove me wild. While he teased my nipples and had me crying out his name, and even though I hadn't forgotten a single moment of that night, being there, seeing that couch brought it all back in vivid detail.

"Show me how you like it."

A shiver rolled through me before I could fight it back, and I took a seat on the chair, the only visible piece of furniture we hadn't defiled.

Davis went to the fridge and grabbed his own water before turning. If I wasn't mistaken, he stared at the couch a beat longer than normal too, before he took a seat farthest from me.

"I have questions, and I'm not sure where to start, but you're one hundred percent sure you're pregnant, and it's mine?"

I'd repeat it as many times as he needed me to. His shock was probably the same, or worse, than mine had been.

"Yes. I have blood test results and printouts of the first scan I had if you need to see." I reached for my purse, but he shook his head.

"Not right now. And the other?"

"The last guy I was with was months before you. Tim and I dated for a few months, and it ended in the spring. I haven't been with anyone since. Well… until you."

His jaw jutted out, and he was again shaking his head. "I don't really want to hear specifics about who else you slept with as long as you're sure."

I held my hands in my lap like I was getting reprimanded by my prep-school Sunday teacher. "We can do DNA testing if you need the proof, and I'm really sorry to drop in here, tonight of all nights, but I wanted you to know."

He nodded at the DNA testing, lifted his head, and stared out to his patio, the night sky of Nashville black, before turning that gaze back to me.

"I was pissed you left after that night."

Not at all what I was expecting him to say, and surprise chilled my body before quickly heating it, probably why I opened my mouth and nothing but "Ohhhh...." fell out.

CHAPTER 7
DAVIS

Goddamn.

First, fuck Tim.

Second… pregnant? Probably should have been first, but seriously, fuck that guy who got to have her and enjoy her before me.

My head was a goddamn mess, which was probably why I went back to that night, but it was the one consistent thought racing through my mind since Roger told me she was downstairs.

And now that I'd started it, I couldn't reel it back in. "I went to get dressed, and you were gone. And trust me, I'd be impressed with the speed of how quick you shot the hell out of here if I wasn't still mad you bolted."

Her fingers twisted together in her lap, and a look of shock changed to something I hoped was regret. "You'd said one night, and it was morning. I didn't want the goodbye to be weird or anything."

Yeah, 'cause nothing was weirder than wanting more and finding silence. "Right. Okay."

Not like I was going to tell her I hadn't wanted her to go at all that day. Maybe should have made that clear while she was riding me at sunrise in the hot tub. My bad. Lesson learned.

"So… um… the baby?"

A laugh broke free. Hot damn. "A baby."

I wasn't sure if I needed to laugh or cry or call my mom or punch a wall. A fucking baby.

What a dumbass rookie mistake to knock up some woman my first year of playing professional football by a chick who was supposed to be a one-night stand.

And oh shit… *my mom*… my dad. And my sisters…. They were going to want to murder Maggie.

My body turned freezing. Then boiling. My hands turned clammy, and my heart was ready to jump right through bone and muscle and flesh and plop itself right onto the floor with the speed it was currently beating.

God freaking *damn*. A baby.

I was going to be a father.

"How far along?" I choked out. I had four, soon-to-be five, nieces and nephews.

"Eight weeks based on my last period and all that stuff…"

My lips turned dry, and I licked them, but my mouth was equally parched, so I grabbed my water and chugged the entire bottle. Didn't help. I shoved to my feet and paced. I could imagine the Christmas conversation tomorrow with my family.

"So hey, kid, what's new today? Having a good Christmas?"

"Oh nothing, just gonna be a dad. Merry Christmas, gotta jet."

Maybe I wouldn't have to tell them. Maybe I could…

"Does your family know?" I asked Maggie. I'd somehow ended up behind the couch in my wild, possibly feral pacing.

She was gaping at me. "Uh. No?"

"No?"

"We're not close." Her lips pressed into a thin line, and still, I was thinking of how they tasted. Definitely not cherries, sweeter. Better.

"That sucks," I muttered and returned to pacing. I'd had a game today and should be resting before heading out to…. "Oh shit." I laughed and shoved my hand through my hair.

There was no way I was going to Broadway *now*. I'd have to call Mason and let him know.

"Are you okay?" Maggie's quiet, hesitant question made me freeze in place again.

"Okay?"

"I mean… I know you're in shock because this is big, huge, and I just showed up and sprang it on you but you don't have to be involved or anything, but I still thought it was the right thing to do. To let you decide…"

Ha. Decide. She'd already made the biggest decision on her own —and totally within her right—but my decisions now sucked. Become a dad well before I wanted to or become a deadbeat. There was only one choice.

"I'm having something to do with this baby, Maggie."

"Oh. Okay." Those hands twisted together in front of her again. "That's good. I'm happy. About that. You know."

"Good."

Perfect.

We were both happy about this. Except she hadn't said that. "Are you?"

A tiny line dug deep between her brows. "Am I what?"

"Happy. About this."

"Oh." A nervous laugh slipped from her, jumping over itself on the way out of her lush lips and a pink rose on her cheeks. "I guess, I'm not sure happy is the word I'd use, and definitely not how I saw it happening at all, by the way, but I've had some time to consider it, start to get used to the idea."

Yeah, happy wasn't really the word I was thinking either.

"How were you thinking it'd happen?"

"Well, I'd actually know the guy."

Right. Knowing each other would have been the best first step.

She chuckled, a nervous little hitch in her laugh that had me joining her.

And it was just that easy for us. Ice broken. In the midst of the maelstrom of emotions racing through me at warp speed, this girl could make me laugh.

"There should be that," I agreed, and a smile tugged at my lips.

"We'd probably be dating for a while. And then, you know, married."

"All good things."

She grinned.

I grinned.

Damn, I wanted to kiss her again.

————

I did not do that. Instead, I asked for a couple minutes and headed to the bedroom after making her swear she wouldn't bolt. When I returned to the kitchen, she was at the kitchen counter and had her purse opened. I cringed at the earlier comment about no phones when I saw hers had been shoved to the center of the island. Had that been a dickhead thing to say?

Probably not all things considered, and now that it was just the two of us, I had no worries.

If she'd wanted money for pictures or any gossip, she'd had plenty of opportunity the last time she was here.

The palm of her hand was at her stomach, and her mouth was pressed into a frown.

"You okay?" I asked.

She jumped and then nodded. "Yeah, my stomach gets upset every once in a while. It should pass."

I headed to the fridge. "I have two sisters, and one is pregnant, due any day, just so you know. And my sisters and I are close, so there isn't much I don't know, at least from their perspective, about pregnancy, so if you're craving anything, or can't eat something, let me know."

I dug through the drawers and found blocks of pre-sliced cheese. I had guacamole I was pretty sure was safe for her, and some orange juice. I grabbed it all, set it on the island, and headed into the walk-in pantry, where I grabbed chips and crackers. Before dropping it at the island, I grabbed some plates off the open shelves.

"Help yourself to anything," I told her as I opened a bag of chips, grabbed one, and plunked it right into the guacamole.

She reached for a chunk of cheese. "Thank you. So, did you want to see this?"

She slid a piece of paper in my direction, and on second glance, it was more than one page, but the one that made my heart start to race again was the curled edges of the thin, silk-like paper.

"You said you had a scan," I muttered, staring at that paper and already knowing what I'd see. "An ultrasound?"

"Doctor wanted to do it to check my dates and stuff, get a better idea."

There'd be a blob of grayness against gray grain. When Annie told me she was ten weeks along this last time, she said her baby was the size of a kumquat, which I'd taken to calling it for the last several months since it was hilarious. If Maggie was eight weeks... well, there was an almost kumquat-sized ball on those pictures, and as soon as I saw it, I'd have to face reality.

She was pregnant.

With my child. I didn't doubt her honesty. I'd only known her one night, but somehow, even with something this big, I trusted her.

I was going to be a dad. Which meant I had to grow up far earlier than I'd ever anticipated. I reached out and pressed two fingers to the edge of the paper like it'd shoot a spark of fire through me and tugged it close.

There it was.

"Looks like a gummy bear."

Across the island from me, Maggie chuckled. The sound was muted against the roar in my ears as I slid my finger over the photos. A tiny blob with stubby little arms and legs already showing.

My throat tightened, and my chest squeezed so tight air left me on a wheeze.

"Holy shit. I'm going to be a dad."

"Yeah," Maggie said. And I was still staring at the picture, but I was pretty sure she was grinning.

What in the hell did I do now?

And what was my family going to do when I told them?

"Okay." Rubbing my hands together, I ignored the fact my palms were clammy. This was a big deal. "What's the plan?"

Thick, perfectly trimmed brows rose on her forehead, and a cracker froze halfway to her mouth. "Plan?"

All right. So I wasn't really a planner outside of football, but I could do this. There were things that would need to be bought. Appointments to be made. Hopefully she could schedule them for Tuesdays when I had the day off, but if she couldn't, I could work with that. Then there was where she'd live—with me if possible so I could be there for her.

"Yeah. Plan. I'm assuming you came here because you want something from me?"

"Want something from you…" She set down the cracker and brushed crumbs off her hands. "What does that mean? Like money?"

"Yeah. I mean, the baby is going to need a lot of things. Money for sure, but what else?"

Her head tilted to one side, and her lips pinched. Was she getting sick? I pushed the plate closer to her.

"Are you implying I can't take care of myself or this child? That what? I came here for your money?"

"Um. I mean, when we met, you weren't exactly employed…"

Her eyes widened to saucers, and she inhaled a deep breath. "Wow." The word came out on a breath, and she was already shaking her head, backing up, hands out, facing me. "You are… you are not the guy I thought you were."

And I was pretty sure there was a tinge of disappointment in her tone, but was I wrong?

"Maggie—"

"No. Stay right there. I'm going to go, and maybe, I never should have come here to tell you."

"Then why did you?"

If she didn't want my help, why *was* she here?

"Because, asshole." She threw her purse strap over her shoulder. "I thought you'd want to know. Want to be involved in this child's life. I didn't come here looking for your cash. I came for you, not some fucking payout. But my mistake."

She flung the door open, and it took a second to take in what she said, and by the time I was rushing after her, hurrying because, of course, I wanted to be there for this baby in every single way, the door to the elevators were closing, and the last sight of Maggie I had was her wiping away a tear.

"I didn't mean it!" I shouted as the doors closed. I slammed my fist into it and shoved my finger against the button, but the door didn't open.

It took too damn long. A lifetime for a second elevator to come, and by the time I reached the lobby and rushed outside, I was met with the darkness of night and the sound of cars. Maggie was nowhere to be found.

And fuck.

She was gone.

Totally misunderstood.

And I still didn't know her last name. Have a phone number. Or an address.

I had absolutely no way to find the mother of my child and fix this, and I wasn't even sure what I'd done wrong or how it went so badly.

CHAPTER 8
MAGGIE

"Boys are stupid." I sniffed and ran another tissue beneath my nose. Ever since I made it inside the elevators, that's all I'd done. Cry. Wipe my eyes and my snotty nose and puke.

Ugh.

Pregnancy was stupid too.

"They are," Belle agreed through the phone.

I shouldn't have called her, but she'd blown up my phone all last night despite me knowing she was spending Christmas with her family in some super duper ritzy gated neighborhood in Brentwood. Country music stars and professional athletes lived on her parents' street, and oh god…. She might have been with people last night who knew Davis. Played with him. Coached him.

The taste of sour milk curdled in my stomach.

I'd texted her to let her know I was home safe and we'd talk after Christmas.

To Belle, after Christmas meant nine o'clock the next morning.

"Can I say something without you getting mad?"

"Of course." I sniffed.

Why would I get mad? It was Davis who went from smiling about being a dad to asking how much money I needed in a split second. I mean, that look he gave me. I knew what it was. It was the same mix of fear and surprise but underlying happiness I'd been sporting since I found out and had a day to digest everything.

He'd done it in moments.

"I don't really blame him, and you kind of freaked out for no reason."

Her voice was soft.

Mine was not. "What?"

"You said you wouldn't get mad!"

"Well of course I'm mad! He offered me *money*, Belle. Like that was all I wanted him for and—"

"I know. I know. But hear me out for a second before you freak out on me."

"I am *not* freaking out. And I did *not* freak out on Davis. I left before I *did* freak out."

"Okay. Okay. Just… let's take a breath, okay, honey?"

"Don't patronize me," I murmured, but I was still listening.

Still breathing. I grabbed my smoothie, raspberry with oat milk and an extra dose of pea protein I'd had delivered every morning for the last week.

A soft laugh came through the phone. She was totally patronizing me, but it was working. As the smooth and cold, tart taste of raspberries hit my tongue, I was able to breathe again.

"Talk to me."

"I work with a lot of famous people, Maggie. I've grown up in this world."

"You *are* famous," I reminded her.

"Hardly. The family name, maybe, but I digress."

This was why I loved her. Her parents had more zeros in their income than I could write without my hand growing sore, and she was still so damn humble about all of it.

I was damn lucky she'd seen me crawling into the back seat of my car that night.

"Do you know how many scandals we hear in a day? How many rumors? How many emails we get saying someone we represent, someone who's done a video with us, has gotten so-and-so knocked up? It's the oldest trick in the book, Mags, and everything comes down to one thing and one thing only—"

"Money," we said at the same time.

Rats. When she put it like that, she had a point.

"That's why I wanted to go with you, to see him and meet him, but I knew as soon as he saw you, he wouldn't be that guy. He'd want to be there for you. Everything I've been able to find out about Davis Hall is that he's as wholesome and down-home as they come."

Right. I bet he was. Until he got naked and had me bent over a bed, palming my ass with his large, strong hand. *That* was not very wholesome.

I shivered at the memory. Enough of that.

"So what are you saying? Besides I freaked out."

And maybe screwed up?

She sighed. "I'm saying, of course, this guy would want to help you. Think about his perspective. He's a rookie, being talked about all the time. The first night you met him, you told him you'd just gotten fired and were getting ready to lose your home. Then you show up telling him you're pregnant?"

I picked at the pilling on my oversized sweat shorts from Goodwill. I mean, the very fact I was wearing old and worn and used sweat shorts from Goodwill made her point about the money.

"I freaked out," I muttered. "Totally lost my shit on him."

"And it's understandable. You're pregnant. Scared. You're alone, and you were nervous about telling him, and your hormones are absolutely raging."

"Thank you. I feel so much better about myself now that I see what an absolutely unstable basket case I am."

She laughed. "Shut up. You know I love you, but I'm not wrong, either."

She often wasn't. "So what do I do?"

"Eat. Get some sleep. Take care of yourself, and in a few days, go see him again. And this time, maybe go on a full stomach so you don't get hangry?"

"Haha. It's a shame you work in music, should have gone the comedy route."

"Love you, Mags. All my heart. You're one of the kindest people I've ever met with the sweetest heart, and you've been through so much, and you're still fighting. You should be proud of all of that. Everything else will work itself out if you give him another chance. I promise."

It would have been lovely growing up in a home like hers. With parents who might have billions but loved her to death and kept her grounded. Sure, their vacations were Mediterranean cruises and trips to Spain and whatever, so she wasn't *normal*, but they were good people, and she was one of the best, too. They gave her confidence and the freedom to be herself.

What a world that must be.

"Thanks, Belle." I sniffed again and reached for tissues. "Just what I needed. More crying."

"Love you Mag-pie. Take a couple days, figure out what it is you do want from him. Maybe if you go to him with a better idea, it'll help."

"Probably should have done that the first time."

"Shoulda-woulda. Next time you'll nail it."

"All right." I blew my nose and climbed off the floor where I'd been sitting since. "I need to get some things done and get ready for work."

With Belle's help after the Franco debacle, I'd gotten a job at one of the premiere steakhouses in Nashville. One phone call from her parents and suddenly, they had an immediate opening for a server, and after a phone call interview, I was hired and started immediately. It was nice to go to work in clothes that fully covered my body, and customers who didn't try to grope my ass all the time. The tips were incredible. By the time this little guy or girl was here, I might actually be able to move somewhere more respectable to raise a child in, somewhere with a working elevator so I wouldn't have to lug groceries and a baby and a stroller up three flights of stairs.

I didn't expect tonight would be busy, but there were three large family groups coming for a late Christmas Day dinner meal, so I at least wouldn't be bored. And it'd help make next month's rent.

———

With Belle's well-loved, if not blunt, advice, I spent the afternoon attempting to follow her suggestions. I ran to the store and stocked up on meals my doctor told me would be good for when I got sick. Fortunately, it hadn't been too bad yet as long as I kept food in my stomach at all times. Which also meant I'd stocked up on small packages of trail mixes and Cheez-Its so I always had something on hand. I did a quick load of laundry and showered for work. It was Christmas, and the streets were far emptier than usual, but that was good because the cold blast of air on my skin as I turned the corner helped me wake up and see that Belle was right.

I hadn't gone to Davis at all thinking of money. Heck, I hadn't gone to him with any expectations. He should know there was a woman out there carrying half of his DNA around in their uterus.

When Davis had clapped his hands together and asked me what the plan was and brought up money, I'd been floored.

Plan? I'd accomplished it. I told him the truth and had done the right thing. I'd expected him to laugh in my face and show me out upon hearing the news. Not smile and ask if I was happy. He'd taken it in stride. I'd sworn, for a second, there'd been heat in his eyes, and he wanted to kiss me before he'd hurried off to his bedroom.

And of course plans needed to be made. The websites I'd taken to reading had lists so long of required and recommended baby gear, my eyes crossed while scanning them. If I wanted to get out of this tiny apartment *and* be able to afford everything this baby would need, some financial help would go a hell of a long way.

Realistically, I needed help. Financial and otherwise. Instead, I'd completely freaked out.

I lost my mind on a guy who didn't deserve it and not only totally thrown him for a complete loop, I'd run out even after I'd heard him shout *"That wasn't what I meant!"*

The whole building probably heard him. Man had a set of lungs on him.

"Well, damn. I did mess that up."

"You know talking to yourself is the first sign of a mental illness? Need to go to the doctor, Maggie?"

I grinned as I recognized the voice and the person who

belonged to it. Will stood in the shadows in an alcove outside the entrance to the restaurant. A red glow made his mouth light as he took a drag of his cigarette. I took a step back.

"I'm good, Will. How's work?"

"Slow as the day is long, my friend. You all right?"

Will worked in the kitchen as a prep cook. He was going to school at a small private college in the city and studying communications. Wasn't sure what he wanted to do with it, but with his tattoos and dark-brown hair he was always shoving out of his eyes, he was noticeable. If I'd met him before I met Davis, I would have been attracted to him, but now—no one else compared.

"I'm good. Ready to get started and then get back home. It's already been a long day."

"Big Christmas plans?" He stubbed out his cigarette against the brick wall and tossed it to the ground.

"No. Never."

Even when I was with my family, the only thing different about Christmas than any other morning was a larger mess my sisters and I had to clean up while the boys went and "did work" with my dad.

"Really? You strike me as the kind of girl who'd go all out for Christmas." He opened the door and let me in first.

"Never had the opportunity." Commercialism was of the devil, and decorations were wasteful when all we needed was Jesus. But now that I was on my own? Getting ready to raise a child of my own?

I could do something different.

After all, if my parents thought kissing a boy and having a beer was enough to send me straight to hell, this child inside me would only seal the deal. What was a little commercialism when I was already branded a harlot and drunkard in their eyes?

"What about you?" I asked him.

We waited for the elevator, and he kicked at the tiled floor of the lobby in the building where Julio's Steakhouse was on the top of a forty-two-story building. On a busy day, the wait could be a while.

"Talked to my parents. Saw my sister, but she was getting ready to go to her husband's family's Christmas, so I didn't stay long.

Kind of boring, actually. Christmas kind of loses its shine after you're done being a kid and before you have your own, doesn't it?"

Mine had never shined in the first place, but I could see his point. "You want some? Kids, I mean."

"Heck yeah, I do." The elevator opened, and I stepped in. "Why? You offering to help me out with that?"

It was a tease. Will didn't really flirt with me. Personally, I think he enjoyed trying to embarrass me. And as far as getting pregnant… if he only knew.

I swallowed down my secret and shoved his shoulder. "Not a chance in the world, Will."

"I'm hurt. Truly." He pressed his hand to his chest. "Even if I was the last man alive?"

"Fine." I'd play his mindless game. "If we were stranded on a deserted island and the fate of the world rested in our hands and procreation was required to save the human race, sure, Will. I'll help you out then."

"So you're saying there's a chance."

I laughed as I walked off the elevator, shaking my head at him. "Have fun back in the kitchens."

"See you later, future baby mama."

Elsie lifted her head from the hostess stand. "Baby mama?"

"It's nothing. Will's joking around."

"Really?" She swiveled and watched as he walked away. It really wasn't a bad view. "Kind of skinny for my usual type, but I wouldn't say no."

"He seems a bit lonely. Maybe you two could end Christmas together."

A mischievous grin appeared. "Now that would be a *gift*."

"I'll let you unwrap that one."

"Thanks." She grinned, and we both laughed.

Several hours later, my shift was done, and my pocket was full of cash tips in addition to the twenty percent required tips included in large groups. I was bone-weary exhausted, barely able to keep my eyes awake, but my shift was over.

By the time I returned to my apartment, I was barely able to stay awake long enough to open my door. As soon as I was inside, I managed to kick off my shoes before collapsing onto the worn, threadbare used couch I'd bought on Facebook Marketplace.

It hadn't been my first Christmas alone, and it hadn't even been my worst Christmas, but as my eyes closed and sleep pulled me under, I didn't think I'd ever felt so lonely.

CHAPTER 9
DAVIS

"I need to talk to you."

Dawson Butler stared at me like I'd just asked him to sell me his soul. He wasn't that much older than me, and he liked to call me kid, which was obnoxious, but I trusted him.

Christmas Day passed with me avoiding everyone, kicking myself for the way I handled the interaction with Maggie. I had no idea how to find her. No way to contact her.

Somewhere in Nashville, there was a woman carrying around my child who thought I only wanted to offer her money, and I was desperate to fix it. Not telling my parents yesterday had been one of the hardest things I'd ever had to do, and then I'd avoided everyone else's texts asking if I wanted to spend the day with them.

Instead, I'd wandered the streets, peering into every restaurant and bar, like Maggie would appear out of nowhere. Hell, for all I knew, she'd had plans with her own family. The problem was I didn't know anything.

It was driving me crazy.

"Talk to me about what?"

"I need some help."

A devilish gleam hit Dawson's dark-brown eyes, and he clamped a hand onto my shoulder. "Okay, kid. So when a boy likes a girl a *whole* lot, and you want to be close to her—"

I should have gone to Cole. Or one of the married guys.

This asshole.

I shook off his hand. "Funny, because I know how that works. And the last time I tried it, it worked a little too well."

"What's that mean?"

I glanced around the locker room, but we'd both arrived early and it was mostly empty. A few defensive ends were at one end, looking at something on Cortland Knox's phone. Probably porn, which meant they weren't paying a lick of attention to us.

"A while back I met this girl. Took her home. And she showed up the other night."

"You do repeats? Huh."

The idea of a repeat to Dawson was unfathomable as people who thought the world was flat.

"She didn't come for that." I leaned in closer, and my hands shook. This shouldn't have been so hard to admit, but it was the first time I realized I was saying the words out loud. "She's pregnant, Dawson."

He barked out a laugh. "Get the fuck out of here. You know how many bitches say that?"

I grabbed his shirt and pulled him around the corner. "She's not like that. I swear it."

"Kid. Just wait. When the rest of the guys get here today, we'll do a poll of how many of them have had some kind of groupie or jersey jumper or whatever show up and claim they were pregnant. Happens to us all, and it's always bullshit."

It wasn't. I knew it in my soul. Maggie wasn't that kind of girl, although it'd make sense. She *hadn't* been in the best place when I first met her. But her friend... Belle?

She wouldn't go along with this, not if she was honest about who her family was.

"She's not lying, Dawson. I swear it. I don't know her well, but..." I told him what happened. A quick rundown from the night we met at Lou's to when she and her friend showed up. What Belle said she and her family did and then how I screwed it up.

"She can't blame you for that," he said, and his arms crossed over his chest. "Her name's Maggie?"

I nodded. "Yeah."

"Maggie's gotta realize that's what any of us would think. Hell, if you don't want me to do a poll, she should. Or she could go to the Avengers and ask them. It's the normal reaction. We get that shit *all* the time."

The Avengers were Tennessee's professional hockey team. I'd met them on occasion, but didn't know any well enough to verify that what Dawson was saying was true.

"Okay, I get that. But I still need to make it right, and I don't know how to find her, where she is, or if she's sick and holy shit, Dawson, this is my *kid* I'm talking about, and I have no idea if I'll ever see her again…"

The room spun, and before I knew it, Dawson's hands were at my shoulders, and he was shoving me into a nearby chair.

"Sit before you pass out."

I did exactly that, but it wasn't like I could stand. My knees turned to jelly, and Dawson crouched down in front of me. "You want my advice?"

"Yeah," I croaked, my breathing ragged. "Yeah, I do."

"First, call a damn lawyer. Call Cole's, actually. He's a good dude. And second, go find the friend. You said she seemed all right?"

Belle was terrifying. Sweet and cute and loud and didn't really appear to care much about me at all, but she had cared about her friend.

"Yeah, I think so."

"And you know where she works, so start there at least. If that doesn't work, hire a private investigator. You'll find her, but before you do anything, have a serious talk with Cole about the importance of custody agreements and that bullshit."

Right. Of course, because Cole Buchanan, our quarterback, had just been put through the wringer by his ex. He was still dealing with the fallout months later, but word was recently his ex had moved to Nashville, and he was still living in his hometown twenty minutes out with his new girlfriend—a woman he'd wanted since high school.

Eden was all right, and we saw them often. Dawson was right. "I'll talk to Cole after practice."

"Good." He knocked his knuckles to my jaw, and I slapped his hand away. "Then chin up, kid. We'll get you all situated."

Cole would help. He knew about the shock of getting a girl pregnant. He understood being a single dad.

Right. I probably should have gone to him first, but as soon as Dawson walked into the locker room, I'd needed to tell someone.

"Thanks, Butler."

"Don't thank me. I'm forever going to give you shit for this. All rookies know to wrap it up every damn time."

Defensiveness rose up in me before I saw the teasing glint in his eyes. He was just giving me shit, so I didn't tell him Belle's theory of the hot tub making things go wonky.

Whatever. How it happened didn't matter now.

Now, the only thing that mattered was finding Maggie and making things right.

Worldwide Music Productions, the company Belle said her family started, was a shiny, all mirrored glass, high-rise building in the heart of Nashville. You could see the building all the way from mine, which was how I came up with this plan. It was Wednesday, and I had workouts in the morning. I needed to get back to the training center later for more film in the afternoon, but every time I looked out the windows from my condo, little Miss *Moral Support* came to mind.

Dawson was right. She'd had the decency to leave us alone the other day, so she had some trust in me not to be a complete prick. She'd help me get an in with Maggie again.

At least, that's what I was hoping as I walked up to the shiny stainless steel door handles, pulled and strolled into the lobby of WWMP. The lobby was as shiny and glassy and mirrored as the outside, and the three-level interior atrium boasted a water fountain in the middle, a gleaming silver electric guitar sticking out from the center standing at least forty feet into the air. The feature was enormous and eye-catching as water burst forth from the top of the instrument and flowed down the neck, over the strings, creating its own form of music.

Before moving to Nashville, I'd been a simple country boy from Nebraska, son to a factory worker and dental hygienist. I'd gone to school at Clemson, and the school had taught me a lot about all things Southern—especially the girls who grew up fawning over Clemson athletes, dreaming of taking home a Clemson ball player to daddy. Nashville was a different beast and there were times the size of this city, the rich musical history, and the money everywhere made me shake my head in awe.

There I was, a rookie and making millions, fascinated and dumbstruck by a musical statue bursting out of an indoor pool, for crying out loud.

Around me, voices echoed along with the click of women's heels on tiled surfaces. I dragged my eyes off the water fountain to the man and woman manning the security desk.

"Hello, I'm here to see Belle Connelly."

This good old Nebraska boy could *Google* with the best of them, so I'd done my research. It wasn't like Belle hadn't been in the media since her mother, Scarlett, entered the CMA's red carpet, showing off her large, round abdomen twenty-four years ago.

"Do you have an appointment with Miss Connelly?" the woman asked. Her bright red painted fingernails were more like claws, and they tapped slowly on the keyboard in front of her.

"No, ma'am, but if you could call her and let her know Davis Hall would like a few minutes of her time, I'd really appreciate it."

Her dark eyes narrowed before she nodded. "One moment then."

"Thank you."

I moved away from the desk, sliding down to give her the illusion of privacy. Not like she needed it. Her eagle-sharp gaze stayed glued to me as she tapped a button on the headpiece protruding from her ear and wrapping around her cheek, ending with a small microphone in front of her equally red and glossy lips.

Shiny.

Everything was so shiny in here. Guess that's what happened

when you owned and ran the world's largest country and rock music production company and multiple labels.

"Mr. Hall?"

"Yes…" I glanced down at the name badge over her maroon and gold-lapeled suit coat. "Vivian. That's me."

"Miss Connelly said she'll meet you outside her office." She tore off a printed piece of paper and handed me a visitor sticker. "She's on the seventh floor."

Huh. Seventh floor out of at least twenty-five. Interesting. Somehow, with her name and personality, I'd expected to take a private elevator straight to the top, where I knew her grandfather was still CEO and president. Her father held the VP title.

I hadn't worn a ball cap like I'd taken to doing in the last couple months when I went out in public, and I'd dressed to impress with a pair of black dress pants, snake-skinned loafers, and a light-blue dress shirt. I felt like I was dressed to go to prom, still unused to the required dress code of suits on travel days, and it was difficult not to dip my head in fear of being recognized as a half dozen more people joined me in the elevator. I was the only one in dress pants, the other men all in frayed jeans and cowboy boots, and the women in equally casual dresses. I almost felt like I was back in Nebraska, getting ready to pull my weight on the Duke's family farm over summer vacation. When the elevator on floor seven opened, it took me a second to realize it was my stop.

"Excuse me," I said, and turned sideways to squeeze through a group of four women gushing over their new Christmas gift jewelry.

A lot of bling. A *lot* of bling on their hands and wrapped around their throats almost blinded me as I stepped off—and almost directly into Belle.

"Hey," I said, and shook off the elevator ride. "I'm Davis."

One side of Belle's lips twisted. "I remember." Her black heeled shoe with the red bottom tapped on the carpeted floor. "Heard you and Maggie had quite the night the other night."

"Yeah. About that."

Employees were standing at cubicles and desks, the phones

were ringing in the background, and in the center of it all were three rows of tables lined with multiple computer screens.

"Any chance we can talk in private?"

"About how you screwed up?"

"You don't beat around the bush, do you?"

"I don't see the point in wasting people's time, and as far as privacy, my desk is there." She pointed to a computer at one end of the first table.

"Can I buy you a coffee then? Or lunch? It's just… I'd like to talk to you for a couple minutes, and I don't really want to be overheard."

She stopped tapping her foot. "You don't just want to ask me for Maggie's number and address and be on your way?"

If this was a test, I wasn't sure how to pass it. "Kind of?"

Belle chuckled. That was probably the wrong answer. "Come on, Hall. I was giving you shit about that desk being mine, and I kind of like you. But I did warn you about hurting her." She spun on those sharp stiletto heels and started walking, telling me all this while expecting me to follow her, and of course, I was. I'd be a fool not to.

"Hurt her? Is she okay… the baby?"

She stopped on a dime, and a flicker of kindness appeared. "Sorry. I didn't think what you would think that meant. She and the baby are fine."

She walked into an office, small with no windows, and again I was sort of surprised. If she really was the heiress to this huge corporation filled with a history of producing some of the best music country artists since its inception, I'd expected more.

"My family isn't big on nepotism. I'm working my way up, learning every possible slice of the company until I've proven myself."

So apparently my surprise and confusion was pretty clear. Made sense. I could never get away with lying, even to my sisters. Mom said I had a crappy poker face.

"Sorry. But that's cool, I respect it."

"I'm not sure I respect you yet. You hurt my friend, Davis. She doesn't have many people in her life to turn to, and I left her with you, thinking you'd take care of her."

"I know." I shoved my hands into the pockets of my pants and rocked back on my heels. "And I'm sorry. I screwed up and want to make it right."

"Good. And also, by the way, I'm totally on your side. She freaked out on you. I blame the hormones."

"Are you fucking with me?" The girl made my head spin. God bless her fiancé. Perhaps I could get him added to my mom's prayer list. He might need all the help he can get.

"A little." She shrugged and smiled, tore a piece of paper off the top of a notepad. "I told Maggie the same. She really didn't go to you for money, her intentions were totally pure, but I don't blame you for thinking that first, either. You're a pro athlete, I deal with celebrities. The amount of fake scams we get about knocking some stranger up is innumerable and they usually want payoffs."

Funny. That's what Dawson had said.

"That thought hadn't crossed my mind. I've got nephews and know babies are expensive, and the night we met, she wasn't exactly in a good place." Emotional or otherwise. *Fuck... had I taken advantage of her?*

It hadn't seemed that way that night, but...

"It's all right." She handed me the paper and as I reached for it, she kept it tight in her grip between her finger and thumb. "Maggie understands, and she'd probably kick me in the shins for telling you this, but she was also pretty embarrassed when I gave her my perspective. Go easy on her. When I tell you she doesn't have a lot of people in her life, I mean she has *me*. That's it."

"Not anymore." I gave the piece of paper a sharp tug until she let go.

"Honest?"

"She's the mother of my child. Our lives will be tied together forever, so yeah. I'll always be there for her, even if what happened to create this scenario never happens again."

A slow, sly smile stretched her glossy red lips. "Good."

CHAPTER 10
MAGGIE

needed a nap. Actually, what I needed was to sleep for at least the next five to six weeks. That's when the doctor told me I should see a return of my energy levels.

As it was, I'd gotten stuck at work through the dinner shift when I was supposed to be home around four. Now, it was eight, well past my bedtime these last couple of weeks. The only thing keeping me awake as I pulled myself up the stairs toward my apartment was the promise of my soft bed and new sheets.

A shadow moved at the top of the steps and I gasped. My heart started racing as there was another movement, no sound of my neighbor's door.

"Hello?"

I was already moving back a step, fully awake and my eyes wide as something moved closer to the stairs.

Another step back and the floor creaked. My neighbor was *never* home. I had never seen them. I didn't even know if it was a her or him or them because my landlord told me the apartment was rented, but that was it. It'd taken me a few days to stop assuming it was some empty place used to store bodies and whatnot.

"Maggie?"

A deep, thick voice called my name and I had half a mind to rush right back down all four flights of stairs—thanks in part to the elevator being broken—when recognition sparked.

I gripped the banister and took a step forward. Then another. "Davis?"

He appeared at the top of the stairs, stealing my breath and bringing tears to my eyes.

"I didn't mean to scare you. Where have you been?"

"Where have I been? What are you doing here? How did you know where I—Belle. You went and saw Belle, didn't you?"

I might not have been the smartest girl in the room, but I wasn't the dumbest. It'd be easy to find her. Much easier than me.

He nodded and held out his hand to help me up the last two stairs, but I shook him off and skated around him at the landing.

"I went and saw her today to find you."

"Figures. By the way, her name's Annabelle. You should call her that sometime, she hates it."

A rough chuckle followed him. "Pretty sure I want to stay on her good side."

"Well, that's all I'm calling her now."

"Are you mad I'm here?"

I already had my keys in my hand, so I inserted it into the lock and glanced at him over my shoulder. "No. I'm not mad, but some warning might have been nice."

"I didn't know if what I needed to say should be done over the phone."

Of course she gave him my phone number too. The heads up would have been nice, at least from her, but my phone had been silent all day. The last place I wanted Davis was *here*. At my home. In my tiny and old apartment after spending time in his elegant and massive one.

As if he sensed my unease, he shoved his thumb in the direction of the stairs. "I can leave. Give you a call. Set up a time to meet."

He'd come all this way.

A yawn hit then and I couldn't hide it. The fear of a stranger being outside my door had momentarily wiped away my exhaustion, but now I felt it everywhere. My eyelids burned and were weighted with lead, and my already sore feet ached with the need to be released from my work shoes.

Heels. Not the most comfortable thing to wear while delivering large trays of food.

Still. He'd come all this way and even though I was desperate for sleep, we probably needed to talk.

"You can come in," I croaked out through another yawn. "But no judging my place."

"Never," he assured me.

I pushed open the door and stepped in, immediately kicking off my heels. My arches screamed with the pleasure of being on flat ground again and a moan of my own slipped out as I lost the four inches of height.

"You were working?"

Davis shut the door behind him with a soft click, followed by the lock of the dead bolt.

"Belle got me a job at Julio's Steakhouse."

"Dang. That's a nice place."

"Money's decent, hours aren't horrible, and at least no one's groping my ass or tits for a fresh drink."

I tried to tease, the reminder of the night we met, but it fell flat as a stormy expression darkened Davis's eyes.

Right. He hadn't liked it that first night either.

"Relax, Cujo." I chuckled and tossed my keys and purse onto the counter. "Need anything to drink? I have to get something in my stomach."

"Please. Go ahead. I'm good." He gestured to one of the two rickety barstools I'd recently found on the curb. "May I?"

"Sit at your own risk. They could break beneath your weight."

He slid onto one, and as predicted, the old wood creaked as he settled himself. Both of us cringed and waited, but the snap of wood never came, so I relaxed and moved toward the teapot.

Ginger and lemon tea after work tended to help as long as I ate it with some crackers and cheese, so while the water heated, I grabbed a box of Triscuits and pre-sliced Havarti cheese from the fridge.

"So, I should apologize," Davis said. "For the other day."

"Pretty sure that's my line." I took a small bite of the cheese and chewed. "Belle told me I overreacted."

"I wouldn't go that far. We don't know each other all that well, and after having some time to think, I can see how that was the wrong thing to say."

"It's fine." It was. So he offered me money, I'd be a fool to say no if he offered again.

"Well, it bothers me to think for even a second you thought I was the kind of guy to throw money at a problem to make it go away, Maggie. My sister's pregnant, due any second actually, and it's not her first child. I know how expensive babies are and how much they require, at least from the sidelines. My mind went to making sure you were taken care of and everything you—we'll—need. That's all."

He was an uncle. I could see him bouncing a nephew on his knee or tossing around the football. Being used as a human jungle gym. He had that youthfulness written all over him that would mean he could spend hours doing nothing but play.

And in nine months—he'd be able to play with his own child. *Our* child.

"Thank you. I appreciate that, and to be honest, I didn't really have expectations of anything after telling you, so I shouldn't have freaked out. It's just… we met on a bad night for me when not a lot of things were going great, so I felt like that was all you saw, but I've come a long way since then, and I have plans for my life."

I wasn't some unemployed screwed up crappy bartender with no home. I was a girl who'd been on my own for three years and whenever life kicked me down, I came back fighting.

If I'd let Annabelle help me out with music, I'd probably be doing even better, but that was something I was determined to do on my own, at least getting my start.

"If it makes you feel better, I'm glad that your crappy night brought you into my life that night, and I'm still pretty happy about it today."

Well… that was unexpected. "Yeah?"

He smiled, that same fun-loving and sexy as sin mixed in one smile that'd made my knees wobble back in October.

"Yeah, Maggie. I wouldn't be here if I wasn't serious about

being involved in this baby's life, but also, I'm wondering about the chances you'd give me to be involved in yours."

My teapot whistled from the small two-burner stove. Perfect timing.

How in the heck was I supposed to respond to *that*?

————

The whistle bought me time, but it didn't save me from Davis's continued inspection. If I was to appreciate his silence while I fixed my tea and settled more crackers and cheese on a plate, I didn't.

All the time did was give me more of it to cast quick, secretive glances in his direction, inhale the muted but spicy scent of him and catalog his flaws—of which there were none.

Shame.

He was utter masculine perfection.

I was too short, too thick, too top heavy due to my large breasts I swore were another size larger this morning.

Soon I'd be a waddling overweight penguin, probably stretch-marked to the max. Davis would still be perfect, which made his earlier statement ridiculous.

In nine months, there was no way he'd want me. Heck, I'd give it five. That was only one of the many reasons I could conjure up that reinforced why we shouldn't go down that road. It'd only make parenting harder when broken hearts—most likely mine— would be involved.

Collapsing onto my couch with a sigh, I forced my eyes to stay open as I took the first precious sip of tea. Another yawn weighed down my limbs, making bringing the cup to my mouth a task and a half.

"You're exhausted," Davis spoke from his seat on the stool.

"I have a hard time being awake these days. My doctor tells me it's normal and will pass."

"Second trimester. Only a few weeks to go."

Great. I'd gotten pregnant by a man who knew stuff. Instead of comforted by it, my jaw clenched. Would it hurt for him to not be good at something? I was still counting weeks on my fingers and trying to figure out how nine months equaled forty weeks.

As the third eldest, my knowledge of pregnancy was extensive, but I'd been sixteen the last time my mom was pregnant and we weren't a family prone to open and honest communication.

Now that it was happening to me, I'd forgotten—or never known—a lot.

"How's your morning sickness?" Davis asked.

He was trying. I'd give him that.

"I don't usually feel like throwing up as long as I have food in me. Mostly I'm tired and my limbs hurt. Along with other aches."

Not like I was going to tell him my breasts felt like they were on fire and stretching with every breath.

"My mom never threw up when she was pregnant either. Doctor says it's normal either way."

"Your mom talks about her pregnancy with you? I mean… does she know?" he asked.

"I don't talk to my mom. It's the seven pregnancies after mine I was thinking of." I covered my mouth as another yawn hit.

"You're the oldest of eight?" Surprise made both his voice and brows rise.

Ha. I wish.

"Third oldest of ten, actually." I sipped my tea and let that settle.

"Wow." He rubbed his hand over his jaw. "That's a lot of kids."

"That's a pretty common response I get."

He chuckled. I joined him.

"Are you calling me common?"

Never. With that thick, lush and soft hair and the lips and that jaw, common was far below Davis Hall.

He pushed off the stool and took a seat on the coffee table in front of me, moving my snack closer.

"I don't want to make the same mistake I made the other day—"

"You didn't. That was mine, and I'm sorry."

He ignored me. "But is there anything you need from me? Anything I can do for you? I want you to know I'm all in on this, whatever you want from me, or need, I'm there. I'm not sure where we go from here, but you're carrying my child, Maggie, and I take that seriously. I take *this* seriously."

With him being so close, it was difficult to remember my earlier decision.

"A friend," I blurted before I forgot it completely. "I need a friend."

It'd be so easy to take him to my bed. Let him further exhaust me. I didn't have the luxury of selfishness anymore.

"A friend."

"Yeah." My teacup hid the quiver of my chin. *Friendship* at least solely, was the last thing I wanted from him.

Friends.

I'd never had a friend I wanted to kiss, or ride, before.

This was going to suck.

"Okay," he breathed out. If disappointment had a look, it was Davis's face as he nodded. "Friends I can do."

"You're sure?"

He laughed, but it wasn't a happy one. "I get it. We're strangers. What we had was great, and I've already told you I wanted more, but there's more to think of."

"More to lose."

"More to gain."

He had a point. Tempting.

"Davis," I said his name through another yawn.

"I should go," he said. "Let you sleep, but before I do, do you have any appointments scheduled?"

"Yeah. My phone's in my purse—can you…"

He was already moving.

"My code is zero-seven-thirty."

He glanced at me over his shoulder, but I only saw him through blurry, half-open eyes. "You're giving me your code?"

"I'm too tired. It's the due date…" I set my tea on the table before it landed in my lap.

"Okay…" It came from a distance, almost a tunnel.

My eyes closed.

They opened to sunshine and the softness of my bed. What the heck? The last thing I remembered was Davis in my living room, agreeing to be friends. Grabbing my phone.

"Oh god," I moaned and reached for the sleeve of salted crackers I kept next to my bed.

Instead of crinkling plastic, I hit warm, softer plastic and frowned.

"What the heck?"

Gone were my sleeve of crackers and instead was a cellophane wrapped plate, two sausage patties still hot enough to steam the covering and some scrambled eggs. Toast. Next to it was a glass of orange juice.

No way. I had to still be dreaming.

I hadn't had a decent breakfast since....

Who knew how long it'd been. I'd been too tired to cook in the mornings, settling for crackers, a bagel and cream cheese and yogurt if I was feeling better. And the fact it was warm? I pushed hair out of my face and ran a hand down my chest to my stomach as it rumbled and felt something softer than I usually wore.

"This is not my shirt." It was Davis's. The one he was wearing last night and a quick check told me I no longer wore a bra or pants, but had on the same underwear.

He stayed? And *changed* me?

Before I could settle how that made me feel, my door opened.

Davis's head, hair a mess and sticking out at the sides, poked in and smiled. "You're awake. You doing okay?"

CHAPTER 11
DAVIS

Maggie gaped at me with the same blank expression as most of the cows on Duke's farm.

I couldn't believe she'd fallen asleep so quickly last night. I debated leaving her, but how could I lock up her apartment? She might have let me help myself to her phone, but I wasn't taking her keys. And in a building like this, it was in no way safe enough to risk leaving it unlocked for the night.

Especially not with how small she'd looked, how helpless, and how absolutely dead to the world she became in seconds. After a few moments of debate, I stayed. I hadn't wanted her alone in the building at all. Her place was old and small and cramped and that the elevator hadn't worked didn't say good things.

It might not have been the most broken-down place in the city, but I still wanted her out of it.

How would she carry everything she needed to with a baby? Leave the baby alone while she hauled up groceries? And a stroller or car seat? I'd hoped to hide my shock last night, and since she didn't catch me judging, must have gotten away with it. I wasn't judging… just didn't want my baby being raised here, with some strange stench of mold or something dirtier lingering in the hallway. I grew up near farms—I knew smells. The second-floor hallway below hers was worse than any stall I'd ever had to clean out.

"You took off my clothes."

She didn't sound thrilled, so I didn't bother pointing out I'd seen everything she had before. Consent was important, and I hadn't had that.

I got it. But in the two seconds it took her to totally pass out on me and not wake when I tried, I didn't want her sleeping in her bra and dress shirt and pants.

"As fast as I could. You passed out while I went to get your phone. I tried to wake you."

"I'm not mad, trying to figure out what happened."

That was pretty much it. She told me she'd changed her phone passcode to our baby's due date—which I hadn't thought to ask yet —and then was *out*.

It was impressive. Wish I could do that on plane trips.

"You stayed." Her voice was still groggy with sleep and she was paling by the second so I moved to her, unwrapped the breakfast I'd set down next to her. I'd only returned to bring her a fork I'd forgotten. She took the plate with a mumbled thanks as I handed it to her and resettled higher on the bed.

"I didn't want to leave and wasn't sure how to lock up safely."

"Where'd you sleep?"

"In a very tight, uncomfortable ball on your couch. I'm all right."

"Hmm." She dug into the eggs first. It'd make me a creeper to stand there and watch her, half-naked since I'd given her my shirt so I didn't have to dig through her dressers, although I quite liked the look of her in my clothes.

"Eat, Maggie. I'll go clean the kitchen. We can talk when you don't look so green."

"Thanks." She rolled her eyes but reached for the plate. "And thanks for breakfast."

I needed to eat before I left, which needed to be soon. It hadn't been any more work to make a little bit more food. "Is that enough? I can make you something else?"

"No. This is great. Thank you so much. And, Davis?"

"Yeah?" I was halfway to the door, figuring she'd want privacy to do whatever she needed to.

"Thanks for staying. That was nice of you."

"I'm a nice guy. And you're welcome."

I headed back to the kitchen repeating *friends friends friends* in my head. It was all she wanted.

I got it. We had a kid involved.

Didn't mean I was willing to be only that for her forever, but for now… it'd work. I'd take my time with the rest because when she'd said that word, she hadn't seemed too happy about it either.

She'd soon learn that this morning might have been the first time I took care of her, but it wasn't going to be the last.

Not by a long shot.

———

I used the bathroom outside her bedroom quickly, running water through my hair to tame it and splashed more on my face to wake me up. My hips were sore from the couch, but I'd work them out when I got to practice. Take an appointment with our team's massage therapist.

After I was cleaned up and gargled with some of her mouthwash, I was back in the living room sipping on a cup of coffee from her one-cup maker I'd found in the cupboard. She came out of her room dressed in cutoff sweat shorts, an oversized T-shirt that looked well-loved and had a faded peace sign in tie-dye colors on the front.

"Here's your shirt." She draped it over the chair. "Thank you, again, for breakfast. It was the best I've had in weeks."

"Good." Her living room was small enough I barely had to push to my feet to grab my shirt, and her eyes dropped to my bare stomach as I did.

Of course I stood to my full height. Tightened my abs.

She could look all she wanted. I understood the concept of friends, but there was no way we'd stay in that lane.

Not with the way she licked her lips as I lifted my arms. I couldn't remember the last time I put on a show while getting dressed, but with Maggie's eyes widening as I slipped on the shirt, I figured it wouldn't hurt to let her look all she wanted.

I tugged down the shirt, covering my body and her gaze was now lower—zoned in on the bulge she'd caused to grow behind my gray sweatpants.

I cleared my throat. "Hey, friend? My eyes are up a little higher."

A furious heated blush rose to the apples of her cheeks.

I spared her further embarrassment. "I set your phone on the table next to your bed. Didn't know if you had any alarms set or anything. Do you want me to go get it?"

"My phone?"

She was still a little dazed. Kind of liked that look on her.

"Yeah. Last night you'd said you had your upcoming appointments on there?"

"Right. You didn't look?"

"Didn't want to be searching through your phone while you were sleeping. Didn't feel right." Although I'd been tempted to check out her recent texts. Pictures. Get a glimpse into how she lived her life, who she was.

"Oh. Thanks. That was—"

"Nice of me. I know. We've already established that I'm a nice guy."

But if she kept pointing it out, I had no problems showing her exactly how *not nice* I could be as well.

"Right." She grinned, and it was shaky, but she turned and headed toward her room. When she returned, another faint blush was on her cheeks. "So, um, Lance told me that for football players, your day off was Tuesdays, so my next appointment is then. And I only have a few scheduled out, but I tried, in case you were interested, to get them those days."

An odd, warm feeling squeezed my chest and made my heart rate increase. Not only about the appointment, but that she'd thought of me. Maybe wanted me there from the start? Or at least hoped for it.

"I do. I want to be there. Thank you for thinking of me."

I took a picture of her appointments with my phone.

This was really happening.

In a month, I'd be at a doctor appointment checking the health of my baby. My head swam with nerves and excitement. "Have you told anyone other than Belle?"

Maggie shook her head. "Belle's all I have to tell, so…"

Right. Because she wasn't close with her family. I wanted to dive into that, understand why that was the case, but not everyone came from normal, boring families like mine and it wasn't my place to pry. At least not yet.

"Do you mind if I tell mine?" It'd been hell keeping secrets from them on Christmas. Visions of Annie's kids and my future child, running around and chasing each other on the farm had been so vivid. I would no longer be solely the fun uncle, but a dad.

Would that change the way I played? Make me more cautious? Would I be too busy and have too many responsibilities to spend hours on the weekends doing nothing but swimming and throwing around a football or playing catch with a baseball mitt and ball?

"Can we wait a couple more weeks? At least until my next appointment? Everything's going fine, I'm not nervous about that, but your family… what will they say? What will they think of me?"

"I…" I hadn't thought that far ahead yet. "I mean, they're not going to be thrilled, you know. At least not at first."

I rocked back on my heels, trying to imagine the disappointment on my mom's face. The anger on my dad's that would definitely make a rarely seen vein bulge at his temples. It'd be the first time in my life I'd earned that look for him in a major way. But after? Once they had time to get used to it?

"I think eventually they'll be excited. They're good people."

"Excited a woman they've never met has gotten pregnant by their NFL playing son?"

"I mean… that might take a hot minute, but my parents are good, kind people. My mom doesn't even kill flies in the house. She traps them and takes them outside. The saying *she wouldn't hurt a fly* came from people like her. I figure once she can meet you, get to know you, then she'll be okay."

"Meet me?" If her eyes grew larger, they'd pop onto the old carpet at her feet.

"I mean, yeah, eventually."

"Do you think, maybe, before that happens, we should get to know each other first?"

I grinned. "Absolutely we should."

———

My phone pinged with the attorney's information Cole sent me.

"Thanks, man."

"Trust me. If there's one thing I've learned, it's to always cover your ass, even if you want to think you don't need it."

"A shame it took you so long to learn that, huh?"

"Shut up." He shoved my shoulder, and I tripped over my feet before I righted myself.

"Too soon?" His ex had put him through hell this last fall and even though things were settled and he'd moved his new girlfriend, Eden, into his house with his son, Jasper, neither Eden nor Cole felt completely settled yet. Selma could turn from sweet to sour with one little flick.

"No. Everything is cool there. So what do you know about this girl?"

"Maggie?"

"No, my mom."

"Oh, well, your mom is cool. Makes the best lasagna I've ever had, but don't you dare tell my mom that. It'd break Kim's heart."

"You're such a shit." He shook his head.

"Yo, loser." Dawson was headed our way, bag thrown over his shoulder.

I shoved Cole. "I think he's talking to you."

"Pretty sure it's you, kid."

"Where are you headed?" I asked Dawson, considering Cole and I were leaving practice and Dawson had already left.

"I was looking for you to figure out if you found your baby mama. Forgot to ask before I left."

Dawson was a pretty grumpy guy. Didn't say much to anyone really although he and Cole were good friends. I hadn't expected him to care much at all about my situation, which was one of the reasons why it'd been easier to talk to him.

Cole's youngest brother was a year younger than me, a senior at Georgia. When I was first traded to Nashville, Cole let me live in his home for a couple weeks before training camp and until the condo I'd bought opened up. In two weeks' time, he'd become like a big brother to me.

"He spent the night on her couch last night."

Sometimes pseudo big brothers were big piles of crap.

"On her couch?" Dawson's expression was one of worry.

"I found her. She was coming home from work and tired. Fell asleep practically mid-conversation. I didn't want to leave without being able to lock the door. That's all."

"So you found her."

"Belle helped me, yeah."

"Good. So what's going on then?" He was now walking with us, headed down the hall to the parking lot with Cole and me.

"She told me about her appointment, we talked a bit before I had to come here, and now, I don't know. What am I supposed to do?"

"Uh… take her on a date?"

"No can do," I told Dawson. "She already said she just wanted to be friends."

"So figure out if she's working and take her dinner or something."

Yeah. I could do that, although this time I wouldn't terrify her by showing up at her house, I'd text first. Might be a good idea, actually. If she hadn't had decent breakfasts, was she eating well for other meals?

I'd have to look into that.

"Where's she working anyway?"

"Julio's."

Dawson whistled and Cole's brows rose. "That's a nice place," Cole said.

"Belle probably got her the job. I have a feeling she knows everything and everyone in this town."

"Make sense, with her family."

It did, definitely, and I was hoping once my parents found out who her best friend was, that'd smooth some of the disappointment. Their love of country music was long and deep.

"So, you're sure she's not playing the long con game here—"

"She's not, Dawson."

"So what else do you know about her then?"

"Um." I scratched my jaw. After breakfast this morning, I ended up showing Maggie some pics of my nephews and my family. Annie's growing stomach. Maggie had paled at that one, so I skipped to the next picture quickly, but really, I spent most of the morning before I'd had to get home and then leave for practice talking about me and my family.

She hadn't said much at all.

"I don't know. She has like nine siblings or something like that. Doesn't really talk about her family."

"Ten kids?" That same whistle repeated.

"I know, right? It's crazy."

"It's like that show. What's it called?" He snapped his fingers, brows tugged in concentration.

"What show?" Cole asked.

"That reality one. My sister watches reruns on Netflix. About some family with like fourteen kids. But they always had friends over and those families have like ten plus kids, too. It's freaking wild."

"You watch reality television about families with massive number of kids?"

"No," Dawson scowled. "Crystal does and sometimes when she visits, she forces me to watch it with her."

"Right." I snorted.

Reality TV was scripted. The only *real* thing on television was a live game.

"Expand your horizons, kid."

Cole was looking at his phone, scrolling and then looked up at me. "What'd you say her name is?"

"Maggie. Why?"

He turned his phone around. "Is this her?"

Holy shit. It was Maggie, all right. A younger version, had to be several years old and her hair was longer, down to her waist. She'd learned the power of makeup and wearing decent clothes since then. I tried to reconcile the image of this still beautiful, undeniably so, woman who'd probably sewed the dress she was wearing with the Maggie who let me ravage her body and threw back shots at Lou's. Well, Magdalene Mary Webber, actually, based on the head-line. "Oldest daughter of Michael Webber, whose family has made several appearances on Webber's sister's family show, *'The Blessed Movement'* has been kicked off future appearances and exiled from the family."

"Exiled?" I rolled the word around on my tongue and tried not to lose my shit.

"Her family kicked her out?" Dawson asked, and there was a growl to his question.

Cole turned the phone back around and it took every ounce of my self-control not to tear it out of his own hands. "Says for drinking or something. *'Making sinful choices with no appearance of remorse'* is what her father says."

"Well, damn," Dawson muttered and glanced at me. "Bet they won't be too happy to hear she's knocked up out of wedlock, huh?"

Well, shit.

This explained some things.

CHAPTER 12
MAGGIE

"Good shift today, Maggie."

"Thanks, Madison."

She was the server shift manager and worked at Julio's for probably half of my life. "See you Friday?"

"Yep, I'll be here."

She glanced around the back hallway. I'd gone into our break room to grab my jacket and was sliding an arm through the sleeves when she stepped in from the doorway that was across the hall from her office. "Um. You don't have to answer me, and I want you to know regardless of your answer, your job is safe, but is there anything you need to tell me? Or anything I need to know?" She glanced out of the break room and back to me. "Last night, after you left, Will said it looked like you didn't feel well, and then made a comment about you being tired lately."

If I wasn't mistaken, her eyes flicked to my stomach and up. Happened so quick I might have imagined it, but even if I had, her implication was clear.

"I'm pregnant," I confirmed.

Her lips went round into a perfect circle and her eyes matched the size of her mouth. "Are you serious?"

"Nine weeks."

"You're dating someone?"

"Um. No."

Wasn't this awkward. Madison knew who I was, knew my past. Belle might have called the owner to help me out, but she had also told him who I was. It wasn't often I was recognized, but it happened occasionally. It'd been four years, and I looked so different. More often than not, I got comments along the lines of, *"you look familiar, do I know you from somewhere?"*

"Oh. Well, this is surprising. I wish you would have told me."

"I'm sorry. I didn't know how it'd be received, but I can still work, Madison, I swear."

"Of course you can work. That's not the concern, but had I known, I would make sure things like last night didn't happen so you could get some rest. You have to be taking care of yourself."

"Ohh. I'm sorry. I didn't think."

"It's okay. Are you okay? I mean, I'm guessing this was a surprise? How are you doing with all of it?"

Madison had been kind to me since the day I started at Julio's. She hadn't treated me any differently because I got the job as a favor of a friend, nor had she questioned my abilities. Sure, it was only serving tables, but Julio's was one of the most expensive restaurants in Nashville, and it wasn't uncommon where we had tables filled with a variety of musicians, artists, or athletes.

The gentleness in her voice made my chin wobble in a way it hadn't since I got over my initial surprise. I adored Belle and was so thankful for her, but a friend's love was different than this... almost a mother's love I'd never really had. "It's a lot, but I'm doing okay with it. Adjusting, still, I think."

"The father?"

"Wants to be involved. I'm pretty sure."

"Well, that's good. I should let you go, but if you need anything, or aren't feeling well, please let me know. We can adjust your schedule as much as we need to. You're most important right now."

Important. I wasn't sure I'd ever felt like it. Invisible, required to work and serve. I'd been a child with a purpose forced on to me before I knew the definition of the word. I'd been needed for sure. Needed to help cook and clean and teach my youngest siblings and I'd been needed to help bathe and diaper them.

My parents would have called those important tasks.

But they were *things*.

I'd never been treated as if *I* was important.

"Thanks, Madison. I really appreciate it."

My chin was still shaking, and she'd gone a bit blurry. When I stepped back and sniffed and grabbed my purse, she moved back into the hallway. As I passed her, she squeezed my shoulder and flashed me a smile so warm I almost collapsed into the sobfest I was trying to avoid.

"Take care of yourself, honey. And I mean it, call me if there's anything you need."

"I will."

"Have a good night."

"You too."

I burst into the cool afternoon air and inhaled a cleansing breath several moments later. That had felt *good*. And it wasn't often I'd had that feeling. Only Davis and Belle as of late. There was a boy I'd dated for a while shortly after showing up in Nashville, but I wouldn't say he left me feeling good—more used, but I learned from that. I hadn't even considered I could talk to Madison about being pregnant and not get fired. Waitressing jobs were a dime a dozen. They could get anyone to take my spot.

My phone rang, and I reached for it, assuming it'd be Belle. She'd called and texted before I left for work. I hadn't had time yet to give her a hard time for handing my information to Davis—not that I was mad about it. But she didn't need to know that yet.

"Hello, Annabelle." I drawled out her full name. She deserved it, even if the night with Davis had gone better than I could have expected our third time meeting to go.

"Ugh. I *hate* that name."

"Then maybe don't give my number and address out to almost-strangers, regardless of how cute they are?"

She laughed. "I promise I won't give your address or phone number out to anyone who hasn't already gotten you pregnant. How's that?"

Considering this was a once in a lifetime situation… "Fine. I agree and forgive you."

"So, how did it go? Did he call you last night? I thought about warning you, but then didn't want to get your hopes up in case he backed out."

"I talked to him. He was at my apartment when I got home from work."

"Oh… well, I hadn't exactly expected that."

"Neither did I. He scared me so bad I almost fell down the stairs."

I told her everything else on my walk home. From Davis showing up and scaring me in the hallway to cooking me eggs this morning. She was all caught up by the time I walked into the building and found a maintenance worker bent down handing something to another worker standing in the open shaft of our broken elevator.

Thank goodness. Four flights of stairs were a killer after a long shift at work.

"I'm going to lose you in the stairwell, so I'll let you go." Cell reception vanished around the second story landing. Another reason I was glad the elevator was getting fixed.

"All right. Have any plans this weekend? It's New Year's."

"Pretty sure I'll be asleep by eight and alone."

"You can come hang out with Lance and me. My parents are throwing a party at their place."

Spend the night in a mansion with a bunch of drunk rich people, while I had to struggle to stay awake? Who could pass that up?

Me. One hundred percent.

"Next year."

"Are you sure?"

"I'm pregnant, exhausted all the time, and just like you said, there'll be people there who might recognize me." It was, after all, how Belle and I became such good friends and why she helped me out the night we met.

"Fine," she pouted. "But I don't like the thought of you alone."

I was always alone when I wasn't with Belle. I'd gotten used to it long before I ever tried going to college.

My phone buzzed and I checked the screen, surprised to see Davis's name appear.

"Hey, I need to go. We'll talk soon, okay?"

"All right. Love you, Mags. Call if you need me."

"Will do."

I ended the call and pulled up Davis's text. When he left that morning, he said we'd talk later. But he was busy with football, and he'd told me this Sunday's game was the last of the regular season. It'd determine who would end up as the divisional champion. I'd smiled and pretended to understand I knew what they were talking about. Either way, I hadn't expected him to reach out so soon.

Any chance you're not working and want to have dinner with me tonight? I was thinking of ordering pizza.

My stomach rumbled as I caught sight of the word pizza. All those chewy carbohydrates? I could probably eat pizza every day. I hadn't even told him it was something I'd been craving.

Crazy.

Which meant there was really only one option.

My place or yours?

Mine.

His response came right on the heel of me hitting send, and I grinned, thinking of Davis staring at his screen, wanting me to text him back so badly he couldn't take his eyes off his phone.

What a dangerous thought. I was the one who said I needed a friend. I hadn't lied, but I didn't really like it either.

Anything else between us would be too complicated. Too risky.

Thirty minutes?

It'd give me enough time to shower and grab a quick Uber ride.

Tell me what you want.

There were a lot of things I wanted—like to see Davis naked again right before he climbed on top of me. Or feel the press of his warm, strong hands as he spread my legs…

Pepperoni, mushroom, and jalapeños, I typed out.

He was asking about pizza. Not my desires… I'd already made it clear where I stood with him.

Now I need to remember it myself.

———

To my surprise, Davis was in the lobby of his building when my Uber pulled up. As soon as I stepped out and thanked my driver, Davis was opening one of the main doors and holding it open for me.

Similar to all the other times I'd first set eyes on him, my chest squeezed and my mouth went dry. That body of his moved with natural grace only someone supremely confident in themselves could move. His worn jeans were slung low on his hips, fitted over the stretch of his thighs and his cream, faded Clemson sweatshirt was oversized, but could do nothing to hide the bulk of his muscled arms I'd clung to. His full lips were stretched wide, curled up into a grin that said this guy didn't live life all too seriously but could when necessary. I knew his family was in Nebraska, and he'd grown up with a simple life.

Probably on land outside a small town that wouldn't have been far too different from mine if my parents' religious reviews weren't cult-like.

"Hey. Good timing. Is the pizza almost here?"

"Don't know." He grinned at me and stepped back so I could enter. "I was waiting for you."

"Oh." How very gentlemanly of him.

"Come on. I want you to meet Roger."

"Roger?"

"Yeah. He normally works security at night. You met him the other day."

Oh… I glanced at the security desk and yep. It was the same older and portly man who had the pleasure of witnessing me fleeing from the elevator, tears in my eyes and rushing like fire was nipping at my feet. He'd barely even been able to ask me if I was okay before I shouted yes and ran through the front doors.

"Roger, this is my friend, Maggie."

"Hello, Maggie." He tipped his chin, making his eyes disappear beneath the brim of his hat. "Pleasure to see you again, miss."

"Nice to meet you."

Davis's hand settled at my back, low and it was a barely there burn of a touch, but it singed my flesh through my thick flannel shirt and tank beneath. "I'd like for Maggie to be added to my permanent visitor's list and given a key."

"A key?" I asked; at the same time Roger's bushy brows rose.

"Mr. Hall— "

"Davis. Please, you know I hate the mister stuff."

"Certainly, um… sir."

I rolled my lips together. It was almost adorable how uncomfortable Davis was being called mister as it was Roger's discomfort calling him Davis.

Davis's hand at my back added pressure to his touch, and when I glanced at him, he was still grinning at me. "I want you to be able to enter whenever you'd like, even if I'm not here yet. It'll be easier for you to just walk in than wait for me."

Oh… well, that made sense, I guess? I wasn't entirely comfortable with his complete trust in me, but the thought was nice.

"I'll need some information from you then, Miss Maggie," Roger said, and his thick, age-spotted hands were clicking on the computer keyboard in front of him.

By the time we were done, Davis had received an alert that our pizzas were set to arrive, so we waited in the lobby for them before returning to his condo.

He'd thrown me for a loop with the full access to his home, and the gold key was currently a heavy weight in my purse.

"You want to do the honors?" Davis asked as we reached his door. He had three boxes in his hands, and while I knew he could handle his door just fine on his own, I sensed he was trying to make me more comfortable with the idea of what he'd just done.

My hand trembled as I slipped it out of the front pocket of my purse. Silly. This was absolutely ridiculous. I was just a friend, having a key to my friend's home in case I ever needed to help them out. The key to Belle's home never made me this nervous.

A green light lit up as I twisted the key and the door unlocked. As soon as I opened the door, I was met with the dark view of the city beyond his private patio and hot tub… possibly the cause for bringing me back to this place. I pushed the door open and gave Davis enough room to come in behind me and as he did, he slipped out of a pair of Under Armour slides. I kicked off my own shoes and followed him to the kitchen.

"I'm glad you were able to come tonight," Davis said. "Did you not work today?"

"I got off at four. I was just getting home when you called."

"Perfect timing then, wasn't it?"

Standing in his kitchen again, watching Davis move to get plates and waters for both of us with those lithe, confident movements?

It really was.

If only I could stop thinking about the other two times I'd been here and how they both ended—with me running out.

CHAPTER 13
DAVIS

Maggie seemed more nervous than usual, and it had started before I'd shocked her into stone cold silence by giving her an extra key and full access to my place. Mostly I just wanted her to know she was welcome whenever she wanted to be here. I had nothing to hide from her. Also, I wanted her to have a safe place to go in case she ever didn't feel safe at her home.

The building in the light of day was worse than I originally thought, and I was pretty certain the men standing on the corner weren't exchanging flour for the cupcakes they'd be baking later. At least I'd gotten confirmation the elevator was being fixed.

I didn't have enough currency with her yet to suggest she consider moving in with me where she wouldn't only be closer to work but closer to the hospital—thanks GPS for that helpful selling point if it ever came up—but for now, I was content with her knowing if she needed to, she always had a safe place here.

She was definitely quieter than she'd been before, though, and while I was trying to give her time to settle into my gesture, I was also trying to figure out how to bring up I'd discovered who she was. She'd said she didn't talk to her family, wasn't close to them, but I suspected the truth wasn't something she enjoyed sharing. I only felt mildly crappy about prying into her life given the work Belle had done into mine.

Also, I couldn't wait to tease her about her choice in pizza toppings.

Jalapeños? It was almost as bizarre as the sociopaths who chose pineapple.

In the end, we spoke at the same time—

"I'm uncomfortable with the key."

"Wanna explain the peppers?"

She chuckled, the discomfort on her features easing into a smile.

"You go first, the key. Why does that make you uncomfortable?" If this was some big deal to her, she'd lose her mind with everything else I needed to tell her.

"I don't know exactly." With two fingers, short fingernails painted a sky-blue color, she pushed the gold key in a circle on the kitchen counter. "I guess it seems… like a lot? We barely know each other."

"Which we're trying to fix with pizza tonight, right?"

Maggie rolled her eyes. She had her thick, dark-brown hair twisted up into a clip, and as I flipped open the pizza and garlic knots boxes, she tugged wisps of hair at her temples out of the clip.

"I didn't mean anything big about it. I just wanted you to know you're always welcome here."

"Even when you're not?"

"If you need to be here, sure." I leaned forward, braced my palms. Her crystal-blue eyes dipped, slowly slid up my arms and caught my smirk when our gazes met. "I have nothing to hide, in my life or my home and we're going to be a part of each other's lives in some way, shape, or form for the rest of them. I *want* you comfortable here and around me."

It seemed to settle her, and maybe it was the reminder of how eternally connected we now were that made her shoulders droop.

"Okay. That makes sense. But I promise I won't randomly start showing up unannounced or anything."

I didn't give a damn if she did. Frankly, the idea of her walking into my house while I was fresh out of the shower, dripping wet with only a towel wrapped around me—if I chose to wear one at all —thrilled me.

"I won't be mad if you did, but let's table the key thing for a minute so you can explain this?" I swirled my finger over her pizza.

"No idea." She laughed and dragged a piece, and then two, onto her plate. "You asked what I wanted and it sounded good."

"So you're craving spicy foods."

"I am today, apparently."

She was laughing now, at ease.

"All right then, spicy mama. Let's eat."

Blond brows rose at my off the cuff nickname. "I'm going to pretend you didn't say that."

"Pretend away."

But I had very vivid memories of how spicy she could be, and she *was* my baby mama.

I think it fit her perfectly. Maybe even more than *Snickers*.

We dug into our food. If she was going to get pissed at me for figuring out who she was, or if it was supposed to be some great secret, at least she wouldn't storm out of my place on an empty stomach.

"How long have you lived in Nashville?" I asked her after she'd eaten her first slice of pizza.

"Three years."

It killed me to ask, but I'd know less had I not read the article about her earlier. "And how old are you?"

Her lips parted in surprise, and then a soft laugh fell from her lips before she wiped her mouth with a napkin.

"What?"

"It occurred to me how little we actually know about each other. I mean, Belle told me plenty about you when she looked you up online, but..." Her head tilted to the side. "Do you even know my last name?"

How bizarre that she was pregnant with my child, and up until a few hours ago, I hadn't.

And since she asked, what a perfect segue.

I set down my pizza slice and brushed the garlic and grease off my fingers with a napkin. "Actually, Magdalene, I think I know quite a bit."

The color on her cheeks darkened. "You know? About my family?"

That they were borderline cultish with their beliefs. From what I'd been able to find, the only thing the daughters were supposed to do were learn how to take care of a home, get married to a man their dad and uncle approved of, and pop out copious amounts of children—ironic, considering? Yeah. I knew. I also knew she was the only child to actually go away to school and that she had two older brothers who went to work with their father in the church and their uncle working a small string of auto parts repair businesses. It was the uncle whose family starred in the *Blessed Movement* television show.

"I found out by accident."

"I was going to tell you."

"I'm not mad you didn't. I didn't want you to be mad I found out. I was talking to my teammates, about well"—I waved a hand between us—"everything, and before you get on me about not telling anyone, they won't tell a soul."

"Davis. It's fine. Belle knows. I was worried about your family, but I'm not mad you needed to talk to someone about this."

Okay. Good. The knot I'd had in my gut started to unwind itself. "When I mentioned something to Dawson, one of my teammates and friends, he said something about how it sounded like those crazy families on TV—and shit. I didn't mean *your* family is crazy."

"They are." Maggie shrugged, like what do you do? "In some ways anyway."

"He said his sister is a huge fan of the television show. So then Cole, our quarterback and another good friend, pulled up his phone."

"And found the article about me being excommunicated from the family due to my multitude of sins?"

I mean, when she put it that way, she had to hear how strange it sounded.

My look must have been answer enough because Maggie shrugged again, picked up a fresh pizza slice and took a bite.

"You're not mad at me?"

"There's no reason to be mad. I made appearances on a show I never fully supported and then convinced my parents to let me go away to college. I'd go where they wanted me to, I'd earn an early education degree so I could help do more formal teaching with everyone else's kids when I was done. At least, that was how I sold it to my dad and uncle so they'd agree—my mom had no say either way, really. I made a deal with them. They chose the college. I'd follow the rules. I'd even let the film crew come show me on campus. The *black sheep*, I think they liked to call me, and that was supposed to be it."

"So what happened?"

"I got to school, started seeing how all these other kids from Christian families lived so differently, and I wanted that instead. They had freedom and were normal. They had their faith, but they also had a life with dreams and goals. I sort of rebelled, well, a lot. Eventually, I got caught. It wasn't really that big of a deal, but I got caught kissing a boy and drinking a beer on a day I didn't realize camera crews were going to be there. My parents flipped out, said I'd embarrassed the entire family and church and our reputation, and I was supposed to go home, marry Patrick, some boy they'd had earmarked me for since I was four, and pretend none of my sinful lifestyle happened—I just had to publicly confess my sins in front of the entire congregation."

"You didn't do that." Didn't take a genius to figure that one out.

"I couldn't. I refused and I was not going to get married at nineteen years old just so I could be forced to listen to another man in my life tell me what to do for the rest of my life and start popping out babies like my mom...." She paused and gave me wide doe eyes. "Which, I guess I failed at some of that."

I chuckled. "I've considered the irony."

"I used to love my mom, and then I got older. I always thought she was this super kind woman, but then things happened." She gulped and her face paled. Whatever it was, wasn't good. "I... well... my dad wasn't nice. He was commanding, at least to us girls. We *had* to do what he said, because all he ever told me was that my job was to make a man happy. As long as I'd do that, I wouldn't be punished."

"Punished?"

"Yeah." She sniffed and stared with a blank expression. "And well, I wasn't great at listening."

My anger pulsed by the second. The thought of a parent's punishment bringing that kind of look in her eyes made me grit my teeth.

"Anyway, I was forced into helping my mom with everything while Jed and Zach could go play. It never felt fair. My college experience was supposed to be my four years away, before I had to go back to that life, but when it came time to do it, I had too many questions about their beliefs and rules they refused to answer. So, no, I couldn't go home. My regret is I've barely been able to talk to my sisters, and they're now going to be married soon too. I wish I could tell them they had choices."

I couldn't imagine being trapped, not being able to make decisions for yourself in regard to your future, and having it restricted further simply because of your gender.

"I'm sorry you went through that." What else was there to say? If she didn't want to go into specifics, I wouldn't push. "Why Nashville?"

"I sang in the church choir and wanted to make it big out here either as a gospel singer or country."

"Is that how you met Belle?"

Another chuckle and adorable shake of her head. Maggie's lips lifted at the corners. "Sort of. I was working at some dive karaoke bar, and she had some friends come in from college. They wanted to have a 'slumming it' weekend, as she liked to call it—where they spent a weekend pretending they were poor instead of filthy rich—because she's ridiculous like that. I was working a shift, and the bar was slow, and my boss let me sing when it was. I hopped out on stage and belted out 'Ain't No Mountain High Enough' and Belle and her friends demanded more. I think I sang like five or six songs while they drank and danced. It was so much fun, and I'd loved every second of it, and I don't know what happened, but my head was in the clouds or something because I dropped a huge case of glasses. Shattered them everywhere and was promptly fired. Belle chased after me. She caught me as I was getting in my car, saw all belongings in the back—"

"You were living in your car?"

"She pretended she was slumming it, I really was. It was only for a short time, but I'd had to live in some pretty unsafe places when I got here. I'd just been evicted from a place because my roommates were too loud, and I'm pretty sure dealing drugs, although I never saw that. My car was better, trust me."

I couldn't picture it. She was too sweet, too innocently pretty to be living like that—and all because she'd kissed a boy and had a beer? I was having a hard enough time getting past the part where parents would just kick one of their children out of their family. Had they known what that decision forced her into? Did her mother lay awake at night lamenting those choices and hating herself for not protecting her child?

The more I thought about it, the harsher fury rose in me. My parents would *never*, under any circumstances or any mistakes we made, not love us, not continue to want what was best for us.

"I'm having a hard time keeping my mouth shut and not telling you exactly what I think of your parents, you know."

"Belle never did. She actually suspected I was from the *Blessed Movement* show—my clothes back then still weren't nearly as stylish as they are now, to put it lightly. But anyway, she'd come out to the parking lot with me to talk about my voice and if I was represented by anyone. Saw me living out of my car, and demanded I live with her."

"And you did?"

"Not for two more weeks. I was trying to find something else, but she kept chasing me down. I don't even know how she did it."

"Belle doesn't strike me as someone who gives up easily."

"She's not, but she wasn't pushy about it, either. She offered to have me record a demo too."

"Have you?"

"No. I wasn't sure I had the guts back then to really do it, and then I didn't want to *make it* only because I got close with Belle. But for the last two years, I've been too busy trying to save enough money to get a new car and my own place, so I haven't done much singing at all."

"There's nothing wrong with taking help when it's offered if you need it, you know."

I thought about her reaction to my offering money. Not following her dreams because Belle could make it happen. There was stubbornness and there was conviction and confidence.

"I know. And someday I might let her, but not until I'm able to try hard enough on my own first."

I had a feeling if she ever went to sing, Belle would ensure influential people were in the crowd. I didn't figure Belle was the kind of person to follow a stranger out of a bar unless there was real talent there. She'd heard and seen too much in her life in that industry.

"So," Maggie said. She tore a chunk off a garlic knot before dipping it into garlic sauce. "Now that we've delved into my entire life history, tell me more about yours?"

CHAPTER 14
MAGGIE

'd always planned on telling Davis who I was, and I wasn't sure yet if he was realizing how this might impact him. If someone in the media saw who I was when we were together, I could very well be recognized. If he had some wholesome good guy image to maintain, I wasn't sure how it would go to be connected to me.

But I wasn't quite ready to delve into that.

Truth was, I'd done a lot of healing, a lot of research, and a lot of work on myself after my parents told me to "take the car and don't come home until you're ready to repent" conversation. The very last one we'd had.

Different and extreme, sure, but their convictions made sense in the context of their teachings. The problem I realized when I went away to college was I didn't think their context was always biblically correct—or, at minimum, necessary. I'd left out the worst parts of the story to Davis, but he could read between the lines. When I told stories on the college campus to friends about how we were disciplined and punished, they'd cried and hugged me. I hadn't even realized until then that it wasn't discipline, but abuse. Funny how a Christian college with strict rules regarding genders spending time together and a list of rules almost as long as the dresses I used to wear was what opened my eyes to see that differences, even among the same religion, were okay.

It also made me hate my parents and their teachings deep in my soul in a way, I'd planned to not return home after I graduated anyway. I couldn't. I'd changed too much and learned too much.

"I'll tell you anything you want to know about my family," Davis said. "If you answer one or two more questions from me first."

He already knew everything.

"Deal."

"What are your siblings' names?"

Well, now that was a common question. One I had no problem answering. "Jedidiah, Zachariah, me, Adam, Timothy, Ruth, Paul, Leah, Joy, and Martha."

"Why Joy? It's the only one that's not a biblical name."

"Joy came after a miscarriage. And my mom was almost forty then. The doctors warned her too many more children could be difficult for her, but Joy was born healthy and normal and her pregnancy was as easy as the rest of them. Any more questions?"

"Do you talk to any of them? Since you've left?"

"Zach called me a few times, but he and I were never close to begin with and he was too much like my father. He's already married with four kids, and they're barely twenty-five. He's working in my dad's church and he only calls to tell me how I'm destroying my internal hope."

"A lovely conversation, I'm sure."

"I've called Ruth a couple of times. She's almost eighteen. She pretty much hates me for my choices because she says now Mom and Dad will never let anyone else leave home and it's all my fault."

Those conversations always stung. Out of the first six kids, we were all born within eight years of each other, but since Ruth and I had been the only girls, I'd adored her. Probably mothered her as much as my own mom did. Having Ruth mad at me was painful, and the only thing I regretted about my choices was the pain it caused her. She was now locked up forever, essentially, and in some ways, that *was* my fault.

"I'm sorry. That has to be hard."

"Your family?"

As I asked, his phone rang. *Mom* lit up the black screen, and he smiled at me. It was a happy one, despite everything I'd told him, which told me everything he felt about his family.

He adored them.

"Speak of the devil. Do you mind if I take it?"

"Of course not."

To my surprise, he tapped the speakerphone button and a woman's voice rang through, loudly, clearly, and *very* happily. "Annie's on the way to the hospital! The baby is coming!"

"What? That's awesome." Davis scooped up his phone and that happy smile he had turned to bursting joy. "How far are her contractions? How dilated is she?"

"She didn't say. She and Max just dropped off the boys a few minutes ago and said she'd keep us posted."

"That's awesome. Keep me updated?"

"Absolutely, dear, she wanted you to be the first to know, but expect a phone call from the hospital later, or tomorrow morning. I know she'll want you to meet your new niece as soon as possible."

"I'll be here waiting."

"Good. I gotta go, love you, sweetie. Be safe this week!"

"Will do. Love you, Mom, and if you talk to Annie, tell her I'm thinking of her."

"Will do! Love ya!"

The call ended and when he turned that grin back on me, I almost fell over from the beauty of it.

If he was this excited about being an uncle again, what would he look like when he was a dad? He was already drop-dead gorgeously handsome.

"My sister's having a baby."

"I heard." I grinned. "Congratulations."

"Thanks. Seems so silly." He scrubbed his hands through his hair, stared off into space and that smile fell before he turned back to me. "I hate missing stuff like this. I love my life, but being so far away and being the only one who's left home—it's hard sometimes, not being able to be there with them."

"I get it."

I did. I'd missed out on my older brothers' weddings and the birth of my first five nieces and nephews. Even Belle didn't know I'd watch my uncle's show when I was feeling lonely, hoping to catch a glimpse of my siblings or their spouses who I'd never met.

"Damn. Well, now what am I supposed to do tonight? I can't just stay here, sitting around, waiting... Annie's last deliveries didn't last that long, the doctors said when her babies wanted to come, they practically slid right out, so it won't be long, I'm sure, but..."

"We could go back to Lou's? Get you a celebration drink."

I wasn't sure I wanted to stroll around the city with him, but Lou's seemed safe enough.

"You can't drink though."

"So." I rolled my eyes. "I can have fun without alcohol."

"You sure? Because Lou's a character, and it's fun there some nights. I can't be out late with practice tomorrow, but yeah, as long as you come with me, being out might help."

"Then let's go."

I helped him clean up dinner, not that there was much besides our plates and a couple of glasses. As late as it was getting, his happiness had caused a spike in my own energy levels. I could hang out with him for a few hours, until he got word.

And I wouldn't tell him I had an excuse for wanting to be there for the news, too.

He was having a niece soon—and it'd be our child's cousin. I wanted to know who they'd grow up playing with.

Lou's was surprisingly quiet when we entered. Seemed like we hit at the perfect time, after the dinner rush and before the late-night drinking rush started, so as Davis and I wove through the tables straight to the bar, Lou spotted us when we were halfway there.

"Well look who the cat drug in," he said and flung a towel over his shoulder. "This is a surprise."

"Hi Lou."

"Miss Maggie, isn't it?" His dark eyes slid from me to Davis and back again. "How'd this happen?"

Well… see I'd gotten knocked up and tracked down the running back…

"We're friends, Lou. It happens."

Davis slid out a stool and waited until I climbed up into mine before taking the seat next to me.

Lou's bushy gray brows tugged together. "People are friends with you? By choice?"

"Back off." Davis laughed and his hands slapped the bar top. "Annie's in labor, and I came for a drink."

"Well hot damn. Guess that means I'll be nice to you for tonight only. What can I getcha?"

Davis glanced at me. "I'll have a lemonade."

"Got it. You?" He turned to Davis.

"I'll take a tequila sunrise."

"What's that?" I asked when Lou turned his back to start making the drink.

Despite the fact I'd met him here, that night hadn't exactly been a typical one for me. Not only did I rarely drink, going home with a stranger had only happened a couple times since I'd moved to Nashville. At first, I'd been so mad at my family, so devastated, I'd tried to rebel against *all* of their teachings to prove to myself how wrong they were. While it helped me see a different view, there were some things too deeply ingrained in me. While I didn't think I was going to hell for having sex before marriage, I had recognized that at least for me, there had to be an emotional connection.

Which was *why* I'd gone home with Davis. I'd never felt so comfortable around another man, especially as quickly as I had him.

That hadn't changed either because even sitting next to him now, I could feel the heat of his body, knew the strength and tenderness of it so well keeping my hands to myself was a new lesson in self-control.

"Annie's favorite drink is tequila. In margarita form usually, but this will work for now. Plus, she'll give me so much shit when I send her a picture of me with the drink."

"Tell me about her. And your nephews."

"Well that's easy. They're all assholes, every single one of them, sisters included." He laughed, and it was clear he didn't mean it. But that didn't stop him from telling me.

Annie and Avery were four and five years older than him. He'd been born the baby to two sisters who took their big sister role seriously and hovered endlessly.

"You know how people always say that like it's a big brother's job to protect their little sister, keep them safe?"

"Yeah…"

"Well, big sisters are so much worse."

"I could see that." I'd been protective of my own little siblings much more than Jed and Zach had been with me. "What'd they do?"

"Um. My freshman year of high school, Avery was a senior in high school and Annie was a freshman at the University of Nebraska. She came home for the weekend to see me and *both* of them went with my parents to a friend's house for pre-homecoming pictures."

"That sounds sweet."

"They were in full camo hunting gear, faces painted, *and* with shotguns strapped over their bodies."

"Seriously? I thought that was only in movies, with dads sitting at the table cleaning a gun or something when boys came over." The scene from *Twilight* came to mind, something I'd now watched a half dozen times ever since I saved the money for my own television.

"Like I said, Annie and Avery are insane." It was said with a heart full of love and a smile on his face so much so my eyes watered.

I sipped my lemonade and let the sour taste of it take away the sting of all I felt watching him.

"And your nephews?"

"David and Luka, those are Annie's boys. Avery has Owen. David was named after me."

"Really?"

"No." Davis laughed. "But that doesn't mean I don't give Annie crap for it, either. No, David was Duke—her husband's—father's name. He passed away while she was pregnant with David, so they did it to honor him."

"That's really sweet. Tell me more."

I listened while he told me as many stories as he could, from the gifts he'd given them for Christmas, to how he spoiled them in the off-season when he went home, and all the trouble the boys gave their parents.

"And this baby? This one's a girl, right?"

"Yeah. A girl… I'm so happy for her." As he said it, his phone lit it up. "It's Avery."

"What's it say?"

"Annie's six centimeters dilated. In her room and getting the epidural." When he set down his phone, there was a look of awe on his face, softening every chiseled line of his cheekbones and jaw. "I was able to be home when Avery gave birth to Owen three years ago, and only because she happened to deliver during my spring break from Clemson. But damn… I can't imagine all you go through during labor. And that's not counting the pregnancy…" He trailed off again and took a sip of his drink.

I could tell his thoughts were on his sister, but mine were solely on him. Not only the knowledge he had, but the depth of how much he cared.

My father hadn't been like that for any of my mom's pregnancies, at least not from what I could remember. Sure, he was nicer to her, but he was never really harsh. The difference was when Mom was pregnant, she was expected to continue doing every task required of her or delegate them to the kids—usually me. Ruth, too, when she was old enough to help out.

I had a feeling that was not at all how Davis would operate.

That key in my purse seemed to pulse with warmth again. Was that why he'd given it to me? So he could take care of me?

I shook the thought away as Lou came over, bringing a plate of fries with him. "On the house, to celebrate your new niece."

"Aww shucks, Lou. Free fries? You shouldn't have," Davis teased.

Lou scowled at him and pushed the plate in front of me. "Never mind. It's for the lady who's probably only here because she pities you."

"Well that's not true," Davis huffed. "I'm a catch and a half."

Lou raised his eyes toward me, a twinkle in them. "That true?"

"Um." I grabbed a fry and shoved it into my mouth and slid my gaze toward Davis.

"I'll take that as my answer," Lou guffawed and then rested his hands on the countertop. "So, big game this weekend. You ready?"

"Weird to think my first season of the year is ending soon, and this one on Raleigh's turf. It'll be tough, but I'm ready. The team *is* ready. I could throw up if I think about it too much, though."

"Your season is over this weekend?"

I knew nothing about football, but I thought it went longer, into February or something.

"No." Davis shook his head while Lou chuckled. "This Sunday we play in Raleigh, but next weekend is our last game. However, next week's game won't mean much. Whoever wins this weekend clenches our division. Either way, both of us will end up in first and second place."

I nodded along like I understood, but he might as well have been speaking computer coding or something to me. I made a quick mental note to go home and study though. I should probably know these things.

"And what happens if you lose?"

"Both of us should make it to the playoffs, which means we'll play each other in the first round of playoffs. Whoever wins this game will have home field advantage that first week."

"So it's important."

"Yeah, Maggie." Davis chuckled. "It's an important game for me."

A customer grabbed Lou's attention at the other end of the bar and he took off.

"Next week, though, that'll be our last regular season home game." His fingers tapped on the sides of his glass and he bit his lip. "If you're around, you could come?"

"Me?"

"There's no one else I'd rather have with me if my family can't be there and my dad might come down, but everyone else will be too busy helping Annie."

"Oh… well, I guess? But I don't really know anything about football. Or sports at all."

"Just think about it, okay? I have a couple tickets if you and Belle want to come."

Oh, well that'd be fun. Belle didn't care about sports either, really, but I knew she went to games. Her company usually rented a box or whatever they're called.

"I'll think about it."

"As long as the answer ends up being yes, take all the time you need."

What a goofball. We snacked on fries, Davis had a second drink, and when we got back to his apartment, I was not only yawning, but Davis was starting to check his phone every few minutes.

"Eight centimeters. This kid needs to get here before I have to go to sleep."

It was only nine, and I was fighting yawns left and right. "I should probably get going home before I collapse on my feet."

"No. Don't. Please?" Davis looked so excited and so stressed at the same time. His hair was a mess from constantly running his hands through it pacing back and forth through his home. The drinks were supposed to calm him down, but from the look of him, they might have been laced with speed. "Stay. I have a guest room, but when I get the news about Annie I don't want to be alone."

My heart squeezed. So cute. So painful. The man was so sexy and so young and sweet at the same time. He wanted me to share this moment with him.

How could I say no?

CHAPTER 15
DAVIS

t was selfish of me to ask Maggie to stay. I couldn't find it in me to care. By the time ten rolled around and she was barely awake, I showed her where the guest room was and gave her a shirt of mine to sleep in. A Nashville Steel shirt that was too small for me, it still hung on her smaller frame and fell almost to her knees when she came out of the bedroom wearing it.

Perfection. I'd hugged her. Kissed her cheek when she asked if I wanted her to wait with me, but while I wanted the company, she needed her sleep.

So I'd told her no, I'd wake her when I heard anything after she made me promise, and then I'd gone back to not paying a single bit of attention to the ESPN highlights on television—mostly showing how awesome Tennessee's hockey team was doing this year with little talk of football—and stared at my phone until the screen lit up.

When it did, it was two o'clock in the morning, I was starting to get worried, but Annie's name flashed on a FaceTime call and I answered it with my heart lodged in my throat.

"Hey," I whispered. She had to be tired. She'd been in labor for seven hours at least. "How you doin', sis?"

She grinned at me, a smile that didn't make her look sleepy in the least. "I needed you to be the first person to meet your niece," she whispered and then flashed the screen around.

"Are you kidding?" Damn. I was crying. Or my screen was blurry.

"Nope." Annie chuckled and then a smushed up face wearing a pale pink hat and slimy goop on her closed eyes came into view. My sister's finger brushed over the puffy, full cheek and those little lips….

"You really did have a girl." And she was so sweet.

"Max and I made sure to check a few times."

Her voice was soft but filled with joy and oh damn… I wiped my eyes. Hot damn they were leaking faster than a kitchen faucet.

"We have a girl," I whispered back. "She's so damn cute, Annie."

"She's perfect. She's already eaten, and Mom and Dad left before she got here so they could bring the boys back in the morning, but I wanted you to see her first."

"Goddamn. You're amazing."

"She's Wonder Woman," came a deep voice I recognized as Max from somewhere else in the room.

"Yeah you are." I stared at the little baby girl's face, so fresh and new.

And shit. That was going to be me soon, calling Maggie Wonder Woman while she held her baby just like this.

"Tell me everything. How big is she? How long? How was it?"

Annie chuckled and then readjusted her hold on her little girl so I could see both of them.

"Meet Reese, Davis. Your niece. Probably should have started out with that part, huh?"

"Reese… she's beautiful."

We talked for a few minutes, both of us teary-eyed. For the first time in maybe forever, Annie didn't give me crap about crying either. Reese was eight pounds four ounces and twenty-one inches of absolute, stunning perfection. When Annie yawned, the move reminded me so much of Maggie and our situation I almost blurted it out right then.

But Annie needed her sleep.

I needed to as well. I let them both go, pressed my fingers to my lips and then to the screen over sweet little Reese's sleeping face and said my goodnights.

Thank goodness for cell phone plans now having all unlimited minutes. If I didn't, my future phone bill was going to be disastrously high.

I wasn't missing a moment of this little girl growing up.

"I'll see you soon, Miss Reese," I said. "Six, eight weeks I promise."

"Better hurry," Max teased and stepped into the frame behind them. "She'll be running by then. Probably working. Dating."

My sister laughed.

I scowled at him. "You're a mean old man, Max."

———

I was in the kitchen, making oatmeal and a spinach and egg omelet when Maggie rushed down the hall, hair a mess.

Her eyes were wild, her face still sleepy. "Did I miss it? You were supposed to wake me up!"

Like hell I was going to wake a sleeping pregnant woman.

"Annie called at two in the morning. I didn't want to wake you then."

"Oh." She came to me then, glanced at the pot in my hand and the empty glasses I had next to orange juice on the island. "So what'd she have? Is she okay?"

"Annie's good. Healthy, did awesome."

"And....?" Maggie was practically bouncing on her toes. I hadn't expected her to be so excited but I wasn't complaining. "Did she have her baby?"

I shook my head, and a grin stretched my cheeks before I could stop myself. Not that I wanted to. This was exciting shit. "I have a niece. Little Reese."

"Reese." She clapped her hands together and then was rushing toward me. "That's so wonderful," she cried right before she threw her arms around me. She was so much shorter, her arms only wrapped around my waist but I let go of the pan and held her tight. "You have a niece, that's so cute. I'm so happy for you!"

"Thank you." I squeezed Maggie back. If being friends with her got me hugs like this, I'd take it. "I think we're all kind of freaking out."

I'd already talked to my parents before they left for the hospital. Mom cried. Dad mumbled something about *here we go again. All this girl shit...*" while tugging on his brown work boots. He didn't fool me. I had no doubt they were headed to Walmart to fill their house with every pink thing they could find for when the baby was at their house. Hell, my own Amazon cart was obscenely long, but Annie had always had boys. Reese needed her own things like blankets and bibs and clothes and pink pacifiers.

"I bet." She gave me a tight squeeze and loosened her hold. When she did and glanced up at me, her cheeks were flushed and eyes bright. I wanted to slip my hand to the back of her neck, tilt her chin up and press my lips to her swollen cherry red ones but refrained. Barely.

Friends.

"How'd you sleep?" I asked instead. Because I hadn't just been shopping like a man possessed for the last hour, I'd been planning.

Reese's birth only reminded me of how much Maggie was getting ready to go through and she might have Belle, but this was my responsibility, and I was damned if I was letting her go through it alone.

Besides, I *wanted* to be involved. Wanted to be there for every moment.

"Like I was sleeping on clouds, your bed might be the most comfortable thing I've ever slept on in my life."

Well... perfect.

"Do you need anything?" As I asked, her eyes went to the omelet in the frying pan.

"That." She pointed at it. "And fast."

"Take a seat."

I plated the omelet that was now close to burning and grabbed a plate. Once I had that in front of her, I poured her a glass of juice.

"I want you to give some thought to something."

"What's that?" She was eyeing the eggs like she hadn't eaten in days.

"Move in with me."

"What?" Her head whipped up and eyes widened. "No. Absolutely not."

I'd expected that. "Hear me out. Please?"

"You're freaking out because of Reese, and that's understandable, but I'm not moving in here because your sister had a baby, and you're missing out, Davis."

Ouch.

When she put it like that, I wouldn't want to live with me, either, but that wasn't exactly the case.

"That's not all there is, I swear it. You're carrying *my* child, Maggie. *Our* child. I want to be there. I want to help you and cook your breakfast and make sure you're eating okay and I want to massage your feet when they're sore after work or run you a bath when you're tired. I know you know this from your mom, and I know it from my sisters, but pregnancy is a *ton* of hard work. I not only want to be there for it, I want to be there for *you*, and my place has more room. The pool for when you're in the third trimester and miserable."

"Thanks," she deadpanned. "Needed that lovely reminder of how horrible this is going to get."

"I didn't mean it like that."

"I know you didn't, but this… I wasn't expecting to wake up to this morning."

I wasn't expecting to demand she did it this morning, either, but here we were.

"So what now? Will you consider it?"

CHAPTER 16
MAGGIE

Consider his offer and move here? To the literal lap of luxury?

Only a fool would say no. Not only did he have to have one of the most majestic views of Nashville, something I was currently ignoring while keeping my back to the sliding glass doors, but that pool… and that bed. I woke up feeling like I'd been dipped in satin and settled onto a bed of clouds.

And yet, for the same reason I didn't accept immediate help from Belle with music, that same two-letter word was currently crawling its way out of my throat. I choked it down. He had points. Valid ones. I should be so lucky Davis not only wanted something to do with the baby, but seemed so intent on taking care of me as well. And I had the baby to consider. What if I started spotting? What if something went wrong? For the pure logic of it I wanted to change my mind and still an agreement wouldn't come.

Suddenly uncomfortable…in my own skin, in this place, under Davis's hopeful but patiently waiting gaze, I brought my hands to my arms, crossed in front of me, and rubbed away the itch beneath the skin. My own fight for independence, forged from the need to prove my worth and success with no help from my family, and the quickening desire blooming to be taken care of.

To be loved.

To not *have* to fight for every scrap, every cent, and every mile.

"I need time." I settled on it, because he'd asked, asked me to consider it.

I could give him consideration when he was offering me so much.

Davis's eyes closed slowly, and when he opened them again, gone was his disappointment, just that steadfast kindness he'd worn since the moment I saw him at Lou's.

"What do you want for being so nice to me?"

"Not a damn thing." He'd said it with unshakable conviction, an unspoken guarantee.

I'd softened toward him then, despite the horrific night I'd had, the man who had touched me, the manager who fired me for not *taking* it because it was *normal*.

I feared I'd been softening toward Davis Hall ever since.

"I understand. Any plans for today?"

And just like that, the conversation was over, there would be no pressure. No manipulation and no anger.

Was it too soon to love this man?

I shook the completely insane thought out of my mind.

"I work later. You?"

"I have workouts and practice and game film later. We'll leave tomorrow for our game."

"But you don't play until Sunday, right?"

"Right. We'll fly out Friday night. Do a walk-through practice on Saturday, have a team dinner and then game film. Coach is pretty strict about what we do with our time the night before games, which means even for home games, we spend the night at the hotel together."

"Wow. I guess I had no idea how much work you put in."

"To play a game where one bad hit could end our career?" He wasn't teasing, but there was that soft curl of his lips and tilt of his head.

Of course. "I should probably spend some time studying football," I muttered and then stuck my tongue out at him.

"I'll teach you everything you want to know."

———

Oh god. Eggs were the devil. Maybe it was the spinach or garlic or cheese. Not that I wanted to think of food at all while I was crouched in the employee bathroom, huddled over the toilet like I was worshipping at the feet of Jesus and my stomach would not stop heaving. It'd started as soon as I stepped into the restaurant and the overwhelming scent of *meat* hit me. I couldn't even distinguish which meat it was, only that there was a *meat* smell in the air. Probably from the grilled steaks but it didn't matter because before I could say hello to Elsie at the hostess stand my hand flew to my mouth and I ran through the restaurant like a track star.

Thank God it was between the lunch and dinner rush and there were only a few tables taken, at least from what I'd seen. At least I didn't actually throw up the incredible omelet I'd had at Davis's until I reached the bathroom stall.

My stomach rolled again, and I vaguely heard someone outside the stall turning on the water. There was a quiet knock on the stall's door.

"I'll be a minute," I croaked, my throat raw, my stomach clenched into a tight ball, and sweat dripping off my forehead. If this was morning sickness hitting at two in the afternoon, it royally sucked.

"It's Madison. Can you unlock the door? I have something that might help."

I'd open the door to a stranger on my doorstep holding a gun to my face if he'd promise to help me.

I pushed off my toes and to my feet, shaking as I stood. "Yeah."

As soon as the door was unlocked, I pressed my back to the wall, and Madison entered. "Here."

She had a wet, white towel in her hand.

"Is this your magic potion?" I teased and took it, pressed the cool wet towel to my forehead and then ran it along the back of my neck. A groan slipped from my dry, and nasty parched mouth as soon as the coldness hit my skin. "I take it back. This is heaven."

"A cold rag always feels good when you don't feel well, but no, that's not what I thought would help you."

"It gets better?"

"I love your sense of humor, Maggie. Even when you're green, you're funny."

"Are you saying I look like shit?"

"You look like a pregnant woman in early pregnancy who doesn't feel good. Not like shit."

Funny, it didn't sound all that different. I hadn't actually thrown up yet, as long as I ate soon after waking, but maybe that was the difference today? I hadn't started with crackers and tea, but eggs and all the trappings?

Perhaps I wasn't used to something so heavy... but I hadn't puked the day Davis made breakfast at my place. Because I'd had toast with it?

Whatever. I could rack my brain all day to figure out the difference and only end up with a splitting headache.

"Feel better?" Madison asked, and with the rag pressed to my face, I nodded.

"Weirdly, yes. I feel a little bit better."

"Good come on then." Outside the stall, Madison had brought in a toothbrush and toothpaste.

"I'd suggest you start carrying these with you, you never know when sickness will strike, at least for the next few weeks, you know?"

Between Davis and Madison and even Belle, I was starting to believe everyone knew more about being pregnant than me, and I was the only one who was actually pregnant. Maybe I did need more help.

Maybe Belle and Davis and hell, practically Madison even though she hadn't actually said the words, were right. What woman would choose to go through this with as little help as possible if she didn't have to?

"Do you need to head home? We shouldn't be too busy tonight?"

I needed the tips and as much money as possible.

"I'm good."

"If something changes..."

"I'll let you know."

Madison's eyes narrowed, and then she gave a quick nod. "Fine, but I'm driving you home as soon as your shift ends at seven, and I don't want to hear you argue."

"Okay."

See? I could accept help. I wasn't entirely stubborn or difficult.

———

"So." Belle rubbed her hands together. "What drawer of his should I peek into first?"

I snorted. This was Belle's idea and if Davis heard I was here, I was blaming her. I'd planned to sit in Belle's living room, enjoy a day off, and struggle bus my way through watching a football game, but as soon as I mentioned it to Belle, she insisted we should have a front-row seat.

And by front-row seat, she meant Davis's living room with her and Lance.

"Come on. It'll be fun!"

So far, my heart was racing, and I was waiting for the cops to show up and drag me out of there, regardless that I had a key, and somehow the woman working at the front desk didn't bat an eye as we entered the building.

"We shouldn't even be here."

"Sure we should. He said whenever you wanted to be here you could."

"And I'd promised him I wouldn't randomly stop by."

"He's not here." She huffed and went straight to his fridge and grabbed some bottled waters. "Here. You grab some snacks. Lance?"

"Yes, dear."

She stuck her tongue out at him, which made him reach for her. He grabbed her waist and yanked her to his chest. Smacking a kiss on her cheek, Belle squealed in his hold. "I just wanted you to turn the TV on! Not assault me with your slobber."

"You two are going to make me puke."

"See?" Belle said and shooed Lance off her, only to follow him back to the couch and climb on his couch. "You're going to make the pregnant woman puke, honey."

Lance laughed and grabbed the remote. "Not sure it's me doing any of that."

I left them to their playful bickering especially since I'd have absolutely no idea how to work Davis's television that took up an entire wall. A miniature movie screen with the massive sectional couch we'd done unspeakable things on, it really would be the perfect place to have a movie night.

Or a football game afternoon as the case may be.

"I never should have let you talk me into this," I muttered, but for reasons only Belle knew, I went straight to the pantry, opened the door, and had to catch my lower jaw from dropping to the floor.

"Did you do this?" I asked, glaring at Belle over my shoulder.

Had she texted him? Planned this in secret?

There was no way... a shiver rolled through me and my eyes burned.

"Do what?" She climbed off Lance's lap, and he swatted her backside as she passed him.

"Come here."

I stood back so she could get a direct shot into the pantry.

She wasn't a liar. If she'd done this, she'd make some sassy comment like, *"well someone needs to take care of you."*

"What is it?"

When I still didn't respond, because the only thing running through my mind was how in the world I was being punked like this.

Her jaw hung down as far as it could go when she saw the madness inside.

"That's amazing!" Her hand hit between my shoulder blades and shoved me forward. I stumbled into the pantry and out of her way.

"Don't push a pregnant lady!"

"Pshh. It was a love tap." I'd lost her attention to the baskets on the shelves clearly labeled. *"Snacks for Maggie."*

Baskets. Four of them. At least a half-dozen chip bags, one basket filled with crackers. Spicy things. Sour things. Sweet things. Peanut butter jars—both crunchy and creamy.

"You can't have him," Belle muttered, grabbing a bag of salt and vinegar chips stacked in front of a bag of dill pickle chips. "I want this man. It's so thoughtful."

"I heard that!" Lance shouted, laughing at us.

"It's weird, isn't it? I mean, he labeled them with my name like he knew I'd be here?"

"Or maybe he's thoughtful and wanted to make sure he didn't eat your snacks?" She tore into the bag of chips and plopped one in her mouth. "Maybe he has some sort of self-control problem."

"Maybe he's psychotic."

"You'll probably feel better once you eat something." She grabbed a plastic bin filled with wrapped peanut butter-filled crackers and cheese-filled crackers.

They did look good.

I grabbed one with a huff. She was probably right about that, too.

"Should I thank him?"

"Only if you want him to know you were here."

I glanced at the floor, at the crumbs trailing behind Belle as she headed out of the pantry.

"Somehow, I think he'll know."

"Four chances. That's all they get to move the ball ten yards." Belle and I, properly confused about the rules of football, had now asked Lance a million questions. I should have been writing them down.

"It really doesn't seem like it should take that many tries," Belle said, a fresh bowl of BBQ chips in front of her. After she spilled the salt and vinegar chips on the floor and cleaned up the mess, I'd insisted she use a bowl—and to quit stealing my snacks.

Seems it didn't take me long to get territorial over them.

Lance, as patient with Belle as always, chuckled. "I know, honey. I'm sure you could do it in two tries every chance you had."

"Probably. What's with all the kicking and the different names, and why don't they all get points?"

I listened intently as Lance explained the difference between a punt, a kick off, and a field goal again while keeping my eyes glued to the screen. The score was tied at eighteen and the Raleigh team had the ball, which meant occasionally when the cameras scanned down the line of the Nashville team standing on the side of the field, I caught sight of Davis, typically with his hands at his hips or curled around the facemask part of his helmet—a term I learned thanks to Lance.

More impressive was seeing him run the ball down the field. I cringed every time he got hit, and surprised myself when he scored and I jumped to my feet to cheer for him.

The Raleigh team hiked the ball and based on the count at the bottom of the screen, it was now third down and eight.

"Hike!" Belle shouted, and in a blink of time after she shouted it, the quarterback for Raleigh was on his back, rolling to his side.

"That means they have to punt, right?" I asked Lance.

"They might. Tied game, that close to field goal range, they might decide to go for the first down."

Well, this just kept getting more confusing. I watched as the teams lined up again, and Lance said, "Looks like they're going for it. Fourth quarter and a tied game, they kind of have to."

"I hope he loses the ball."

"That's called a fumble."

Right, right. It had to be a basic thing, but I'd never watched any kind of sports before, and Lance was so kind in explaining.

I committed the new term to memory, cringed as they lined up again. Raleigh threw the ball and the guy who caught it was taken down.

"No first down," Lance cheered. Thank goodness he liked the game we were watching. "That means Nashville will get to line up with the ball where that guy was tackled."

"That's good, right?"

"It gives them a good chance for at least a field goal, yes."

"Awesome."

"I need more food," Belle said and stood from the couch.

"You're eating like you're the one who's pregnant," I teased, unable to take my eyes off the game even though they were going to a commercial break.

I didn't, however, complain when she returned with a single

serve bag of tortilla chips and guacamole. "Did you search his fridge, too?"

She plopped back down on the couch and Lance leaned over to kiss her cheek. "He bought you tortilla chips. No one eats them plain."

Of course they didn't. Belle was too much.

Lance gave her the same adoring smile he always did when she was slightly unhinged. "She has a point," he agreed.

The game came back on, and I sat at the edge of the couch. The quarterback, Cole, got the ball, and threw it to the guy named Butler.

"Five yards. Come on…" Lance's knees bounced violently, and he cupped his hands together.

I'd thanked them for spending New Year's Eve with me, but if I wasn't mistaken, this was probably where Lance would have preferred to be anyway. His fascination with the game was intense, but as Cole got the ball again and handed it off to Davis, it was me who jumped to my feet first.

"Go, go, go," I chanted. He dodged around one guy. Then another, and after he shook off a third guy, he lunged into the end zone. "Touchdown!"

"Holy crap, they did it!"

Lance threw his hands in the air and gave me a high-five. "Your baby daddy is incredible."

One hand, on instinct, went to my stomach. There was nothing there except maybe some bloat late at night, but that didn't mean his words didn't pierce straight to my soul.

Davis was proving himself incredible in many ways, both on and off the football field.

CHAPTER 17
DAVIS

"We did it!"

Cole slapped my back, and Dawson threw himself on both of us. There was a minute and change left on the clock, but our defense had successfully held Raleigh scoreless in this final quarter.

We had this. This was *our* comeback.

"Hell yeah, we did!" Cole screamed, wrapping his hands around my shoulder.

Our offense was a relatively young team. Cole at quarterback, me at running back, and hell, even Mason only had a couple years in the league himself. But it was our defense that helped us most of all, veteran players who were currently screaming their heads off on the sidelines, knowing just as well as I did that the game was done.

They were going to take the field, kick some ass, and we were returning home, clenching our division title.

Complete with a hat and T-shirt to celebrate.

Which is exactly what happened, and three hours later, our team's plane touched down back in Nashville. Next to me, Charles Carr jumped into the aisle as soon as the plane hit the tarmac.

"Carr, get your ass down!" Coach shouted from the front of the plane

"As soon as I get a headcount for whoever's joining me at the Big Ass Honky Tonk, Coach!"

"The honky tonk again?" one of the guys several rows up complained.

Oddly enough, that was the bar I was supposed to go to the night I met up with Maggie instead. I hadn't been back since, and now was not the night I was going.

Honky Tonk on Broadway on New Year's Eve?

"You took one too many hard hits to the head if you think I'm going anywhere near Broadway tonight."

It'd be closing in on eight o'clock by the time we got there, and people would have packed the bars as soon as they opened. When it came to knowing how to party, the people who swarmed Broadway were champions. Except it also meant the streets would already be reeking of vomit and piss.

"Hard pass, Carr," Dawson said from in front of us. He slapped Charles's chest and grabbed his overnight bag from the overhead compartment. "You heading out?"

He turned and asked me.

"No. I don't think so."

"What?" Mason shrieked from halfway up the plane. "What the hell, man? You never head to Broadway with us, and you're the one who started this idea!"

It ate at me I hadn't told more of the team about Maggie—either meeting her or seeing her again. It'd only been a week since she popped back into my life, but ever since that first night, I'd barely gone out to the bars with the guys. A drink or something with dinner, sure, but other than that, this wasn't the first time I'd backed out. Based on the way Mason was glaring at me, I needed to fix that. And I would. Soon.

"Leave him alone. He's got a chick."

"What?" asked Sam, who'd spoken up.

"Why else would you not be hanging with us?"

He shrugged like it was obvious and as the guys started ribbing me about having a girl I was hiding from them, I told them to fuck off and turned back to Dawson.

"What are you doing?"

"Going home. Crystal's in town."

"Your sister is here? Why didn't she come to the game?" Sure, it was an away one, but she'd done it before.

"Because she didn't want to."

From what I knew, Dawson and his sister were really close, but she was also pretty damn selfish and easily manipulated him. His parents were divorced due to an affair from his mom and after that ended in a giant crap show, every time he talked about his family, it sounded to me like his sister was following in her mother's footsteps instead of being a decent human.

Crystal lived in Ohio, where they were from. She'd randomly show up at Dawson's and usually left with a wallet heavy in cash and a brother in a shit mood.

Exactly what we needed with our season coming to an end.

It really wasn't my problem, and I had my own ideas on how to ring in the new year, but he'd always had my back...

"Need back up?"

He scowled at me, telling me exactly how his visit with his was going to go. "No."

All right then.

I waited until I was in my truck, luggage loaded in the back and my phone connected to the truck's CarPlay before I made my call.

"Hey. Good game today."

And just like that, hearing Maggie's voice through the phone got me all excited about the win all over again.

"Thanks. You watched?"

"I did. You're really good."

She knew nothing about football, so the compliment shouldn't have meant so much, but from her, with that sweet lilt in her voice, it did. I wanted her.

"What are you doing now?"

"Oh... um, vacuuming?"

"Why is that a question?"

"Because Belle had the idea to watch the game at your house, and I'm sorry, but she made a mess, and I'm cleaning it before you get home."

"You're at my house?"

"Yeah… is that okay?"

I didn't care if she threw a rave in my house. I was more surprised she'd taken me up on the offer to go there whenever she wanted. If Belle was involved, I shouldn't have been surprised.

"So you and Belle sat around and watched football today?" I tried to imagine it.

"Yeah. Is it okay that she was here? Lance came too, so he could explain everything."

"I said you were welcome, and they're your friends, it's cool. Are they still there?"

"No. Belle's parents always throw some huge New Year's Eve party so they just left to go get ready."

"What are you doing?"

"Well, I was going to go home."

"Want to spend time with me instead?"

"I figured you'd have plans with your teammates or friends or something."

"The only thing I have planned is to take a dip in the hot tub to relax. I can do that tomorrow. Stay there for me?"

"Sure. Davis. I'll spend New Year's with you."

"Good. I'll be there in thirty minutes."

———

I'd known Maggie grew up sheltered, with little access to television and internet and now video games or sports… things she quickly told me earlier her parents called the devil's tools for causing idle hands, which I took to mean made people lazy. Couldn't really blame them fully for that one, but I learned that she absolutely *sucked* at video games and looked adorable while playing them.

"Oh come on! Why do I keep crashing?"

She slammed her PlayStation controller into her lap and pouted, coming in last place for the fifth time.

"We can do something else." After I got home, ordering Chinese takeout on my way for both of us, we ate a quick dinner.

Since I didn't exactly have a booming supply of board games or cards, there wasn't much else left to do once Maggie insisted she wanted to try to stay awake until midnight. After vetoing a movie she was sure would knock her out quickly, I suggested the PlayStation.

I was almost surprised she jumped at the chance to learn. I wasn't quite sure if she was regretting it or not yet.

"Anything easier?"

"Mario Kart is about the easiest game in existence."

"Huh." She pouted and then shrugged it off. "All right then. Let's keep trying. Maybe I have a sucky teacher."

"As if." I laughed outright. "It's not my problem you lack hand-eye-speed coordination."

"Says the man who missed three tackles in that last run."

I tossed my controller onto the coffee table and leaned back against the couch. Hearing her talk about my game was a turn-on. Yeah, it happened a lot. In college for sure, girls would be tripping in their heels to throw their arms around me and be all, *"Oh you're so amazing." "So fast."* But Maggie was actually trying to learn and she didn't have to.

"Have you given any more thought about coming to next week's game?"

She tugged on the corner of her lip with her teeth and shrugged. "Belle can't go. I don't know if I want to be alone. Would that make you mad?"

No. Not mad. Disappointed, sure. There'd be other games. Other seasons. If being alone was the only thing stopping her, I had a solution for that.

"Our quarterback, Cole Buchanan's family, has awesome seats, and with the passing of a dear friend early in the season, he hates that seat being empty. It'd be with his parents, his fiancée, Eden, and son, Jasper. I usually go to their house for dinner on Sundays after home games, so you could join us for that, too…"

It'd mean her getting to know my friends. People I thought of as a second family.

"You're giving me a lot to think about these days, you know."

"Yeah, but you came here willingly, so I'm betting you're already going to move in with me."

"You think?" Her brows rose right as a yawn hit. Screw staying up until midnight. She needed sleep. "Sorry."

"Don't apologize for that, and yes, I'm pretty confident that will happen."

"Why?"

Oh, that was an easy one even if we were getting off topic. "Because you like me, even if you're trying not to. Because you want me involved in this pregnancy and even though you're working on your independence, which is awesome, by the way and not something I'd change, you still want the help. Want to be taken care of."

She blushed then, and I fought against leaning in, brushing my thumb along her cheek where color rose the more she gaped at me. I had her pegged easily, and we both knew it. Getting her to admit it would be a different story altogether.

"How do you know all that?"

I sat up and moved closer. She hadn't denied a single thing. "Because I listened to you that night we were together. I felt something. *We* had something, and I know the kind of woman I want to be with would be all of those things. The kind of woman who could make me laugh and have my respect, the kind of woman who I'd want to be the one having my children. I *want* you, Maggie, and I'll play this friend game as long as you insist on it, but don't for one single second that I'm not holding back, waiting for that moment when you tell me I can kiss you, that you're ready for something more."

"I'm scared."

"I know that, too, which is why you're in charge of the pace here, and nothing has to be decided tonight—not even going to the game next week. But if you *do* want to head to the game, I've got the tickets for you. They're great people, and I have a feeling you'll love Eden, his fiancée."

I could practically see her mind spin with my shift in conversation. But she'd soon learn I wasn't a liar. I wanted her. Wanted her more than I could imagine I could ever want someone and it wasn't purely about having her body in my hands again, or beneath mine.

She'd set that pace, though. I had no problems waiting.

"I'll consider it," she whispered, and her eyes fluttered close.

"Go to bed, Maggie. I'll see you next year."

She laughed and pushed to her feet. "I'm not a very fun New Year's Eve date, am I?"

"You're the best date, and we'll have more of them."

I sat back on the couch and draped my arms over the back of it to stop from reaching out for her.

"Good night, Davis," she yawned as she spoke, blushing again.

"Night, spicy mama."

Her chuckle followed her down the hall and as soon as she was gone, I groaned with pent-up frustration. I could wait. Had no problems doing it. Didn't mean my libido had the same patience. It was screaming at me to chase her, haul her to my bed and kiss her senseless until we were ringing in the new year with her calling out my name.

CHAPTER 18
MAGGIE

I should have gone directly to bed. Should have used the restroom, slipped into the T-shirt Davis had left for me on the dresser in his guest room and gone straight to bed. Actually, I should have called an Uber and headed home, not that I thought for one second Davis would let me do that that late or on New Year's Eve night when the streets would be insane.

What I absolutely should not have done was slip into Davis's Nashville Steel T-shirt and brush my hands down my stomach, pretending it was *him* touching my body or kissing his way across my sensitive flesh. My body was equal parts exhausted and *awake*, and I shuffled on my feet, staring at the closed bedroom, trying to do the right thing versus the thing my body was seeking.

Pleasure.

Excitement.

To remember the feel of him around me and on me and in me.

I definitely should not have taken the second to peek outside. The lamp was on next to my bed, but the curtains were open, giving me a gorgeous view of the city lit up at night.

And Davis. Standing at the edge of his pool by the hot tub, body turned to me in profile so I could see every inch of him. It was also the exact moment Davis, in all his bared upper body form, was stripping out of shorts. There he was—bare freaking naked.

Over the last two months, I'd gone to bed at night, remembering

Davis's body. Remembering the strength in his muscles and the ridges on his abs and those arms... the curve of his biceps and the bulge of his triceps when he moved. I'd convinced myself I was exaggerating his perfection.

If anything, based on the way he stepped over the ledge, hand cupping himself for a mere smidgeon of privacy, my memory was operating at under capacity.

I had drastically undersold the way he looked in real life.

The pulse at the tops of my thighs from the feel of his shirt on mine grew heavier, deeper, and my mouth went dry as I watched him sink into the hot tub, throw his hands to the edge and rest the back of his head at the ledge, eyes closed and face tilted to the sky.

Oh, how I wanted to know what he was thinking.

More, the tiredness I'd been fighting turned into an altogether type of need.

Two choices. Climb into bed, ease the ache being around Davis for so many days had created.

Or take a gamble. Throw caution to the wind.

Gambling might have been a sin where I came from, but I'd been rolling the dice since getting in my car in Missouri and plugging Nashville into my GPS. So far, when it came to Davis, I hadn't lost a hand.

Not only was he kind and oh-so perfect and thoughtful and funny and patient and sexy as hell.

He was the only man I'd been thinking of for the last two months.

The only man I could ever see myself with again because after him, no way could anyone else compare.

So I took the risk, and I walked down the dark hallway toward the living room that was darkened by the glow of the lamps next to the couch and a light on in the kitchen, but the brightness of the overhead lights were turned off, and the television was dark.

If he opened his eyes, he'd see me hesitantly stepping toward the sliding door, but due to the lights on inside, I could no longer see him.

Was he thinking of me? Replaying his game? Was he soaking

sore muscles he'd tried—and failed—all night to hide? Or was he thinking of Reese? His family he didn't get to see?

I had to know.

The door unlatched, the soft click a bomb compared to the silence and the racing of my heart, and as I stepped out onto the patio, letting the door slide shut behind me, Davis hadn't moved an inch from where I'd seen him in my bedroom.

It wasn't until I was halfway to him that he turned his head in my direction, and the gentle lines of his face gave way to furrowed brows and a hardened jaw.

"What's wrong?"

"Nothing. I didn't feel tired anymore and saw you out here."

One brow lifted in interest, and that throb at the tops of my thighs returned. "You saw me?"

My teeth found my bottom lip as I nodded. If he needed to hear everything I saw, the perfection of *all* that was him, I'd share, but based on the way I fidgeted on my feet, he knew.

I was learning I didn't hide much from him, and though I was taking this game, I didn't have much of a poker face.

He sat up straighter in the hot tub, hair swept to the side and though it was dark, there was no missing the desire heating his eyes. "If you're not tired, then what are you feeling, Maggie?"

He was going to make me say it, but the words wouldn't form and my throat thickened with nerves, so instead of *telling him*.

I showed him.

I took several steps closer, his eyes raking down my skin, my legs, and back up to the swell of my breasts barely concealed by his overly large shirt.

And then I removed the shirt.

I'd left my bra and underwear on, both modest and cotton and full coverage, and stood in front of him, showing him more than my flesh—my vulnerability and my desire was on bold display.

"Come here, then."

He scooted back to the other side of the hot tub, giving me plenty of room, but I hesitated. "I don't think I'm actually supposed to be in a hot tub."

"It'll be all right. Sit on the edge and put your feet in."

Which probably wouldn't make me too hot, and there was no way I could overheat more than I already was, so I listened.

Davis's gaze didn't move from my face while I climbed up and in. His body was tense, ready to help if I slipped. Once I was sitting at the edge, my feet resting on the seat in front of me, I groaned as the warm water washed over my lower legs, warmed my feet and made my entire body shiver.

"I turned it down the other day," he said, moving closer to me until his hands were running up my legs, my thighs. "I read about water being too hot, at least for your first trimester, and in case you ever wanted to use it, wanted it to be safe for you."

I was no longer sure giving myself to Davis was any gamble at all.

"That was nice of you."

"I know."

His hands settled at my hips and he used my body as leverage to pull himself closer until he was on his knees in front of me. The warm water dripped off his chin, his chest, rolled down his body as he lifted himself up onto his knees while I sat there, caging him in with my legs and his hands making large, firm but tender sweeps down the outside of my legs and back.

"I'm a nice guy. We've already agreed on that. So tell me, what'd you come out here for?"

"You. I came for you."

His full lips kicked into a grin and his hand at my hip brushed up my back, pushed away my hair until his hand was cupping the back of my neck and he was tugging me down until our lips met.

"You sure?"

"Yes," I whispered, my lips brushed his as I did, and then there was no more time for words or talking or asking because his mouth pressed to mine and he stole my nerves and my indecision with a kiss.

Our lips parted, tongues slid together and there was a sound from my throat as soon as there was an almost contented sounding sigh from his.

Yes, Davis was no risk. Not tonight anyway.

My hands settled at his shoulders, ran through his hair while he held me to him, and his other hand explored my body, down my side, my leg. He brushed his hands over my stomach and then up to my breasts. As soon as his fingers ran over my hardened pebble beneath the cotton of my bra, a gasp escaped me, and I arched into him.

"No one can see us out here," he reminded me. He slowed our kiss and tugged down one of the cups of my bra and pinched the nipple he'd barely grazed before.

My hips bucked, and who cared if the whole world saw this. Davis kneeling in front of me, dipping his head to take that nipple in his mouth while he removed my bra at the back. As soon as it was loose, I wiggled it down my arms, used the edge of the hot tub to steady myself, and Davis came back.

Kissed my clavicle, my shoulder. He slid to the side, only enough to hide me if anyone had any possible view of us, and I clung to his hair while he worked my breasts, taking time with each. His mouth. His fingers.

"Touch yourself," he said, and I obeyed before I realized I was doing it. My fingers slipped beneath my underwear and found me soaking wet for him, so needy I groaned, and pleaded with him as my head fell back and my face tipped to the sky where city lights hid the stars, but I didn't need them.

As my eyelids closed, light exploded behind my eyes as Davis tugged at the edges of my underwear, tugged them down my legs and tossed them somewhere—who knew—who cared before his mouth replaced my fingers.

I came like a rocket, so wet, so primed for him as he sucked my clit into his mouth, and pressed a finger inside of me. My entire body lit up the night with ecstasy, and I bit down on my tongue so I didn't scream his name to the heavens.

His lips pressed against my thighs, the curve of my hip and to the other side as I slowed and came down. "Please tell me this means you're giving me a chance."

There was hesitancy there as if he knew ahead of time this might have been for one night but was still willing to give me what I needed, regardless of risk or cost to him.

"Yes." My hand slipped through his hair, to the back of his neck and over his shoulder. "What can I do for you?"

"You've already done it." He glanced at me from between my thighs. "I'll do my best to make sure you never regret it."

There was a lot I could regret in life. A lot of choices I'd made and wished I wouldn't, but regardless of how this ended, I would never regret Davis.

His hand settled on my lower stomach and he rose so his mouth met mine. "I'll make sure neither of you regret giving me this chance."

Tears stung my eyes at his words, the richness of his voice, and I kissed him back, sealing his promise with a kiss until I felt the hard length of him brushed along my legs. I reached down, found pleasure when he jolted and then groaned from my touch and wrapped my hand around his thick, perfect length.

"Shit," he rasped as I began working him.

Wet from the water, my hand easily slid up and down his length, and my mouth watered to taste him. To taste *all* of him.

"Can you stand?"

"You don't have to." His hand covered mine. "This is enough."

"I want to give you more." I pulled my mouth away from his, looked down to where he threaded his fingers between mine and we jerked him off together. "Please?"

I'd never done this. Never wanted to, and even when I tried to learn about sex, watching or imagining this act had never once made my heart race the way it was now.

"I can guarantee I'll never turn you down or make you ask for this again."

He stood then, and it was my turn to rake my gaze over his body, the rivulets that ran down sinew arms and chiseled abs but it was the kindness on Davis's face that grabbed my attention and held my focus as I looked up at him, our hands still tangled together around him and brought it toward my mouth.

"I've never done this."

"You can do nothing wrong. Take as much as you like, don't be afraid of pressure and use your hand near the base."

I opened my mouth and slid my tongue over and around the

curve of him that was wider at the top than the rest. An unknown sound fell from Davis's parted lips as he glanced down at me, held hair out of my face with his free hand, and kept his hand at the back of mine, fisting my hair, keeping me steady.

"So damn good. Yes, just like that."

He encouraged me with words and direction and the sounds most of all that I caused him to elicit.

Me. I was doing this. There was power here, sitting exposed to the weather and the night, completely bare, and yet it was Davis who was vulnerable right now as he let me learn the feel of him, taste him, and take him until his noises became grunts and his fist tightened in my hair.

"Going to finish, Maggie, you don't have to…"

I took him deeper, gagged as he hit the back of my throat and only moved back enough to do it again.

"Fuck. Maggie."

My name was a grunt, and he swelled in my mouth, hardened further if possible, and then there was a warm wet stream from him hitting my throat. I swallowed it down as he came, chanting yes and so good on repeat until his knees in front of me shook and he released his hold only hair.

"Was that okay?" I asked when he'd stepped to the bottom of the hot tub, splashed warm water on his face, then stood, leaned over the side, and draped my shoulders with a towel he must have brought.

"Yeah, Maggie." He kissed me gently, a smile on his lips. "That was better than okay."

"Good."

"Better than good, too. You're fantastic. Every part of you."

CHAPTER 19
MAGGIE

I woke to bright light, and if possible, an even more comfortable bed than before when I spent the night at Davis's. I curled to the side, opening my eyes in search of him, and found his side of the bed covered with rumpled sheets, but no man. As soon as we'd finished in the hot tub, he'd brought me inside, where he took time drying me off and offered me a fresh T-shirt.

I fell asleep almost immediately, not even aware when he'd come to bed after taking care of himself, but at some point during the night I'd woken to his arms around me and the soft snores he made at my shoulder.

He hadn't even asked me to spend the night in his bed, I'd just collapsed right into it, but from the way he held me while I slept, he hadn't seemed to mind.

Which left the other offers he'd made me more difficult to answer.

Move in here?

I liked Davis. Liked him more every time we spent time together. He came from a family he adored, and if the way they raised him was like how the rest were, I'd probably feel the same way about them. Logistically, moving in with him would be a good idea. At least until the baby was born or in the months after. Belle and Lance were getting married in August, right after I was due. I wouldn't be able to depend on her for much help, not when they'd be on their honeymoon and newly married. The summer would be Davis's off-season, so he'd be around to help out before his next season started.

The only risk was my heart or us not working out and having to adjust after being gifted such luxury.

"Ugh." I groaned as my stomach rolled, and then I jumped to my feet and lunged toward the bathroom.

"Crap," I coughed right before I reached the toilet, dropped to my knees, and started puking into it.

I was an idiot. Got lost in my thoughts instead of taking care of myself, and now, the tiny bean inside me was revolting in anger for their immediate morning needs being ignored.

Once I was done, I flushed the toilet, closed the lid, and then collapsed back onto the tile floor, my back to the counters.

Which was exactly where Davis found me. Still sitting with my back to the counter, my head tilted so I was staring at the ceiling. His footsteps were heavy, alerting me to his presence well before he appeared in the doorway.

I turned my head to face him, and he glanced at me, the toilet, the rug I'd slipped across the floor in my rush to not puke on his floor, and then back to me.

"Are you okay?"

He was dressed to work out. Probably already had given the sweaty shirt clinging to his chest and the wetness of his hair.

"I waited too long to eat when I woke up." My stomach rolled again.

"What do you need?"

"Toast?" I swallowed and cringed. "And some toothpaste?"

Davis quirked a smile. "That's a strange pregnancy craving."

I gawked at him. He couldn't really think I meant…

"Kidding, Maggie. I'll be back in a few minutes. Stay here, okay?"

Since I hadn't planned to move for a while, I didn't say anything and a minute later, Davis returned with a toothbrush, still in its packaging, and a travel-size tube of toothpaste. He set them on the counter and crouched next to me, brushing hair off my cheek. My eyes closed as his warm hand brushed over my face, soothing me in ways I didn't know I needed.

In ways I'd never really had.

"Bread is in the toaster. Need anything to drink?"

I allowed myself one cup of coffee, but never before I ate and after brushing my teeth, orange juice would taste janky.

"Water, or Sprite, if you have it, would work."

"All right. Take your time. I also brought in your clothes from the other room and set them on my bed. I'll be waiting for you in the kitchen, okay?"

"Thanks." He stood to leave. "Davis?"

"Yeah?"

"What time is it?"

"It's after noon."

"Noon?!" Holy crap. I never slept in. Rarely past nine, and I couldn't remember if I'd ever slept until noon.

He tossed me that smile of his that did funny things to my stomach in a much different way than it currently felt. "You were up late, and you need the sleep. It's okay. It's not like I have much to do anyway. Rest. Wake yourself up. I'll have something for you to eat when you come out."

It didn't take me long once I managed to pull myself off the floor. A quick brushing of my teeth, and I climbed back into the sweatpants I'd worn the day before since I hadn't planned to see him. I kept on his shirt, too lazy to change it and when I found him in the kitchen, he looked freshly showered, hair a different kind of wet than before, and in different clothes.

"Did you shower?"

"Quick one in the guest bathroom. Here."

He slid a plate of buttered toast toward me with a can of Sprite. It was like the man had stocked his home with every possible craving any pregnant woman on Earth might possibly have.

I wasn't complaining.

Grateful, more like it, as I popped the top on the can and took a first, testing sip. The bubbles slid down my throat and didn't upset my stomach, so I took a bite of toast, and as soon as I had that smallest bite of food in me, I already felt better.

"I was thinking this morning," I said, and tore off a chunk of toast while Davis was busy pulling fruit and a bag of spinach and a container of protein powder out of his fridge and cupboard.

"Yeah?"

He bent down on the other side of the island and reappeared with a blender in his arms.

"I was thinking my apartment isn't so great. Not the safest, really, and it's a lot of stairs."

He'd been working on twisting the top of the protein powder, but as I spoke, he stopped moving. Blue eyes focused on me with such intensity I fought squirming beneath the weight of it. "Those are all true…"

"There's not a lot of room there after the baby comes, either, so I'm going to need to save more money to get something nicer."

"Okay…"

God, this was killing me. He told me I could set the pace, but I didn't think he'd force me to drag it out like this. "So, yeah." I swallowed another torn-off piece of toast. "I was wondering, if you know… that offer? It wouldn't have to be forever…"

"Yes. If the offer you're talking about is moving in with me, or at least into my home, then yes. Absolutely yes, it's still on the table."

I wasn't really doubting it. Not after last night. Not after I was beginning to learn that he might not only be the sexiest man on the planet but also the most thoughtful. He might say he hated growing up with bossy older sisters, but I sure as heck appreciated them. Their mom and them had raised one hell of a good man.

"Okay then."

His brows peaked, and his palms pressed to the counter, bracing himself. "Yeah? You mean it?"

The veins in his arms were pronounced. The smile on his face endearing. For a moment, I was speechless and nodded. Because this guy… so damn cute. Sexy. Perfection.

Davis pushed off the counter, smoothie concoction forgotten and stalked around the island slowly. I'd never felt the shivers from feeling like prey until that moment when he swiveled the barstool until I was facing him and his finger pressed to the soft flesh beneath my chin.

He tilted my chin up, that small pressure sending a racing heat through me. I licked my lips as his gaze dropped to them. "I really want to kiss you right now."

He leaned in slowly, giving me time to move away, but I was arching, moving closer to him, aching for the brush of his warm, full lips against mine.

We connected, a soft press of his mouth to mine, and I inhaled the crisp scent of his cologne or body wash that smelled like lemons and mint and fresh air and peace.

"Thank you," he rasped against my mouth. "It's killing me knowing you're in that building, and I really hoped you'd give me this chance."

I leaned back on the stool, and his hand left my chin. The loss of his touch was a sharp ache in my chest, and I swallowed it down before I looked too much into it.

One night together months ago and a few days this last week meant it was too soon for me to be feeling such insanely deep reactions to him.

Wasn't it?

Davis licked his lips as if sealing in the taste of me or craving one more and stepped back to his smoothie almost like nothing happened. A moment of disappointment arose before he threw his ingredients into the blender, slammed the top on it, and with one palm pressed to the lid, grinned at me.

"So, we moving you in today?"

Turned out, by the time we ate and I showered and got redressed in the clothes I wore to Davis's home the day before, he was cutting it close to needing to get to the practice facility for a light practice and game film. He dropped me off at the door to my apartment, refusing to allow me to walk up alone. The elevator still wasn't working, and the workers weren't inside, and the clench of Davis's jaw told me he wasn't exactly thrilled to see either of those.

Fortunately, he didn't say anything and promised to talk to me when he was done with practice.

I had the day off work, so I called Belle to fill her in, which meant, after a lengthy shrieking squeal of happiness that almost ruptured my eardrums, she dragged her hungover butt to my apartment, arms filled with moving boxes and packing tape she'd stopped to purchase on the way.

"I'm so damn glad you're getting out of here. Know you didn't want me to help, but it's been killing me to know you're in this place. This building." She was talking more to herself than me, so I let her ramble because, for once, I was moving with people at my back, a safe place I could trust to go to, and I wasn't quite sure I ever had that except for the months I spent with Belle.

"I don't even know what to pack." Almost all the things I owned were bought on Facebook Marketplace or found on the curb. Someone else's junk became my temporary furniture, like the couch I'd had Lance haul up four flights of stairs with unknown stains on the cushions that'd been covered by a sheet from a garage sale.

I wasn't even sure how Davis spent the night on that couch or how he'd been able to hide any sort of cringe when he was at my apartment the first time. Looking around now, scanning it even though I tried to keep it clean and tidy, all of it made me feel like a thin layer of dust clung to my skin.

I wouldn't have to live like this anymore.

My *child* wouldn't have to grow up living like this.

"We can store it all or donate it," Belle said and stood from the box of books she was loading. She wiped her hands along her hips, and her gray shorts became smeared with a light covering of dusted handprints.

Yeah. Moving anywhere would be good.

"What if it doesn't work? What if... what if I get there and this doesn't work, or we just don't belong together, and then I have to move back out, and then my child gets to live with some poor mom while her father can offer her everything in the world?"

"Her?"

"I don't know."

Of course that's what Belle would cling to, and I hadn't even realized I'd gendered my baby before the results came in. There was a way Davis smiled when he talked about his nephews. And then the way he looked when he talked about his brand-new niece. A tenderness softened his features and while I imagined him running around and tackling boys and tossing them in the air, my hand went to my stomach as I envisioned him holding a little baby girl with that same look, intensified because it was *his*. "And either way, thinking of if I'm carrying a boy or a girl doesn't help me. This could blow up."

"It could." Belle nodded and grabbed a handful of more books before placing them in the box. "It might not, too. Or maybe it works for a while and you and Davis reach an agreement, but do you really think he'd toss you out and make you live like this again? Not at least provide for his child?"

When she put it like that…

"No."

Of course, he wouldn't. I didn't know him well, but I'd already decided that was no gamble. I only needed to keep reminding myself of it.

"Then let's get packing."

———

"Long day?"

I fought a yawn and could see Davis's smile through the phone. Belle and I packed for hours, and the smaller furniture we could move out ourselves, we moved to the curb. Most of it, at last check, was long gone. Every time a car pulled up and someone jumped out, or someone walked by and grabbed a small end table or lamp, I prayed a quick little prayer it was going to someone like me who needed the help. Who was fighting for independence. Who was working on bettering themselves and the lives around them.

"I called my landlord and left a message for him. My lease has a penalty for leaving early, but I'm hoping since he can turn around and rent this tomorrow, he'll give me a break."

"Don't worry about it, Maggie. I can help."

"I know. But…"

He was sitting back on his couch, one arm flung over the side of his chair. From where he held the phone, I assumed his elbow was propped onto the armrest. He looked as tired as I felt, just more recently showered.

"You want to handle it."

I was still trying to figure out if I'd saved enough money to cover it, but I was close. It might mean taking away all my savings, but I could do it. It would hurt, though.

"Yeah."

One soft laugh left his mouth and lifted his lips at one edge. "You do know I'm at the end of a first-year contract for four years, and the total of that is almost forty million dollars, right?"

I couldn't remember the exact amount of the contract Belle told me he signed or how much he made, but that number sounded awfully simple and obscene falling from his lips.

"Oh. Is that it?" I twirled a chunk of hair that had fallen out of my ponytail around my finger. "Seems kind of low."

"Brat," he teased and sobered. "Let me do this for you. I asked you to upend your life. Think of it as a loan if you have to, but I *want* to do this. It was my idea in the first place. I can at least cover the expense of it."

I was going to be out almost five-thousand dollars, a bit more if I decided to store the rest of the things, just in case. It was pennies compared to what was probably in his bank account.

"I'll pay you back," I told him, and I must have been more forceful than intended because his eyes widened before narrowing again.

"Maggie."

"I know. I know you can do it. I know I don't have to worry about a thing, but I also need this. To take help and make this work with you without feeling like I'm giving everything I've worked so hard for up."

"What are you thinking then?"

"I pay you the same amount of rent I'm paying now. And I help with food."

"That's it?"

"That's it."

"Okay."

He made everything so easy, so willing to follow my terms. I wasn't sure I'd ever met a man who would allow himself to not be the one setting the terms for any kind of deal.

"Are you sure?"

He bent his arm, ran his hand through his hair, and tilted his face toward the ceiling before looking back at me through the screen. "I don't have the hang-ups about money or a need to be independent like you do, Maggie. I had parents who loved me regardless, who put my happiness and reaching my goals above the dollars that would follow. I send them things, I help with my nephews. But they love me. Unconditionally. I have everything I need right now, and my parents always made sure I did, so yeah"—he gave a little one-shoulder shrug,—"if you need this and it's in my nature and abilities to give it. Easy as that."

Easy as that.

Huh.

He certainly made it so.

Which only made my decision this morning to give this a chance that much more appealing. A relationship with Davis would be easy. Fun.

"I also need to keep working."

"Maggie." He laughed and leaned off the couch. His face grew closer to the phone before he resettled it, and I imagined him with his elbows on his knees. "You're not getting this. I want *you*. I want to take care of our baby. Nothing else matters and however I need to do that, whatever you're willing to take from me, it's not a burden… it's a privilege. You want to work, I get it. Work as long as you're able. All I ask is after, you make sure you're physically and mentally ready to return or don't. Again, if there's something you need and I can give it, it's yours. No questions asked, no expectations in return. It's just how I believe relationships are supposed to work."

A relationship.

I was in a relationship with Davis Hall. First-year running back for a professional sports team I barely remembered the name of before a month ago, and now I was having a baby with him and he was more incredible than I hoped.

Which made the next decision I made earlier easy to say.

"I want to go to the game on Sunday. With your friends."

CHAPTER 20
DAVIS

Nerves mixed with excitement were thrumming beneath my skin, making me bounce on the soles of my feet and shake out my arms. Sure, it was to keep them loose. But any second, we'd return to the field after warm-ups, and for the first time since I took the field since my freshman year of college, there was something larger than football on my mind.

Maggie would be there... sitting by Eden and Jasper while Cole's parents, Kate and Dave, sat behind them. She was taking Marley's seat, a beloved friend of the family who passed earlier in the season, and yet Cole hadn't hesitated when I asked if Maggie could join them. Of course he wouldn't.

Cole Buchanan, our quarterback and one of our team's captains, wasn't only one of the best quarterbacks I'd ever witnessed, he ranked in the top five of the best guys I knew. He, and Dawson, who was currently standing in our locker room, half-dressed, back to the team and on his phone. He was standing three seats down from me, but I could still hear the harsh whispers coming from him. The white-knuckle grip he had on his phone and the clench of his jaw made it obvious who he was talking to.

Crystal. It had to be. She was unlike any other and any day now she would most likely end him up in a world of trouble. Or drain his bank account.

As for me, my blood was pumping. Couldn't sit still. Maggie

hadn't been in her seat when we were out there on the field earlier, stretching, warming up, and I'd looked. Looked for her and the seats I'd always saved for my parents. My dad—who was running late due to a storm in Chicago, would be there for sure, and all I was thinking about was how he would react to Maggie when I introduced them.

He'd be nice and respectful, and probably love her on the spot because he'd see how happy she made me, but if I was given the go-ahead from Maggie to tell him she was pregnant, that could change on a dime.

Shit.

"Hey." A slap hit me from behind, making me stumble toward my locker.

"What?" Sam Denmark, our backup quarterback and all-around All-American guy, shoved his brows together.

"What's wrong with you?"

"Nothing's wrong." Everything was perfect. Or had the potential to be. Or turn to an irrevocable pile of shit I couldn't fix. What could be wrong?

"You ready for this?"

"Are you?"

He threw his head back and laughed. "I stand on the sidelines and cheer, ready to play but knowing I probably won't. Are you kidding me? I'm living the life right now."

As long as Cole was healthy, Sam would always be on the sidelines. Everyone knew it. But there was always the chance. A wicked tackle. A messed up hit during the pass that tore out Cole's elbow. Broken thumb. Even a sprained ankle that could take him a game or two. Anything could happen at any time. Assuming best case scenario though, Sam was right.

He'd be able to cheer us on with little to no pressure.

Me?

My first year and I'd already broken not only three team records but currently held the rookie all-around yards and touchdowns made. And we were a passive offense. Still, eyes were on me. Critics were picking up. Comparing me to the greats.

I shook it off and focused on Sam. On Dawson, who tossed his phone into his locker and flinched from the sound it made as the screen shattered.

Damn.

"I'm good." I was. I would be.

Might need to throw up, but I tried to inhale through my nose, exhale through my mouth, and take Cole's advice before our first game.

Play like it's high school when you're playing for glory and fun and not the paycheck or the sixty-plus thousand people who would be in the stadium. Watching me. Waiting. Hoping I scored or praying I fucked up.

"Shit," I muttered, as bile rose in my throat.

I took off toward the bathroom, shoving lineman and defensive ends out of my way like I wasn't half their size or weight, and managed to hit the toilet right as my nerves appeared.

"Fuck," I grunted, puking my brains and my courage, and probably all my football knowledge out into the toilet.

"Dude!" Cole. He pounded on my door. I'd seen him earlier. He was cool. Calm. Collected. "What the hell?"

The prince of Nashville who wore our team's uniform like he'd been born in it even if life hadn't gone his way a time or twelve.

"I'm good."

"You're screwed in the head and you're not thinking of the game."

I coughed, made sure everything I was terrified about was already expelled, and flushed the toilet. What twenty-three-year-old man puked before a game?

"My head's in it, I promise."

I flipped the latch and shoved open the stall door. Cole followed me to the sinks while I splashed water on my face and washed my hands. Cupped them with water so I could rinse out the vile taste of my nerves.

"Hey. Talk to me." His hand landed on my shoulder and even though we were both padded, his touch was a comfort. An anchor.

I glanced at him in the mirror and his concern was obvious. Not as quarterback. Not as captain. But as a friend. The guy who let me stay with him and his son, Jasper, for weeks before I could move into my penthouse. The small-town guy who'd done everything right after a really shitty and difficult past.

The guy who cared.

"Maggie's pregnant, moving in with me, and I barely know her and I don't want to screw it up but I'm afraid it's going to be when my parents find out because shit… who fucking knocks up a one-night stand and then moves her in and actually really likes her?"

Me. That was who. The idiot and corn-fed boy from Nebraska who no one really expected much from besides himself and his family. But that could go to shit when said family learned what I did.

I expected a laugh. Anticipated and braced for it even, but Cole stared at me with eyes that had seen more than me, a wealth of understanding in them considering his own son had been born from a similar, if also very different circumstance.

"Come on." He tugged me toward him, his arm landing over my shoulders and slapping my pads. "You've gotta see this."

"Coach is coming soon."

"We've got time."

We headed down the hall, toward the tunnel that would take us to the field. Inflatable towers were set up that would blow smoke and the noise of the crowd would soon encompass us all. Soon, for the next hour of playing time, we would be gods and heroes and I was buckling quickly under the pressure to be everything to everyone but most importantly… the only thing that mattered to the few who needed it most.

"Look." Cole pointed. His arm flew out and I followed the direction and *there.*

There she was. She was across the field, near the corner behind the end zone on the side of our team's bench but the spot I'd memorized hours ago was now filled with the person I wanted—needed—to see the most.

"Do you know why I'm always the last guy in the locker room before Coach shows up?" Cole dropped his arm from my shoulders and stood, hands on his hips.

We were still in the tunnel but far enough out no one would see.

No media. No photographers. Like he knew the exact place to stand and it made sense in a blink of my eyes.

"Because you're here."

"Always." He turned to me. "I'm here. Always. Looking at my reason for why I do this. Why I want to be the best." He curled his hand into a fist and punched it to my pads over my heart. "You have your own now, you know? And I get it… trust me. I get that whatever you're feeling right now is absolutely, one hundred percent scary as absolute fuck. But she's your reason, yeah? The baby she's carrying?"

"Yes."

Unequivocally. Always. Even if Maggie fucked off and wanted nothing to do with me, the child we'd made would forever be my reason.

"Then take this moment, Hall. Take it. Soak it all in. The experience. The sound. The excitement, the hope, the joy. It could be over tomorrow or last for a decade, we never know. You could be here for years or traded in March. We *never* fucking know what life will bring. But this? Right now? Everything you're playing for is *here*, supporting you. Cheering you on. You know what that makes you?"

"The luckiest man alive?"

I couldn't see her, but she was there, and it was all I needed.

"Damn straight." He slapped my shoulder. "Now let's go listen to Coach tell us how much he loves us and then go kick some Rough Rider ass."

We were not kicking Rough Rider ass.

Down by eight, one minute to go. At the forty-five yard line, which was good enough for a field goal and three points but no way would we kick in this situation.

Short, under twenty-yard touchdowns and long, over sixty were my jam, but I'd been sat down all night by Raleigh's defense. They were on me like bees on honey and I couldn't shake off their defense or shove my way through it.

Not a single touchdown for the running back who'd been described as the best rookie in twenty years.

I could only imagine the criticism, the shock, the talk from Monday morning quarterbacks that they were wrong, I wasn't all that great or special. None of it was true. Even without being able to find a hole in their D-line, I'd still run over fifty yards. I hadn't punched in a goal, but Dawson had two.

Yet every time he returned to the huddle, he appeared pissed, like his touchdowns were fuel, not celebration.

"All right, men." Cole slapped his hands together, appearing unfazed and relaxed.

I was anything but. Sweat dripped down my spine, clinging to my compression shirt, and for the first time since maybe Pop Warner football, I doubted myself.

Until Cole stared right at me, confident as all hell, and shouted, "Forty-two draw."

"No." I shook my head. "Won't work."

"You can do this. We've got you."

Shit. The faith he had in me. I hadn't broken through a hole in the line all game and now with the game actually ticking down, only a few more plays up our sleeve... this could work. They wouldn't be expecting me to get the ball, not with how well they'd shut me down. At worst, I get us a few yards and we regroup.

"Forty-two draw," I repeated with a nod.

"Let's get it, men. I can already smell the parade the city will have for us!"

A few offensive linemen grunted out their agreement and we released from the huddle to our spots. A draw, where Cole would fake a pass to JJ, or Jefferson Jameson who'd already scored a touchdown. He'd be double covered for sure, loosening up the defense in the backfield if I could break through, and the defense would be running to block the ball and slap it out of Cole's hands.

Which meant I had to tuck and run, maybe juke one out, and I'd have this.

I had this.

Cole called the play, dropped back, and like every time a play started, it moved in slow motion for me, tunnel vision where the only thing I had my eye on was the ball, my speed, and any obstacle in my way.

As soon as my fingers touched the cool leather of the ball, I was off. We'd moved quick, our offense blocking like they'd done all game and there. The hole. A slight squeeze.

I was shoved to the right, my left foot slipping but I regained control, pummeled and shoved my way through the beams that were some of the largest arms I'd ever seen in my life but my force was more powerful than their strength and I slipped through. The field wide open, the defense read our play wrong meant the two backs who were supposed to double team JJ were rushing me, men fast on their feet, but no doubt I was faster and I turned, missing one, kept the left foot in play as I reached the sideline and I was at the thirty. The twenty-five. The twenty, the fifteen. The crowd was probably on their feet, losing their minds, but all I saw was that thick white line moving closer with every split second and my own racing heart.

I had this. A touchdown… until a shadow took to my side and the hell? I couldn't glance, but my jersey was tugged, killing my momentum. I threw my left arm back, shook him off. The last defender tripped over my feet and I did the same, tripping. Slipping.

And sliding right over the goal line.

"Touchdown!" I screamed from where I'd belly flopped my way into the end zone.

Not pretty.

But I scored.

A massive weight slammed into my back. "You did it, you little fucking shit! Thought for sure you were down at the ten."

I rolled to my side as Yeets continued to scream at me and shoved him off, hopping to my feet.

"Hell yeah I did!" Arms were thrown around me. Dawson slapped my back and I threw my arm in the air still holding the ball while the entire stadium roared with approval, their happiness like they'd been physically involved.

And in that moment, I turned the corner.

Found her.

Maggie, sitting a few rows up, on her feet, face shining and teeth beaming with her large smile as she clapped and screamed with everyone else. Next to her, Cole's son, Jasper was jumping up and down, massive noise-canceling headphones on his ears, but it was Maggie who grabbed my attention and held it.

I pointed the ball in her direction before flicking it toward the ref and then pointed my index finger back at her with a smile I hoped she could see behind my face mask.

I did it.

"One more play. Let's tie this game up and close it down."

Dawson caught an easy shovel pass into the end zone as we went for two and then we were on the sidelines, lining up to watch the kickoff.

Still more than thirty seconds to go, enough time to get off a few plays. This game was far from over. Our place kicker, Jassen Moore, lined up for the onside kick.

Cole stood on one side of me. Dawson, the other. The entire offense held their breath while the kick went off. Raleigh's special teams fell on it, but … no fucking way!

"Holy shit!" Cole grabbed my arm and jumped.

The guy had fumbled. Touched the ball so it was live and there was a massive dog pile for it. The ball slipped out, and our team landed on it.

"Yes! Holy crap! They've done it!"

"Game is ours!"

"Let's go, boys!"

Coach Paul Bowles jumped up and down, throwing his fists into the air so hard and fast he knocked his mic off his ear. "Yes! Goddamn, yes, that is how you play, men!"

Our team erupted in another round of furious cheers as the refs called it officially our ball and Raleigh's special team slunk back to their sidelines.

Thirty seconds. Less than thirty seconds left in the game and we were already in Jassen's field goal range, although it'd be long. Tight. The wind was minimal and he had the least amount of misses of any field goal kicker in the NFL this season, but we could make it easier for him to lock in the win.

"Quick run play," Cole said to me as we hustled out to the field. "Get me eight to ten, Hall."

"Let's go, Captain."

That was the trust he had in me. No doubt. No hesitation. I rose to the challenge and the ball was in my hands. Six yards. Four to go. Twenty seconds and we called our last time out and hustled to the sidelines.

"Get the ball to the sidelines and get out," Bowles said, and he glanced at all of us.

He was intense, but he was a good man. Loved each of us. Made sure we knew it and when he criticized our mistakes, he always made sure to start with what we'd done right. He was the kind of man who reminded me of my dad. Unconditional love and respect was given to every one of his players. "Butler. JJ. Everyone get open. Get me six more yards so Moore can nail it. Everyone got it?"

There was a round of *yes, sir* through our huddle and then Bowles settled his hands on the shoulders of Cole and Mason. "Love you, men. Told you once, and I told you a thousand times this season you men have something special. It's not only your talent, it's your heart and your drive we've seen every day since pre-season began. Since camp, and even since the off-season. You've worked for this, you've earned it, and now you just gotta finish it out but even if this game goes into OT or against us, know, down to my soul the love I have for each and everyone of you is the love I have for my sons."

"Yes, sir!"

"Now go end this and get us to the next round!"

We clapped hands together, hustled back to the sidelines.

Cole lined up. Play was called.

The play moved to slow motion, and as I looked, heading toward my spot, I got tripped up by a defensive end, and a yellow flag flew in my peripheral.

Shit!

Play ended with Yeets getting the ball. The six yards turned to eight as he stepped out of bounds but it was the flag that had my stomach knotting. It was too close to our side.

The field judge hurried to the other refs, nodded, and tucked the flag back into his pocket as he ran toward the side of the field. "Holding! Offense. Number ninety-four."

"Shit!" Cole shouted. Fifteen seconds. Enough for one more play, but with losing ten yards, we'd put Moore in a tricky spot. The ball would be right at his longest field goal all year.

"All right. Shake it off," Cole told Gibson, the guy who'd caused the penalty.

"Bullshit penalty," he grumbled. We always liked to believe they were. "Let's go. Do this."

Lined up. Ball snapped. Adrenaline raced through me and as the play looked to be similar to the last one, at the last second, Cole spotted me. I had a defender coming up on my ass and one barreling toward me from the backfield but he let loose. The ball sailed through the air and dropped right into my hands. I was hit almost immediately, managed to fight the first tackle and then was shoved out of bounds.

"Yes! Good job!" Bowles slammed his hand to my helmet where I'd stepped out of bounds and I risked a quick peek at the clock.

Ten seconds.

Twelve yards.

I'd put us right back where we were pre-penalty and hopefully gained a couple extra yards.

"Field goal! Field goal!" It was time. Ten seconds.

We'd still have to kick off and pray like hell for those seconds that something batshit crazy wasn't hiding up Beaux Hale's sleeve but this was it.

Our final chance.

The field goal team took the field.

Moore lined up.

The ball was snapped and he let loose with a forty-two yard kick that sailed high and tight straight through the middle of the bars.

"Yes!" Our team went wild.

He was tackled where he'd kicked the ball and hauled off the field as the stadium shook from the cheers and applause and absolute mayhem. I scanned the stadium, felt Maggie's happiness radiating off her but kept looking until I spotted the man I hoped to see.

My dad was somewhere up there, probably losing his complete mind.

This was it, though. Those moments Cole had told me to remember. To lock into my memory so I never questioned, never doubted, because anything could happen—the good and the bad and as the seconds ticked down and our defense managed to shut Raleigh down from scoring—this was what I'd worked so hard for.

Not just a game in the NFL. Not just a win—but a trip to the post-season and the dream of a little boy to win the Super Bowl was within our grasp.

Within *my* grasp.

And with those I loved most, those I wanted to impress most in the stands as the clock reached zero time left, there was absolutely no better feeling. Nothing would compare to that moment.

CHAPTER 21
MAGGIE

learned about more than football watching the game and sitting near Cole Buchanan's family. First, I learned Kate and Dave treated every human under the age of thirty like they were their own children. As soon as I found the seat my ticket stated, Kate was on her feet, already searching for me. How she knew what I'd look like, I had no clue. As far as I knew, Davis hadn't taken any pics of me, but once I got close to the row, she was already waving her arm, calling my name. She welcomed me with a hug and her name, insisting I call her Mama B like everyone else, and her husband Dave did the same thing. We spent the time alone with them, telling me all about Cole and their other son, Graham, who was still in college, playing football, but not the same position as Cole. And then Eden showed.

She hugged them like they were their own parents, held Jasper's hand, and got him situated. She welcomed me with a smile that didn't quite reach her eyes and a handshake that was a little too hard, a little too suspicious.

She had to know, right? Cole would have told her... which made everything make sense.

She wasn't suspicious of me because she didn't know me... she basically gave me the cold shoulder all game *because* she knew I was pregnant and she absolutely didn't trust me.

It soured my mood. I was being judged in ways I hadn't been

since I stopped wearing floor-length skirts and homemade dresses and first stepped foot into the "real world."

I didn't blame her, but the assumptions she made about me weighed heavily on my shoulders. Throughout the game she made ignoring me an art form while she fussed with Jasper, turned and smiled and laughed with Kate and Dave all while Jasper was firmly planted between us. She jumped to her feet and cheered during every great play Cole made, gave high-fives to Jasper and Dave, spinning while she did so and skipped her gaze right over mine.

Needless to say, by the time the clock was running down, we weren't all just on our feet, I was starting to get a pit in my stomach growing with dread because after this game, Davis promised Kate and Dave—and his own father who was also somewhere in this stadium—we'd all head to their home in Marysville, north of Nashville, for their Sunday family dinners.

All that surety I felt earlier in the week when I agreed to move in with Davis so he could help me out and all the confidence I had in what I thought we were growing was quickly replaced with an anxious, constant stream of doubts. If I stayed with Davis, this would be how everyone treated me. Friends. Family. Strangers online probably tearing me apart from my hair and eye-shape to the curves of my body. I would forever be known as a gold digger. Or worse.

I might have really liked Davis, but I wasn't sure I had the stomach for the rest of it.

None of it was enough to ruin my excitement as Davis scored a touchdown with less than a minute left in the game, and I swear, for one brief second, our eyes met across the field, and he pointed at me.

"That's Uncle Davis!" Jasper shouted. He pointed right back at number eleven and waved even while Davis was running to line up for another play.

I leaned back and made eye contact with Dave. "I thought he was done after the touchdown."

An unfriendly smirk curled Eden's lip in my peripheral. A fan of my questions she was not, but fortunately, Dave seemed thrilled to help me out. "Usually they come out and kick an after point kick for one point. But once they're still down by two, if they score one more play, they can tie the game up."

"Oh. Okay."

I spun back around just in time to see Cole hike the ball. Next to me, Jasper's little hand wrapped around mine and he squeezed. "Come on, Dad…"

My heart leaped into my throat and while I didn't fully understand the game, it didn't diminish the absolute electricity on the field. The complete silence as Cole hiked the ball or the mass hysteria that followed in a blink as one of the Steel players lifted his hands and the ball dropped right into it. He ran three steps and was caught in a dog pile as the rest of the team threw themselves on top. For one brief moment, as Jasper and I cheered and Eden turned around to hug Kate and Dave, she smiled at me, cheered and even managed to catch my hand in a high-five, which helped settle my fears.

At least, until it was time to walk through the stadium and head to where the players would leave the locker room and by the time we arrived, there was already a man outside the doors, apart from the rest, hands shoved into jeans and worn work boots on his feet.

I spotted him immediately, due to his pacing and his size, but it wasn't the fact he didn't seem to know anyone.

He was the spitting image of Davis, an exact replica only thirty-some years older. I had a flash of future Davis, maybe a little less muscled straight in front of me. The man who would be my child's grandfather.

And he had absolutely no idea.

Making me feel like an absolute pile of crap for forcing Davis to keep this secret from a family he loved and adored so much. The day I'd asked him to hold off had seemed so minuscule. He was still someone I barely knew, and his family was half a country away.

We had time.

But as he turned and spotted Kate and Dave, who again welcomed him into their arms with warm hugs and greetings, I couldn't force my feet to move.

"You look like you're going to throw up."

As far as first willing words, Eden spoke to me all afternoon, they weren't the greatest. Neither comforting or exactly kind, even if she wasn't wrong. "Davis hasn't told his family, and now I feel like shit for asking him to wait."

"Huh." She peered at me with narrowed eyes, inspecting me and then her features softened before she turned and walked off.

I opened up and got a *huh* in return and as she reached to shake Mr. Hall's hand. I had the utter urge to slap their hands apart and push her down the hall so she couldn't spill my secret or Davis's well before he was ready.

Before *I* was ready.

Instead, she turned, and with maybe the first non-judgmental smile she wore in my presence all day, waved me over. "Jim, this is a friend of ours, Maggie. Maggie, this is Jim, Davis's dad."

"Hello there, Maggie. Pleasure to meet you. Any friend of Davis's is a friend of mine."

I glanced at Eden, searched for something hidden, anything to figure out her motive, and found nothing.

Weird. So weird.

Fortunately, I didn't have long to wonder because the doors to the team area opened, and players started streaming out.

I hadn't seen Davis since Friday before I went in to work. I'd stayed there Thursday night, worked an afternoon shift yesterday, and he'd had to get in a workout before heading to the hotel where his team always stayed the night before games. It'd been less than forty-eight hours since I'd been in his presence but I felt it as soon as he pushed through the doors, dressed in a tailored, dark charcoal-gray suit with light pinstripes and his hair already perfectly styled but still wet from his shower.

His blue eyes lit up as soon as he saw his dad, and he dropped his bag he'd had slung over his shoulder and rushed to him. Emotion burned in my eyes and I willed them back while Davis threw his arms around his dad, so damn glad to see him and threw him back and forth in a manly bear hug that Jim returned with equal vigor.

"Great game, son," Jim said, squeezing Davis tighter. He

slapped Davis on the back before giving him another hearty hug. "So proud of you."

"Thanks, Dad. Glad you could make it. How was the flight?"

"Bumpy. Your mom says they've already gotten five inches with another eight expected. Might be stuck here for an extra day."

"Not mad about it." Davis slapped his dad's back and then saw Cole's family still waiting nearby and for Cole to come out. He grinned at Eden. "He's almost done. Just talking to Coach for a second."

He turned to me. "Hey. What'd you think?"

"I think you were great. It was fun."

"Everyone good to you?"

"Yeah." Mostly. The small little white lie got stuck in my throat and Davis frowned before taking the few steps toward me.

"Dad, did you meet Maggie?" As he asked, he slid his arm around my lower back and pulled me close to him.

My spine straightened with steel and my mouth went dry. Davis told me his dad was going to try to come to the game, but I hadn't been fully prepared and we hadn't talked about *what* we were or who I was to him.

Jim, smart man, didn't miss the gesture and he flashed me an amused grin. "Seems maybe I didn't get the proper introduction."

"Maggie's my new girlfriend." He said it with all the proudness his own father had just spoken to him and I grinned up at him.

This was important news. And surprising because we hadn't talked about any of this, not that I was complaining. I imagined my look was as surprised as Jim's mixed with the happiness he'd so boldly proclaim me as his.

"Girlfriend? Well, heck, dads are always the last to know the good stuff, aren't we?"

"If it makes you feel better, you're actually the first."

"Oh hell." Jim tossed his head back and laughed, brushed a hand over his clean-shaven jaw. "Can't wait to rub this into Avery and Annie's face when I get back. Come on you two, you can drive me to Kate and Dave's and tell me all about it."

I flashed wide eyes to Davis. He wasn't going to tell him *everything* now was he? In a car?

Seemed dangerous.

Davis winked at me and when his dad turned his back and started heading down the hall, kissed my temple. "We'll only tell him what he needs to know for now. Your pace, Maggie. Your pace."

The reminder was just what I needed. I reached to where his hand was at my back and gave it a squeeze.

"We'll see you soon?" I asked Kate as she grinned at me.

"We'll be right behind you, sweetheart."

———

"So, how'd you two kids meet?"

I knew the question was coming. It still didn't help my nerves as Davis headed north on I-24 out of Nashville toward Marysville. He'd spent time this week telling me about Cole, how Cole grew up there and how he'd hoped to stay nearby because of Jasper and when he was drafted he realized it didn't make sense to move anywhere else, so he'd built his own house on the opposite side of town instead of closer to his parents.

Although with a town barely skirting four thousand, I wasn't sure how far apart that could be.

Shockingly, it was still three times the size of my own hometown and my family had taken up at least fifty of those.

Davis chuckled at his dad's question. Which was *such* a dad question. "Lou's. I went in for a meal after a game a couple months back and met Maggie instead."

"Huh. Seems to be as sweet as the food is there. Probably not a bad deal you got."

I laughed. Jim was a character, cracking dad jokes left and right so far. He ribbed Davis half-heartedly about a couple tackles he says he should have gotten free from, but it didn't matter what he was saying. He had the look of a man who worked hard, loved harder, and enjoyed his easy life as much as possible and through all of it, his love for Davis shined the brightest.

"Not a bad deal at all, Dad."

"So what do you do, Maggie?"

Ah. All the questions I didn't want to answer. My fingers trembled as I pushed hair out of my eyes and turned around in the chair in Davis's truck enough so I could see him.

"I work at a steakhouse in Nashville? Just serving for now, but I like it okay."

"Customer service is hard work. Be proud you can do it, not everyone can. Pretty sure I'd quit three hours in if I had to be around that many people at one time."

"Um. Thanks." Was he for real? I'd just told him I was a waitress, and he hadn't batted an eye. My eyes grew with surprise. I tried to catch Davis's but he was focused on the road.

"Worked a factory my whole life. Didn't go to college, in fact no one in my family until my kids ever saw the need. We've done just fine. And my wife Kim's been a dental hygienist long as I known her. You think I'm gonna assume anything because my son makes millions and you're not right up there with him, don't. Don't care what you do as long as you do it with character and a sense of purpose. Don't care what anyone does as long as they don't step on others to get there either. Can't all be athletes and doctors and senators, but we can all be kind and decent. Least, that's what I always say."

My dad would say if you didn't know God, you were going to hell anyway, so it didn't matter what you did or who you were.

I liked Davis's dad better.

"Thanks, Mr. Hall. That's really kind of you."

And I wasn't quite sure I needed to hear it until I did.

"Jim, sweetheart. Name's Jim to my family and friends, that's for certain."

"And Paw-paw," Davis teased, glancing at his dad in his rearview.

"And Paw-paw, which might be the best name if I'm honest. Being a parent is too much hard work. Being a paw-paw is all fun and games."

"How is Reese?" I asked him. "And Annie?"

"Sweet as pie and tired as a mother with three little ones, but Annie's doing all right, and I'm not sure I'm gonna be able to set Reese down once I get her in my arms when we get back. You'll understand someday, both of you. Boys are great. Wonderful. Would have loved a dozen boys running around our land and causing mayhem, but a man gets a hold of a precious little girl in his arms? Well, if he's any kind of man at all, he's a completely different man from that point on. Breaks all of us, I figure. Builds us back up, too."

Yeah, I liked Davis's dad.

And equally hated the secret I was forcing Davis to keep from him.

I caught his eye as he glanced at me out of the side of his and mouthed, "Tell him."

His brows rose in question.

I nodded.

I hoped like hell Jim would still feel all those wonderful things about character and hard work when he learned I was pregnant with his son's child, and that we barely knew each other.

CHAPTER 22
DAVIS

Being in Cole's house was like being in my own except it was larger, and somehow given there were a bunch of men currently in it watching the late football game and having a couple beers and hanging out, quieter than a home with me and my sisters ever was.

Or maybe it was me, lost in my head, because Maggie had given me the go-ahead to tell my dad the full truth, and now I had no idea what to tell him.

I knew he'd love her because my parents were good people.

But liking her and then liking I'd gotten a girl pregnant before I really knew her or cared about her? I was more afraid they were going to be ashamed and disappointed with me than not like her. My sisters, on the other hand, would probably take a while to come around, although I was still holding out hope everyone would see the good in her and realize I was equally culpable, not tricked.

Maggie was in the kitchen, helping finish up dinner with Kate and Eden, who was being quieter than usual and kept shooting glances at Maggie which didn't help anything. She'd have her own baggage considering Jasper's Mom tricked Cole into having sex with her, got pregnant because she'd believed he'd finally date her and then marry her. They might have had all of that worked out now, but I wasn't exactly surprised Eden wasn't welcoming Maggie with open arms. She wasn't that kind of over friendly person anyway.

Still, with dinner almost ready, my knee was bouncing with anxiety, worrying myself until a pit filled with unease grew in my stomach. My dad was sitting near me on the couch, his eyes glued to the Arizona and San Francisco game. Bound to be a good one and either team would be hard to beat if we made it to the championship game, but I had barely paid attention to anything all game.

"Hey Dad."

The two words came out on a croak, immediately garnering my dad's attention he whipped his head in my direction.

"What is it?"

"Can I... can I talk to you? Outside?"

Dave, sitting in his beloved rocker recliner, watched us with concern tugging his brows together. "Everything all right, son?"

"Yeah."

God I loved that man. This whole family. Almost as much I loved my own.

I shoved off the couch, unable to sit still and caught Maggie's gaze from the kitchen. I gestured for her to join us with a nod of my head toward the back door and she rolled her lips together while wiping her hands on a kitchen towel.

She made her way toward me with the steps of a soldier heading into a deadly battle and my dad was now watching both of us.

"What's going on?" he asked.

"Outside. Please?"

Because if there was drama or cussing or crying, heaven forbid, we didn't need it in Cole's parents' living room.

"All right. Of course."

I opened the door and we let Maggie exit first, then my dad and I followed. Maggie was twisting her hands together, shuffling on her feet.

She was wearing my shirt. A T-shirt with my team's logo on it and jeans with tears at the thighs and knees. She looked damn good in both, the shirt clinging to her curves and the small swollen section of her belly I wasn't sure anyone else could see but was becoming more noticeable to me.

Given her height, or lack it, her doctor had told her she might show earlier than most women.

I tore my eyes off her stomach and cringed, trying to find the words to tell my dad.

"Maggie isn't just my new girlfriend, and actually, before I said those words to you earlier, we hadn't actually talked about what we were, but there's something you need to know."

Thick, bushy brows arched on his forehead as his eyes that mirrored mine bounced back and forth between us. He crossed his arms over his chest.

"What is it?"

I held out my arm, a gesture for Maggie to come to me, and she did with those same, slow hesitant steps. There was no easy way this and I had a sudden appreciation for what Maggie felt like the night she and Belle showed up at my condo. "She's pregnant. She's having my baby."

If I thought my dad's shock was evident when I said the word pregnant, it turned epic when I told him it was mine.

"Oh." He blew out a breath, glanced at both of us again, nodded. Hands went to his hips. Back across his chest. Swiped down his face. The number of seconds that passed while he was silent was a killer.

And next to me, Maggie sniffed.

God, please don't make her cry. I couldn't handle being screamed at and having a woman cry at the same time.

"Pregnant," my dad muttered like it was the first time he learned the word, and he had to test it out.

"I'm really sorry, Mr. Hall," Maggie whispered, and her voice shook as she spoke to him. "I didn't mean it. And it just happened—"

He held up a hand, palm out, and silenced her while he stared at the deck beneath his feet, puffed out his cheeks, and blew out another breath.

"That's... that's a lot to hear," he admitted, before finally lifting his head. When he didn't, he didn't face me, but stopped at Maggie. "Did you do this on purpose?"

"Dad…" I warned.

"No, sir." Her back straightened against my palm even as I wanted to tug her behind me. If my dad became the kind of guy I couldn't respect…

His head tilted to one side. "Then what are you apologizing for?"

Of course he wouldn't become that guy. I shouldn't have worried.

"No apologies, dear, okay? These things, well… they happen."

"Thank you," she whispered, and there was a tremor in her voice where I knew she was starting to cry.

"Hey." I slipped my hand to her hip and drew her in closer until she had to face me. "You're good."

"We're good," she replied, and she was absolutely right.

We were good.

"So, I'm assuming you're keeping it, and you're healthy? Everyone is healthy?"

For the first time, my dad had a tiny grin on his face, and Maggie caught it, smiling up at him and settled her hand on her stomach. "We're healthy."

"Well, I think that's the most important thing, then, right?"

He pressed a hand to my shoulder. "Can't lie. I think we can all agree this isn't how you would have liked for this to happen, but I raised you to be a good man, and I have no doubt you will be. And a father, too."

Damn it. Now it wasn't only Maggie on the verge of tears. I was fighting them back too and raised my free hand to my mouth and coughed to clear them away.

"That's really kind of you, Mr. Hall."

He smiled down at her, one he reserved for his grandsons and his daughters. Soft and sweet. My dad was the *best*. "What'd I say about calling me Jim?"

"Right." Her head fell to my arm, and I took her weight as my dad asked us more questions.

We told him how far along she was, that we would be going to her doctor's appointment next Tuesday. I told him I'd call Mom and my sisters as soon as he was back home with them so he could fill them in as well, and by the time Eden opened the sliding back door, it felt like things were good.

I hadn't disappointed my dad, just surprised the hell out of him, and like I knew they would be, he was fully supportive, including happy that Maggie was moving in so we could do this together.

"Everything all right out here?" Eden asked, peeking her head through the door.

If I wasn't mistaken, she lingered longer on Maggie as she asked before flicking her gaze toward my dad and me.

"We're good," I told her. "Dinner ready?"

"Been ready actually, Mama B thought you might need more time."

"I'm starving!" Jasper's shout, on the verge of tipping the kid into the hangry zone, echoed through the house, and Eden flinched.

"Can't keep Jasper waiting," I said and went to guide Maggie toward the door.

We entered, and Eden hadn't been lying.

The food was all on the table, the dishes covered with towels and lids to keep them warm and everyone's drinks had been moved to their places. An extra leaf settled into the table to make it longer and like we'd done every family home dinner time since the fall with their neighbor and good family friend Marley passed away, there was a small bouquet of lilies laid across the place setting where Marley had always sat.

I ushered Maggie inside and to the chair next to me, where she'd had a glass of lemonade set for her, and held out her chair. "Sorry for the wait."

"No apologies necessary." Mama B slid into her own chair at the foot of the table while Dave pulled out his at the head. Across the table from me, Cole was standing with Eden at his side, Jasper on his other. "Good?"

"Perfect." I grinned down at Maggie, kissed the top of her head and took my seat.

I wasn't hiding secrets from my dad, he actually liked Maggie as I knew he would, and the rest of the family would come with time.

CHAPTER 23
MAGGIE

Dinner was an event, and while I was used to large family meals, it'd definitely been a few years, and back then, we'd all been kids, proper, kind and gentle manners forced on everyone so even though we were only seven adults and a child, the meal was much louder, much more chaotic with Cole's mom telling stories about his and Graham's childhood, sprinkling in memories of their friend, Marley. I'd wondered about the empty seat on the other side of Eden and was quickly filled in on her passing.

"That was what brought Eden back to town actually," Mama B said. "Which only further proves to me that beautiful things can come from any darkness."

"Thanks, Mama B."

Kate, I learned, refused to allow anyone younger than her to call her by her name and instead, preferred Mama B.

"Stop thanking me, Eden. You know we love you."

"How'd you all meet?" I might as well have dropped a bomb into the center of the kitchen table for as cool as the room turned.

"Um." Eden glanced at Cole, and their eyes locked for a moment too long before they both laughed. "Silly," Eden said, still laughing. "We've known each other since high school and the rest, truly, is the longest story of all time."

"And not nearly appropriate for the dinner table," Dave said.

"At least not certain parts. Sorry." He glanced at me. "It's a happy ending with a lot of difficult parts for some of us to still talk about. You'll learn, though, in time."

Jasper, across the table and who was in kindergarten, talked around a bite of green beans. "Someone died. Eden left. Mom had me, and then Eden came back to help Miss Marley while she was dying, and now Dad and Mom don't really like each other, and then Marley died. And it sounds bad, but it's not all that bad because we all still have each other, right?"

He chewed his beans, and everyone's eyes widened, including Davis's. His hand he'd had resting on my thighs for most of the meal, tightened in a way that wasn't so much about comfort but surprise.

It was Jim that spoke first, clearing his throat and taking in the frozen pulse of everyone around him.

"Sounds like you gotta lot of love in your life, Jasper. And you're right... as long as you got that in your life, you can pretty much get through everything."

"Sounds about right, Jim." Dave raised his glass toward him. My gaze ping-ponged around the table, trying to take in what everyone else was thinking, but it was Mama B and Eden, who were staring at that empty place setting with tears in their eyes but smiles curling their lips that was a punch to my chest.

The women *loved*. Hard.

It was no wonder why Eden was suspicious of me.

There was a quiet clinking of glasses as Dave raised his glass for a toast for people loving us, but my hand trembled as I brought my drink to my mouth.

I'd once been so worried about the people in Davis's life not loving me, not liking me and not trusting me, but I couldn't have been more wrong.

It was *my* family that was going to lose their minds when they found out what was going on, and I had no doubt they'd turn it into a media production of all the ways I'd abandoned them, turned my back on my faith, and was readying myself for eternal damnation.

Awesome.

Davis and I were probably going to have to figure that out sometime soon, too.

———

Jim and Dave were on the Buchanan's front porch, and Davis had his keys in his hand, saying good night to Mama B at her front door when Eden came around the corner with her teeth digging into her bottom lip.

"Can I talk to Maggie really quick?"

"Everything all right?" Davis asked.

"Girl talk." Eden grinned, and it looked awkward on her face, something Davis noticed.

"What is it?"

I settled my hand at his bicep. "It's fine."

"You sure?" It wasn't like she was going to *hurt* me, but considering she'd only marginally thawed toward me at dinner, it probably wasn't going to be a conversation that turned us into besties.

"Go wait for me outside. I'll be right there."

He kissed my temple, murmured *"hurry up"* and I couldn't fight the shiver the brush of lips or the gravel in his voice elicited.

Eden nodded her head toward the formal dining room, and I followed her there.

"What's up?"

"I'm sorry," she blurted, and it must have surprised us both because we both let loose a giggle.

"What?" I asked.

"I'm sorry. For earlier, for being rude to you. It's... I mean, Cole had told me obviously, about you and Davis, but Jasper's mom...." She paused then and tugged at her hair that was in a ponytail at the back of her head. "Anyway, that's a long story, but basically, she *did* try to get pregnant to try to get together with Cole, so when he told me what happened, and well, I like Davis, don't know him well, but he's kind of like everyone's little brother, you know? And such a good guy, I was just... triggered, for lack of a better term."

She shrugged like she wasn't quite so sure what to do with herself, and since I didn't quite know what to say to all of that we stared at each other until it was awkward, and both of us chuckled again.

"I didn't do it on purpose."

Although I was starting to wonder how many times I'd have to say that to people.

"I believe that."

"Why?" Because I hadn't exactly *done* anything to make her think differently.

"Because Davis believes you, and he's a good guy. And Cole trusts him."

Right. So this wasn't exactly about me at all, or anything. Couldn't really blame her for it, and at least she was being honest.

"Anyway, I'm sorry. For not being nicer today and I'd like for us to hang out someday, get to know each other. You and Davis could come to our place some night, or we could go to Davis's if that's easier."

"I would think I'd need to talk to him about that first." I might have been moving in with him, but it was still his house. His friends.

"Of course." She smiled, and this time it was real and soft, and I could tell she was *trying*, but there was still something…

"You know who I am, don't you?"

She cringed and blushed. "Kind of?"

Which was at least an honest answer because no one *really* knew who I was who'd watched the show.

"So, you're being nicer because of that, or…"

"Because I think you're brave for leaving a life you didn't want and fighting to make one on your own. Trust me, we hang out, I'll tell you how much I can relate to that, so yeah… I know who you are, and I'm glad Davis has someone that strong in his life, I'd just forgotten that earlier and let stuff that doesn't matter get in the way."

Well… there was a whole basket of things to unpack with that…

"Maggie?"

Davis poked his head around the corner into the dining room. Behind his back, the door was open, telling me he'd left and come back in.

"Coming." I turned back to Eden. "We'll talk. And we'll let today go?"

"I'd like that."

"Good. I'll talk to Davis and get your number from him then. Maybe we could do lunch someday?"

"I'd love that."

———

"Your dad is *staying* here?" I whisper-yelled when Jim headed off toward the bathroom. The bathroom in the bedroom that I'd been using, and even though I wasn't fully moved in, that was still where most of my stuff was. Since I hadn't known his dad was staying there, I hadn't thought to clear out my things... or stay the night at my own apartment. Davis's third bedroom was his office and held workout equipment.

"Where am I supposed to stay?" I asked, panic flaring. "Or do I need to get an Uber?"

Davis twisted off the top of a water bottle and handed it to me. "Why would you leave?"

"Because your *dad* is staying here, sleeping in the bed where I normally sleep."

"Not sure I see the problem." He had a wicked little gleam in his eye and if he found this humorous, I was going to kick him in *his* humorous bone.

"I am *not* sleeping with you with your dad fifteen feet away."

He grinned, eyes dropping to my stomach that was trying to shove its way through denim and zipper and a button to let loose. Dear God, my doctor had not warned me nearly enough how painful the bloating at night could be, or that because of how short I was, how quickly my stomach would start to balloon.

"I think he knows we've already done that, Maggie."

He chuckled.

Argh... this man! I grabbed the kitchen towel piled on his kitchen counter and whipped it at him. It slapped his bicep, and he jumped back, both laughing and rubbing his arm.

"Ow. What was that for?"

"Because it's your *dad,* and it's us sharing a bed! He can't... he won't... he'll..."

"Think we're sleeping in a bed? Yeah, Maggie. He's not going to think anything wrong about it at all."

"But..."

The glimmer in his eyes died. "Okay, let me say it this way. If you're concerned about my dad knowing we've shared a bed, I will absolutely either take you back to your apartment or sleep on the couch tonight. If this is about your strict upbringing, I can understand that. I can guarantee you my dad won't think anything of it, and it will not change his already wonderfully positive opinion of you in any way, but if you're not comfortable with this, that's what matters."

Darn it. How could he possibly be so absolutely wonderful and why was I always such a mess?

"I don't want to mess up, and today's been a lot."

"What do you need?"

He came to me slowly, settling his hands at my arms and holding me while keeping his distance, peering at me like whatever he'd asked for, he'd hand to me on a newly polished silver platter.

I was falling for this guy, right then... right there. Because my comfort would always be more important to him than anything or anyone else, and he'd never once not shown me that's what he'd give me forever.

"Davis—" I rasped his name, my throat dry and so many emotions racing and tumbling their way through me.

"What do you need, Maggie."

"I need to sing."

"Sing?"

"Not now. Not tonight, it's late and nothing's open and..."

Whenever everything got to be too much for me, I sang. In the shower, in a park, on a jog, while cleaning. It was the one place where I could be me. Be free. I could stand in front of a church and belt out the hymns and it never mattered if there were a hundred eyes on me, all I had to do was close mine, feel the beat and the rhythm and the passion in music, start singing, and I was transported somewhere else. It was my escape, one I hadn't taken in far too long.

He chuckled. "It's Nashville, Maggie. There's always something open." He grabbed his keys off the counter and pocketed his phone. "Let's go."

"I don't… I'll be okay. We can wait."

"Nope." Snagging a ball cap off the table near his entryway, he tugged it down over his forehand and then spun it so the bill was facing backward.

And suddenly, I didn't need to sing anymore.

I needed to see Davis in nothing but that backward cap. He went from a ten to a full knockout with that thing on and wasn't that the way with men.

"I'll text my dad on the way, and bonus for me, I get to finally see you doing something you love. Only fair with you getting to see me do mine."

Well, when he put it that way.

"Your dad won't mind?"

"He'll be asleep in twenty minutes anyway. Man always goes to bed before nine." He held out his hand, palm up, and wiggled his fingers. "What do you say?"

CHAPTER 24
DAVIS

could die a happy man.

Which was not the song Maggie was currently belting out at that hole-in-the-wall karaoke bar she insisted we head to, but I was enamored.

Totally knocked onto my ass as soon as she took to the stage, still wearing the jeans and shirt she wore at my game earlier. With a curl of her fingers around the microphone, all the fear I'd seen simmering beneath the surface of her most of the day vanished and a calmness and confidence I didn't often see from her poured forth.

She currently had every person in the bar captivated, drinks frozen halfway to their mouths and all conversation ceased as she belted out the song lyrics to "Shallow."

Her tone gripped everyone, arm flung out wide to the side as she squeezed her eyes closed and sang about crashing through the surface. Goose bumps rose on my arm as I watched her, standing near the bar, unable to move to a chair or move closer. No, I was rooted to my spot.

This was not a young woman who should have been busting her ass, waiting tables or sleeping in her car.

This was a woman who was destined to take a stage much larger than this, singing songs meant for her to deliver to the masses who would be utterly destroyed by her strength and her beauty, and the emotions pouring off her.

The song slowed, she quieted her voice as she sang the rest of the "Shallow" chorus. Quiet rang through the bar. Not a clink of a glass on a tabletop. Not a click of a fingernail and not a whisper until every single person, man, and woman, burst out into a round of applause.

Maggie jerked, eyes opening wide, and she scanned the bar in surprise until a smile broke out on her face and a blush stained her cheeks.

Beautiful. She was so damn beautiful and innocent and devilish all wrapped in one, and more importantly…

She was *mine*. We'd be talking about this dream of hers to sing and why she was hesitating, why she was singing at karaoke clubs instead of open mic nights on Broadway. Why she hadn't yet taken up Belle on her offer to help. Independence was one thing, refusing to take the steps necessary to make her dream come true a completely different one. I'd do everything possible to help make this dream of hers a reality. After everything she'd already survived and fought for, there wasn't anyone who deserved it more.

My own hands were clapping and I brought them to my mouth, cheered her on as the bar called for more.

"Thank you," Maggie said, laughing into the microphone.

"More. More. More. More!" The entire bar rang out in a chant, calling for an encore even though there had to be a list of people who had wanted to go next. Fists pounded the table tops, and drinks were lifted into the air.

Even the bartender was clapping for her, swinging a towel around in the air.

My guess… no way was anyone in there stepping up onto that stage after her.

No one could compare.

"Okay, okay." Maggie laughed again, tucked a piece of dark hair behind her hair before dragging her fingers through the length of it. She went to the DJ and spoke with the man in charge of the music and the words on the screen prompter. Maggie hadn't once looked at those lyrics last time. Probably wouldn't again.

Four songs later, I was proven correct. Maggie sang "Walking On Sunshine," "Ain't No Mountain High Enough," Dolly Parton's "9-

5," and sang every single song without once looking at the screen, but she had the entire bar on their feet, dancing and jamming to her singing like they'd paid for a live concert of popular cover songs.

She was on fire. Undeniably, incredibly talented, and even as her voice turned husky and thick from the use of it, she still managed to power through Shania Twain's "Any Man of Mine" before finally thanking the crowd, the entire bar.

"Thanks for this tonight."

She slipped the microphone into the stand, grabbed the last glass of water I'd taken to her before the song and ducked her head as everyone cheered and clapped for her, seemingly nervous or embarrassed as she made her way straight to me.

The smile on her face couldn't be hidden though, nor could the tiredness soaking into the skin beneath her eyes.

"Hey," she said, in that raspy, tired voice, and tilted her head to look at me.

I wanted to tell her how incredible she was. How absolutely gorgeous and sexy as hell she'd been up on that stage, instead, nothing came out.

I bent down, sealed my lips to hers, and tasted the sweetness of her lips as well as the hint of salt and coolness from the water. She gasped in surprise before melting into me, a hand at my chest she had to feel the racing of my heart and I hadn't done anything but stand still in complete awe of her and her talent for the last hour.

"You… there are no words that can describe how blown away I am by you," I said and cupped her jaw with my palms. My thumbs went to her cheeks, and I brushed them along her skin, forcing her to meet my eyes. "You were so damn incredible, Maggie. Absolutely amazing."

"Thanks." Her teeth dug into her lower lip and I tugged it free with my thumb before swiping my thumb along that bottom absurd lip.

"Let's get home."

I'd shared her long enough. "Feel better?"

She nodded and slipped her hand down my arm until she laced our fingers together.

"Sometimes, whenever I have too much on my mind or too much emotion, the singing helps, so yeah."

"Well, I'd say you released a lot of that, and every person in this bar is a better person for being here to hear it."

"That's not…"

"It's true."

It absolutely was. I glanced at the stage, now empty and dark. The crowd was still talking about her. Women with jaws opened in surprise and men glancing at the back of Maggie like they wanted her for their own. Made me want to slam my mouth to hers again and carry her ass out of there.

I restrained myself.

Barely.

"Thanks, Chuck," Maggie called out to the bartender.

"You know you're always welcome here."

"Come on. Let's get you home."

And out of the view of others. She'd stirred more than a desire to have her body. She'd stirred up a need to have her. All of her. Her body, her mind, her soul, her passions, and her heart.

———

My home was dark and silent when we entered, only the gentle hum of the heating turning on. The kitchen light was left on, and I went to the fridge to get Maggie something to drink while she headed to the pantry to get herself some food.

It was only ten o'clock, but between the game, the dinner, and the incredible concert performance, my body was quickly slowing. I needed sleep. I needed to wrap my arms around Maggie and hold her while doing so.

I needed her to be okay with that, knowing my dad was sleeping in a room down the hall.

But most of all, I just needed her.

"Can I ask a question?" I grabbed waters for both of us, along with a pasta salad I'd made earlier in the week, and set it on the island.

Maggie's eyes lit up as she saw the food and grabbed a fork from the drawer and a bowl off the shelf.

"Sure."

"Why aren't you doing open mic nights and things like that on your nights off work?"

It'd been killing me. She'd been here for years and never let her voice be heard outside karaoke clubs? She was so much more than that.

She chuckled. "Because that takes work and marketing and demos to even get your foot in the door, and I've been focused on finding a safe place to live and getting money in the bank."

"But Belle…"

"Belle's my friend."

"Who would do anything for you, wouldn't she?"

This was the girl who offered to let a near-practical stranger move into her apartment after seeing she was sleeping in her car.

"I know she would." She stabbed some pasta and popped it into her mouth.

"I don't understand. You're not taking advantage of her by taking her help."

"I need to know I can do it on my own."

Stubborn. So stubborn and maybe, too naive, too. "Maggie. No one, not a single person on the planet, reaches their dreams by themselves, completely on their own. Everyone has someone helping them, rooting for them, encouraging them. Why do you think you have to go it alone all the time?"

Her eyes narrowed and twitched with irritation. It was late. She was tired. We were both exhausted, and we'd had a hell of a long physical and emotional day.

I could have dropped it.

Probably should have.

But something told me she needed a push. That Belle had stood back and waited for her friend to come to her, and now there was so much more on the line. Providing for our family. Showing our child how to pursue their passions and being willing to have an army at their back and standing at their side while they did it.

"I don't want to take advantage of her," she said finally and frowned down at the pasta.

"There's a difference between taking advantage and having support."

She shrugged and moved her fork around her food like she was no longer really seeing it. "I feel like I've always been alone and never had anyone listen to what was really important to me, or that I mattered, that the things I wanted mattered. Maybe it's just easier this way."

"To struggle when you don't have to? You're not alone anymore. You have Belle and Lance and me."

Her eyes flicked to mine.

Was she surprised by that?

"You have *me*. Baby or not, Maggie, I'm yours."

A wet shine filled her eyes, and she swallowed thickly. "I don't know what to say to that."

"You don't have to say anything." I went to her, closed the space between us, and cupped her cheek with my palm. My thumb brushed at her jaw, down her throat, and I reveled in the way she trembled beneath my touch. This woman owned me. Every single part of me.

"I would give you the world and all you have to do is ask for it. It's not taking advantage, it's giving me the pleasure and honor of being able to make a part of your dreams come true like I've always had family doing for me. Just tell me you'll think about it. You want to keep working, do it. You want to take time off to work on your singing, go for it. You're not taking advantage of me or my money, I'm investing in *our* future, and I want to make sure, way down the road when our child is growing, they will see both parents finding happiness in their passions."

Her eyes flared in panic. "I can't just quit my job, Davis."

"Why not?"

"Because..." She trailed off, and I watched her argue, and counter-argue every thought she had before she pressed her lips together and scrunched her nose. "Because it doesn't feel right. We're not *together. Or married.* Aren't I supposed to work?"

"We absolutely are together."

I kissed her. If she was having doubts again, I'd kiss her until I kissed them all away. We'd talked enough. She knew what I felt and where I stood.

She was the mother of my child and the woman quickly claiming my heart.

The rest would come with time.

CHAPTER 25
MAGGIE

Davis's kiss stole my worries and my doubts, and my fears. His lips, so full and warm and tender against mine, warmed me straight down to my toes, making them curl in my shoes I hadn't yet removed and brace myself for the onslaught of the passion he'd ignite as soon as he took it further.

Everything he said made sense, and yet there'd always been something holding me back from taking Belle's help.

Maybe because I want to prove to my parents that when they kicked me out, they didn't ruin me. Maybe because when it became known about my past, I didn't want anyone saying I'd gotten a handout due to the television show I rarely starred in.

I didn't want to hear, "She only made it because...."

I want to hear. "She's incredible. Where has she been?"

Still, with Davis's mouth on mine, his tongue sweeping the seam of my lips and seeking entrance, the last thing I wanted to be thinking about was my past....

Not when my future was standing in front of me, moving me backward until my hips hit the counter and my back bowed to keep our connection.

A sigh slipped from my throat, and my hands went to his hips. His arms. I ran my hands up and down every part of his covered body I could reach while he kept his hands at my cheek. My jaw. Cupping my throat and holding me still.

Kissing Davis was a gift I would open and treasure for as long as it lasted.

We *are* together. His words echoed through me. Telling me I was his. That he had me. That he was there. No one in my life had ever made their need for me so completely, openly known, and I was a fool for doubting him. For worrying about him.

If his family had a problem with us, he'd take care of it.

If my family discovered anything about us, he'd be there and help me.

Davis would always be the kind of man who would give his life for those he cared about, and I was a fool for thinking otherwise.

"I'm sorry," I whispered, as that truth settled inside of me, knit together broken, mistrusting pieces deep in my soul.

"What?" He pulled back, lips so close to mine and too far away at the same time. "Sorry for what?"

"For struggling to believe you're as good of a man as you really are."

Lips kicked up at the corners, and his blue eyes sparkled. "There's nothing to apologize for, honey. I have the rest of forever to get you to believe it."

The rest of forever. How wonderful.

He kissed me again and bent down. Before I knew it, his hands were at my backside, and he was lifting me easily. "Come sleep with me. Spend the night in my arms."

I'd forgotten completely about Jim being there, sleeping in the room where I'd spent nights before until Davis's look turned worried.

"Okay," I whispered. He'd promised me it was okay.

I'd trust him.

"We don't have to do anything but sleep," he told me and carried me down the hall.

I was quiet until he set me on my feet in the bedroom and closed the door behind us. Darkness filled the room until he flicked on the light.

I blinked from the harshness of it.

His bed, massive and oh-so deliciously comfortable and wonderful, was the only thing I saw as Davis moved toward his dresser and pulled out a T-shirt before handing it to me.

Suddenly, sleeping was the last thing on my mind.

Between that kiss. His word. *Him.*

I wanted Davis. Wanted him to know how badly I craved him.

"You sure your dad's asleep?"

"My dad can—and has—slept through tornado warnings and sirens. He's out."

I took the shirt he held out to me and tossed it to the floor. "Then maybe we don't have to go to sleep quite yet?"

His tongue came out, licked along his bottom lip and his eyes dropped to mine, swept over my breasts where my nipples were hardening beneath my bra and lower before he scraped them back up my body. Every inch of me grew tight. Too hot. Too needy and I shuffled back and forth on my feet to quell the ache that inspection created without a single touch from him.

"You want me?" he asked, and if I wasn't mistaken, he stepped back before his hands went to his dress pants, pants he'd worn after the game.

"Yeah. I do."

"Show me. Take off your top, Maggie, and strip."

Oh dear. As he flicked open the button of his pants and the *zip* of his zipper going down roared in my ears, my hands went to my shirt.

I pulled it up and over my head, holding it in my hand as I shook out my hair.

"Let me see your tits. They're fucking perfect and I've missed them."

He was going to kill me. His words. The steely look in his eyes. I was going to explode right in front of his eyes.

I reached behind my back and unclasped my bra. Davis hadn't removed a single piece of clothing yet, but pulled his dress shirt out of the waistband of his pants.

As I pushed down a bra strap, he undid a button. When I dropped it to the floor, he sucked in a breath.

"Can I see you, too?" He was still fully clothed, and I was before him, in torn jeans and shoes, while he looked immaculate in his suit pants and shirt.

"As soon as you're done." He dipped his head to my jeans, and another shiver racked my body. My spine heated, and my throat was thick.

How could words and direction do so much to me without a single touch?

It didn't matter. I listened, stepped out of my shoes, and shoved my jeans down my legs until I had to step out of them. He lifted a hand and steadied me while I removed the rest of my clothes, and then I was in front of him, bare, dressed in nothing but flesh and desire.

"Go lie on the bed, feet at the edge."

Bossy. He was so bossy. I'd seen glimpses of it that first night together, and it *did* something to me. I wouldn't have thought I'd enjoyed being bossed around in bed, not when I worked so hard to not need anyone, but every time Davis spoke a command, my body complied before I could think.

Even then, I turned and felt absolutely no embarrassment or worry at what he saw as I walked from him and climbed on the bed. Once I was how he wanted me, I settled my hands to the bed and waited, licking my lips while he slowly, much too slowly, divested himself of his shirt, the tank beneath, and bared his chest to me. Those muscles. That tanned and toned skin and the bricks that appeared as he raked his gaze all over my body.

"You're perfection," he muttered and bent down, pressed his lips to my inner knee, hands curling around my thighs and spreading me open. "I crave you. Every day I've thought of you and how good that first night was, how good you felt when I was deep inside of you." His fingers drifted up my thighs, skimming my flesh and the goose bumps he caused before brushing over where I was soaked and throbbing for him.

A whimper escaped me, and Davis's grin turned wicked. "You'll need to stay quiet, honey. Can you do that for me?"

Absolutely not.

Still, I nodded. I'd try. We'd need to.

And then he pressed two fingers deep inside me. He filled me in a moment, and my body rolled, my toes curled as the press of his fingers ran along my inner walls, my head pushed back into the bed and my teeth pressed into my lips.

It was amazing, and as I throbbed around him, Davis bent over me and brought a nipple into his mouth. He sucked it into a wet, tight peak and kept his hands steady while his mouth at my breasts, paying equal attention to both drove me to distraction. This was maddening, and every time I rolled my hips, I tried to find the pressure to take care of it myself, he slid his fingers out, making it more difficult.

"Still, Maggie. I'll get you there."

I trusted him. It didn't matter. "You need to do it faster."

He huffed against my breasts, bit down on my nipple, and I cried out in an equal mix of pleasure and stinging pain before he sucked it back into his mouth, laved my nipple with his tongue before sliding off, down, and it didn't escape me he was still mostly clothed while I was fully exposed.

I'd never been in a more vulnerable position, and yet I was completely safe.

Trust him.

I opened my eyes and reached for him, uncurled my fingers from their grip on his bed, and ran my hands over his shoulders, up the back of his neck, and scraped my nails through his hair, along his scalp while he kissed my stomach, my ribs. He played with my body like we had all the time in the world until both of his large palms curled around the backs of my thighs and with one quick tug, he had me practically bent in half, my bottom lifted off the bed.

He swiped his tongue along my seam to my clit, and my mouth dropped open in complete, obscene pleasure.

He dove in and then ate me until the sounds he pulled from my body were too much to fully hold back. His teeth scraped my clit, that quick burst of pain before he sucked it into his mouth while, at the same time, he moved those fingers deep inside of me, fucking me with his fingers in such a forceful way, it showed how much he'd been holding back before.

He was a man who wanted it *rough* and had probably held back for fear of scaring me.

Little did he know, there was nothing he could do that would scare me.

"Yes," I hissed right as that first wave of my orgasm barreled down on me.

I rolled wave after wave, my body exploding with heat and excitement and so much pleasure I was spun out to sea, pulled back, and yanked under again. I rode each wave Davis pulled me through with his fingers and mouth until I was listless, and he was pressing gentle kisses along my inner thighs, brushing his hands down my legs and setting me back to the bed.

"Fucking perfection," he grunted and stood.

In a blink, he was naked, his hand wrapped around his thickness, stroking himself and moving toward the nightstand. I quickly rolled to my stomach to not miss a single second of the view of his perfect body and when he saw me on my knees and hands, crawling toward him, a pleasure low growl rumbled through him.

"Stay like that."

I froze on the bed, so instantly attuned to what he needed and dropped my head to the mattress. My hair fanned out around me, tickling my back and shoulders, and the bed dipped while Davis climbed onto it. The weight of him on the bed rocked me back and forth, and then his lips were pressing to my spine.

"I don't know if I love your ass or tits more," he murmured, as his palms went to the globes of my backside and he squeezed.

I, frankly, didn't give a damn what he liked more because every touch from him turned me on, made me feel cherished and treasured. So completely taken care of.

His knees knocked against the inside of mine, forcing me to widen, and then he was there, the condom-covered head of his thick length pressing into my opening. The stretch was incredible, and as he slid inside, a groan escaped my parted and parched lips.

"Feels so good," I whispered, and my hands went to the bed in front of me. My fingers curled into the covers as he filled me so completely.

"Perfection. You're so damn perfect for me." He grunted the

words, and as much as I wanted to look back and see his face, watch his features distort as he began moving inside of me, one of his hands slid up my back, curled around my shoulder. The other settled at my hip, holding me against him, and he used me, yanking me against him while his hips slammed into me over and over. The slide of him so deep inside, the pain when he hit the end of me, the stretch of him forcing me open, all of it ignited a completely different sensation deep inside my core.

He moved like the hounds of hell were chasing him, forcing him to be harder. Rougher. Faster. And with each thrust, he went deeper. Deeper into my body, straight to my soul where I wasn't sure I'd ever be able to kick him out if I wanted.

My body lit up with sensation, my thighs shook, and right as I felt another orgasm cresting, Davis slipped his hand at my hip to my front. His fingers pressed against my nerves there, so swollen and wet, and as he worked me from inside and outside. I bit down on the sheets beneath me, cried out in pleasure as it took me over again.

My heart was racing, thundering in my ears, and still Davis moved, grunted as I pulsed around him.

"That's it. Squeeze everything I have out of me. Take it, honey. So good. God, you feel soo…" His hips bucked wildly. Once. Twice, and then he was squeezing the flesh at my shoulder to the point of risking bruises.

I did not give a single crap if he marked me.

I wanted his marks everywhere.

He slammed into me, forcing me to my stomach, and his lips came down to the top of my head. "Shit, Maggie. I think I might have died." He emptied himself inside of me.

The throb of him against my settling pulses, and we lay there, me covered with his weight and scent and him pressing soft kisses to the back of my neck, the side, over to where he'd clung to my shoulder. He kissed each red mark from his fingertips, apologizing.

I had no words left to tell him it didn't matter. That I loved every minute of it and when he slid out of me, I whimpered at the loss of him.

"Did I hurt you?" He rolled me to my side, skimmed his hand down my stomach, over my hip.

"No. It was incredible."

"You're incredible. Stay there." He kissed my hip bone, the swollen area of my lower stomach with a soft smile and pushed off the bed. "Let me clean you up."

Good thing he remembered. By the time he returned and pressed a warm cloth to my core, I jumped from the surprise, already half-asleep.

"Come on, honey." He tugged my hand and helped me to my feet. "You'll feel better in the morning if you brush your teeth and get ready for bed."

I'd feel perfectly fine in the morning as long as I woke up next to him. Still, I listened. Brushed my teeth and chugged some water, and Davis brought me the shirt I'd thrown to the floor earlier, and we climbed back into bed together.

He slid in behind me, wrapped his arms around me, and pressed a kiss to my shoulder, letting his lips linger there.

I was half-asleep, drained from the day and orgasms and life, and still he had to know.

"I'm yours, too, you know."

His hand squeezed mine at my stomach. "Good."

I was pretty sure I fell asleep to his contented sigh.

CHAPTER 26
MAGGIE

I woke in the same position I fell asleep without the heat behind me and the arms surrounding me. Like every other morning, I'd woken up after a night with Davis, I was quickly realizing the man was not someone to lounge in bed. It was only seven, the sun wasn't close to rising, and next to me on the nightstand was my phone, a glass of juice, and a plate of crackers and cheese.

The juice was still cold and as soon as I brought it to my lips, sitting up in the bed, the chilled tang was delicious as it slid down my throat. I quickly followed that first sip with a cracker and unplugged my phone.

He thought of everything, and I was smiling as I unlocked my phone only to have it buzz in my hand with an incoming call.

No Caller ID shone on my screen. Too damn early for anyone I knew to call me. I went to ignore it but paused.

The last time I spoke to my sister, she'd called from a phone she hadn't wanted me to know she had and blocked the number.

I tapped the green button and brought the phone to my ear. "Hello?"

"Magdalene?"

"Ruth?" Her voice was a harsh whisper, making it hard to hear. "Are you okay?"

"What are you *doing* out there?"

"What?"

I sat fully up in bed and tugged the sheets at my hips further up. "What are you talking about?"

"Daddy's mad, Magdalene. So mad, and I keep hearing him and Uncle say your name and how could you do this to us. What are you doing?"

"I don't... I have no idea what you're talking about?"

"Singing?" she hissed. "In a bar? And that boy Daddy said you saw at the game? What is going on?"

My heart dropped to my stomach, which rolled. I didn't have nearly enough food in me, nearly enough preparation for any of this.

"Ruth, calm down. Just a second, okay? Take a breath and talk to me."

"You're in trouble. Daddy said they never should have let you leave, and you're embarrassing everyone all over again and he's going to come get you. He's going to make you come back, and he said once you're back here, you're going to be punished worse than anything he's ever done before, and you can't, Magdalene. You can't come back here because I don't know what they're going to do to you, but you won't like it."

"Shhh...."

My sister was on the edge of a panic attack, and it was so very unlike her. The last time we spoke, she'd told me she hated me. Because of me, none of the girls would ever be able to leave. It'd left me feeling like she wished she could and despised me for taking away her chance, but since then, we'd rarely spoken. But she was almost eighteen. Old enough to make her own choices, and she was the last person I assumed would ever be willing me to stay away.

I ignored the part of my dad punishing me. There was the paddle and his hand and the willow branch and the thin reed he'd used on us, usually girls, more than once in my lifetime. Rarely the boys, though, because every time they did something wrong, they were exploring being leaders and would learn through mistakes. We were breaking our submission and being willfully defiant.

My jaw gritted together as I thought of that last time. When I'd told my father I wouldn't be courted by Peter unless he let me go to college. He'd allowed it at the time because I put my foot down in public, but that night, well… I'd had to stand for a week until the bloody lashes on my backside healed. No one was allowed to help. No one was allowed to see, but that first night, it was Ruth who'd crawled into my bed and asked me why, if Daddy loved God so much, why was he so horrible.

A shadow grabbed my attention right before Davis appeared in the doorway. He was smiling, but whatever he saw on my face erased the smile completely.

"I'm putting you on speakerphone, okay, Ruth? And then I need you to take a deep breath, slow down, and tell me what's happened."

"Okay. Okay… give me a sec." She sniffed, and her breathing trembled through the phone.

I waved Davis toward me, and he hurried before climbing into the bed and sitting next to me.

After changing the phone to speaker, I clasped it in my palm between us.

"Okay, Ruth? You're okay? Where are you?"

"I'm in the shed. Supposed to be doing chores, but I saw Zachariah's phone—"

"Okay. What's he doing?"

"He's in the office at the church with Daddy. I don't think he knows he forgot his phone."

The church was a half mile from the shed, across the field. She'd see them coming. We had some time.

"Okay. It's okay. Now, tell me what you know, okay? And then I'll answer any questions you have."

"Alright." Another trembling breath came through the phone. "Uncle Brandon came over this morning. I was doing the morning chores, you know, helping Joy and Leah with their hair and getting dressed. He stomped right in, didn't even knock or anything and he shook something at Dad's face and said *'have you seen what your whore daughter is doing?'*"

Next to me, Davis straightened, spine as rigid as steel. I shook my head, pressed a finger over his lips to get him to stay silent. If she knew he was here, she'd stop talking.

"What was it?"

"I heard something about the devil and the bar and you singing and…"

I glanced at Davis. Damn. Things moved so fast I hadn't even considered. "If it was last night, I was singing karaoke, Ruth. Just some songs on stage. They weren't church songs or anything, but they weren't bad."

"Well, Uncle's pretty mad about it because apparently a whole bunch of people put you up on YouTube or something, and it's all over the internet and there's a lot of comments and questions asking if it's you."

Crap. I bit back the cuss word that wanted to fall. Ruth would hate it and I didn't need another sin on top of the singing until I knew where she stood. Was she helping me? Or threatening?

You can't come home…

The only way I'd return home, ever, was if I was dragged, kicking and screaming, and I'd make the world know I was there against my will.

"I hadn't even thought that would happen. I'm sorry, Ruth. I'm sorry they're mad, but you know this will blow over, right? I'll take care of it and everything."

"Blow over? Are you kidding? You have no idea how mean Daddy's gotten since you've left. It's bad, Magdalene. And every time he gets mad at you he says because I look so much like you, I must have you in me—"

"What the fuck?" Davis bit out, and my sister choked over her sobs.

"Who's that?" she rasped, panicked, and now, I could tell she was crying.

I was going to get her hurt. She'd take it because she had no other choice, and she'd hate me more for it and all I wanted to do was help her.

"Ruth. What do you mean?"

"Who's with you?" Damn. Her voice. It shook with terror.

"It's my friend, well, my boyfriend. He's next to me, but he's a good guy. The best and he's mad because Daddy's a jerk." I *hated* calling him Daddy. To me, he was my father. A man I barely knew because once you disobeyed, you saw his truly evil side.

"The boy Daddy says took you to that *game?*" She spit out "game" like he'd taken me straight to a trip to hell.

I should have thought this would happen.

"I went to a football game, Ruth. That's not wrong. There's nothing wrong with it."

"Well, according to what I heard Zachariah saying to Daddy before they left, you're on Instagram. Cameras saw you and people are wondering how you know some hero guy or something..."

"Cole," Davis whispered in my ear. "It's because you were sitting by Cole's family."

"Ruthie."

"Don't call me that." She sniffed, and I flinched. She'd always been Ruthie to me. Every time we were spanked or beaten or forced to go without supper because we hadn't done our chores perfectly. It was Maggie and Ruthie. Together.

"Ruth. You need to get out of there. Before Daddy's done with Zachariah. What will they..."

"All of them. All the older boys. Daddy makes them all do it."

"Do what?" Davis growled, and his tightly banked tension and anger almost made his skin ripple with fury.

Ruth cried, cried into the phone and said something about how she shouldn't have called. This wouldn't help, but I needed to fix it.

"Ruth. Come here. Just come here. Get to the Clancey's house, and they'll help get you to me. I swear it, but you don't have to stay and let me help you since it's all my fault—"

"The fuck it is," Davis rumbled, and I hoped like hell my sister couldn't hear, but it was.

She wouldn't be at risk of being beaten by multiple men if I had stayed. If I had taken it.

No one knew.

No one knew why I left and ran and was so desperate to get

away, but it was this. Because the first time, I was fifteen years old, and I hadn't done something my brother, Adam, a year younger, had told me to do and stood up to him and said he wasn't my husband, so I didn't have to submit to him, he'd gone straight to Dad.

Dad took me out to the shed and already had Adam, Jed, and Zach lined up. Handed them each a *discipline* tool, strapped me down... and taught me the very painful lesson that as a female, and under his leadership, I needed to submit and obey *all* men in my life until he handed me off to my husband.

The Clanceys left right after that. They had six kids, a daughter the same age as me, and apparently, when my father had shared what happened in the men's study group, using it as a lesson on how to raise willful girls, Mark Clancey had gone home and thrown up. Three girls. They had three girls out of six, and he left our church, saying he would never run the risk of his girls being abused and beaten by any boy or man in that church who agreed with my father.

"I can't. I can't leave, Magdalene. There's Martha and Joy and Leah."

"They're too young." Martha was only twelve. She was safe for a few more years. "Come here. Let us save you from what's coming. *Please*, Ruth. Let me help you since this is all my fault. And then we'll figure something out so none of our sisters get hurt like this again."

"I don't know."

"You have to. Please. Remember when you were so mad I got in trouble because it meant you couldn't leave? I can help you now, Ruth. I swear it. Please. Go to the Clancey's. Tell Mark and Beth what's happening and they'll keep you safe. They'll get you to me."

I hoped. I hadn't talked to them since they left, but I knew what happened to me was the reason and their eye-opening moment to realize what my father preached wasn't all that biblical after all.

She sniffed. "Are you sure? Because if they go to Daddy..."

Mark Clancey would only ever talk to my father again if it was to punch him in the face. I was certain of it.

"They won't tell. I can call them."

"No!" she shouted and then quieted her voice. "I gotta go. But I don't know when Zach will be done with Daddy, and if I'm not here…"

"If you are, you're going to be beaten, and you've done nothing wrong. It's not right, but I'm sorry. There's no way I'm ever going to return home again unless it's to grab you and our sisters and run like hell. No one deserves to live like that. There's so much more to life than what Daddy teaches. So many more people who love Jesus and show it without rods and paddles and bruises and rules."

"That's the world talking."

"No, Ruth. It's biblical. I swear it." Not that I did much studying anymore, and I hadn't been able to come close to forcing myself through the doors of a church since then. But Mama B prayed before the meal yesterday and talked about her faith and she and Dave weren't people who I could see raising a hand to their children.

"I just wanted to warn you. What Daddy is planning and how mad he was, that's all. If you fix it, if you never do that again… if you stay off television, I won't get in more trouble."

It killed me to know even now there were consequences to my actions far away from Missouri. But I wouldn't give up the life I was creating, and once they knew I was pregnant. Well, Ruth might not survive it.

As much as I wanted to protect her, I couldn't do what she was asking. "I can't do that. Davis, that boy, he's on TV all the time, and I want to start singing. It's going to happen, but it's cruel and wrong for Daddy to beat you because I'm not there. Don't you see that?"

"If you'd never left…"

"We'd all be black and blue. I couldn't stop that. I'm sorry I couldn't protect you from it, but if you come to me, I'll keep you safe, and then we'll figure out what to do. I promise you. To the ends of the earth, I promise you that."

"Do they still live on Willow Wood?"

She meant the Clanceys, and I choked over a sob clawing its way out my throat. "Last I knew. Yeah. Just through the field and across the creek by that boulder."

"I know how to get there. Daddy says we're not allowed past the creek."

Because of them. Because they strayed from the flock, and now the entire church was cut off from them.

"Please, Ruth. You need to go."

"Okay. Can I… can I call you when I get there?"

"Please. Definitely. But go before Zach and Daddy are done with their meeting. You know exactly what's gonna happen to you."

"You promise we'll help Martha and the rest?"

"I'll help everyone or die trying."

She laughed, a small chuckle over a sob that tore at my throat and ripped at my heart. None of us deserved any of that life. Not even for my brothers, for growing up and thinking any of this was okay.

"I'll try, Maggie. I'll try."

"Good. Now delete this from the call log, put the phone back where you got it, and *run*, Ruth. Fast as you can."

We spoke for a few more minutes. I had her stay on the phone when she went back to the barn to replace the phone. At the very last moment, I whispered I loved her.

She said *yeah*, hung up.

I turned to Davis.

Tears in my eyes.

His own were shimmering. The anger had changed to something else, and he threw his arms around me and yanked me to him until I was sitting across his lap. I buried my head in his shoulder and sobbed.

For my sister, who would hopefully get safe. For my own past he now knew way too much about. For the secrets I'd hidden that would now have to come out, and for the mess I was going to make of his own current life.

I cried because I'd felt more kindness from his dad and Mama B and Dave in twenty-four hours than I had from my own parents in twenty years. I cried for all of it, and as the tears slowed, I pressed my hand to my stomach. Sniffed.

Took Davis's hand at my back and moved it on top of mine.

"I'm so glad you're the man who's going to be the father of my baby, Davis. So very glad I don't have to live with that fear anymore."

He cleared his throat and held me tight. "No one should have to live with that fear, Maggie."

CHAPTER 27
DAVIS

had to unleash it. I had to get the fury boiling beneath my skin and tightening every muscle in my body somewhere else so I could be the man Maggie, and hopefully soon, Ruth needed.

Fortunately, my dad was a big man with even larger shoulders and wouldn't collapse under the weight of it, so when I saw him in the kitchen making eggs and bacon and toast for breakfast like it was his home, I gave it all to him.

He took it, jaw clenching and white-knuckling the spatula as I told him about Maggie, the past I'd known about before, and the phone call I sat through. All she'd given me before was a skeletal outline compared to that conversation.

"That's how you know she isn't lying. She wouldn't risk that."

"It wasn't at first, but yeah. That's what made me one hundred percent certain." Because she might not have thought about it, but I had the night she told me about her family's show. Hell, I'd thought about it as soon as Dawson mentioned his sister watching that same show. Given her past and the media attention she'd already lived through, she would not have walked back into my life for attention or money.

She'd want to stay hidden, and I figure knowing who I was actually kept her away, might have been one of the reasons that sent her running that first night.

"That's not really the point though," I told my dad as he grabbed a pair of tongs and flipped the bacon.

"I know. But I'm thinking on that part and how sweet she is for you instead of wondering if I need to get home so you can take care of that girl when she gets here without me around or if I need to call your mom and get her down here so she can live here. That cruel... sadistic... what in the hell is wrong with people? Men. To treat women so damn horribly when it's women who give us kindness and help teach us empathy and compassion. Who give up so much of who they are, their bodies, to carry our children, to raise our families and take care of homes and families, all while most of them still work careers. I don't get it, son. Never have."

Thank *God* I'd been raised by a man like him and not someone like Vince.

"I don't know what to do either." My hands were braced on the counter, arms tight and tense. Telling my dad what was going on had eased some of it, but I knew as soon as I saw Ruth, it'd all come rushing back. There were more secrets Maggie was hiding, or rather more nightmares she didn't want to talk about. There was so much more going on than I'd ever considered and now her need to make it on her own with absolutely no help made sense.

How many times had she been refused the simple privilege? How many times has he been told she couldn't do a thing without a man?

The very idea she'd lived that way for so long and had been willing to take my help in small measures so far suddenly meant everything.

She *trusted* me.

I'd make sure to treasure that trust for as long as she let me.

"For now, let's eat breakfast." He set bacon on a plate as he said it. "Perhaps with good food, we'll have a better understanding of what comes next for you two."

"Thanks, Dad. For being so incredibly awesome about everything."

"I love you." He shrugged and wiped his hands together. "It's that simple."

For him, it certainly was.

Behind me, soft footsteps echoed from the hall, and I glanced over my shoulder. Maggie was there, dressed in clothes she would have had to grab from the guest room. Loose-fitting sweatpants that hit at her shins and dressed in a black sweatshirt, she had her hair piled on top of her head, and color was back on her face.

A gift after that phone call.

"You okay?"

She smiled at my dad, who was grabbing pates from the open shelf. "I'm good. Food smells delicious Mr.... Jim."

"Just Jim, Maggie," he teased and flashed her a wink.

We gathered food, took everything to the table, and sat down. Maggie had her phone next to her plate and was taking small bites of bacon, testing to see if it'd sit well in her stomach.

"So, what do you two have going on today?"

"I need another workout and have film later. Not until three though."

"I have to work from two to eight, but I'm thinking about calling in." She flicked her gaze toward me, uncertainty flaring.

"I told him, Maggie."

"Oh."

"Is that okay?"

"I won't tell anyone, sweetheart. Not even when I want to."

"Oh." A pink stain hit her cheeks. "That's. Well, thank you. But that's okay. I don't know if I want to be at work. What if Ruth can get here tonight?"

"Do you think she will?" I didn't want to cause doubt, but she had waffled back and forth on the phone.

"I don't know. I think if she can get to Mr. and Mrs. Clancey's they can convince her, or at least keep her safe there for a bit. I don't know if I want to be at work if she calls, but if she does come here, even for a while, there'll be things I need to buy her. Clothes, that kind of stuff, and I don't know what my dad will do if he finds her missing."

She started rambling, words falling from her lips faster than I could follow her, and it was my dad who reached across the table and took her hand, squeezing it.

"Breathe, Maggie. Take a breath. You don't have to have

anything figured out and solved right now. What's important is you eat for that baby of yours. I'm sure it's awfully hungry this morning."

"Especially after all that singing last night." I kicked her chair with my toes playfully. Anything to get her to calm down. Dad was right.

The worry and stress wouldn't be good for her.

"Which reminds me." Dad wiped his hands with a napkin and pulled his phone out of his back pocket. "If your singing is causing all this mess today, I need to see what all the fuss is about."

"Oh, you don't have to."

"You wouldn't have ended up filmed and online if you weren't good, so let's just see how good you are, huh?"

"Jim…"

"She's incredible. Powerful and beautiful on stage, even in jeans and a T-shirt. She had them completely raptured."

"I did not," Maggie whispered, stabbing at her eggs and avoiding eye contact with both of us. The tips of her ears were pink.

I'd feel bad for embarrassing her, but she deserved the praise and needed to get used to hearing it.

In a few swipes of his fingers and thumbs on his phone screen, Maggie's voice, tinny through the phone speaker, came through and I smiled as the lyrics to "Ain't No Mountain High Enough" came through. My dad's face lit up and Maggie buried her face in her hands.

"This is embarrassing. It's so bad."

"It's beautiful," Dad said and set the phone down to smile at her. "You should be proud of that voice, do everything you can to make your dreams come true using it."

"You told him?" She peeked out behind her fingers to glare at him.

"Voice like that needs to be heard by everyone. Not ashamed of bragging about your talent."

"Damn talented, for sure." Dad hit his phone screen and turned off the sound. "Can't quite figure out how that'd make our own father mad, though, and I definitely could live the rest of my life without ever thinking of him again. You say your uncle has that television show?"

"*The Blessed Movement.*"

He scoffed. "Don't know a man who can truly believe he's blessed and treat others the way I hear those men treat your families. How do they get away with not getting this stuff on camera?"

"I don't really know how my uncle treats his kids. He didn't have any girls my age, mostly boys, so it's not like I had anyone to talk to over there, and for the most part, my uncle's the one with the show. My family's on it occasionally, but one of the rules has always been no cameras inside the church or studies. They mostly record the daily life and good times."

"Makes sense why your dad would want that rule in there, then, huh?"

"Honestly, I'm not sure my dad cares. He's not worried about anything. He's the shepherd of a flock that since I've left, learned might be small, but the families involved carry a lot of weight in our county and some even in the state. There are senators, mayors. Business owners. I'm not sure how strictly every family follows Dad's teachings, but very few families have ever left."

"This Clancey family?"

Her eyes widened in surprise. If she was shocked, I told my dad everything, she shouldn't be. Why would I hold anything back from one of the best men I knew? In truth, only Cole and Dave Buchanan and my sister's brothers rivaled him in down-home goodness.

"Yeah, they'd heard about a teaching my dad gave me, said they had daughters and wouldn't ever let a boy or man in that church touch them like that, even once they were married."

"What about your mom?" I asked.

"What about her?"

"Does your dad....?" I couldn't finish the question. Couldn't consider it.

"I guess she learned early on to submit and follow the rules, but no, I never saw him mean to her. He's actually really nice to her. Polite and sweet most of the time."

"He's still evil," Dad muttered, and Maggie's phone rang.

Maybe: Elizabeth Clancey lit up on the screen, and Maggie croaked. "Oh god. She made it. She actually went."

Tears were already falling down her cheeks as she answered the phone, putting it on speaker and thank God, because if I only had to listen to one side of this conversation, I was screwed.

"Hello?"

"Magdalene. How are you?"

"I'm good, Mrs. Clancey. I'm okay. How's Ruth?"

"She's here, sweetie. Told me to call you. I have Jenna getting her packed. She's grown so much, well you all have since we haven't seen you, but she and Jenna are just about the same size. Mark and some of his friends are outside, keeping an eye just in case we see them coming. You sure it's okay for her to go to you?"

"Yes. Absolutely, yes, please."

"'Cuz we can keep her. Trust me, I can still get so angry when I think about what your father… well." She sniffed, and it might not be only the women who were crying by the end of this phone call.

Ruth was coming here. It was all that mattered.

"I won't speak poorly of the man. But let's say Mr. Clancey and I and our kids, all of them, have never felt so free since we left. The stories we know now, the things we've discussed. Wish I could walk right over to his land and scoop all of you young ones up."

"Thanks, Mrs. Clancey. That means a lot."

"You and Ruth need any help, you let me know, okay? We'll send you a text once we're on the road. Should be a few hours, but if you can text me the address where we're headed, that'd be great. It's only about five hours, so we'll be there by dinner if we leave soon. I just thought you'd want to know we have her, and she's safe. Scared, you know, and questioning if she should be here or go back home, but I'm gonna do everything to keep her from doing so."

"Good. That's really good. Thank you, I was hoping you'd help her."

"Oh, sweet child. We should have caused a bigger fuss over what's going on in that church and in your family much sooner. The fact we can help now is a blessing. Mark beats himself up all the time, wondering what's happening to y'all and not knowing how to fix it, so you let us know. You want our words or witness or anything, you come to us, okay?"

"I will. Thank you, Mrs. Clancey."

"Don't thank me. Day we heard you were kicked out and were taking off was the best news we've ever heard. And from what Ruth says, sounds like you got yourself a pretty good man there. Mark says he's a great ballplayer and everything, really nice and good. Seems to have his approval. Not that you need ours or anything."

Maggie laughed into the phone, and when she caught my smirk, rolled her tear-filled eyes.

So, I liked hearing people think I was a good guy. It would always be a better compliment than if it was about my talent. Character mattered more.

Always.

"That does mean a lot to me. Thank you."

"All right now, child. Didn't want you worrying. You save this number, and I got yours now. We'll talk soon, okay?"

"Okay. Thanks again."

"It's our honor. Trust me. Speak soon. Bye."

She hung up, and I yanked Maggie into a hug. "We'll keep her safe. I swear it, Maggie, and we'll make sure none of your sisters are hurt ever again."

"Damn straight," Dad muttered, and when I peeked at him, his eyes held their own shimmer.

I fought mine down and held Maggie tight.

We'd figure all this out.

Together.

CHAPTER 28
MAGGIE

"Thank you, Madison. Thank you so much for understanding."

Did I feel bad lying to my boss about being too sick to work today?

Yes. Was I doing it anyway?

Absolutely.

"It's no worries, Maggie. Come in tomorrow or call me if you don't feel well. It's truly not an issue."

Fortunately, Mondays were the slower nights of the week.

We said our goodbyes, and after I ended the call, I tossed the phone to the bed and scrubbed my hands through my hair.

No way would I focus on taking orders or care how someone wanted their steak or what type of addition they'd like to it while I waited for an update about Ruth.

It was after breakfast, after I'd showered. Davis and his dad were cleaning the kitchen and sounds of the television filtered down the hallway to his room while I had called my boss.

Davis's offer to quit rang in my mind. I couldn't. Not with Ruth hopefully coming, and oh god…

I hadn't even considered where she'd stay. Would I have to move back to my apartment? She wasn't eighteen for three more months, and I only had one bedroom. And with Davis…

"Damn," I whispered. This was all happening so quickly, and a part of me still couldn't believe it was.

My sister had called me for help. Or at least to warn me.

What had happened in the last three years that she'd feel comfortable doing so? How *bad* had it gotten for her that she called to warn me? And what were my father and uncle going to do? Hunt me down in Nashville and kidnap me back to Missouri?

There was no way, but I needed a plan.

Once they found out Ruth was gone, if they hadn't already, I'd be the first person they thought to come find.

I hurried out of the bedroom and practically slid across Davis's wood floor in my socked feet. I'd changed from the sweats I threw on that morning into another pair of jeans. I had on a tank top beneath my oversized red and black flannel shirt that was only halfway buttoned and as I slid, the shoulder of the shirt slipped off mine, so I ended up sliding into his living room like a maniac, pinwheeling my arms like a crazy person.

Davis jumped off the couch to grab me, but I found my balance before he could.

"I'm okay." I was breathless and shaking with nerves.

"What is it? Did Ruth call?"

"No. I have a bigger problem."

"Life sure isn't boring around here, is it?" Jim kicked his feet up on the coffee table and rested back on the couch.

I loved that man.

It had to be an effort to calm me down, and it worked. Nerves popped like a pinprick on a balloon releasing some of my near-hysteria.

"Dad—" Davis warned him, but I placed my hand on his arm.

"It's okay. I needed that. I was just starting to freak out. I mean, I just invited my seventeen-year-old sister, who I haven't seen in three years *here*."

"I know. I was there."

"*Here*, Davis. I mean, you just asked me to move in with you, and I still have that apartment, but you didn't sign up for this. A woman with a baby and a younger sister who's on the road from god knows who and..."

"Woah. Slow your roll, sweetheart."

His hand came up and covered my mouth. I inhaled the coconut scent of the hand lotion he kept by the kitchen sink and stared at him.

"I'm gonna keep this hand here and talk real nice and slow, so listen to every word I'm saying, okay?"

I glared at him, to his dad beyond him who was trying very hard to not look like he was paying attention.

"Hmmphf."

Davis grinned. "Good. Now, I wanted you to move in with me so I can help take care of you and our child, right?"

I opened my mouth beneath his to speak before remembering I couldn't. I mean, sure, I could, I could pull away, and he'd let me. But for some reason, I wasn't.

I nodded instead.

"That hasn't changed. And you're not *some woman*, you're mine. We've talked about this, right? Nod if you remember."

My glare hardened, and yeah, we had, but...

"Just a nod, Maggie."

I nodded. Something was happening to my stomach. My nipples. Was I *liking* this? Another humph left me, and I couldn't bring myself to check to see what Jim was doing, but I swore... if he was seeing me get turned on by this....

"So you're mine. My girlfriend and the mother of my child. We're good. You're moving in here. Right?"

"Yeah," I mumbled beneath his palm.

"That doesn't change. Ruth needs help, we're helping her. That's it. Simple as that."

My brows rose on my head, and he smirked.

"It really can be that easy when you've got the right people at your back. What would Belle do?"

Belle would pack her up and move her in with her like she'd done to me. Or take her to her parents and never let her leave. She'd probably have her dressed in Free People and Lululemon and enrolled in the local high school before a plane touched down.

Which... was exactly Davis's point.

My shoulders slumped, and I wrapped a hand around his wrist

and pulled it from my mouth. Before I could speak, he leaned in and kissed me slow. Sweet. Tender. No tongue but his lips lingered on mine until I wasn't worried about becoming turned on in front of Jim, I *was* turned on in front of him.

"Davis," I rasped against his mouth. "Are you sure?"

"Never been more sure of anything in my life." His hand cupped my cheek, and he grinned. Those blue eyes of his popped as he waited until I blew out a breath.

"It's a lot, and we're still strangers, and our life keeps getting more complicated."

"Easy is boring, Maggie. We've got this, okay?"

Right. "You have it, not me. I'm on the hot mess express and I've thrown you on the train for the ride."

"Better than being alone."

Gah. "Do you always have to be perfect?"

Behind him, Jim barked out a laugh. "Ain't no such thing when dealing with people."

"Yeah?" I pressed to my tiptoes and found Jim behind Davis's side shoulder. "When isn't he perfect?"

"Almost shot me in the ass one day when we were out duck hunting. Missed me by inches. That wasn't very perfect of him." He winked at Davis. "Missed the damn ducks, too."

Davis rolled his eyes to the ceiling. "You weren't wearing your orange vest, and I saw movement, Dad. That was your fault."

"Still missed the damn ducks. Didn't get any that day, did you?"

I chuckled. These men. They were just what I needed.

I headed into the living room.

"Fine," I agreed on a mumble. "No one is perfect."

Jim was looking back toward the kitchen and nodded at my agreement. "And everyone has their shit. Sometimes it's big shit, sometimes it's small shit. But everyone's got time in their life when that's their lot. Yours is now. Someday it will be someone else's shit. I figure, girl as sweet as you, you'll help them carry it all, too."

I wasn't quite sure I'd ever heard someone use shit so many times in a sentence or so eloquently.

"Am I wrong?" Jim pressed.

"No. I would probably help someone else with their shit, too."

"Then that's that. We do those things for people we love."

My gaze darted to Davis. His eyes were round but not scared. "Dad," he warned again.

"Said my piece. Think I'll head out, see the town for a bit, give you two some time alone." He slapped the back of Davis's shoulder. "Call your mom, though. She and your sisters will want to talk about the game, and it might be time to tell them the rest, yeah? Sounds to me they might hear it from someone else first, and you don't want that."

Fear drained the color from Davis's face. "No. Annie would kill me. You mind?" he asked me.

What had I been convincing myself of?

In for a penny, in for a pound?

"Go for it." I shrugged.

After all, what else could go wrong?

———

I left Davis in the living room to call his mom first. Once Jim left, I decided to take the time to clear my things out of the bedroom he was sleeping in. If he was heading back to Nebraska soon, I would have kept it, but with Ruth coming... guess I wasn't heading back to that room for a while. I had my phone in my pocket in case she or Mrs. Clancey called again and had my arms filled with the clothes I'd hung in the closet, crossing to Davis's room when I could hear him laughing at something his mom said.

A grin broke out on my face.

This was the kind of guy who would *always* be there for me. He'd move heaven and earth to make sure I was happy and taken care of. He'd do more for our child.

I'd be a fool to not give him back everything he was giving me, and maybe it'd only been a couple weeks. Maybe we barely knew each other, but every time Davis grinned down at me, teased me, laughed with me, or held me... I saw something more than a good guy doing a good thing.

He was *my* guy taking care of me, loving me so easily and

effortlessly I wasn't even quite sure when it happened… when I realized I was falling in love with him.

It could have been that first night we spent together.

The way he smiled when I first reappeared at his door on Christmas Eve.

The way he'd taken all of this in such an easy stride, no matter what I kept throwing at him.

I would need to find a way to repay that, ensure he received everything from me he was giving to me, and with Davis, that would not be a hardship.

Falling in love with him was as easy as breathing. It happened without thought or plan.

My phone rang in my hand, and I tossed the clothes on the bed, grabbing it. It fumbled in my hands and fell to the floor.

"Shit." I dropped to my knees, dug it out from where it slid beneath Davis's bed, and then groaned.

"Hey Belle," I answered.

"Well gee, don't seem all that excited to hear from me. Probably tired after your big night, huh?"

"What?" I fell to my backside and rested against the foot of Davis's bed. "Do you mean meeting Davis's family?"

"Ha! As if, silly. You know a video of you posted on YouTube already has five million freaking views? You're going viral everywhere!"

There was excitement and nerves mixed in her statement.

"I didn't know it'd gone viral," I admitted and pushed my feet straight out in front of me. "It's been a wild morning."

"Well, it's about to get even more wild because my *dad* was forwarded that video first thing this morning, and after he yelled at me for not telling him how talented you were, he told me I have to offer you a contract to get your ass in the studio, or I'm disowned *and* fired."

"What?!" I shrieked.

She was joking. Had to be.

"You're lying," I accused her and she burst out laughing.

"The hell I am! I'm not lying about any of it."

"Belle… I've always said…."

"Uh-uh. You said you didn't want my help, which was still stupid, by the way, and because of that, I never said a word to my dad. He didn't know anything, and this isn't help. Technically, I've been given a task to do for the CEO of my company and I must carry it out."

My head thumped against the footboard, and I flinched, rubbing the back of it. "I can't think about this right now."

"Well you're going to have to because Dad and Mom want you over here for dinner this week to talk about it. I told them I'll have to figure out when you're working and let them know. But if you don't come to dinner, Dad told me to drag you here kicking and screaming anyway, so..."

"Thursday," I said without thinking. "I don't work Thursday."

"Perfect. So what made you go singing last night? Things not go okay with dinner?"

"It was fine. I just needed to sing."

She understood. I'd told her how it was my way to release stress and deal with my problems.

"So why don't you sound happy? What's going on?"

"Ruth called. My sister."

"She scream at you again?"

"No." I busted out crying. How could I not have cried all the tears inside my body yet I was uncertain, but Belle listened to everything. To how bad it'd really been with my family, to everything Ruth had said and what I was waiting for. She cursed through it, hugged me with her words when I needed it, and by the time I was done, we'd both cried more than humanly possible.

"We'll figure it out," she said when I was done. So confidently. So much like Davis.

This time, I was starting to believe them.

"Thursday," she stated. "I'll let you get off the phone but promise me. You're coming to dinner on Thursday. And you're bringing Ruth and Davis."

"I don't know, Belle. It's a lot."

"And they're your family and we're going to make sure Ruth knows how loved you are, show her how normal people can treat those they care about, and Davis is coming because he's going to help me get you to agree to the damn contract. Capisce?"

I didn't have any fight left in me. "Capisce," I grumbled.

"Good. Love you. Ciao!"

She ended the call, and I stared at the screen.

Since when did Belle become Italian?

————

Leaving now. Haven't seen anyone in your family yet. Should be there by seven.

A valve released in my chest. I still wasn't over the call from Belle, and now I was back to dealing with this. Heck, I was still sitting on the floor against Davis's bed, my clothing on top of it forgotten.

So many things I needed to do.

Ruth would be here tonight.

Where in the heck was everyone going to sleep?! I couldn't kick out the Clanceys after they drove so far, and they couldn't go home while it was so late. The condo was already full with Jim being here. Unless Ruth and I crashed on Davis's couches. The sectional was large enough for both of us.

I climbed to my feet, grunting as I did. The button of my jeans pushed into my stomach, making me uncomfortable.

I'd need bigger clothes soon.

More things Davis would need to help me with or I'd need to work for.

Quit my job. Yeah right.

I needed the money now more than ever.

But if what Belle said was the truth….

No way. I shook my head. I hadn't bothered pulling up the viral video or whatever she called it, and I had no idea what anyone was saying about me. If they even knew it *was* me for sure. If her dad wanted to sign me though, I'd be all sorts of a fool to say no.

I popped the button on my jeans and sighed at the immediate relief and once again went in search of Davis to tell him how my life had become a soap opera drama.

His voice was quiet but strained as I reached the hallway. I couldn't make out what he was saying, but I could already picture his cut jaw, jutting forward and muscles tightening on his arms. Crazy how I knew him so little and so well.

"I'm just saying, Davis…"

It was a woman's voice coming through his screen. His mom? I checked the time on my phone. He couldn't still be talking to her. That was a while ago.

"Annie. Don't."

He reprimanded her in a way my back flattened to the wall and I moved toward the living room slowly so as not to get caught. He loved his sisters. There's no way he would talk to one like that.

Not unless…

"I'm not sure I like it. You can say she's good all you want, but you and Dad like everyone. There's something going on, and now she's going viral? You know she had to plan that, right? How else could she get her foot in the door with music, as hard up as you say she is. And who gets busted and *discovered* at some karaoke bar."

She scoffed, and I was certain that use of discovered was in air quotes when she said it. My pulse raced with the desire to run. Everything she was saying was everything I would have to defend from now until eternity.

I stayed still, inhaled slowly, and counted to ten. Davis promised me we'd get through this together.

He cared about me.

More—I could trust him. Already had more than anyone in my life, even Belle.

Yesterday, Annie's comments would have sent me into a spiral. Heck, two hours ago, those words would have crushed me to the floor. Amazing how quickly things could change.

"You're wrong," Davis said, and he was so vehement about it I didn't stay hidden. I could fight this battle. I'd have to do it repeatedly.

I headed into the living room with purpose and Davis's jaw dropped, gaze yanked from the screen and on me the second he saw me moving toward him. Straight to the couch where he was sitting on a video call with his sister.

"I'm saying you need to think about this—"

I plopped onto the couch with purpose, Davis cringing, and the look on his sister's beautiful and natural face with the same blue eyes as Davis's turned to regret.

"I'm sure you're really nice, Maggie, is it? But you have to understand our concern."

"The only one concerned is you," Davis pointed out.

He dropped his arm from the back of the couch, hand settling to my lower back. "Maggie. It's okay, she's—"

"Completely within her right to be worried about you. About this." I pressed my palm to his cheek and turned him so he was facing me and no longer glaring at his sister. The glare wiped away immediately as he smiled down at me. "It's okay. I get it and understand. You had to know we'd get this."

"Yeah. But not from my family."

His eyes narrowed and flicked toward Annie. She was so pretty. Her skin was flawless, and I doubted she was wearing makeup. It was only the frown and slightly embarrassed expression she wore, even if she'd spoken first. Even with that, she was so similar to Davis I had to fight against smiling.

I dropped my hand from Davis's cheek and held his in his lap.

"Annabelle Connelly is my best, and really, only friend I've made since moving to Nashville after my family refused to allow me to come home and pulled me from college. If you don't know who she is, she's the future heir and great-granddaughter to WWMP's empire. WWMP, as in Worldwide Media Productions. They're the largest music producer, primarily with country music in the world. I'm happy to give you Belle's number so you can call and talk to her, but all she'll do is confirm that for the last three years, I've refused any of her assistance in getting started in the music industry. I've *wanted* to do this on my own. I've needed to, for me. I haven't even seen the videos, although your dad pulled one up earlier, but that's all I know about what's going on. Belle's dad, Christian Connelly, learned at some point today that I could sing. Someone sent it to him." I turned to Davis. "By the way, if you're not busy Thursday night, we're invited to their house for dinner."

"Belle's?"

"No. Christian and Scarlett's."

"Scarlett?" Annie asked and then sputtered, "Are you… are you talking about going to Scarlett Drummond's house?"

Ahhh, so she listened to country. Or old school country. While I knew Scarlett as a Connelly and Belle's mom, most of the world knew her as a nineties country sensation, breaking records women had never held and having more CMA awards than any female country performer in history and still held to this day. She was an icon in the country music world.

And the sweetest woman I'd ever met.

"Yes. That's Belle's mom."

"Shit," Davis muttered. "I'd forgotten about that. That they were related."

I turned back and faced Annie. "I know this can look bad, and I'm still terrified the rest of the world will think exactly how you have, that I'm not some gold digger, jersey jumper, or whatever. We met by chance—"

"Fate," Davis cut in.

I pressed my hand to his face to silence him. He frowned behind my hand on the screen, but I was focused on Annie. She smirked at him, and that move over any I could have done might have actually had her liking me.

"We had a great night that ended with a baby, and now we're trying to work things out with a lot of issues popping up along the way. I really care about him, Annie. I do, and I know he loves you so much because every time he mentions you and Avery, he gets stupidly happy."

He grabbed my wrist and tugged it down. "I resent that."

On the screen, Annie sighed. Pouted. "You're making it really hard to hate you."

"So don't." I shrugged. "Sometimes, it's just that easy."

Davis tapped my shoulder, and I looked at him on the screen. "I feel like I've been the one saying that."

I grinned at Davis. "Maybe I'm finally learning."

CHAPTER 29
DAVIS

Was it possible for her to become any more beautiful or incredible? I doubted it. As soon as Maggie appeared and I realized she'd heard all, or most, of the horrible things Annie was saying, I figured that was it…

That was how we ended.

Being with me was too hard, the risk too high. Look at what already happened? One night with me and I'd hijacked her future. I'd convinced her to move to a whole new home, and now I'd put her sister in danger. And *her* if her father actually intended to come here and take her back home.

Like hell that was happening. My blood boiled at the thought of it, but the last thing I expected Maggie to do was plop her ass down and put my older sister in her place.

She also managed to do it in the most spectacular way.

Annie was still talking, but I couldn't take my eyes off Maggie. Didn't want to. I reached out and gave my sister one quick glance. "Gotta go. Talk later."

I slapped my hand down on the *end call* button and my computer screen went black.

Maggie's jaw dropped in shock. "What'd you do that for? Now she's really going to hate me!"

"Don't care."

I curled my hand around the back of her head and slammed her lips to mine, cutting off her argument or retort or scolding or whatever else was going to come out of her mouth. Nothing mattered more in this moment than showing my absolute appreciation to Maggie for only sticking up for herself, but for me—for us.

We would get through all of this together.

She gasped in surprise, and I took the opening, slipping my tongue into her mouth and tilting her head to take the kiss deeper. Fire lit deep inside me, making my heart pound and my dick harden. Every time I touched her, it was like this and kept getting better.

"Come here," I growled against her mouth and pulled her toward me until she was straddling my hips.

"Oh." Maggie hummed when she pressed against my dick, and goddamn, I wanted to be inside of her so bad. Wanted to live there, spend the rest of my life drawing those pleased sounds from her throat and feeling the heat of her around me. "Davis… your dad…"

"Don't care. Make out with me for a bit. We'll hear him come back."

I could have moved her to the bedroom, but then I'd get too lost in her. My dad would probably return to the sounds of her screaming.

Not comfortable for anyone. Instead, I pressed my hands beneath her T-shirt, held her at her sides, and rocked her against me.

Every time I pulled her toward me, she whimpered into my mouth, and soon her hands weren't settled on my shoulders, they were raking through my scalp as her moans grew higher as I pressed my dick against the seam of her denim shorts. She rocked against me, clung to and soon, her entire body quivered and shook. Her thighs clamped down on mine as her orgasm hit.

"Davis," she whimpered, and I growled in response.

"Fuck. Yes, Maggie. So damn good. Take care of you."

Another shiver racked her body, and she yanked her mouth off mine and buried her face in the crook of my neck as she came, moaning *yes* and *more* and *oh god….*

I couldn't handle the sounds and was so close. With one hand at her lower back to hold her steady against mine, I used my free hand to work my shorts down. I held her to me as I lifted, shoved them and my boxer briefs down far enough so I could wrap my hand around my length.

"What are you… oh…"

Her hand met mine, and we wrapped it around my dick together. Sliding up and down, Maggie grinned and licked her lips. "I can take care. Of that." She went to move and slid off my legs but no fucking way. I wanted her breasts pressed against me and her hot breath skimming my heated flesh.

"Another time," I grunted it out, pushed against my hand and together we jerked my dick until I pulsed, pressed my forehead to hers and we both watched as I came, shooting my seed all over my stomach, our hands.

"Ew." Maggie laughed and wiped her hand off on my stomach and climbed off my lap. I was too worn out to care about keeping her close. "I'll get you a towel."

"Kiss me first."

She pressed her lips to mine, eyes open and hazy from her orgasm, and lit with happiness.

A look I wanted to make sure I put on her gorgeous, innocent and trusting and independent, and breathtakingly beautiful face every damn day for the rest of my life.

My dad was right.

I loved her.

Had no idea how it happened so damn fast, but there it was.

Now I had to find the time and a way to tell her so she wouldn't doubt for a minute I meant it.

My hand and stomach covered with my cum in my living room, not the best place.

———

"You distracted me earlier," Maggie said, coming into the kitchen. We'd both cleaned up, and now we were back in the kitchen where I was pulling out lunch meat and fixings to make sandwiches. I had two chicken breasts for me in the air fryer along with some orzo and quinoa boiling on the stove.

"I think you distracted me with how sexy and brave you were with my sister."

It wasn't only what she said, either. It was how adamantly she told Annie she didn't have to hate her. Simple as that. Taking what I'd told her only a few hours earlier and proving she'd not only listened to me but was on the same page.

"Who distracted who argument aside, I was coming to tell you that Mrs. Clancey called, and they're on their way. Driving. Said they'll be here tonight."

And the reality of our horrible morning returned in a snap of a moment.

"That's good. How are you doing?"

The front door opened and my dad walked in, armed with two shopping bags from local tourist shops.

"What are you doing?" I asked, chuckling. They've been to Nashville several times since I was drafted and rarely left without more souvenirs. "How many times have I told you that you need to stop wasting your money on that crap."

"Well I don't think this is crap." Dad dug into one of the bags and pulled out a pink onesie. The words *Nashville Steel's biggest fan* written in white across what would probably take up Reese's entire tummy. "I think this was needed."

He had me there. "You're right. I'm wrong. Blah-blah-blah."

Next to me, Maggie hid her giggle behind her hand.

"So what'd I miss?" Dad asked and dropped his bags onto the kitchen table. "Any more earth-shattering dramas happen?"

"Annie was pissed," I admitted and shoved my thumb in Maggie's direction. "Maggie calmed her down, and I think Annie now secretly loves her."

Maggie snorted. "Doubtful."

"Eh. Not many people can put Annie in her place as easily as you did."

"Annie's a tough nut to crack," Dad said to Maggie. "If she didn't throw anything at you through the screen, Davis here is probably right."

"I'll take that into consideration. And to answer your question, Mrs. Clancey called. Said they were on their way and will be here tonight." She turned to me. "Where's everyone going to sleep? I mean, I can't let them come and then not give them space, and with your dad here, I guess Ruth and I can sleep on the couches? There's plenty of room—"

"Nope." Dad was already shaking his head. "Don't worry about me at all. I'm headed to a hotel. Gotta catch an early flight anyway, but I *am* pretty sure your mom is heading down soon to take care of all these new girls of hers, so be warned about that. But don't you worry about me. You need the space, and I need to be awake around five for the airport. Hotel next to it I'll be easier for me, anyway."

"Seems we've got it worked out, then." I gave the orzo and quinoa a quick stir.

Maggie was gaping at my father. If she thought any of this was a problem, she'd soon learn.

I expected her to argue, but instead, she scrunched up her face. "Are you sure?"

"Yep. Need to get back and get my arms around Reese anyway."

"Okay. If you're sure…"

Dad chuckled and grabbed the things off the table. "I'll pack and head out before they get here. Probably go better for you tonight with Ruth with less company, men especially around, I gather."

"Thanks, Jim. That's really sweet of you."

He went to her, and my throat went tight. She really had to start seeing how kind people could be if given the chance.

She swallowed as he pulled her into a hug and resisted for a moment before she wrapped her arms around him.

"We're family, you and I," he said, patting her back. "That means so is Ruth. You'll trust us all soon enough."

He let go and left, leaving Maggie stunned and staring off into the distance. "He feels like more of a father to me in the last two days than my own has ever been."

She turned to me with tears in her eyes but a hopeful smile stretching her lips into a soft smile.

I didn't bother telling her her own father was a giant piece of crap I'd love nothing more than to stomp into nothing until he quit existing in the world.

————

"Calm down." I squeezed her hand in mine and tried to settle her jitters. We were in the lobby after getting a text from Beth Clancey saying they were about ten minutes out. Since then, Maggie had stayed on the edge of hyperventilating. "You're going to freak her out when you see her, and you have no idea what kind of mood she's in."

"I know. You're right. I can't stop, though. I'm worried and scared and excited."

Tear-filled eyes looked up at me and stole my breath. "I haven't seen any of my family in three years, Davis. Three long, horrible years, and the only phone calls I'd had with them weren't good. Not even this one."

I settled my hand on her cheek and nodded. "I know. But she called you, and she *listened* to you when she needed it the most. That means something. Trust me."

She blew out a breath and shot out her arms. "I know. It was huge she called me at all even if she was calling to warn me, but...."

Headlights pulled up to the curved valet drive of my building and stopped.

"That's them," she whispered.

We had no way of knowing that, but Maggie took off and was pushing through the circular doors before the valet at the front door could help any of them out of the several year old minivan.

As soon as the back door to the aged minivan opened, Maggie was there, yanking it open the rest of the way.

"Ruth," she cried out and threw her arms around an almost spitting image of Maggie, save for the ankle-length denim skirt, plain T-shirt, and hair that might not have ever been cut in her life.

The reality was a jolt to my gut. I had yet to watch an episode of the show, but Maggie had told me small details, like how they sewed their own clothes and weren't allowed to cut their hair, but I could never picture Maggie like that until Ruth's arm hung at her sides while Maggie rocked her back and forth.

Goodness. My girlfriend was terrifying her sister.

A woman stepped out of the front passenger seat and settled her hand on the back of Maggie's head, kissing her softly. She then turned to me.

"You must be Davis Hall." Her smile was kind, if not worried, as she kept glancing back at Ruth and Maggie. "I've heard a lot about you on the trip. Safe to say my husband's a large football fan."

"Davis Hall." I held out my hand for her to shake, and she took it easily.

"Beth Clancey. So thrilled we could help these girls out today." Beth had an even kinder face than her smile, and she covered her other hand with ours, already shaking. She gave me a quick squeeze and pulled her hand back before glancing over her shoulder.

She had her hair pulled back in a loose ponytail, and it flipped over her shoulder as she turned to watch her husband come around the front of the minivan.

The man was dressed like every Nebraskan farmer I'd ever met with worn denim jeans, even more, worn cowboy boots, and a plaid flannel shirt buttoned up and tucked into his jeans with a wide leather brown belt and even larger brass belt buckle.

"Mark Clancey. Nice to meet you."

"Davis Hall. You, too. Thanks for getting them here so quickly. I imagine that wasn't difficult."

"Pisses me off to say it, but we should have done this years ago." He worried his lip and frowned in Maggie and Ruth's direction. They'd been joined by another girl, I assumed, their daughter Jenna. She was the spitting image of her mom and dressed in leggings and a sweatshirt. Simple but fashionable, and so drastically different from what Ruth was wearing.

"Tried to get her to take Jenna's clothes," Beth whispered. "Refused any of the pants at all, said she's not allowed but we managed to get her to have a couple of sweatshirts and things. She'll need to go shopping."

"We'll take care of it."

Maggie would know and understand. I'd give her my credit card and take her where she wanted to go with it, no limit.

"How is she?" I asked because Ruth hadn't yet smiled nor hugged her sister back, and Jenna was shooting Maggie a worried look while she said something to Ruth, who shrugged. Expressionless.

"She's been pretty quiet. Embarrassed, but I think mostly she's pretty damn terrified."

"You heard anything yet?"

"No," Mark said. "I've had men, friends of mine, on the land all day. There hasn't been any activity we can see, so I don't know what's going on. There *might* be people still in the church we can call, but I don't want to tip our hand."

"Don't." Especially not while they weren't there to protect their other kids still left at home.

"Maggie!" I called out. "How about we get your sister inside?"

"Come meet him, Ruth. Please?"

Ruth's gaze slid toward me, and there was nothing there. No happiness or nerves or worry. Just blank.

I sighed.

This might be a bigger battle than Maggie had anticipated, but one thing was for sure—

I was there to help her win it.

CHAPTER 30
MAGGIE

My sister. She was here. I couldn't stop touching her and smiling and forced myself not to badger her with a list of a million questions swarming my head all day, but I was trying to keep calm.

For her.

Because she hadn't hugged me back, and when I asked if she was okay, she simply said, "don't know," and then didn't say another word.

"Hi," she said to Davis as he opened the door for all of us, and then "thank you" when she walked through the door to his building.

The valet had taken their van to the parking garage beneath the building, and Davis instructed them to leave the ticket at the front desk.

Once we were all in the elevator, I couldn't stop glancing at Ruth. I was pretty sure the skirt she was wearing had been mine years ago, and her hair was in desperate need of a cut, and while surfaces looked similar, that was where the similarities ended.

She was me all those years before I tried to leave, and it felt like a lifetime ago I'd been so afraid of every single little thing. I was pretty sure the only reason I'd had any chance of adjusting to life on my own, outside the church and my family, was because I'd been desperate for it. Desperate to see the world, knew there was more than the way we lived, and I wanted to experience it, if even for a short time. Like a Mormon on their two-year mission or an Amish child on their Rumspringa.

Given the way Ruth was acting, she'd neither had any desire nor hope of ever having such experience.

It'd come with time.

Or maybe not.

And if she wanted to live the simple, clustered life she'd been raised in, I'd help her do that, in a church that was safe. With people who would protect her and not abuse her. There had to be churches similar to ours who didn't behave the same way.

I'd do whatever she needed to feel safe and happy and fulfilled however that meant. For now, she was safe.

Here.

Not screaming at me like she'd done on the phone.

It was enough.

"Well, isn't this a lovely place?" Beth's eyes lit with wonder as we stepped into Davis's home.

Funny how I'd thought the same thing, and yet now, it didn't feel majestic or incredible or lavish.

It was *home*. Warm, inviting, with a gorgeous view and luxurious sure, but more than any of the rest, it was home.

Funny how that'd happened so quick and I wasn't even fully moved in yet.

"There's a pool outside," I told Ruth quietly. We'd been allowed to swim growing up as long as we wore full-body swimsuits that came down to our knees. "And a hot tub, if you ever want to sit in it. It's gorgeous when the sun sets."

"Okay."

"How cool," Jenna said on my other side.

Unlike Ruth, she sounded excited by everything, and while we'd never really been friends due to our age difference, she felt a lot like how I used to be. A small-town girl with dreams of seeing the world.

At least she had parents who seemed willing to help her with them instead of squashing them.

"Would anyone like anything to drink?"

"I'll take a water, please, Magdalene. And thank you."

"You're welcome. And Maggie. Magdalene isn't someone I know anymore."

Ruth scoffed and walked toward the windows. The inky black night was peppered with lights, but that was pretty much all you could see.

"Probably shouldn't have said that," I muttered to Beth, who was giving me an understanding smile.

"It'll be okay. Give her time. Today's been a lot, and I'm betting she's second-guessing herself right now, but it is the right thing." She settled her hand on my shoulder tentatively, like I'd be afraid of her touch, but I leaned in instead and gave her a hug.

"Thank you."

"Anything for you, Maggie."

I grinned against her chest and pulled back.

Davis stepped up behind me and handed the water to Mark. "Would any of you ladies like anything? We have some snacks, or I can make a quick dinner—"

"You cook?" It came from Ruth, who'd spun so fast her hair whipped around her. "You cook." She glanced at the water Mark was holding. "And you got him water."

"Sure, I can cook."

Davis said it easily like he couldn't fathom the problem.

"Lots of men cook," Mark said softly to Ruth.

Her face screwed up, and she rolled her eyes.

It was a defiant gesture, something she'd *never* do in front of the men in our house, which gave me hope she wasn't as scared as she looked, but I understood, especially when she glared at me. "What do you do then? If he's cooking?"

In truth, I hadn't cooked a meal at all since I started spending time with Davis. He was always in the kitchen, taking care of the meals and me.

Davis stepped up next to me, either prepared to handle her wrath on my behalf or explain himself. Neither necessary.

"With my job, I have to follow a very strict diet plan. Most of the players cook their own meals, or maybe their wives do it, but I'm not married. If I didn't learn to cook, I'd have a hard time following the requirements from our team doctor, and I need to do that to stay healthy more than most."

She understood. I saw the moment she got exactly what Davis was saying, but I also knew what her struggle was. The boys in our family had *never* stepped foot into the kitchen. Not to load their own plate or grab their own knife. They had never so much as poured their own glass of water or milk. She *had* to see how insane that was, but I wouldn't push her, either.

She might have wanted me safe and to save her own hide today, but that didn't mean she wanted to throw away an entire lifetime of teaching, either.

"Ruth..."

She turned eyes that mirrored mine on me. "I don't know what to believe. What's right and what's wrong. Mark and Beth said so much—"

"No one's asking you to change your entire worldview, Ruth. We wanted you safe. If you have questions, ask them, and we'll answer anything. I can sit with you any day you want and tell you what I've been through, why I've changed and what I haven't changed my ideas on at all, but all I'm asking is that while you're here, you ask those questions *nicely.*"

She flinched and managed a chagrined look after a moment. "Deal. You like it here though?"

"I love everything about my life."

I didn't realize it was true until I said it. I had a job I liked, my dream on the horizon. An incredible man, and more... I settled my hand on my stomach and her eyes almost popped right out of her head.

"You're *pregnant?!*"

Oh dear.

I hadn't even thought to warn her.

———

"Well, that went well." Davis was staring at the doors outside, where Ruth stormed off to after screaming at me.

Not that I blamed her.

Beth Clancey was out there with her, and from what I could tell, both women were sitting in chairs, staring at the pool or the dark sky, not saying anything.

I hadn't even seen Beth's lips move once since they went out there, and yet Ruth didn't seem to mind her company.

"I'm not sure what to do."

"Well, she pretty much thinks if you weren't going to hell before, you're on a straight ticket now, and you can't really blame her for that one."

"Jenna!" Mark scolded.

"What?" Jenna was next to me, not trying to be cruel, and at any other moment, I'd appreciate her honesty.

If only she didn't have to be so brutal about the delivery.

"You can't just say those things."

"She can, Mr. Clancey. It's okay. I get it." The drinking was bad. Kissing a boy was worse. But sex before marriage? My father and his church were going to *freak*, and it'd come out eventually. It'd have to, especially with that stupid singing stuff going viral.

Next to me, Davis had taken my hand at some point and squeezed. "You should go talk to her."

"Yeah. How about I shove toothpicks beneath my fingernails and call it even."

He chuckled, brought our connected hands to his mouth and kissed my knuckles. "I think we can hold off on personal torture for a bit."

"Fine." I might as well have been walking to my doom as I stepped outside. The cool air skated across my skin. I crossed my arms over my chest, rubbed my upper arms, and Beth stood as I approached.

"I'll let you two talk."

"Thanks."

I slid into her chair. "I'm sorry. This has been a really bad day for you and a really long one. I didn't mean to throw that in your lap as soon as you arrived."

"Because acting until morning would have been better?" Her look could freeze a lake. Terrify small children.

"No, and to be fully honest, I hadn't figured out how to tell you yet at all."

She humphed. "You've … you've … had sex."

"Yeah."

I let that linger. I wouldn't apologize for it, but knew the difficulties in her understanding.

"How long have you been dating him?"

Oh. Okay. So she was really starting with the hard questions. I thought we'd start with *why*? Or straight to scripture that proved Jenna's ideologies true.

"We care about each other." So much for being fully truthful.

If she noticed I dodged her question, she didn't show it. Or push. Not surprising since she wouldn't have been allowed to do so when she woke up this morning.

"I'm really glad you're here. It's so good to see you."

I sniffed as I said it, surprised at the emotions bubbling. This was my sister. We might have been drastically different, and maybe there was a chasm between us too wide to build a bridge across. But she was here, and when she needed help, I was there for her.

"I don't understand your new life at all."

"You don't have to. And I'm not trying to say my life should be yours, either. I want you healthy and safe, free to figure out what kind of life it is that you want. That's all, Ruth."

She nodded, facial features softening. "You're having a baby."

This time it wasn't an accusation.

"Yeah. I really am."

"That's really kind of exciting. Isn't it?" She grinned softly. It shook until it stretched wider across her face.

My own matched hers. "Yeah, Ruth. It really is exciting. And scary, but mostly exciting."

"I can't believe you're dating a man who cooks." I snorted and then chuckled. Wait until I told her he did his laundry, too. "Is he good to you? Is he nice?"

I reached out and pressed my hand to her knee, making sure I had her full attention. "He's the best man I've ever met."

Full truth. That time, anyway, no hesitation.

We'd get to the story of how Davis and I met when she could handle it.

CHAPTER 31
MAGGIE

Next to me, Davis's knee was bouncing like he was getting ready to start taking off down the field. He kept bumping his knee into mine, folding a pamphlet he grabbed from the table in front of us titled, "What to Expect..."

We were at my doctor's office for the first appointment I'd invited him to, and to say we were both a ball of nerves was an understatement.

I squeezed his knee to still the bouncing, and his hand clamped onto mine. "Sorry. I'm excited, have been, but I don't know why this is so scary to me."

"Because this will make it all completely real."

"It *is* real," he stated and held my hand tighter. His palm was clammy, but I didn't let go. If he needed to touch me to calm his nerves, I'd let him every time. "But now I'm thinking of all the things we'll need to buy. There's a lot to do, you know? And it'll be here so fast, and we have so much else going on right now."

"We'll figure it out."

A chunk of his hair fell onto his forehead as he turned his head in my direction. "How are *you* the calm one?"

I laughed. Funny how we'd come full circle. "Because you keep telling me everything will be okay."

"Right. I'm the calm one, got it."

In the last few days, neither of us had been calm. With the whirl-wind arrival of Ruth, we hadn't stopped. Mr. and Mrs. Clancey stayed the night in Davis's guest room. Jenna, Ruth, and I camped out on his couches. There were three full-grown young women on the sectionals, and we'd still had room to spread out and invite more had we wanted.

Davis hadn't argued that night about me not sharing his bed with all the company we'd had, but right after the Clanceys left that next morning and Ruth went to shower, he'd whisked me into his large walk-in closet, bent me over the dresser island in the middle of it and ripped off my panties.

He'd then murmured, "Never again. Never again do you sleep on the couch in your own home," while he drove me over the cliff and out to see with his fingers and tongue and then his dick, all while forcing me to stay silent so Ruth didn't hear.

Davis had then spent the day on the phone with his lawyer, trying to find someone who could help us, especially if my family showed up for Ruth. We then spent the afternoon searching for private investigators to take the case, see if anyone could find any information on what was really happening in my father's home or uncle's or in the church in general. The abuse of these young girls would stop, and the toxic treatment and teaching to males would as well.

As far as Ruth, she was settling, and while I'd told her more than once that she didn't have to be on kitchen cleanup duty or constantly walk around the condo with a dust rag or mop in her hands, looking constantly for messes to clean, it was Davis who'd pulled me away to quietly tell me to let her be. Her world was upended, and she was doing what she knew.

Since then, I'd backed off, taken her to lunch at Lou's yesterday when Davis had practice. Tonight we would go out for dinner and then get her a cell phone. She'd declined to come to the appoint-ment with me. Even though I wanted her in my sight at all times so she couldn't do something rash like hop on the first bus back to Missouri, I was thankful for this time with Davis.

"Miss Maggie?"

Davis jumped to his feet at the mention of my name and I was still shaking my head, smiling at him as he hurried us down the hall.

After she took my weight and settled me into the room, and the round of common questions regarding how I was feeling, I left Davis to do a urine test, and when I returned, he was staring at a plastic set of rings on the doctor's table.

"What is this?" He pointed at it, pale-faced.

I climbed onto the exam table. "They're the circles that show what each centimeter of dilation means."

His eyes widened so large he looked like a cartoon character. "I don't... I can't... I mean, my sisters have done this, and it's amazing, but you're going to be stretched *that* big?" He pointed to the largest circle.

"Trust me, not something I enjoy thinking about either. But it is a muscle that retracts."

"I can fit my whole fist in there."

"Let's not try that out in real life, k?"

His head whipped in my direction, and his jaw dropped. He was still gaping at me in shock when a knock rapped on the door and it opened.

"Hey there, Maggie. How are we doing today?" Dr. Sally Flecks squeezed my shoulder as she walked by. "Oh, and you have company today. Hi there, I'm Dr. Sally Flecks, but please call me Sally. Doctor seems so impersonal given the relationship we'll have over the next several months."

She held out her hand, and Davis took it. "Davis Hall. Nice to meet you."

"You too. I'm assuming you're daddy?"

His cheeks turned a further sheet of white, and I reached out to hold his hand. He was falling apart and a part of me was grateful for it. He'd always been the put-together one.

Apparently, Davis Hall turned into a nervous fool when faced with the reality of being a dad.

Good to know.

"Yeah." He cleared his throat, squeezed my hand so hard I had to wiggle my fingers to get him to loosen his grip. "I'm the dad."

"Davis," I whispered it to get his attention, and when his eyes met mine again, there was a wet sheen in them. "We've got this."

He broke out in a smile. "Yeah, we do."

"Okay, then." Sally sat in her chair and pulled up my chart on her iPad. After a round of questions about how I'm feeling, how I've been eating, and my general level of energy and stress, she then moved to grab the monitor.

"Since you're almost through the first trimester, we'll try to check baby's heartbeat externally. If we can get a good reading, we won't need to do the internal this time, okay?"

"Sounds good."

"Dad, how about you move up to the edge of the table there." She pointed to where I was shuffling my head toward the pillow.

As I lay down, I lifted my shirt to beneath my breasts and pushed down the waistband of my leggings.

"This will feel cool," she reminded me and then covered my belly with a clear, jelly-like liquid.

"Heartbeat," Davis muttered, and he had my hand in his again.

Gone were his clammy hands, and now they were so hot he might have had a fever, but as he grinned down at me, nothing else mattered. We would both be nervous. We would both have moments of fear.

But we would get through them together.

I winked at him, and he chuckled right as Sally clicked the machine on and then ran the wand in a small circle on my stomach.

"This is safe, right?" Davis asked.

She grinned up at him. "Totally and completely. I prom—"

She cut off as the rapid thump of quiet drums came through the speaker in her hand.

My hand tightened in Davis's as I squeezed him tight.

"There we are." She smiled at me. I loved this woman. She was so kind, so sweet and reassuring. She almost appeared as happy as I was to hear the baby's heartbeat, even though she had to hear dozens every single day.

"Wow," Davis breathed out. "That's…"

"That's your baby's very strong, very healthy heartbeat. One hundred and forty-two beats. Sounds absolutely perfect to me."

"Oh my god. I'm going to be a dad."

Numerous emotions raced through Davis's face, from fear to elation, and then a softness settled over him as Sally removed the wand and handed me paper towels to wipe up the goop.

"I'm going to be a dad."

"Yeah, you are."

"Thank you," he murmured and bent down, kissed my forehead while Sally moved back to the small desk and worked on the chart.

"I think you did all the work," I whispered right back.

Davis's grin stretched, and he kissed my forehead again before pulling back. "Good thing I have you to help me with all the rest."

"Yeah. You have me for sure."

"Okay then." Sally stood. "Everything looks great. We have your next couple of appointments scheduled, and you should see a burst of energy as you settle into the second trimester. As long as you watch what you eat, get some exercise, feel free to continue with any other normal activities. But remember, if you feel any cramping, or see any spotting, make sure you call us immediately."

"Will do, Sally."

"Thanks, Doctor."

She left Davis and me alone in the room, and it heated as he helped me sit up and threw away the paper towels for me.

"That's it?" he asked.

"That's it. As long as things are good, I've been told these monthly check-ups are usually pretty quick."

"Good. That's good. That's wonderful."

"What's wrong now?" He was starting to pace, scraping a hand through his hair until it was totally disheveled.

"I thought of something, but I don't want you to freak out."

"Okay…"

"I want to move. Out of the city. I want our baby to have a home and space to run and not grow up with a cement patio, and I want him or her to have all the things I did growing up, and—"

"Davis." Oh dear sweet goodness. This man was having a day and a half for sure.

"What? Don't you want that?"

"Of course I'd love that. It doesn't mean we have to have it *today*." I laughed and tried to get him to see how ridiculous he was being, but he only scowled at me.

"We need more space, especially with Ruth, and what's going to happen with your other siblings, and then we'll have our child. We can't have them in the city, and I can't fit them all in my condo."

My siblings?

"What are you talking about?" I jumped off the exam bed. There had to be a better place to have this discussion, but since he'd started it…

"Your little brothers and sisters, Maggie? What do you think will happen if it's discovered your dad has been abusing children? Or at least the girls?"

"He'll go to jail?"

"And be out in a few years, might not be able to have contact with them, but who would take care of them? Your mom, who allowed it to happen? Your brothers?"

Well, crap. I hadn't considered any of this.

I wrapped my hands around Davis's still flailing in the air until he relaxed, exhaled a breath that practically shook the room.

"Let's go home and talk about this, okay? We don't know anything yet."

He scolded me with a look that basically told me to get on the same page with him, that I was being naive, and maybe I was. But we had more immediate concerns. My sister. This baby. His *career*. He had a month left of games if they made it to the Super Bowl.

That's where I needed him focused.

"I want to show you and Ruth something. Then we'll go back home and talk."

I was thinking of finishing a pregnancy and getting him through the rest of his season. He was thinking of moving and taking in my siblings if it came to that?

Who was this man, and how did he get a gazillion steps ahead of me?

CHAPTER 32
DAVIS

t was all perfectly clear. The night Maggie showed up at my door telling me she was pregnant was only weeks ago and felt like a lifetime. There was too much happening, too quick, and while I appreciated her protests earlier of wanting to go back to the condo and hang out with Ruth all day, she'd reluctantly agreed to this idea of mine.

She hadn't even considered what would happen to her siblings, but I've thought of little else since Ruth arrived at my home, timid and scared, and so screwed up with the mindset of what women did versus men. I wanted to prove to all of the people in Maggie and Ruth's family that life didn't have to be that way, and there was one sure-fire way to do such a thing if it came to that.

Was I a twenty-three-year-old who not only recently found out he knocked up a girl but was now preparing to build a life with her and her family if it came to that?

Hands down.

Without question or hesitation.

Yes.

Unequivocally.

Maggie would, too, as soon as she realized the alternatives, if it came to that. Which really made the idea I had that popped into my mind as soon as I heard my baby's heartbeat the best idea ever and because I had such incredible friends, they wholeheartedly agreed with me without hesitation.

Which was exactly why Eden and Cole were standing on the front porch on the home next door to his parents. The home where Eden had returned to after seven years last fall to help take care of the woman everyone in this small town of Marysville loved.

The home where Marley Bickerstaff passed away last fall.

Eden and Cole, and his parents had been torn on what to do with it since. None of them wanted a stranger to move in. No one wanted to see the home fall apart further and yet none of them wanted to renovate it, either. It was too soon. There were too many memories inside the walls of the home that sat at the top of the hill with the gravel driveway.

Rocks clinked against the undercarriage of my truck as I pulled up and behind Cole's.

He and Eden stepped to the top of the front porch stairs.

"Why are we here?" Maggie asked. "Isn't that Cole's mom's house?"

"Yeah." I hadn't known Marley well, and not for long before she fell ill, but she'd still treated me like I was a grandson she'd known my entire life. "So, I have an idea…"

Before I could say it, Maggie's door was opened, and Eden stood there. "Come on, come on. I have to tell you, I think this is wonderful."

"What's wonderful?" Maggie asked her.

Eden's steely gaze smacked right into me, and she scowled. "You didn't tell her?"

"I was getting to it," I muttered.

Eden rolled her eyes. "Boys. Come on, Maggie." She glanced into the back seat. "You must be Ruth. Hi, I'm Eden, and that guy on the porch is Cole. He's friends with Davis here, and they play on the same team."

As she spoke like a whirlwind, something I hadn't anticipated from Eden, ever, Maggie slowly slipped out of the truck and Ruth followed.

"What's going on?" Ruth asked.

"No idea," Maggie muttered, but they followed Eden up to the porch.

"Give me a second," I called out to all of them and reached for Maggie's hand. "Before we go in there, hear me out, okay?"

She smirked and then stared at the house with the grand front porch. "Do I have a choice?"

"I'm serious, Maggie. Please?"

She must have caught the serious tone in my voice. We could joke all we wanted, have all the fun in the world, but when it came to my family, I would always be serious.

"What is it?"

"The home. Remember hearing about Marley the other night?"

"Yeah."

"This was her home. She left it to Eden in her will, but Eden hasn't been able to decide what to do with it. She lives with Cole, and they haven't been able to bring themselves to sell it or anything, and it's not huge, but it could be a great start. Needs updating and renovating, new floors that kind of stuff, but the land is perfect. The bones of the house are perfect."

"Davis, what are you saying?"

"I think we should buy it from them, and they're actually good with the idea."

"Davis!" she shrieked, and everyone on the porch was staring at us.

So okay, I should have brought this up in the car, but truthfully, I'd wanted Maggie to see the cute downtown that was growing and feel the warmth in the small town as we drove through it. It was three times the size of where she grew up, half the size where I did, but the proximity to Nashville and to the stadium still made it easy for me to commute.

We wouldn't have to raise a child in the city.

We could raise them here on acres of land with a lake they could swim in. Build treehouses and explore nature all they wanted. Put in a pool and hot tub. I could afford to go anywhere, get a home in Brentwood like other players, and live among the richest people in the state.

But that wasn't where Maggie would be comfortable.

Here we'd have family and not the one we created, but the one we could choose.

"Davis," she finally whispered and her eyes shone with unshed tears. "You're insane."

"I'm just asking you to look and think about it, okay? That's all."

"Well, I'm already here…"

"Perfect." I kissed her, uncaring her sister was watching or we had an audience. I kissed her because she was Maggie and when she was this close to me, adorable with a scrunched-up nose and still cracking jokes, I couldn't *not* kiss her.

———

"That lake was really pretty."

"It was, Ruth, wasn't it? What else did you like?"

In the back seat of my truck, she shrugged. "The town feels nice. Everyone was smiling."

After we looked at the house, Eden and Cole talking about what had been updated and what would need to be done, I drove them back through Marysville, past the high school and elementary, down the streets. It was a Tuesday afternoon, and school was in session, but that didn't mean the little downtown wasn't bustling.

There was something comforting about the place that I didn't have in Nebraska, where all the shops were in strip centers and spread out without a downtown, central town area. It was like a movie, almost.

"I still think you've lost your mind," Maggie mumbled next to me, but she lost the heat as soon as Eden took her through the tree line and showed her the lake where she and Cole had spent a summer swimming in when Eden lived there in high school.

She might not have been fully on board with my idea, but she wasn't protesting. Not really, anyway.

"We have time to think about it," I said, but I was already compiling a list of what needed to be done. Popcorn ceilings and wallpaper stripped. New countertops and floorings. The bathroom vanities needed updating since they were old Formica trimmed with gold circa nineteen-seventies.

There were other things too, but mostly, I envisioned everything I wanted to add. A screened-in porch, an outdoor fireplace and kitchen. A pool. Hot tub. I couldn't live without either after having them.

"The bedroom downstairs would be really great when company came, though," Maggie said. "They could have their own space at night, especially with a baby who might cry or something. Your mom and dad would love to visit and be close to Mama B, I'm guessing."

There she was. She was seeing it exactly like I did.

"I like that room at the top of the stairs," Ruth said, and when I caught her reflection in the rearview mirror, she was smiling. "I wouldn't have to share a room?"

Maggie choked down tears at the question. "No, Ruth." She turned and grinned at her sister around her chair. "You won't have to share a room."

"Davis?" she asked.

"Yeah, Ruth?"

"Any chance we could get some chickens?"

I shot Maggie an *I told you so* look. She rolled her eyes and then hid a smile behind her hand, but her eyes didn't lie.

She was *loving* this idea now.

"We can definitely get you some chickens, Ruth."

CHAPTER 33
MAGGIE

Belle's parents' home was seven-thousand plus square feet of majestic white-painted brick, black windows, and sharp peaks. Double two-car garages framed the enormous wood front door with a curved driveway in front to make the entrance and exit smooth for visitors. Back in the Governor's Club neighborhood of Brentwood, their neighbors were other musicians and CEOs and professional athletes, among others.

It never ceased to amaze me how Belle could grow up in this home, amid such extreme wealth and how her entire family was the kindest and sweetest people alive. Especially given her own mom's iconic past and her father's incredible success.

"This is a *house?*" Ruth rasped from the back of Davis's truck.

He'd already pointed out three homes where his teammates lived, but it seemed each home in the neighborhood grew larger and more impressive.

"It looks like a hotel," she whispered, and I rolled my lips together to hide my smile.

There were moments Ruth was morose and quiet, where she watched Davis fold his own laundry and scowled like she should have been the one doing it. There were others where she showed her youthful innocence.

I much preferred these moments to the others.

"And they're so kind," I told her. "But if you get uncomfortable with anything, let me know, okay?"

"Will they be drinking?"

"Probably."

"Dad says that's a sin."

"Technically, the Bible says drunkenness is a sin," Davis said, and when Ruth talked like this, it always surprised me of his knowledge of the Bible. For some reason, he seemed to be able to help her more than me.

Although that could have been because, in our world, women were taught by men. At least about important matters.

"And having a drink or two, or for some people three, doesn't make them drunk at all."

"Yeah, but…"

"And there are verses about people being drunkards, which means they're essentially drunk all day. But Jesus drank, didn't he? And he made more wine so people could keep celebrating at a wedding?"

"Well, yeah…"

"No one's going to be drunk here," I told her. "But it is pretty common for people to have a drink or two of wine with dinner. It's not like *you're* going to get to a drink. You're not even legal age."

Ruth rolled her eyes, but her smile had returned.

Perfect timing because as Davis stopped his truck, the front door opened, and Belle rushed out.

Dressed in a midi-length floral dress, it flew in the wind behind her along with her blonde hair.

"Is that Belle?" Ruth asked.

"The one and only tornado," Davis muttered.

I slapped his chest and hopped out of the truck as Belle wrapped me in a hug. "You've had the craziest week of craziest weeks."

"Tell me about it."

Since we were going to dinner at her parents' house, both Davis and I dressed up. I think part of it helped Ruth feel better in her own floor-length skirt, even if it was clear the quality was no match for Belle's designer labels.

Davis, for his part, had made me drool upon seeing him. Dressed in a deep, royal-blue but not quite navy suit, his tan shoes shined as he stepped toward both of us. All of it fit his body to one hundred and ten percent perfection.

"Hey Davis," Belle said.

"Trainwreck express," he greeted her with a laugh. Funny how he'd met her so few times and knew her so well.

"This is my sister."

"Ruth." Belle reached out her arm to shake her hand. Belle was a hugger, but I think everyone knew Ruth wouldn't be receptive to hugs from strangers. Might have been the most insightful thing Belle had ever done. "I'm Belle. Annabelle, actually, but nobody calls me that. Welcome to my parents' home."

"Thank you."

She trailed behind us, and once we stepped through the front door, it was Lance who met and greeted us. Like Davis, he was dressed in suit pants, slim fit but black and wearing a light gray dress shirt rolled up to the elbows.

"Look at you, little Miss Famous."

I rolled my eyes and let him sweep me into a hug. "Hi Lance. Good to see you."

"You too. Sounds like your life has gotten a lot more interesting and I didn't think that was possible a few weeks ago."

I slapped his back and stepped out of his hold. "Shut up."

He held out his hand and introduced himself to Davis. "Huge fan of yours," he said. "I followed you in college too, but now I'm a bigger fan, learning the kind of man you are."

Davis blushed from his cheeks to the roots of his hair. I'd never seen such a thing. "Thank you. Nice to finally meet you too, Lance."

"There you are!" Scarlett Drumond swept into the entryway in a gorgeous ivory dress. It was a halter top tied at the back of her neck, a tight empire waist and a flared-out skirt. The dress shone beneath the entryway chandelier, exposing a slit up to her thigh and thin, shimmering threads. But what I loved most about her was her bare feet, non-painted toes or anything. Instead, she introduced herself first to Davis, then Ruth. She gave her a gentle hug like Ruth was fragile porcelain.

Surprisingly, my sister hugged her back like she meant it before ducking her head and stepping back as Scarlett cupped her cheek and said, "Why aren't you just so beautiful and sweet? Gorgeous, child. Absolutely beautiful."

"Umm. Thanks?" Ruth shuffled back and forth on her feet, and I went to her to take her hand.

She never would have been called those things. They were superficial and worldly, and while I knew she'd struggle with them, the easy praise seemed to boost her spirits. Which means she was blushing and smiling as Christian Connelly, Belle's dad, swept into the room with the grace and confidence of a man who knew exactly how important he was, and the kindness of a man who'd do anything for someone he loved.

"Hello! Hello! Welcome to our home!" He introduced himself to Davis, shook Ruth's hand, and when he came to me, scowled play-fully. "You've been hiding secrets, young lady, and we're going to talk about this tonight."

"Yes, sir."

He barked out a laugh, throwing back his head.

"Christian, Maggie. How many times have I told you to call me Christian?" He threw his arm around me and swept me toward the kitchen.

Everyone else followed, and soon the dinner table was a hot mess of laughter, conversation, food being passed around and drinks being poured.

———

"So, tell me about this singing of yours my daughter neglected to mention before."

We'd talked about Davis's upcoming week off and the playoffs. The Steel's chances of making it all the way and bringing home a Super Bowl win to Nashville for the first time ever. Scarlett, with a skill I wished to possess, managed to drag conversation out of a very overwhelmed Ruth until she appeared at ease with the chaos.

Both Scarlett and Christian had peppered me with questions regarding my pregnancy, something Belle and Lance *had* mentioned to them, along with many offers to help with anything I needed.

For the second time in a week, I felt at home.

It never ceased to amaze me how strangers could become friends and then family, and yet especially in the last month, that's what Davis had given me.

As the meal had slowed, it was Scarlett who suggested she and Ruth and Belle clean up, so they were in the kitchen. Lance had excused himself not bothering to mumble an excuse, leaving Christian and Davis and me alone.

There was no doubt this wasn't pre-orchestrated, so I wasn't surprised by the question. It didn't make it less intimidating.

"It's something I've always done. And you can't blame Belle. I told her not to say anything."

"Oh trust me, she spilled that can of beans as soon as I recognized you on that stage. I'm not mad. I understand, although I'd hope you know we would have gladly helped as soon as Belle came to us and told us of your talent. You've had no formal training?"

"No. I've just always done it. Started singing nursery rhymes and then hymns. When I was twelve, my father had me start singing in front of the church. When I went to school, I went for a music education degree, so I had some voice coaching then, I guess. But we all know I wasn't there for long."

"I've spoken with some agents, because as much as I'd simply love to sign you, I also want to make sure you find someone you trust to help you along the way."

"I trust you, but are you sure? I mean, it was a karaoke bar." A ridiculous nervous laugh escaped me. An agent?

"With your talent and your look, people will be climbing over themselves to represent you the first time I get you on stage. I want you in the studio recording music, but I also want to work on getting you a following. I have dozens of agents in my office, as you know, and I'd like for you to meet with a few of them I think would be best. Of course, if you want to go elsewhere, I'm happy to do that for you, too."

That was… well, my head was already spinning. "Why?"

"Because your natural talent is unparalleled and with the right amount of extra coaching and teaching, you could be a star, Maggie. Unless that's not what you want? Unless you'd rather squander your gift?"

"No, I don't want that. But I guess I wanted to do it on my own."

Next to me, Davis huffed. He'd been very vocal about how very few came to success without any help.

"Your effort alone is yours to give. The depths of how far you want to go is your decision alone. But your talent? That deserves to be shared and if it's your dream, it is well within my abilities to help you reach it. Why wouldn't I?"

He said it so matter of fact as he sipped his bourbon, not seeming to realize he was completely knocking me off my feet.

"You want to get me on stage?"

"As soon as possible. I've made some calls, talked to some people and we can get you on stage doing covers within the next couple of weeks. Which I would recommend seeing as how those viral videos will slow and people will forget. You know the saying 'strike while the iron's hot?'"

"Yes, sir."

"That's what I'd like to do. I understand, though, if the timing with your pregnancy isn't ideal. But if you take off as quickly as I believe, we could have you releasing an album before you deliver, on tour as early as next year."

An album. A tour. On stage, singing music.

He might as well have slid a silver platter across the table toward me with my dreams piled on them and said, "Here. Take it."

"I don't know what to say."

"Think about it. Let me know when you're ready. We'll get the wheels moving then, but in the meantime, I'd like you to at least meet with some of our agents. I think Brianna would be the best fit for you. If you want someone else, though, that's fine, like I said. I want to sign you, get to helping make this happen, but if you're not ready, we won't force it."

"Thank you, Christian." My eyes welled with tears and I sniffed them back. I brought my lemon water to my mouth and practically drained it. I was ready.

And terrified.

So would it be smart to wait?

There were so many things to consider. Davis's schedule. The pregnancy. My sister.

"I'll give you time. Let me know whatever you decide, but in the meantime, tell me about this sister of yours? Belle said your family might pose some problems?"

His dark brows puckered on his tan face.

"Her father's a monster," Davis said, face pinched with anger, and I didn't blame him, but…

"Davis—"

He glared at me. "No. You've lived this and have hidden it and spoken of it enough. Someone needs to be protecting you and Ruth, and if it's me from saving you the pain of talking about it, I will."

"Tell me everything you're comfortable with," Christian said, and his grip had tightened on his glass along with his lips.

I nodded to Davis, giving him the go-ahead.

And then I clenched his hand while he told the most horrific of stories I'd shared with him, what Ruth had said on the phone. Other things I'd talked about since that morning of her phone call. The beatings. The strictness. How overwhelming all of this was for Ruth and why.

Christian's face was bright red with fury. He held up a hand, halting Davis in the middle of a story where Ruth had told us yesterday morning about how dad had locked her in the shed for twenty-four hours, only water and bread, because she hadn't had lunch made on time for the younger kids which had made them whiny and difficult.

"Stop. Right now." He grabbed his phone, stabbed the screen so forcefully it was a wonder it didn't shatter in his grip, and put it to his ear. "Michael? Yes. Not good. I've just learned information I need you to know." He went on to tell him my father's name, the church, the connection to the television show, and my uncle's name.

I was almost impressed with how much he remembered without having to ask for any clarifying questions but was stunned.

What was he doing? And who was Michael?

"I want a goddamn report on my desk by Monday with all the details of everything. I don't care how it needs to happen, but this asshole is going to be stopped, and I'm going to enjoy throwing him in prison where he belongs."

Oh god.

"Davis," I rasped and squeezed his hand. I was shaking.

"He's right." He pressed his lips to my temple. "He's right, and Christian can get this taken care of faster than we can. Your siblings deserve to be safe, and he can make that happen."

I knew that. Obviously I wanted that and was determined to do it.

But…

"My mom. And the kids… what will happen?"

"We'll be prepared for anything. But this is what family does, Maggie. A real family who loves each other. You're family to him, a daughter, and right now, I'm guessing he's raging at the very idea of anyone touching Belle like that. How horrific a man needs to be to do such things, and he's reacting the way a decent man does. Let him help you. Let him help save Ruth."

"Monday, Michael, I want this shit taken care of, and I want it done now."

He tore the phone away from his ear, stabbed a button, and with eyes blown black with anger, Christian took a large chug of his drink. If the burn of alcohol affected him, he didn't show it.

"I am so very sorry you've had to live like that," he finally said, chest heaving but voice calm and tender. "That should never happen. I will fix this for all of you."

I shoved my face into Davis's shoulder and cried.

How could I have gone so long with ignoring what was probably happening and not asking for help when I knew it was so desperately needed?

It was happening now, though.

That had to be good enough.

CHAPTER 34
MAGGIE

The days flew by. After our dinner with Christian and Scarlett, Davis and I returned home, talked through everything that was happening, and made some decisions.

My first decision was to call Madison and quit my job.

Between Ruth, the drama I knew would be coming with my family, the pregnancy, and the possibility of me singing, Davis convinced me to let him take care of me so I could have the energy to fight for everything good.

She was upset but understanding, and since she hadn't done the next week's schedule, I finished out the weekend, working Friday through Sunday and then turned in my apron and name tag.

She'd given me a hug, made me promise to keep her updated on my baby's arrival and told me to call her to grab lunch sometime.

Funny how it hadn't hit me that my boss had actually liked me, that Will and Elsie and several of the other servers were sad to see me go. They were upset about missing me, but not about being short-staffed. I hadn't realized how closed off I'd been to people until Elsie threw her arms around me, hugged me, and told me she'd miss me.

Davis was right. I hadn't been alone, I'd chosen to be to protect myself, but he barreled into my life and ensured that would never happen again.

I wasn't complaining.

The last week was spent mostly with Ruth. I took her to a few baby stores, and we *oohed* and *ahhed* over all the tiny little, store-bought baby clothes we'd never had, and we went shopping for some maternity clothes. I convinced Ruth to upgrade her home-made clothing to some store-bought skirts and even dresses that still allowed her to be modest and comfortable, but definitely started showing off her figure, which was taller and leaner than mine. A breakthrough, small as it was, came through the day she asked me to put makeup on her, not a lot. Some blush and mascara to start with. I straightened her hair and gave it a little trim. Halfway through, she told me to take more off, so her hair was still long, well past her shoulders. However, we looked it up online, found out how to donate the length we were cutting, and she was thrilled she could help have her hair go to an organization that made wigs for children going through chemo.

Now, every morning, before she came down for breakfast, she was wearing a light covering of blush and mascara and her smiles seemed to come easier and more frequent.

Christian called me Monday morning, first thing, to tell me it was going to take longer to find information on my uncle and father. He had someone talking to the show's producer, demanding footage that hadn't aired to see if the production company knew and hid any of the abuse happening. It would take more time, and I was anxious every day, but for Ruth, who we'd only shared neces-sities with, I kept it to myself.

Someday, when we know more, I'd share everything.

By the following Wednesday, I had driven Ruth so crazy with my need to be busy since I wasn't working and Davis was at prac-tice every day, she told me if I didn't call Mr. Connelly and accept the help for singing, she was going to call him herself.

"If I have to hear you singing one more song while you grocery shop or standing stupid in the kitchen or walk outside, I'm going to scream at you for wasting this talent."

She'd stopped me in my tracks mid-chorus to "These Boots Were Made for Walkin'" by Nancy Sinatra and hit me with a real-ization without saying anything else.

If I wanted to prove to my family and my siblings I could live my life without their church and their rules, I needed to start living by mine and chasing my dreams. What kind of example was I setting otherwise?

"Fine," I'd told her and then texted Christian to get Brianna's number.

The next day, we were sitting down for lunch at WWMP, and she was showing me a plan she'd already drafted along with a contract. She then took me into one of the recording studios to have me sing some of my songs to get a feel for my range and my voice.

In three days, I was going to make my debut on stage, not at an open mic night, but as a paid singer at Miranda Lambert's restaurant on Broadway, *Casa Rosa.*

My opening song was going to be one of hers, one of my favorites from an older album, *Little Red Wagon.*

I'd been practicing and singing the set list ever since my meeting with Brianna, who worked with me to sing songs I already knew and loved, and more than once mid-song, if Ruth was otherwise occupied in her room, Davis hadn't missed the opportunity to whisk me to our bedroom and show me how talented he thought I was, by proving his own multifaceted talents with his hands, his tongue, and his dick.

In the last two weeks, my life had been entirely upended in ways almost as drastic as learning I was having a baby.

On a good day, I was a frazzled, anxious mess even when everyone around me told me to relax.

Today, I was a mess of nerves for an entirely different reason.

Davis and the rest of his team were warming up on the field. Hosting Raleigh, who won their first playoff game. Today's game was going to be an absolute nail-biter and since I'd convinced Ruth to join me, I didn't have Kate and Dave and Eden and Jasper to keep me company.

We were sitting on the twenty-yard line behind the team's bench, ten rows up in seats Davis got for us.

My heart was in my throat.

My palms were clammy.

My pulse was racing.

And down on that field, every time I caught a glimpse of Davis, the jerk had the absolute nerve to appear as calm and unfrazzled as always.

CHAPTER 35
DAVIS

Dawson tore off his helmet chin straps, ripped off his helmet and sent it flying straight into his locker.

Cole was pacing the length of the locker room and back, and our defensive ends were huddled in a corner of the locker room. Fingers were being pointed.

Cussing was at an all-time high and our frustration levels were off the charts.

Raleigh was winning by ten points at the half in a game we should have been kicking ass in, but we were making mistakes.

I didn't want to ask Dawson what was up his ass. He'd missed two routes he had memorized. Wasn't getting open, and that was only with single coverage. He was playing like half of him showed up, and it was the half of him that wasn't talented in football and hadn't been the number three tight end in the league at the start of the season.

For my own, I'd barely been able to get more than two yards a carry. We knew their defensive line would be tough to crack, but I'd spent hours watching their game films. I knew their holes like the back of my hand, but our timing had been off.

The door slammed closed behind us, and our coach walked in, hands on his hips, lips pressed into a thin line. He yanked off his hat, swiped his forehead and resettled it before shoving his hands back to his hips and meeting the eyes of every single player who turned silent at his entrance.

Even Dawson went and grabbed his helmet from his locker and held it at his side.

Coach Paul Bowles was a man who I'd always admired, mostly for the character that made him decent and aboveboard. He rarely cussed, didn't have to to get his point across, and believed in motivating and encouraging over disparaging and criticizing. It worked for him. For us, because it made us feel more like a team, like his sons and brothers and family versus a means to a paycheck like other coaches in the league who honored records over growth.

I would lay down my life for this man.

Right then, I could practically see the cartoon thought bubble over his head, filled with four-letter words and symbols, cussing each and every one of us out.

"Does anyone have anything to say for themselves?" he asked, gaze scanning the room again.

I dropped my head and shook it. Disappointing him was like disappointing my own father.

"Would the defense like to explain to me how you let their second-string wide receiver score a touchdown on a forty-yard pass?"

Oh, this was bad. The questions he asked forced guilt into our chests and the pain of remembering our mistakes.

"Would the offense like to tell me why you haven't been able to push Hall through the line for more than two yards at a time and can't open a hole to save your life?"

Another round of grumbled *"no sirs"* continued to follow as he questioned each and every one of our mistakes.

"Would someone then, please explain to me, how we can be the best damn team in the league, with the closest teammates, and the love we have for each other and the respect for the game and be out there, playing in one of the biggest games of your lives and acting like it's your first time ever suiting up in pads?"

Bowles yanked off his hat again and slapped it against his thighs before sending it sailing across the room like a frisbee.

"What in the heck is going on with you men? You're better than this! You're faster than them. You're more prepared, I guarantee. You want it more, that I have no doubt. You're experienced. You're deadly. You haven't shown this amount of disarray and lack of focus at any point in time I've coached any of you. So what is it? Nerves? The pressure? You caving to that, Dawson?"

Butler practically growled at him. "No, sir."

"You?" he asked, turning to Yeets and as everyone responded with a required *no sir*, that he asked a handful of men randomly spaced throughout the room, the tension in the room mounted.

Changed.

Switched to something altogether warmer and more determined.

We weren't caving to the pressure. We weren't playing as well as we could. We all knew we could do better, and listening to Bowle's voice, filled with disappointment, was exactly the motivating factor we needed.

Not a single one of us wanted to disappoint him.

"I have some news to share with you." At one, the already quiet room turned silent. He took off his ballcap, swiped his forehead and resettled it before he pulled his gaze from his shoes and met ours. "I've been debating when to share this information, but I'm hoping now is the right time."

He swallowed thickly, wiped his hand over his face and then turned to the assistant coaches fanned out around him.

"I've spoken with management and while this breaks my heart to tell you, win or lose this game or win or lose the Super Bowl, the last game we play this year will be my last game being the head coach of this team."

"What?" Dawson all but shouted. "You're lying." He wasn't the only one who was shocked.

My own blood turned cold. I'd wanted to come to this team primarily because of the environment Bowles created. In the last five years, he'd taken a mid-range team to being a Super Bowl contender.

"I'm not, and trust me, I'm as sad and upset as the rest of you, but for me, it's time. I'll give you all a few minutes to process this alone, and I won't answer more questions, but what I'm asking is for you to think of this in the next ten minutes before we get that ball in our possession again. This is *not* the kind of game I want to go out on. This is not the kind of playing I want as the memory of my final game. I want to go out winners, confetti falling on us and holding a trophy and waving it around at a parade next month. That's what I want for me, selfishly, but I want it for all of us, together. I have a team of men, of brothers in this room with the talent to get this done. All you have to figure out is if you want that, too."

He met each of our gazes, nodded, and then turned, taking the coaching staff with him.

"Well, fuck," Cole said, and like the captain he was, of course he'd step up into the center. "My timing has been slow, and I've missed a few bad passes, undershot you, Butler, more than once, and overthrown to Yeets. I don't know what's going on with us, but Coach is right. We will not go out like this, at home, with *our* fans in the stands cheering us on and knowing what we're capable of. Will we?"

"Hell no!" The shout came from Knox, our defensive end. Big as a bear and built like a steel wall, he might have been the only one doing his job correctly.

"I slipped on my last kick. Made it, but it wasn't pretty. That won't happen again." That was Moore, nodding once to Cole.

"I'll make my own goddamn holes in the line if I have to," I promised every single one of them.

The locker room filled with men acknowledging their mistakes in that first half, and their determination to improve.

All but Dawson, who still looked ready to charge after Coach and demand answers.

"Hey." I nudged him, earning a feral growl for the effort. "Whatever's going on, you have to kick it to the curb right now."

It was Crystal. Had to be. His sister's drama or any mention of his mother could send him into a rage it could take weeks to bring him back from. Usually it was a benefit to us on the field because he'd take it and play like an animal.

Sometimes, like I suspected today, it was having the reverse effect.

His nostrils flared. "I'll do my part."

"Good."

He was barely six years older than me and had treated me like a baby brother all season. I'd come to hate him calling me kid or telling me I'd understand things when I was older, but now, I'd kill for that treatment. Instead, all I got was his back, stained with paint from a few sliding tackles he'd taken, and an attitude rolling off him.

"Need to punch me? Or throw me in the ice bath?" One of our tackles, Charles Carr, had done that to me earlier in the season. It'd seemed to make Dawson laugh then. Wouldn't be good for me to be tossed in during halftime, but it couldn't make things worse.

Dawson glared at me, then huffed and finally the hint of a grin broke loose on his hard lines. "Maybe later, kid."

And all was right with the world.

———

Third and ten. We had the ball at kick off and our returner ran it to Raleigh's forty-yard line. It put us in contention for a field goal, which was good but not what we needed to get the crowd all on their feet and at our backs, helping us win this. Since then, we hadn't been able to move the ball an inch. A run for zero yards from me, an incomplete pass to Yeets, and the third quarter was starting to feel an awful lot like the first half.

We would *not* go out like this. That determination had been decided in the locker room and we'd left pumped, as one team. When we met Coach in the tunnel to take the field again, he'd been smiling at all of us, cheering us on and slapping shoulder pads and helmets as we ran past him.

"Hall," Cole barked my name. "To you. They won't be expecting it. The rest of you make whatever goddamn holes you need to do for him, but I swear to any of you, you get a holding call on your ass, and I'm kicking it after this game. On one!"

He gave us no time to laugh and no time to argue with him as we lined up in one of least used, but incredibly effective players where he'd fake the pass and hand it off to me as I ran straight through the other team's center line.

It'd work if it didn't get me landing on my ass five yards back.

He hiked the ball, I ran, grabbed the leather in my hands, and I turned up the field in two strides. And there it was. The small opening I needed. I ducked, barreled through it, and forced my weight into the defensive tackle, shoving at his hip. It slowed me down for a moment, and then I stumbled, my foot slipping. I set a hand to the turf, tucked the ball in tight to me in case I went down, and then found my footing.

I was free of the hole, and there were men coming at me from every direction but like Cole had demanded, they were stopped. Pushed off course and shoved out of the way and the only thing suddenly between me and the end zones was nothing but green turf and white paint.

Thirty yards. Twenty. The speed of their safety was coming at me from an angle, so I turned it up, ran faster and closer to the side-lines in case he reached me.

Ten.

He dove for me, missed my heel by inches, and then I was in the end zone, collapsing to my knees before jumping to my feet.

Dawson reached me first, jumping all over me.

"Way to fucking go, kid!"

Cole grabbed me next, fisted my pads at my chest, and shook me back and forth. "This is how we fucking win this game!"

I tossed the ball to the ref as we ran to the sidelines so our special teams could kick the field goal.

Down by three with plenty of time left in the game.

As long as our defense got their act together, we had this.

Thirty to twenty-three.

Our defense kicked ass. Held Raleigh to a field goal in the second half and while we didn't take control like we hoped, a win was a win. Given our ugly start, I was pretty damn thrilled with the twenty points we managed to score in the second half.

Could have been much, much worse.

As soon as Cole and I showered, we were hauled off to speak to the press with Coach, which meant celebrating would have to wait. By the time we returned to the locker room, most of the guys had headed out.

Our locker room was a disaster zone with towels, water bottles, and jerseys thrown all over the place. We were animals, but we were currently happy animals.

"Great second half," I said to Cole. "Almost can't believe we pulled that win out."

"I can't believe Coach is leaving."

I grabbed my wallet and shoved it into my pants pocket. "You really think he will? I mean, if we lose, don't you think he'll want one more year? And if we win, yeah, maybe, but I don't know. I don't see it."

"So what, you think Coach lied to motivate us?"

"Worked, didn't it?"

Cole huffed and grabbed his bag, slung it over his shoulder. "I'll believe that when I see it. He'd do a lot, but risk us giving up? Seems like a risky move."

I didn't want to think Coach would play us like that. I also couldn't imagine being coached by a man I respected more. One thing was for certain, if this was his last year, he'd ensured we'd give it everything we had. Blood, guts, and all.

"You're probably right."

"Sucks to lose him, though," Cole said and pushed open the locker room door.

I was immediately greeted with a sight that squeezed my chest in the best ways.

Maggie was there, laughing with Ruth as they stood together and talking with Eden. Jasper was next to them, back against the wall, looking like any surly, tired child his age.

At the sight of them, Maggie turned that dazzling smile on me.

"You won!"

"We did."

I grabbed her, kissed her like her sister wasn't there staring at us and held her to me.

This was all the congratulations I needed.

CHAPTER 36
MAGGIE

They won. I spent most of the game trying to explain what I knew of it to Ruth. Admittedly, it wasn't a lot. I really need to talk to Davis more about it. Outside the basics Lance taught us that night, I hadn't really bothered to ask, and what a crappy partner that made me.

At the end of the first half, Ruth had asked, "That's bad, right?"

Yeah. It'd been pretty bad. Even I, a novice and pretty ignorant in the knowledge of any ball game, could acknowledge that, but whatever happened during halftime brought the team back to the field and fired up. It showed in every play, and it felt like the crowd knew it because they spent the second half on their feet. I joined them.

Ruth followed, and when Davis ran the ball thirty yards down the field in the fourth quarter, being tackled before he could score, she was on her feet, squeezing my hand and cheering just as loud as the rest of the stadium.

"This is exciting!"

"I know, right?" I bumped my shoulder into hers, and for the first time, we were kids, laughing and chasing each other around the acres of our land, having fun without all the worries and fears and drama getting between us.

By the time the game ended, Ruth had laughed and screamed

and cheered and been more vocal about the game than I'd heard her be in the last two weeks.

By the time we were in the tunnel, waiting for Davis, it was me who was standing back while she talked to Eden and bent down and spent time getting to know Jasper. That hadn't surprised me. My guess, she was feeling pretty useless without a handful of children to help take care of. The way her eyes lit up when Jasper was equally talkative with her back proved it.

Happiness filled me as I took in the peace on Ruth's face and I was still filled with it as the door to the locker room finally opened, and Davis followed Cole out the door.

I was in his arms in a blink, his mouth seared to mine and his tongue diving inside.

I didn't stop to think about what Ruth would think.

I didn't hesitate.

He'd played an incredible game, and I was more than thrilled to show him exactly how proud I was of him.

"We'll continue this later," I whispered in his ear before he set me back on my feet.

His smile was wicked. "Damn straight. What'd you think of your first game, Ruth?"

If I hadn't been watching her so closely, I would have missed the blush on her cheek. "Oh. It was fun. Loud? Exciting though. Good job."

His returning smile was sincere. God, he was incredible. So sweet to her. He would only ever be kind like this. "Loud and fun sounds like fun to me. How about I get my girls home?"

Ruth blushed again. My grin was so wide it nearly split my face.

Oh yes. I was definitely showing Davis my appreciation sooner rather than later.

———

"Please. More, Davis." My fingers dug into his scalp as his mouth and tongue did wicked things to my body.

He threw me on the bed, slammed the door, and turned on music before he tugged down my jeans, muttered something about needing to get me a real jersey to wear, and then buried his face between my legs.

Heat was building, throbbing, zings of arousal zipping down my spine to my toes.

He shoved two fingers inside of me, and I was done. I clawed at the sheets beneath me with one hand and bit down on my lips, curled toes into the sheets and cried out as my orgasm barreled down on me. It rolled through, spinning me with unending pleasure while Davis worked me through it.

Davis pressed soft kisses to the apex of my thighs, my inner thighs as he climbed up my body to my stomach, my breasts, laving both with his mouth and flicks of his tongue until my overly sensitive body ached with the pain of his attention.

"You're an animal," I whispered, cupping his cheek.

His eyes were blown black with desire and seeing that rapturous look on his face forced me to say the one thing that'd been growing in me, only fear keeping it choked down.

"Davis."

"What is it, Maggie? Mother of my child." His hand went to my lower stomach. Over the last week, I'd started to swell. Not all day, but as it progressed and more so at night.

Thankfully I'd bought the clothes, but I was still mostly wearing leggings and sweats, so I was comfortable.

Davis had taken to pressing his palm there every day for a few minutes, brushes along my swollen abdomen as he passed me in the kitchen.

Him doing so quelled the last ounce of fear I held.

"I think… I think I might love you."

His eyes closed, and he pushed up so his forehead rested against mine. "Say it again without the might or the think."

I laughed against his throat and inhaled the delicious scent of his sweat and body wash. Something cheap, like Old Spice he kept in the locker at the arena. His simplicity made me feel the way I did even more. He was just as likely to order everyday clothes on Amazon as he was to purchase them from Neiman Marcus. He loved Lou's po'boys, but the couple of rare times he took me out, it was to upscale restaurants.

He was a man who enjoyed the simple things in life he was born and bred from while he didn't hesitate to enjoy the pleasures of the blessings he'd earned.

Yes. My risk had turned into a winning hand.

"I love you, Davis. So much. Thank you… for being you."

"It is easy to do all I do for the woman I love," he replied and sealed away my gasp of surprise with a kiss, his tongue diving inside.

My hands went to his hips to still him, to continue talking, but in truth, there was nothing left to be said.

We loved each other, so we said it with actions and not words.

And the actions Davis used the rest of the night proved every word he said true.

———

Peeking out from behind the wall, my nerves tied a knot in my stomach. I jumped back before anyone could see me even though I was well hidden.

"Are you okay?" Ruth asked.

"There are more people here than I expected."

"Really? That's good, isn't it?"

It *was*. In theory. In reality, I wasn't sure I'd be able to take that stage.

Brianna came around the back hall, dressed in black cowgirl boots and short white shorts, and a gray and white flannel tied in a knot at her waist. Her jewelry was wooden and clunky and she had matching earrings dangling from her ears, partially hidden behind her thick head of wavy, copper hair. Belle was at her side, dressed in ivory, wide-leg pants, and a tan crop top tank. She had on matching ivory heels. Gorgeous as always, my best friend came right to me and smothered me with a hug.

"You doing okay?"

Brianna took one look at my face and flinched. "Do I need to grab a puke bucket?"

I hadn't needed one until she said it. "Maybe."

She grinned wider. Next to me, Ruth giggled.

"You've got this, sister. Pretend you're at church or at those bars you sing at."

"This isn't karaoke, Ruth."

"It sort of is," Brianna cut in. "You're doing songs you know, covers you'd sing anyway. You can do this, absolutely, but is there anything you need from me before you go on stage?"

"Davis. Where is he?" I hadn't seen him since he drove me here.

I'd been swept into a room where Brianna made sure I was plucked and tweezed. She'd dressed me in an emerald-colored dress that had rouching at the waist and flared at the hips. It hid my belly while allowing me to breathe easy. The neckline was low, and my ever-growing breasts were shoved together, almost bursting from the top half. Every nervous, ragged breath I inhaled pushed them against the seams so much so Brianna had insisted on using double-sided tape to ensure they didn't make their own appearance and turn my show into a different kind of one.

She'd tried to shove me into tan boots that were similar to her black ones, but I'd put my foot down at being able to wear my own shoes, ones I'd already broken in and were comfortable.

"I'm here," he called from behind Brianna and made his appearance in worn denim jeans and a skintight light-blue shirt. It showed off his biceps and clung to him like a second skin, and like every time I saw him, my body reacted like his hands were already doing wicked things to my body.

"Where were you?"

"Guys are here. I was out front having a drink with them."

"Guys?"

"Dawson and Cole. Eden. Mason and Sam and Charles Carr. More are coming."

"Good grief. Why?"

He rolled his eyes at me like I was the ridiculous one. "Because it's my girl's debut on stage, and my brothers will always support those closest to us."

My heart fluttered, and I reached for him, cupping his cheeks and pulling him down while I lifted to my toes to kiss him.

"Thank you. Thank you for everything. Thank you for loving me so well."

The words came so easy now.

"Love you, too. Now go knock them dead. And if you're nervous, find me. Sing only to me, sweetheart. Okay?"

"I will." I would always sing only for him.

"Good. We'll see you out there." He escorted Ruth away and winked at me over his shoulder before he disappeared.

"I'm going to be out front, okay?" Belle's hands did a calming sweep up my arm, but it wasn't my arms that were freaking out. It was my insides. My guts had never been twisted so tight. "Just like always. And you have Ruth and Davis there, too. Sing to us, but like Brianna and Davis said, you're going to kill this. Got it?"

"Got it." I'd try, at the very least.

The band Brianna had set up for me showed up, guitars slung over their shoulders and drumsticks in my female drummer's hands. She spun them in a fancy circle and the colorful tattoos running up and down her arms danced with her movements.

"Ready to rock this, beautiful?"

"I'm closer to throwing up," I admitted.

Stella threw her head back and laughed. "Nah. You won't. As soon as that first chord is played, you'll own that stage."

"How do you know that?"

"Because I've been doing this for a decade, and Brianna's the best. We've practiced. I've seen your confidence. You've had it all week, so it might be hiding for a moment, but it'll be back."

She swept off onto the stage, long blonde hair flowing in a straight sheet at her back as she took her seated place and double-checked the height of her drum kit.

"You ready?" I asked Carter. He was my lead guitarist.

Amazing how Brianna could throw a band together for me, and everyone had been so kind. We'd played together like we'd been doing it for years and had from the very first song. Sure, it helped that they were all songs everyone would know, but our personalities had meshed together as well. Stella was outgoing and bright and sassy. Dayne, the electric guitarist, was a quintessential rocker with tatted arms and long hair and facial piercings. Halfway through practice, his shirt was usually tossed somewhere, and I had no doubt it'd end up somewhere in the crowd by the time my set was done. My bassist, Joshua, who insisted on Joshua not Josh, was quieter, focused, and talented.

And then there was Carter. He could have been a brother to me for as well as we instantly clicked. He seemed to understand me on a deeper level. Knew how badly I wanted this and let it be known his job was to help make me shine, not take the spotlight.

"Always ready, Maggie. You?"

I glanced at the rest of the band, doing quick final sound checks and tuning their guitars.

Davis, Belle, and Ruth were out there. Friends I'd only recently met and already cared deeply for.

This was my chance. My opportunity.

I settled a hand to my stomach, glanced down at the bulge there, and nodded.

I was ready—to make my own dreams come true to prove to my siblings they could do it, to make the best life possible for my child, and most of all, to be my own best self so I could be the best partner to Davis.

"Let's do this."

CHAPTER 37
DAVIS

Holy freaking hot damn in a basket. My mouth was dry, my gut tight, and my dick? Well, he was all sorts of confused about what he should be feeling right then. He was absolutely not enjoying being confined behind the tight denim and zipper of my jeans, that was for certain. I'd been semi-hard since Maggie took the stage.

She was halfway through her set and absolutely killing it. The bar was packed, grew packed the longer she stood on that stage and sang her heart out, as if people walking by had been drawn to the sound of her voice as it filtered through the doors. My team-mates had come to make sure there was a crowd, but two songs in, I was pretty sure they were all ready to shove a knife in my back to get me out of the picture. Mason couldn't shut up about how hot she looked, how lucky I was.

And if Carr licked his lips one more time while Maggie swished her hips back and forth, he'd end up with my fist in his face. Ruth hadn't left my side, and while she'd looked terrified at the crowd and uncomfortable in her surroundings, at a bar with alcohol being freely drunk in excess around her, she was now clapping right along with everyone else, singing the choruses to songs she knew.

Goddamn, I was so damn proud of Maggie. My heart swelled every time she nailed a note she'd been worried about, but she'd never needed to worry. She was absolutely mesmerizing. She was so pure, so energetic, and the beams of light bursting from her eyes captivated every person who listened to her.

"You have found yourself a babe!" Mason threw his arm over my shoulders and yanked me against him.

"Don't call my girl a babe." I shoved him off me, only to have him laugh and shake it off.

Moving to Ruth, he held out a hand. "What do you say, Ruth? Want to dance with me?"

Her eyes went round and turned to me, back to Mason. "Um."

"I'll be a gentleman. Promise."

Yeets was no damn gentleman, but it wasn't like half the team hadn't heard and learned of Ruth and Maggie's past in the last couple of weeks.

"Can I?" she asked me.

And goddamn, I really wanted to shove my fist into her father's face, more so than Carr's. What a fucking asshole he was. I understood strict religious rules. I understood biblical principles, but the more I learned about Ruth's upbringing, the more I believed her family's church wasn't a church family, it was some goddamn strange cult.

I couldn't wait until Christian Connelly's lawyers and investigators found all the dirt on them and took them down.

"You can do anything you want, Ruth. A little dancing is okay, I think. As long as Mason keeps his distance?"

"I'm going to teach her some two-steppin', calm down, *dad*."

"You two-step?"

"Learned in middle school PE class. I was the best, obviously."

This idiot. "Obviously."

I turned back to Ruth. "You don't need my permission. Whatever you're comfortable with."

She slipped her hand into Mason's in almost slow motion. "I think I'd like to learn?"

"Then we'll do that." He held her hand and moved closer to the stage, backed up, shoving the crowd back around him. He bent in, whisper-yelled something in Ruth's ear.

I stayed focused on them, the way he guided her hand into his.

The way he formed her arms into squares and then the way he kept a full arm's length of space between them.

Maggie noticed, and her gaze fell down to her sister with surprise as she sang the chorus to "Any Man of Mine" by Shania Twain and then broke out into a wide grin.

Mesmerizing. The next time I slid deep inside of her, I wanted her wearing that grin and that dress.

Movement and clatter came from behind me, and I was jostled forward. Stumbling, I threw my arms out and hit the people in front of me. I curled my hands around them, pulled them back as they gaped at me over my shoulders.

"Sorry. Sorry. My bad." I turned. What the fuck had happened?

It was mayhem behind me, pure chaos, and I caught sight of Dawson, shoving his way through the horde of people on his way to the bar to our right.

Oh shit. I grabbed Carr. "Come on!"

"What?"

"Dawson!" I shouted and pointed in his direction, and of course…

Of fucking course. Crystal was at the bar, and before Dawson reached her, she threw a glass of whatever she was drinking at some guy standing by her, who already had his hands out, palms facing her like he was backing down.

"Fuck. Butler," Carr groaned, and we joined the rest of our teammates, shoving men and women out of the way to get to him.

Dawson was a lunatic when it came to his sister. And Crystal was the ringleader of completely shitty and narcissistic behavior.

By the time we reached him, Dawson had the man's shirt gripped in his fist and he was screaming at him.

"What'd you do to her?"

"Nothin', man. Back off. I didn't do anything!"

"Bullshit."

Crystal was smirking. That freaking bitch.

Dawson swiveled and pinned her with eyes blown black with anger. "What'd he do?"

"I offered to get her a drink, and she lost her shit!" the guy yelled.

Crystal's smirk vanished in a blink, and she shook her head. "I told him no thank you, and he didn't listen, Dawson."

"The fuck I did!" the guy screamed. "You lying bitch! I asked, and the next thing I knew, you were fucking slapping me."

"Dawson!" I called out his name as I got closer and settled my hand on his shoulder that had the guy's shirt in his fist. "Let him go before you get kicked out."

"No one treats my sister like shit, especially not this bachelor-partying wannabe playboy."

He did have the guy tagged pretty damn close. Looked like he'd just stepped off a golf course before coming in.

"Fuck you," the guy said. "I didn't do shit, but if she's your sister, she's batshit crazy."

Around us, phones were out, cameras already recording. If this guy antagonized Dawson further, it'd get attention for sure. As of now, he looked like a bull ready to rage.

"Carr. Pull him off."

He stepped around me, grabbed Dawson from behind, wrapping his massive arms around Dawson, and yanked. The guy came with, slipping on his feet and his face slammed right into the corner of the wooden barstool.

"What the fuck!?" Another guy pulled him back, and blood gushed from the guy's forehead. "You're all fucking dead! All of you! What the hell is wrong with all of you? He didn't do anything. That fucking cunt started it!"

"She's not a goddamn cunt!" Dawson shouted, kicked his feet, and struggled in Carr's hold.

The blood and the screaming had finally got the attention of security, and they stepped in between them.

"Fucking hell," one of them muttered and brought his mouthpiece closer to him. "Call the cops. Maybe an ambulance."

The security went to haul Dawson out of Carr's hold, but he stopped them. "Let me," Carr told them. "I've got him."

Considering Carr was two times the size of any of the beefy security guards that showed, they allowed it, and soon, Carr was outside, in front of the glass windows. Dawson was still seething as

Carr released him, and he was slammed chest first into the window. The guards surrounded him, and hot damn fucking shit.

This was going to be bad.

So very bad.

I turned to check on Maggie and caught sight of Crystal, still sitting on her stool, sipping a fresh drink. "What in the hell is wrong with you?"

"What?" That goddamn smirk appeared. "My brother loves me. He'd do anything for me."

"That asshole was right. You are a fucking cunt."

It was words I'd never said, could never imagine myself saying to a woman. Crystal was no woman.

She was a viper in Louis Vuitton clothing... paid for by one of my best friends now being questioned by police with an ambulance pulling up.

What a fucking mess of a night this was going to be.

———

"Get outside!" I grabbed Mason off Ruth. Out front was mayhem, absolute madness, and before I left the front of the bar, someone had yelled, "Hey, that's Dawson Butler!"

It brought even more attention and *shit shit shit*. Coach was going to be pissed.

"What's going on?"

At least the drama and madness hadn't extended to the full bar yet. A miracle considering the bar wasn't that large.

"Dawson's outside, maybe getting arrested. Need you to go calm him down." Half the team was already out there, and I needed to find Cole and Eden. They'd be able to help more than anyone.

"What is it?" Ruth yelled.

"Nothing to worry about, but I want to get you backstage, okay?"

I'd let the guys handle this. My job was to protect Maggie and Ruth.

"Davis."

"Not now, Ruth. Yeets, you going?" He gave a sad look to Maggie and then winked at her.

"See you later, darlin'. Yeah, I'm outta here."

"Come on, Ruth."

"What happened?"

I didn't answer until we were around the corner, Maggie's beautiful and strong lyrical voice in the middle of "Before He Cheats" that had every woman in the club screaming along with her.

Talented. So damn talented. Thank God I'd taken her to sing that night.

This was going to change her life. Ours. Hopefully all for the better.

"One of my teammates got in a fight," I told Ruth as soon as we were granted access through the door leading to backstage. "I have no idea what's going to happen, so I wanted us back here."

"A fight? Why?"

Because sometimes blood family could be the most toxic of all. I couldn't tell Ruth that.

"Not exactly sure." No doubt Crystal had started it though.

That guy hadn't been lying. When men were rejected by women, they typically turned it around on them, said she wanted it, or asked for it, or whatever other bullshit they came up with. That guy hadn't touched her, and I believed him.

Crystal left a disastrous mess in her wake every time she came to stay with Dawson, left with a half-million dollars once he got tired of her shit, and then returned when she blew through the cash.

She was a waste of space, and I didn't doubt for a second half of those funds went to their mom, who Dawson refused to have anything to do with.

We stayed backstage until Maggie was done. My phone was blowing up with updates of Dawson, who was getting a courtesy backseat trip to Nashville's closest police department. I turned off my ringer once Cole told me that and didn't look at it again.

I would not allow this to ruin my excitement for Maggie.

She jogged off the stage and threw her arms around me. I

grabbed her ass and picked her up, swinging her around in a circle. "I did it! I really did it!"

"You killed it," Brianna said. "Absolutely wonderful. Everything okay out front?" she asked me.

"Drama. It's all good." It wasn't. Not even close.

"What drama?"

"Someone got in a fight!" Ruth said, and was she happy about that? "I think with like fists and everything?"

"What?" Maggie gasped. "Who? Why?"

"Dawson," I admitted and set her on her feet. "But we'll talk about that later. You were incredible up there, Maggie. So damn beautiful and sexy. Everyone out there absolutely *loved* you and the bar was packed. They came in off the streets like you'd hypnotized them."

"Stop." She blushed and smacked my chest.

"I'm not lying. You didn't see the crowd?"

"I was too afraid to glance past the first few rows of people."

At least that kept her from seeing Dawson basically shove a guy's face into the bar. Nasty shit. That'd take a hot minute to scrub from my brain.

"Oh my gosh!" Belle rushed her and threw her arms around her. "Amazing! My dad is going to be so pissed, again, at me for not bringing you to him sooner! Love you girl, Lance and I are getting a drink. Need anything from me?"

Maggie shook her head, laughing at her friend. "I'm good."

"Damn straight you are. You *rocked* this entire place tonight." Belle gave her cheek kisses another squeeze and before I could get my hands back on her, Stella was there.

"Hey. Awesome work, babe!" Stella hugged Maggie, squeezed her so hard Maggie choked. "Proud of you. Told you you could do this. Just say I'm right."

"You're right, Stella," Joshua drawled as he stepped past.

"Awesome set," he said. "Happy to play with you anytime you need it."

He tugged his bass guitar over his head and moved straight back toward the band's room.

We stayed while she chatted with the rest of the band, Stella declaring she needed a drink before she took off, so she headed to the bar, tucking her drumsticks into the back of her cutoff denim shorts.

Once Maggie and Ruth and I were alone again, I slipped my hands to the sides of her neck and kissed her. "You were a sight to behold."

"I don't remember a single second of it. I was so scared. What'd you think?"

"I was pretty proud of my sister," Ruth said. "And that Mason boy taught me how to dance."

"He did! I saw that. Did you have fun? He looked like a good teacher."

Ruth shuffled on her feet and blushed to the tips of her ears. "He was. Very nice."

"Cute, too, huh?"

"Maggie," I warned her.

Mason Yeets was probably the biggest playboy on our team. Action followed him night after night. He was not the guy to help Ruth get a crush on.

"What? He is."

"I don't know," Ruth said. "But I did have fun with him."

"Good." Maggie squeezed her. "I'm glad. Let's go get some water in me, help me change out of this dress and then we'll head home. Where you, Davis, will tell me absolutely everything that happened."

Hell, by the time we got home, she could probably watch it trending on TikTok.

CHAPTER 38
MAGGIE

I couldn't believe what Davis told me. I couldn't believe I'd missed it all.

I was still living on the high of coming off that stage, the thrill of people singing along with me and the extreme excitement the band and Brianna and Belle showered on me afterward, I was having a hard time imagining everything Davis told me happened.

Stepping out of the bathroom after a quick shower, my face was clean of my makeup, and my hair was wrapped in a towel. My bones were tired and my body felt like I could either crash for two days or run a half-marathon. It was such a different feeling than I had experienced after singing at church or karaoke, but hell, the entire night had been so different.

Never had I stood in front of a crowd of people, singing other people's songs while they danced and jumped and screamed along with me.

What would it be like if it was my *own* music?

Davis had stayed in the living room, checking his phone while I hauled off for a shower after he finished telling me about Dawson's arrest. We had so much more to discuss, so I tugged on a pair of sweat shorts, grabbed one of his T-shirts from his freshly folded laundry on his dresser and tugged it on. My hair could stay in the towel until it dried more.

I found him in the kitchen, gripping both handles of the refrigerator in his hands and staring but seeing absolutely nothing inside.

I pressed my hands between his shoulders. "You okay?"

The doors slammed close. "I'm pissed at Dawson for acting like this at this point in the year. I'm more pissed off at his sister and how she continues to get under his skin. I'm worried as hell this will be suspensions and we cannot lose him right now, and I'm so damn proud of you I don't know whether to throw a celebration party for you or head down to the police station to see what's going on."

"So, not a lot on your mind." I went for teasing, hoping to break through the seriousness tightening his muscles.

"Yeah." He chuckled and swept his lips over mine. "Nothing on my mind at all."

His hands went to my waist, and he lifted me, set me on the island's countertop, and I gasped as the cold marble seeped into the backs of my thighs.

I ran my hands through his hair. "It'll be okay. The team will come together to help Dawson. Your coach will figure out what to do if he can't play, and you'll continue filling in the gap for him. And as far as a party goes, let's wait until my first album comes out."

Davis's hands ran up my sides, around to my back, and up to the backs of my shoulders. His hands were warm. Strong. Heat flared along my skin in their wake, making me squirm.

I now understand the adrenaline rush he felt after a football game.

Every nerve in my body felt more alive than I'd ever felt before.

"Your first album…"

"I'm planning on keeping this dream going, so yeah."

"Good. About Dawson… I'm so damn sorry that happened tonight. It shouldn't have."

I pressed my finger to his mouth to silence him. "It's not your fault, nor your apology to give. I'm sure Dawson feels like shit about it, too."

"He better. Because I have half a mind to kick his ass myself for causing that kind of scene."

"Let's just wait until you know all the information, okay?"

Behind me, his phone rang, and he cursed. "I would love to be able to ignore that…"

"Don't."

He bent around me and grabbed the screen. "It's the lawyer."

"Hello?" he answered on speakerphone.

Jordan Love's voice, Christian's attorney he'd hired to help Ruth and dig into my family, came through loud and clear. "Davis. Is Maggie with you?"

"I'm here," I said before Davis could, and all that heat Davis had riled up chilled. "What's going on?"

"I've already spoken with Christian, and he suggested I call you. I apologize for the late hour, but my investigators have finally gotten back to me with more information than I feared we'd receive."

"What's that mean?" I gripped Davis's hand at my side.

"Tomorrow, police in Waskin County Sheriff's Department will be moving in tomorrow to arrest your father."

"What? Really?"

"Yes, and while I can't share many details with you yet but will as soon as I'm able, your uncle, aunt, and mom are also included."

"My mom? Why? She never did anything."

His voice was thick, full of regret. "Unfortunately, what we've learned is both women not only knew what was going on, but in order to keep it off the cameras, they would have the men abuse the girls at the church. Often, they brought them to your father and uncle during the study times."

"No." My stomach rolled and my hand went to my stomach, felt the roundness of the baby growing in me. Tears dripped down my eyes and Davis's own face was a mix of fury and sadness.

"I didn't know," I rasped through my tears. "I swear I didn't know."

"The good news, if there is a silver lining to any of this, the younger children will be taken from their home. We can figure out the rest of this as the courts proceed and I'm sure both your uncle and father will have lawyers, but some of the things we've discovered that even the show knew about aren't pretty. I'm sorry to be the one to tell you all this, and I'm even sorrier you've had to live like this. You and Ruth are both incredibly brave. You should know that."

I wasn't brave. I'd abandoned those who had needed my help and didn't step in until far too late.

How many girls had they hurt? Or worse?

Bile rose in my throat, and I choked it down. Davis held me, my forehead falling to his chest as he ran one of his hands in large, sweeping circles on my back.

"I want to know everything."

"Soon. I'll make sure as much as can be is shared, but some of it's going to be sealed due to the ages and circumstances of the punishments. Also, I want you to know I'm including paperwork for your father to sign and for Ruth to fill out. It's an emancipation form, and I have no doubt the courts will approve it."

"Emancipation?" Ruth asked, and both Davis and I jumped. "What's going on? What does that mean?"

"It means, if you want, Ruth, courts will agree that living with Mom and Dad isn't a safe place and you're capable of living on your own. You wouldn't be their dependent anymore but could live anywhere. Even on your own if you wanted."

"We'll get to that," Jordan said. He was a gruff man, but his voice was low and thick. "No need to rush anything, any of you. I wanted to give you an update though, seeing as how all this will go down tomorrow, soon as they can get out there."

"Thank you, Mr. Love. At least, I guess?" This wasn't good news. It was sad. And that feeling of being a failure continued to grow thicker despite his kindness.

"You're welcome, Maggie. And Ruth? You're a brave young lady for telling us all you did. You've done the right thing."

Davis ended the call and stepped back. I held out my arms for Ruth. She only hesitated for a brief moment before she threw herself into my body.

"I'm not brave. I'm so scared."

I cupped the back of her head and held her tight to me. "You are brave. And it's okay to be both scared and brave at the same time. That's often when we're the bravest."

"Mom? I didn't know…" she sobbed against me.

"I don't think any of us did."

"Why would she do that? To other girls?"

"Maybe, in her own way, she was protecting us and herself." She jerked in my hold, but I held her tighter. "It's not right and none of it's okay, Ruth. But in a weird, roundabout way, it was possible she tried to keep us from even more beatings."

"I don't know if I like any of them anymore."

I despised them, but I'd had more years to see their ugly lies and hideous behavior.

"I think it's okay to be entirely confused on your feelings. It's okay, Ruth. I'll be here, with you, whatever you want to do. And I'll be by your side for all of it, okay?"

***

Davis was stretched out in bed when I joined him. One arm shoved beneath his tousled hair, he was naked from the chest up but had his light gray sheets pulled up over his stomach. Any other moment, any other night, I'd take it as an invitation to crawl into bed next to him or straddle him.

Not happening.

"She okay?"

"Sleeping at last."

The exhilaration from singing for the first time was long since gone. My bones ached, my eyes burned and were probably swollen and red, and every step made my limbs ache.

Tonight had been a long freaking night, and I said nothing else to Davis, barely spared him a second glance as I headed to the bathroom.

Yep. Swollen and red eyes. Comforting Ruth had sucked. We clung together with tears, worried and fearful of what tomorrow and the future would bring. I tried to tell her what Davis had said, that we'd take any of the kids who wanted to come to us, but she wanted nothing to do with talking about it.

"Dad will go get help, everything will go back to being good again."

Somehow, all the progress she'd made evaporated at the thought of our father being arrested, even as she admitted she didn't like them.

We'd talk more. We needed to.

But no more talking tonight. My throat ached from singing and then the emotions that followed.

Tomorrow might bring a tsunami of problems. Dawson's arrest. My parents.

I shoved down my shorts and climbed into the bed next to Davis in only his T-shirt and clicked off the lamp he'd left on for me.

"You hanging in there?" He didn't turn to hold me. Didn't move, but the warmth of his gaze was a gentle caress I desperately needed.

"No more talking about it tonight."

"I'm sorry all of this overshadowed the celebration you should have been having."

"Not like I could really celebrate the way I would have liked to." With a couple margaritas and Belle and I staying out until two in the morning to see who sang after me.

Three months ago, that's what we would have done. Had I been bold enough or trusting enough to take what she'd offered to help me.

The bed shifted and Davis rolled toward me, slipping his arm beneath my shirt until his hand settled on my stomach. My muscles ached as I shifted on the bed to grin up at him.

He was propped on his other arm, smiling down at me. "We'll get through all of this."

I dropped my hand to cover his, linked them together over my swollen abdomen. "Together."

"Damn straight, sweetheart."

His lips brushed mine, soft and gentle. I doubted either of us had the energy to take it further. Tonight had been a lot.

And the best—and worse—was still left to come, but Davis was right.

We'd conquer it all.

Together.

CHAPTER 39
DAVIS

This was it. The dream of a lifetime and I reached it at the age of twenty-three. How in the hell did I get here? How would anything beat this moment?

Super Bowl in Houston. We were playing Philadelphia. Any moment, our team would be announced and while we were crammed into the tunnel, bouncing on the balls of my feet, I tapped Cole on his shoulder.

"Remember that first game where I almost puked?"

"Remember what I told you?"

"Just like the high from high school."

"Damn straight, kid. You gonna puke today?"

"I might."

He chuckled and turned back to the tunnel opening. Smoke was billowing across the field. Philadelphia was taking it. We'd been considered the home team, and we'd go out second, but once we hit that field, home field meant nothing.

Next to me stood Dawson. Jaw tight and visible. Eyes steely and visible through the face mask of his helmet.

He'd been suspended for a game due to his behavior, but the guy he'd hurt didn't press charges. It'd all been, in effect, one large accident between being pulled and pushed and slipping. Dawson had to pay a six-figure fine, and the coach had him on his shit list for bringing such a distraction to the team at this point in the season, but at least he was still *on* the team and not in jail.

Although at the moment, he didn't seem like he cared much about the game ahead at all. Probably not the best time, but I couldn't help myself.

"You all, right? Things with Crystal… she gone yet?"

"Do not fucking talk to me about this before the biggest game of our lives, kid."

There was a time I would have backed down. I'd been fighting too hard and too long for Maggie, now it was my nature.

"What happened? After that night?"

"Fine, fuck it. Yes, Crystal's fucking gone, and the GM says I need to settle the fuck down."

"What?"

Rick Marchand was a big family guy. Part of why the players on his team respected him and Coach and all the players. We were a team from the top down. Always.

Not that I was *surprised*, but Dawson was as settled as they got. Broody, especially this last month, but he'd always been settled. More morose than most but still a decent friend when needed.

"What does that mean?"

"Wants me to date if you can believe that shit. Like I don't have women—"

"Having women and dating aren't synonymous."

"You're fucking telling me. Doesn't change the fact he told me to spend the off-season finding someone to show off on Instagram. Give people what they want—the feeling that I'm a good, kind gentleman. Can you believe that shit?"

Dawson, a gentleman, was a stretch and a half.

But he was kind. He also needed his head in the game and not on his sister or the drama she's once again caused in her wake.

"You'll figure it out." I grabbed his shoulder and gave him a quick shake. "Want to know what else you need to figure out?"

His glare could set forests aflame. "What?"

"How many more yards and points I'm going to get than you tonight in our first ever Bowl win."

"You little shit."

At least I got him laughing as the horn blew and our entrance was announced.

Like everything else that had happened in the last month, most importantly and wildly, was preparing for Maggie's three youngest sisters moving in with us next week with more maybe to come, we'd get through it if we leaned on each other.

Everything else was gravy, as my grandma would have said.

———

Holy shit. We were doing this.

Thirty seconds left, and we were only up by two, but we were still doing this. Mason jumped on my back as we hit the sidelines after he scored a touchdown to put us ahead. The entire game had been a battle. I could practically hear the announcers losing their minds. There hadn't been a Super Bowl game like this in decades. So close that the risk of overtime was imminent.

We wouldn't let that happen.

We'd hold them. Our defense had done a helluva job all game even if the points didn't show it.

We'd block a field goal if necessary, but no way were we losing the momentum we had going after grabbing a punt to us on the third line and driving all the way down the field. We tore seven minutes off the lock on that last possession. Had penalties that put us at a disadvantage and then penalties that gained us a first down. Yards lost. A fumble Cole managed to recover for a gain of one.

My heart was racing so hard I might have been having a heart attack.

"We're winning!" I flung Mason off my shoulders and slapped Dawson's as he passed me.

"Damn good feeling," he said and strode to the bench where he'd spent the entire game while we weren't on the field.

I felt for the guy. I did. He'd missed out playing in our last game and now it sounded like he had cement blocks pressing down on his shoulders. He scored our first touchdown tonight and was met with boos from half the crowd instead of a stadium full of cheers.

I let him go, because no way would he listen to my pep talk and refocus on the game. The field goal was good. We were kicking off. Up by three.

Twenty-eight seconds.

Kick off.

They grabbed it at the one. Ran. Tackled at the seven.

"Yes!" I shouted and grabbed the closest player to me. Didn't know who it was. Didn't care, didn't even look.

Hell was being on the sidelines as the clock ran down and trusting the rest of your team to bring the win home.

———

Even though I showered, I smelled like a mixture of champagne from the locker room and Gatorade dumped on the coach while I was standing close to him on the sidelines. We'd won. Celebrated on the field and we'd probably be finding confetti in unmentionable places for days to come. The celebration continued in the locker room, and once we were showered and changed and ready to find our families, more celebrations.

Maggie waited with my dad and mom, Ruth, my sisters and their husbands, and all of their kids. Tiny little Reese was tucked tight into the wrap my sister was carrying her in and as soon as I hugged my parents and shook my brothers-in-law's hands, I swooped Maggie into my arms.

I slammed my mouth to hers and swung her around the family room where they'd had to wait for hours. Fortunately, the teams spared no expense, and there was a buffet of food and drinks and a large television with announcers still talking about our nail-biting win.

When we caused a fumble on Philadelphia's last play, Nashville recovered.

Incredible. It would take days for my heart rate to lower to a normal rate.

"I'm so proud of you," Maggie said, still grinning. Still laughing.

It'd been hours since the game ended. It'd taken over an hour since Coach Bowles was able to talk to us all in the locker room.

Longer until we were finally able to shower and get to our families.

We had to board the team bus to get back to the hotel via police escort, and I imagined it'd taken even longer to get back to our rooms. But once we did, she was going to be all mine.

But our family was here now, and while I'd wanted to keep this moment private for the two of us since we would soon lack any privacy once Martha, Joy, and Leah came to live with us, I'd waited long enough. Spent the last four hours debating. Thinking.

Screw the waiting.

Maggie and I hadn't done anything yet by a standard timeline.

With that, I set Maggie back on her feet, keeping one hand at the back of her head, while I bent to kiss her, and dug the ring box out of my pocket.

"Davis," she whispered when I pulled back. "I love you."

Perfect. Absolutely perfect.

I opened the ring box and dropped to my knee. "I'll love you even more if you agree to be my wife. What do you say, Maggie? Wanna spend forever with me?"

There were gasps around the family room, but Maggie's was the largest of all. Her hands flew to her face, covering her mouth in surprise and then dropped to her belly, which was still small but growing more obvious every day. At sixteen weeks, we'd soon find out the gender.

Secretly, I was hoping for a boy. I was about to be overrun with tiny little girls already, but it didn't matter.

"What?!" she gasped again and tears streamed down her cheeks.

Next to her, Ruth's smile was enormous. The girl was coming out of her shell and was even decked out in jeans and a Steel sweatshirt.

"I mean it, Maggie. I want to be married before our peanut gets here. I want the kids we're going to raise, *all* of them, to see a healthy, loving marriage. But mostly, I want to spend the rest of my life with you. Marry me."

My knee ached from the cement floor. I'd stay down on one knee until she said yes.

Nothing mattered except her.

"Yes," she finally screamed and threw her arms around me.

"Way to fucking go!" someone shouted. "Let's party!"

Had to be a teammate, but behind Maggie, everything in the room was a blur as I stood, kissed her again, and finally managed to get the ring on her finger.

"You'll marry me? Really?"

Her dazzling smile gaped at the ring Mom and Ruth helped me pick out. "I'd marry you tomorrow if I could, Davis Hall."

Which could be arranged if it was what she really wanted.

———

I'd been right. The streets were packed. The hotel lobby more, with fans and families and friends. By the time I was finally on the elevator, alone, I was ready to fall into bed in the room where Maggie would be joining me for the first time in a week and pass out.

Except I'd gotten engaged a few hours ago, and I wanted to shower Maggie with all my love and devotion while she wore nothing but the emerald-cut diamond. I'd wanted to go larger. Get her the biggest damn diamond anyone had ever seen, but Ruth convinced me otherwise. It wasn't Maggie's personality nor what she would want, so I'd kept it at two carats, which Ruth still thought was insane, but Mom assured me she'd love.

Based on the way she kept grinning down at it like a fool until we'd been separated earlier, I figured Mom was right.

I used the keycard, and once the green light flashed, I opened the door. Quietly, in case Maggie had fallen asleep because as well after one o'clock in the morning, but what awaited me was even better.

The second-best surprise Maggie had given me since she showed up at my door and told me she was pregnant.

"You're a dream." I dropped my bag from my shoulder, and the door slammed shut behind me. "Absolute perfection. This was exactly what I wanted."

She was naked. Gloriously naked, exposing every single inch of her body unashamedly to me, standing in front of the bed wearing nothing but her ring and a smile.

Her hair was draped behind her shoulders, her boobs, already large to begin with growing larger with every week, and that round stomach I now loved so much on display for my viewing pleasure only.

"I was hoping you'd get here soon before I fell asleep."

Some days I thought we were starting to share a mind.

"We can if you need to." I'd give her anything.

She reached for me and grabbed my hand, drawing me to her, but it wasn't like it took effort. I was already hard beneath my suit pants. "I'm suddenly not tired anymore."

I brought her hand to my mouth and kissed her knuckles where her ring sparkled on her finger. "If you weren't already pregnant, I'd want you knocked up tonight, too."

Might as well go with a hat trick—championship, engagement, and baby all in one night.

Maggie laughed and brushed my hair back before pulling her hand from mine and shoving my suit coat down my shoulders. I shook it off and let it fall to the floor as her fingers went to work on the buttons at my shirt.

"I think we have enough kids to think of for a while."

As she always did when she thought of her family, the light in her eyes dimmed with sadness.

There would be none of that tonight. All I'd see was her glassy eyes after an orgasm, a satisfied smile, and flush on her cheeks by the time I was done with her.

"Get on the bed and spread those legs for me."

She swallowed thickly and flashed me a sassy little smile. "I thought you'd never ask."

What could I say? I was a starving man.

For her body. Her heart. Her soul. I was desperate for her in all the ways she'd give herself in a way I knew it would never end, only growing stronger and fiercer with time.

EPILOGUE
MAGGIE

"Did you girls get your beds made?"

Joy, Leah, and Martha scrambled onto chairs at the dining room table in our new home.

"Yes, Maggie." My sisters were the sweetest, kindest little creatures to ever roam the planet. They'd come to us in tears and uncertainty, clinging more to Ruth in the first few weeks. Expected, considering Martha was only three when I'd gone away to college. She barely knew me.

"Good." I gave them all kisses on the tops of their heads and then set waffles and eggs and bacon onto the table in front of them. They dove on it like they hadn't eaten in days. At six, seven, and nine, these girls could *eat*.

We'd moved in next door to the Buchanan's in March, a few weeks after the Super Bowl and after we were busting at the seams in Davis's condo. That sold in a matter of days, and we invested some of that money from the sale into a home in the mountains outside Knoxville, close enough where we could spend weekends whenever we wanted. The rest would go to an addition on our home.

That was taking some time to find the right contractor, but until that happened, we were working on updating the inside. New wood floors had already been laid, new carpet for upstairs. The floral wallpaper was all gone, and Ruth was settled in the downstairs bedroom.

She'd offered to stay upstairs so she could be close to the kids, but Davis and I put our foot down.

She was now eighteen, an adult, and it was time for her to find her own way in what she wanted. She was no longer the provider of her siblings, outside anything she *felt* like doing but we were not expecting it. Ruth took it to heart, too, because as of yesterday, she'd enrolled in a cosmetology program in Nashville. She was going to stay living with us while she completed it, which was the reason for the addition of the home. We were building a separate garage slash pool house for the pool we were going to install, and above the garage there was going to be a two-bedroom apartment for Ruth and any family who came to visit.

Besides, it made more sense for Davis and me to take the upstairs primary bedroom with the baby coming in a couple of months.

At thirty weeks, I was almost as large as the house we lived in. I'd been right early on. Given my shorter size, my stomach kept stretching forward and around to my ass. I was as huge as the mountains we visited last weekend, and I groaned every time I had to pick something up off the floor. Forget tying shoes at this point. Thank God it was spring and I could live in sandals. Not to mention the swelling. My ankles were as large as my thighs.

Not that Davis minded my size at all. He was making it work for us, every night, in all manner of creative ways, but I'd truly love it once I could enjoy a simple night of missionary sex again. I couldn't remember the last time I'd been able to be on my back without feeling like a watermelon was crushing my diaphragm.

"Eat up, girls. It's a busy day, and I'm going to need lots of help, okay?"

"When can we put our dresses on?" Joy asked. As the oldest of the three, she was taking her flower girl responsibilities seriously.

I bopped her nose with the tip of my finger. "As soon as I can be certain you can wear them without getting them dirty."

"I won't get *mine* dirty," Martha pouted.

"I'm sure you won't."

Lies. Martha was as likely to run straight into the pond behind our yard and swing from the tree branches as she was to paint everyone's fingernails a pretty pink color or experiment with makeup I'd bought for her. She was rough and tumble and sugary-sweet all wrapped up in an adorable package.

"What do you need help with?" Ruth stole a piece of bacon from the kitchen table. "I've already been working with Mama B and Annie and Avery on the flowers. They're gorgeous, by the way, and the guys are setting up the chairs now."

Today was my *wedding* day, and what was supposed to be a private, quiet affair had steamrolled into madness.

Almost all of Davis's teammates insisted on coming, their wives or girlfriends. Davis's entire family had made the trip from Nebraska. Not to mention there was Belle, her parents, Brianna, my *band*, that still made me laugh to say out loud. Their partners and so many more people who were currently helping me work on my first album were also now attending. I'd done weekly live singing on stages all over Broadway until my stomach grew too large and uncomfortable. For the last month, we'd been in the studio.

What was going to be fifteen to twenty people on a quiet after-noon was now well over a hundred. I'd tried to insist Mama B let us move the wedding and reception to somewhere in Nashville, but she'd insisted on hosting it in her backyard, which was where I'd wanted to be married.

On our land, where we were starting a family. I might have been as big as a house, but I'd agreed with Davis. Before our baby arrived, I'd be a Hall.

Davis's mom and dad had been staying at the Buchanan's house next door for the last week helping get everything prepared and they'd stepped up like I was one of their own daughters. A thought that made me cry every time I hugged them.

I blamed the hormones.

"Belle will be here soon with the hair and makeup team," I told Ruth. Our sisters cheered at the table. They were more excited about hair and makeup and *brand-new* dresses than they were anything else. "Then there's pictures. But I think we have an hour or so before things get crazy, right?"

"Perfect. Then I get to have a moment alone with you." Davis swept into the house, screen door slamming behind him, and like always happened when he entered our home, the girls shoved out of their chairs and dove for him like he was their own personal tackling dummy.

Soon, he was squatting, hugging all three of them.

It'd taken a month to get them to smile around him, to go anywhere near him.

He'd broken through with ice cream cones and a shopping trip to the American Girl Doll store. Now, I was pretty sure he was their favorite.

Not that I minded… he was destined to be a *Girl Dad*.

He stood after giving them all hugs, and I burst out laughing as I saw his shirt.

"You're a fool." I laughed, my hands going to my stomach to hold up the weight of it.

"I'm *your* fool."

"Nice shirt," Ruth teased and grabbed another slice of bacon.

He brushed his hands down his rock-hard abs and shrugged. It was hot pink. Bold white letters. **Future husband and girl dad forever.**

"Who gave you that shirt?" I asked, still laughing.

"Mason."

I shouldn't have been surprised. Mason Yeets was a giant goofball and a great guy. If I had to pick my favorite teammate, it'd be him, hands down. He was single, a year older than Davis, but if we ever needed a night out, Mason was first to volunteer. Not that it happened often, but he was a frequent fixture in our home.

"How's Luella feeling today?" he asked after he ushered my sisters back to their chairs and refocused them on eating. His hands went to my stomach, covering mine and he bent to kiss it. "Good morning, sweetheart."

My pulse kicked up, and my core tingled.

There'd never be a time when Davis didn't turn me on but watching him love our unborn daughter drove me *wild*.

"She's kicking." I moved our hands to where one of her feet was pushing against my sides. "See?"

"Feisty, beautiful, perfect little thing." He stood and kissed me. "Just like her mama. You ready for today?"

"Isn't there something about bad luck and seeing the bride before the wedding?" Ruth had a waffle in her hand and tore off a chunk as I glared at her.

Davis didn't take her bait. His blue eyes were glued to mine, excitement and anticipation and most of all peace, radiating from him.

"We make our own luck," I said, staring at him. "And mine isn't running out anytime soon."

"Damn straight. You and me forever, sweetheart."

"Together." I rolled to my toes, and he met me halfway. His lips brushed over mine and we kissed until the girls groaned and moaned about us being gross and then we all laughed.

We had a lot of battles left to fight.

My parents had been arrested, as well as with my uncle and aunt. They'd been bailed out by my oldest brothers, who were also facing charges. None of them were allowed to be around children until their trials. Jed and Zach's wives had all the kids in my parents' house after it'd been clear they hadn't known what was going on.

They were standing by their husbands, for now, anyway, but occasionally, I'd receive emails from them asking me questions I knew they wouldn't dare ask their husbands.

My other brothers were with them for now, but Davis and I were preparing to bring them all here if necessary.

At a minimum, my brothers would receive a small amount of jail time and required parenting classes as well as anger management, but so far, they'd shown little remorse. The fact they were still standing by my parents was telling enough.

There was little I could do, my hands tied until the trial in the fall, and for now, I was focused on giving all four of my sisters some normalcy.

"You didn't answer my question," Davis whispered, skimming his lips along my jaw. "You ready for today?"

"I would have married you months ago, and you know it."

"Yeah." He nipped at my ear, and I bit down so a needy sound didn't escape my lips. "But I didn't want a quickie in Vegas. I want everyone we know and love to celebrate with us."

And like he'd do anything for me, provide it multiple times and in massive ways—like being so willing to take in my sisters—I was always willing to do the same for him.

Hence, the massive party and wedding.

I cupped his cheeks and grinned. "Today is going to be the best day of our lives, and I can't wait to walk down that aisle and marry you."

"Every day I spend with you is the best day of my life. Good thing we have forever to make more, huh?"

"Good thing," I agreed.

He whisked me out of the kitchen to the front porch where we had a moment of privacy, and he kissed me until my lips were swollen and my chest was heaving until Belle arrived and we needed to part ways.

He was going to the Buchanan's to finalize setting up for the reception and to get dressed, and me to our bedroom where I'd be made over to look like some form of an Oompa Loompa princess.

"Love you," he said, going in for one last kiss.

"See you soon, husband."

"Forever." He winked, dashed down the porch, and I met Belle at the front door.

"Ready?" she asked.

"To marry the best man I've ever met? Absolutely."

I'd taken a chance on Davis and found my happiness. Our foundation might have been built quickly, but it was firm. Long-lasting.

What had become one night of passion had turned into my fairy tale. I was only a few hours away from saying my "I do's" and starting my happily ever after.

———

Thank you for reading *Time Out*! More Nashville Steel books are headed your way later this year. Dawson's book, *Tight Spot*, is up next, releasing in August and you can pre-order it here: http://bit.ly/3Zu3JZO

If you never want to miss a sale, release date, or new series announcement, sign up for my newsletter here: https://bit.ly/3nC4exd

Thank you, always, for loving my books and giving me a chance!

THANK YOU

HUGE thank you to Nina and all the incredible women at Valentine PR for throwing your full enthusiasm and support behind me and these books. I've loved working with you and can't wait to see what the future brings us.

Ellie and Virginia, as always, thanks for putting up with my mess and spit-shining each manuscript until it sparkles. Thank you especially during this crazy time in our world for your flexibility and your extra hard work.

Shannon, you're the best. Always. Forever. Your talent is astounding and I'm thankful I can call you a friend.

To my Sweeties! I love you ladies and your excitement for my books!

To all the bloggers who devote their time and passion into reading books, book tours, release events, leaving reviews, promoting and pimping – you are all rockstars! Thank you for all the love over the years.

My family— I love you all to the moon and back. I don't know what I would do without you in my corner, cheering me on every step of the way. Your support is everything to me and I love you all with all of my heart.

To my girl crew— Tamara, Lauren, Niccole, Cassy, and Bree. What would I do without you ladies? Thank you for blessing me with your friendships. My life is a hundred times better with y'all in it, and a gazillion times more entertaining! To the SteelP! May we forever reign.

And last but definitely not least – to you, the reader. I'm blown away with every release how much you adore my books. You have made my dream a reality and I hope I can cheer you on with yours. Please don't forget to leave reviews on Goodreads or whichever retailer you've purchased this copy from. It helps us so much!

ABOUT THE AUTHOR

Stacey Lynn likes her coffee with a dash of sugar, her heroes with a side of bossy, and her wine a deep shade of red.

The author of over fifty romance novels, many of which have been best-selling titles, she loves being able to turn her vivid imagination into a career that brings entertainment and joy to her readers. Focused on sports romance and emotional, small-town romance, she also loves stretching herself in different genres.

Born in Texas and raised in the Midwest, she now makes her home in North Carolina and loves all things Southern. Together with her ultimate tall, dark, and handsome hero, she has four children. Her life is a loving, chaotic mess, and she wouldn't have it any other way.

Subscribe to her newsletter so you can stay up to date on all her new releases. www.staceylynnbooks.com

OTHER BOOKS BY STACEY LYNN

Nashville Steel ~ football romance

Sneak Attack

Time Out

Tight Spot – releasing 2023

Risky Game – releasing 2023

Las Vegas Vipers ~hockey romance

Final Shot (free on all retailers)

Game Changer

Dream Maker

Rule Breaker

Shot Taker

Goal Chaser

Secret Keeper

Ice Kings Series ~hockey romance

Playing With Fire (free on all retailers)

Playing To Win

Scoring Off The Ice

Hooked One Her

Hard Checked

Fighting Dirty

The Rough Riders Series ~football romance

Dirty Player

Filthy Player

Wicked Player

Cocky Player

<u>Love and Lies Duet ~angsty slow burn, romance</u>

<u>All the Ugly Things</u>

<u>All the Beautiful Things</u>

<u>Love and Honor Duet ~angsty, romantic suspense</u>

<u>Twisted Hearts</u>

<u>Unraveled Love</u>

<u>Love In The Heartland ~small town romance</u>

Captivated By You

This Time Around

Long Road Home

Before We Fell

<u>Crazy Love Series ~small town romance</u>

Fake Wife

Knocked Up

28 Dates

Weekend Fling

<u>The Fireside Series ~small town romance</u>

His to Love

His to Protect

His to Cherish

His to Seduce

<u>Tangled Love Series ~erotic romance</u>

Entice

Embrace

Enflame

<u>The Luminous Series ~BDSM romance</u>

Dominate Me

Crave Me

Long For Me

Just One Series ~rockstar romance

Just One Song

Just One Week

Just One Regret

Just One Moment

The Nordic Lords Series ~MC romance

Point of Return

Point of Redemption

Point of Freedom

Point of Surrender

Standalones

Remembering Us

Don't Lie To Me – billionaire romance

Try Me – A Don't Lie To Me Novella